They Never Expected To Meet Again, But A Dangerous Past Haunts Them

Standing in the presence of Matt's never-stay-at-home dad, relief flooded her. "Oh, Mr. Crandall, thank heavens. My name's Melanie. My son, Luke, is a friend of Matt's. Call me a flake, but I'm out of gas."

He reached across the seat and opened the passenger door. Light flooded the interior. "Happens to the best of us. There's a gas station on the corner. Hop in."

Even though his voice seemed kind, she hesitated. After all, taking rides from sweet-talking strangers had been her downfall. But that had been a lifetime ago, and she knew this man. Or at least his son. The decision made, she rounded the car. Sliding in beside him, the scent of coffee and his musky fragrance filled the air. "I can't thank you enough. I wanted to start . . . dinner."

That's when she saw this was no ordinary vehicle. A laptop computer was bracketed to the console, and above it a radio. The world seemed to slow as she focused on every detail. The dash . . . the console . . . and finally the man behind the wheel.

Her gaze took in his long legs, the veins in his powerful-looking hands, his rolled-up sleeves and at last settled on the sizeable scar on his inner forearm.

Shock made her numb.

It wasn't possible. How had she missed the connection? She hadn't thought of the man in years. The cop who'd arrested her, his name had been . . . *Crandall*.

Somehow Mel found the strength to look into his eyes. And when she did, she came face to face with what could only be a mutually shocked expression.

"You," she whispered.

"You," he replied.

D1445755

The Past Came Hunting

by

Donnell Ann Bell

Bell Bridge Books

This is a work of fiction. Names, characters, places and incidents are either the products of the author's imagination or are used fictitiously. Any resemblance to actual persons (living or dead,) events or locations is entirely coincidental.

Bell Bridge Books
PO BOX 300921
Memphis, TN 38130
ISBN: 978-1-61194-048-0

Bell Bridge Books is an Imprint of BelleBooks, Inc.

Printed and bound in the United States of America.

We at BelleBooks enjoy hearing from readers.
Visit our websites – www.BelleBooks.com and www.BellBridgeBooks.com.

10 9 8 7 6 5 4 3 2

Cover design: Debra Dixon
Interior design: Hank Smith
Photo credits:
shadowy figure and background (manipulated) © Constantin Opris | Dreamstime.com

:Lptc:01:

Dedication

To my children, Audra and David, the two of you inspired this novel. No mom could be prouder of her children. It was my absolute joy to watch you grow on and off the court. This is for you.

1995

New River, Arizona, State Hwy. 89

Dead if you stay, dead if you jump . . .

Melanie Daniels hadn't been asleep ten minutes before she felt the truck driver's miserable paw on her crotch. Grandfather her ass. She'd hitched a ride with a filthy, wrinkled perv. Instantly awake, she slapped it off. "What the fuck are you doing?"

"That any way for a pretty young thing to talk?" He grinned, revealing a wad of chewing tobacco in his mouth, and slid his hand back to her thigh. "Just collecting my fare."

Gagging, Mel yanked off her seatbelt and yelled, "Pull over."

"There's the door." The sleazebag laughed and grabbed at her breast.

Forget *this*. She clawed his arm and drew blood.

"You little bitch." He backhanded her so fast, she never saw it coming.

All fury and nails, Mel went for his face. "Pull over this damn truck."

"I don't think so." He shoved her off of him, covered his watering eye and mashed down on the gas. "Besides, tease, the next time I stop, I'm gonna teach you some manners."

Tease? Were they even riding in the same vehicle? Noting his furious scowl, she watched the red-rock desert speed by. How fast were they going? Sixty? Seventy? Oh, god, she was desperate, not suicidal. He might've originally planned to cop a feel, but by fighting back, she'd lit the fuse of a rapist. Forcing back tears, she demanded, "Let me out of this truck."

He threw her a malevolent glare. "No fucking way."

Heart ramming against her ribcage, Mel dug her fingers into the armrest the way she wanted to tear into his flesh. But the last time she'd dove at him, the semi had swerved.

A half-mile down the road, the truck driver rounded a curve. And when she saw the diamond-shaped warning, *Steep Grade Ahead,* she'd never read more beautiful words.

No way in hell could this lumber-hauling rig maintain this speed. Sure enough, the driver recognized the problem, down-shifted and the big diesel engine whined to a crawl. As they trudged up the mountain pass, she shoved open the door.

Ignoring his bellow of surprise, and hanging on for dear life, she almost wretched at how far it was to the asphalt below. But as bad as things were,

1

she hadn't lived on this earth for seventeen years to check out of it now—or to let someone rape her, either.

Screw you, Grandpa Pervert.

Mel jumped.

She hit pavement, wincing and rolling, finally landing on her butt as the truck slowed, then picked up speed again and lumbered away. Obviously, the mangy creep had decided she was more trouble than she was worth. She stared at the skin beneath her fingernails and wiped a smattering of his blood on her terry cloth shorts. She dragged herself upright and tugged on her tattered cotton top. With gravel embedded in her palms, her legs cut and oozing, she gradually came to her feet. Then it hit her, and she whipped around in the direction of the semi, now just a spot in the distance.

Great. Just fucking great.

The bastard had driven off with her money and clothes.

Now what? Gritting her teeth, she considered thumbing a ride back to Phoenix. But no matter how much crap she had to deal with in this pitiful world, home no longer existed.

From the southbound lane, an engine purred. A car this time. Certainly not the grinding gears of an eighteen-wheeler. Much as she needed a ride, Mel couldn't bring herself to stick out her thumb again. Limping in broken sandals, she scurried through foot-high weeds toward a copse of trees. A silver Corvette with California plates rounded the bend and immediately slowed.

She moved fast, but not fast enough.

Kicking up rock, the driver skidded to a halt and got out of his car. "Hey! Hey you, wait up."

Each step was agony as she broke into a run. "Go away. Leave me alone."

It didn't take much for him to catch her and spin her around. "Hey, wait. What's happened?" He touched her face where the trucker's fist had caught her cheekbone. "You're hurt. Let me help you."

This was too much. Maybe when she jumped, she'd died after all. A guy with sandy blond hair falling into his eyes held her at arm's length. And, holy shit, he was hot.

She jerked away from him. "I said, *leave me alone.*"

"I'm not going to hurt you." He held up his hands as though to say he was harmless. "Let me give you a lift."

Surrounded by the evergreens lining the highway, she stepped back. In a few short hours the sun would go down, leaving her to deal with more than predatory humans. She took in his good looks, the fancy clothes and expensive car. Why would some Ivy Leaguer living off of Mommy and Daddy's money bother with her?

"I won't sleep with you."

His gaze roamed over her shredded top and filthy shorts and he

2

dropped his hands. "Who's asking? Like you're some kind of prize."

Mel flushed. The truth hurt almost as much as she did. "Where're you heading?"

"Colorado. Boulder. Where's your stuff?"

Her stomach sank. "Probably in Flagstaff by now. Look, I'm messed up. If I go with you, can I trust you?"

"Baby, I'd say compared to the last guy you were with, I'm a boy scout. Let's get you cleaned up and into some new clothes."

"I don't have any money."

"Did I ask you for any?"

He had an answer for everything and said all the right things. But if a grandpa trucker could let her down, what made her think she could trust this guy? Folding her scraped up arms, she said, "You're not some serial killer?"

He laughed. "You found me out. I'm working on it, but not yet."

"Very funny. You got a name?"

"Drake Maxwell."

The name even sounded preppy.

"How about you?"

"Melanie Daniels." Then, looking for a hole to crawl into, she said, "Back when I had friends, they called me Mel."

He lifted a brow. "You comin' or what?"

"I've always wanted to see Boulder. Guess I'm coming."

True to his word, Drake stopped at a travel stop down the road, bought her a pair of sweats and a couple of T-shirts, then led her to the bathroom in back. There, he propped her on a wobbly metal counter and cleaned her injuries. His touch was light and his hands never wandered. Mel wondered if he was gay, or if she simply wasn't good enough, still, the college boy intrigued her.

On the way out, the pretty salesclerk who'd sold him the clothes came on to him and he flirted back.

Mel muttered, "You two should get a room," but Drake caught the comment and winked at her.

Inside the sleek Corvette, dressed in fresh clothes, she leaned against the luxurious leather, and after days and nights of sleeping in snatches, she fell into an exhausted sleep.

She awoke to pitch darkness and the steady drone of the highway beneath her. Stretching her aching body, she asked, "Where are we?"

"Colorado. We made it. You alive over there?"

"I feel like I jumped from a moving semi."

He reached down to the floorboard and came up with a bag. "I can fix that." He opened the sack to reveal a stash of pot and black beauties.

She clumsily rolled a joint, having recently taken to smoking dope on the streets—another in-your-face moment to her father for stabbing her mother and Mel in the heart. "I thought you were a boy scout."

"I am. Can't you tell? I come prepared."

For the first time she smiled, and her hero smiled back. They shared the joint, downed a couple of black beauties and got off on the buzz.

They arrived in Colorado Springs a few minutes before dawn. "Hungry?" he asked.

"Starving. Know what I'd love? About a million chocolate donuts."

He laughed, and no question about it, he had a great smile. "I'll spot you a dozen. I could use some smokes and caffeine. Reach behind my seat and grab my jacket, will ya?"

It wasn't the least bit cold outside. Still, Mel did as he asked. Surprised by its bulk, she said, "What's in here, Fort Knox?"

"Spare change."

He pulled off the interstate and into the parking lot of an isolated convenience store.

Normally pot relaxed her, but the beauties had brought out the jitters. Man, she needed something to eat. Through the glass plate window, she saw a young man behind the counter. He was all by himself, and she felt a kindred loneliness.

Perhaps Drake sensed her emptiness because he glanced over at her like he was sizing her up. "I'm glad we hooked up, Mel. Let's make this quick, okay?"

Some of her melancholy lifted. She smiled at the guy who'd treated her like she was something special. She wasn't stupid enough to think this was love, but, hey, she could do a lot worse. He had money and he hadn't attacked her. If he wanted her around for a while, she was willing.

Leaning over the bucket seat, she kissed him. "Whatever you say."

He left the motor running and got out of the car. She followed Drake, he held the door open for her and they entered a store so well-lit it could've been daytime. The smell of pastries, hotdogs and coffee made her mouth water. "Aren't you afraid someone will steal your ride?"

Glancing behind him at the empty parking lot, he laughed. "Like who?"

She rolled her eyes. "Be right back, I'm going to the loo."

"All right. But hurry it up, damn it. We don't have much time."

Stunned by his suddenly angry tone, Mel moved quickly. What was his problem? If he was worried about the Vette, he should have turned the damn thing off.

She used the bathroom, then opened the door to a madhouse of screaming. Racing back the way she came, she encountered the shock of her life. Oh god, why hadn't she read the signs?

The college boy wasn't a hero, and he certainly wasn't a boy scout. He had the clerk face down on the floor, and Maxwell stood over him. In his hand, he held a gun.

Chapter One

Fifteen Years Later

The kid looked like he'd lost his best friend. Probably because he had.

From the passenger side of the vehicle, Melanie Norris glanced over her shoulder and forced back the stirring of tears. Slumped in the backseat, her teenage son stared wordlessly out the window. She ached for him. Not only had he lost his father, she'd taken him away from his school and his friends.

As if the boy were deaf and not depressed, the realtor murmured, "How long has his father been gone?"

"Three months." Before Luke tuned into the conversation, Mel added, "The properties you've shown me are out of my price range, Mrs. Sims. I need to stick to the budget I gave you."

The trim, silver-haired saleswoman cast Mel a look as if to say, *but your budget's so low.* "I think the next house will better suit your needs. It's more modest than some, but the neighborhood's safe. It's in District 11 and the high school's a few blocks away."

Years ago, Mel had learned the value of remaining silent. She'd bide her time. One more house. One more stop, which would prove a huge waste of time, and then she would demand the woman take them back to their car.

Dark gray clouds hung low in the sky, threatening to unleash snow flurries at any time. Dreading to forsake the warm vehicle again on the brisk October morning, she snuggled deeper into her coat and suppressed a sigh.

Mrs. Sims steered the red Honda onto a street called Serendipity. Crisp golden leaves littered the ground, aspens with barren limbs lined the narrow lane and snow-capped Pikes Peak loomed like a sentinel over the city of Colorado Springs.

Four houses from the corner, however, she saw the for sale sign, and beyond the sign, a path led to a pristine white two-story structure with forest green shutters and trim. And for a moment, she dared to dream.

Until her gaze fell to the flyer stating the price, a full fifty thousand above her pre-approved loan amount. She was set to protest when the realtor pulled alongside the curb, and Mel caught sight of a teenager close to Luke's age shooting baskets from the driveway next door.

From the backseat Luke made a shuffling noise. She turned to find his eyes lit up and that he'd suddenly straightened.

Mrs. Sims looked between the two and smiled. "Shall we go inside?"

With her son bolting from the car, what else could Mel do?

The realtor took her through a property that had been vacant for almost two years. Though musty and layered with dust, the house had so many good points Mel almost strayed from her common sense. The kitchen with its wood floors was airy, the back yard immense, and although the upstairs bedrooms were tiny, the house came with two full baths and an unfinished basement. The landscaping wasn't much, but since that was Mel's strong suit, she wasn't worried about it.

She found herself mentally calculating the additional mortgage payment when she and Mrs. Sims returned to the front door. Luke would start college in three years, and although there'd been talk in Cañon City of an athletic scholarship, she couldn't count on that. And no matter how much she liked this house, she couldn't risk his future.

Her heart sank when she stepped onto the porch and found the boys engaged in a rowdy game of one-on-one. The neighborhood kid showed moves that said he wasn't a novice. Twice he even stole the ball from Luke and drove to the basket. Not many boys Luke's age gave him a challenge. Obviously Luke agreed. It had been too many months since she'd seen her son smile.

But a game of basketball and a neighborhood kid had made it happen.

Out of breath, Luke and his new pal came running. "Hey, Mom, this is Matt Crandall. He lives next door. He's a sophomore like me."

She shook the boy's hand. "Nice to meet you, Matt."

"You gonna buy the place, Mrs. Norris? If you are, better hurry, basketball tryouts start in November—"

"Whoa, whoa, slow down." Mel laughed. "Talk about being outnumbered." Both boys towered over her, Luke fair and blond as his father, Matt a head shorter, dark and brunet.

Luke's youthful expression remained ever hopeful, but too soon she would disappoint him again. Buying time, she said, "Give me a moment will you, sweetheart?" She turned to the realtor. "I'd like to see the backyard again, if you don't mind."

By the time they reached the rear of the property, pressure squeezing the life out of her. A sweater she'd paid too much for snagged on a diseased Juniper bush, only adding to her frustration. She gritted her teeth and worked the fabric free. "I can't afford this house, Mrs. Sims. I work for a florist. I earn enough to pay my expenses. I have my husband's pension and a savings account, but I've set it aside for Luke's college tuition."

"I understand," the woman said. "And, of course, your son's education comes first. But the listing does say motivated seller, and I have it on good authority she'll negotiate."

"But will she come down fifty thousand dollars?" Mel asked dismally.

"Maybe not the full amount. For the right buyer, though, she's been known to make things happen. She's made a nice living buying and selling properties like these, and the house has been vacant awhile, so she's willing to deal."

"You sound like you know the owner personally."

"Let's just say we're acquainted." Mrs. Sims stuck out her hand. "I'm ready to do business if you are, Melanie. The owner of 39 Serendipity Lane is *me*."

Lieutenant Joe Crandall suspected his trek around the cubicles of the Police Operations Center resembled the acid churning a path through his gut. This morning's briefing had held one surprise after another. Joe hated surprises.

He also hated premonitions, and as he stared at the third shift's list of callouts, the bad feelings just kept on coming. He'd entered his office, dumped the reports on his desk and logged on to the Op Center's computer. His second in command chose that moment to waylay his suspicions.

"Mornin', L.T. Got a second?"

Joe waved the sergeant inside. "One second's all I've got, Chris. What the hell happened last night?"

Chris Sandoval looked between two chairs, then chose the one closest to the door. "I wish I had an answer. Can't even blame it on a full moon, there wasn't one. But Dispatch was on overload."

Some cops were superstitious. Joe wasn't one of them. Like most growing cities, Colorado Springs had its share of drugs, gang activity, domestic violence and other sporadic crime. Typically, multiple events going down all at once were anomalies.

He clicked on the police activity reports and scrolled to a weekend earlier in the month. A liquor store holdup, a burglary, a convenience store robbery, all reported within minutes of each other, all in various sectors of the city. Add to this barrage, a surge of seemingly unrelated 911 calls were phoned into the call center.

Now the previous evening, a Thursday, an identical scenario had happened again, the events severely diluting police resources and slowing backup. Not one arrest, not one positive I.D. Joe set his jaw. By the time help arrived, it was too late. The only difference, it wasn't the weekend.

"This is orchestrated," he said. "One incident I wasn't sure. Twice, we've got a gang on our hands. Let's increase second and third shift patrols, alert vice to contact their snitches. See if we can't shake something up."

"Right."

"Anything else?"

Chris leaned forward. "Ran into Bruce Bennett at the courthouse yesterday."

"He ask for your vote?"

"He didn't have to. He's been a decent D.A. He'll make a fine attorney general." Chris grinned. "Speaking of which, he mentioned I may be looking at the division's future commander."

"*May* being the operative word." Along with not being superstitious, Joe wasn't into wishful thinking. "We were talking about Bruce."

"He wanted me to tell you a prisoner by the name of Drake Maxwell is up for release. He said you'd want to know."

Intimately familiar with the California bad boy, soon to be a Cañon City ex-con, Joe nodded. "When?"

"First of next month."

"Is the victim aware of the timeframe?"

"D.A. said he and his family haven't missed a hearing in fifteen years. But come November, Maxwell's a free man. He's done his time."

Joe grimaced. As a convict who'd served his sentence, Maxwell reported to no one. "Appreciate the heads up."

"No problem." Chris started to rise, then hesitated. "Sir, I understand the vic's involvement. But why you? I mean, you've put hundreds of these types behind bars. What's so special about this bad guy?"

A knot formed at the base of Joe's Adam's apple. "Drake Maxwell was my first violent arrest. When his gun jammed, he pistol-whipped the clerk and left him for dead, all for a measly hundred dollars and change."

"Ouch, L.T., that's tough. But if the clerk survived, why'd Maxwell get fifteen years?"

"One of his previous victims wasn't so lucky." Joe held the man's gaze. "He had an accomplice, you know, a real babe."

"Babe, sir?"

"Literally. Seventeen."

"She do time?"

"Oh, yeah," Joe replied. "Bruce Bennett was an assistant D.A. in those days. Judge sentenced her as an adult. Real smart-ass. Drug user, anti-establishment everything. Claimed she never knew what Maxwell was up to."

"Did she?"

"The clerk remained conscious long enough to identify her. Accomplice claimed, of course, she tried to stop Maxwell."

"If I had a dollar for every time I heard that one," Chris said, standing. "Let's hope the sentence turned her around. I'll let you get back to work."

Joe nodded and reached for the reports.

Turned her around.

It could happen. *Maybe.*

The girl, a runaway, had run like the devil to avoid apprehension. He'd chased her into an alley. Tackling her, he'd discovered a juvenile reeking of marijuana, wearing too much makeup and using language that would make a cellblock proud.

He'd thought of the girl often over the years. He had no choice; she'd left a five-inch scar on his inner forearm.

He glanced at his watch, then opened his briefcase and stashed the reports inside. His day was jammed with budget meetings and the need to provide justification for additional patrols. If no problems arose, he might make it home for dinner. Raising a teenage son alone was proving harder than expected, and his ex-wife was just waiting for him to screw up.

Joe flipped the lights and closed the door to his office. He could only hope a burgeoning crime spree and soon-to-be-ex-con didn't give her the opportunity.

Chapter Two

On the first day of basketball tryouts, Joe changed his open door policy to closed. If someone dropped by, he cut the conversation short. His phone was an albatross; his pager an anvil. This week Coronado High School selected its varsity players.

Joe left the office, warning that short of a homicide, he wouldn't be available for the next several hours. Parents had been invited to observe the tryout process. For once, he planned to be there.

Now sitting beneath a huge mural of a snarling cougar, he and other anxious onlookers watched the coaches and hopeful players run drills. A propped-open side door only half-eliminated the smell of rubber and sweat as the sound of screeching sneakers and dribbling balls filled the air.

At five-ten, Matt was still growing and Joe only had him by a few inches. His son wasn't the tallest on the court, but he was one of the quickest. And since he'd been practicing with their new neighbor nonstop, the two knew each other's moves.

Joe searched the room for Luke's mom, but had yet to see a woman he didn't recognize. Luke Norris was all Matt talked about these days, and Joe wanted to thank her for taking his son under her wing. As soon as his schedule let up, he planned to return the favor.

Clad in his ever-present warm-up suit, Head Coach Rick Hood called for a time out, talked briefly with spectators, then climbed the steps to sit beside Joe. Stretching his long legs in front of him, Rick crossed his arms, leaned back and said, "So, what do you think?"

Joe had met Rick during a police investigation years ago when a disgruntled ex-player had shot out the coach's windows. Sports fanatics, they'd shared their frank opinions and love of basketball ever since. "Mighty tough choices, Coach."

Rick furrowed his brow. "Yep. My job gets harder every year. I'm losing six seniors after this season, and there's been speculation, so I'll make it official. I'm bringing up two sophomores for Varsity. One happens to be your son."

It took everything Joe had not to stand and beat his chest. He was a cop to the bone, but a parent to the marrow. He'd hoped Rick would see Matt's potential, but one never knew what went on inside a coach's head.

"If you have any objections to him being a nonstarter, tell me now. He'll step up his game playing with these older kids, but he'll ride the pine a lot this year. Next year, though, he'll be a leader."

Tamping down his excitement, Joe said, "He'll work hard for you, Rick."

"That's why he'll be part of this team."

A lump formed in Joe's throat as he focused on the boy working his ass off on the court. Matt needed this accomplishment. After the divorce, his mom had transferred to Chicago, taking his little sister Trish with her. Karen had begged Matt to come, too. He'd staunchly refused. He wasn't leaving his school or his friends.

Secretly, Joe harbored the hope Matt had stayed because of him.

"He'll be back-up to Kinsey," Rick explained, referring to a talented senior point guard. "But Matt needs to get his grades up. They're border-line."

Guilt twisted Joe's insides. "I'll talk to him." It had been too easy to blame the divorce. The plain truth was he hadn't been paying attention. "I take it the other sophomore's Luke Norris?"

Rick grinned. "Hardly a guess. Kid's a coach's dream. At six-two he's still growing, says 'yes, sir and no, sir'. Good god, Joe, I've watched him and Matt in open gym. The way they read each other's amazing." The coach paused for a moment. "Have you met Mrs. Norris?"

Here came the guilt again. Joe shook his head. "I haven't had the pleasure."

Unsmiling, Rick leaned forward. He placed his elbows on his knees and clasped his hands together. "You're going to like her."

"You say that like it's a bad thing."

"Could be. Young widow. Divorced cop. The boys are like glue. She's a looker, Joe. It could get awkward around your place if you get involved with the mom."

A smile tugged at his lips as he resisted the urge to laugh out loud. Was Rick out of his mind? Finding a woman wasn't Joe's problem, finding time to spend with one was. "The woman's lost her husband. I'm never home. I wish I had time to spend with my neighbors."

The coach stood, glancing around. "Good. Just thought I'd mention it. Your lack of free time might get us to the playoffs. By the way, now's your chance to prove me wrong."

"And how can I do that?"

"She just walked in. C'mon, I can kick myself later, but I'll introduce you."

Joe came to his feet and turned in the direction the coach indicated. As a woman with auburn hair, wearing jeans and a green jacket, crossed the gym, his preconceived notion of what Mrs. Norris looked like died instantly. With Luke's coloring, he'd envisioned a tall, full-figured blonde. This woman stood somewhere between five-six and five-eight with honey coloring and a slender build.

This was Luke's *mother?*

Joe's collar grew tight, and all at once he appreciated the coach's concern. Still, he had no choice but to meet her. The way Matt had taken up residence at her place, Joe should be paying her rent.

He descended the bleachers as a few of the players' moms intercepted her, and Joe paused mid-stride. One woman, in particular, he wasn't anxious to see. "Tell you what, I'll meet her some other time."

Amusement lit the coach's eyes. "I'd heard the rumors. This is a first. Joe Crandall scared?"

"Terrified."

One of the returning varsity player's moms, Lydia Ryerson was also a recent divorcee. From the amount of calls he'd seen on his Caller I.D. arising out of one dinner date, she'd apparently taken an interest in him.

"Suit yourself," Rick said, laughing. He sauntered down the bleachers and onto the gymnasium floor.

Joe lingered long enough to listen to the coach's informational spiel, then headed to the parking lot toward his unmarked unit. He replayed his excitement over Matt making the team as well as his curiosity over the attractive widow he'd seen on the court.

Incredibly, his pager was clear, and only two calls were logged on his voice mail. The sun had set and sodium streetlights illuminated the parking lot. Joe pushed the vehicle's interior light to check the numbers as people exited the gym.

Mrs. Norris strode to a white late model Toyota Corolla located a few spaces down from his. He watched her get safely inside and proceeded to return his calls.

An uneventful status report later, he noticed the Corolla was still in place. His interest further piqued when Mrs. Norris left the vehicle and appeared to survey her surroundings uneasily. Joe ended the call to the patrol sergeant and started the engine.

Ready or not, it was time to meet the new neighbor.

Drawing a deep breath, Mel massaged a pounding temple. She'd stayed late at the shop to make a last-minute arrangement for a long-time customer, then rushed to get to Coronado for tryouts. Of course, she hadn't noticed the gas gauge. Why would she? Didn't all cars run on fumes?

Someone pulled alongside her, and instantly she regretted getting out of her car. Life had made her an untrusting soul and she stepped back.

"Problem?" the stranger asked.

"Not at all." She held up her keys for emphasis. "I was just leaving."

"Mrs. Norris?"

The shadows hid his face, and at the use of her name, her heart did a flip-flop.

"Joe Crandall," he said. "Matt's my son."

Standing in the presence of Matt's never-stay-at-home dad, relief flooded her. "Oh, Mr. Crandall, thank heavens. My name's Melanie. Call me a flake, but I'm out of gas."

He reached across the seat and opened the passenger door. Light flooded the interior. "Happens to the best of us. There's a gas station on the corner. Hop in."

Even though his voice seemed kind, she hesitated. After all, taking rides from sweet-talking strangers had been her downfall. But that had been a lifetime ago, and she knew this man. Or at least his son. The decision made, she rounded the car. Sliding in beside him, the scent of coffee and his musky fragrance filled the air. "I can't thank you enough. I wanted to start . . . dinner."

That's when she saw this was no ordinary vehicle. A laptop computer was bracketed to the console, and above it a radio. The world seemed to slow as she focused on every detail. The dash . . . the console . . . and finally the man behind the wheel.

Her gaze took in his long legs, the veins in his powerful-looking hands, his rolled-up sleeves and at last settled on the sizeable scar on his inner forearm.

Shock made her numb.

It wasn't possible. How had she missed the connection? She hadn't thought of the man in years. The cop who'd arrested her, his name had been . . . *Crandall.*

Somehow Mel found the strength to look into his eyes. And when she did, she came face to face with what could only be a mutually shocked expression.

"You," she whispered.

"You," he replied.

She swallowed hard and reached for the handle. Discovering it locked, she said, "On second thought, I'll walk."

The cop just sat there.

Louder this time, and with more resolve, she said, "I'd like you to open the door, Officer Crandall."

"It's Lieutenant."

"What?"

"It hasn't been officer in years, and you're not walking anywhere. The closest gas station's on Fillmore. It's a mile away and it's dark."

"I'll walk *fast.*" She glared at him. "And next time I'll stick to my promise never to accept rides from strangers." Mel pointed to the door. "*Now,* Lieutenant."

Ignoring her demand, he continued to stare. "The change in you is incredible."

Forced to relive a time she'd vowed to forget, humiliation wound its way through her. She'd been high the night that had changed her life forever, and scared out of her mind. None of the cops on scene would believe she had nothing to do with the robbery. She'd acted out of desperation. She must've said horrible things, but in truth, drugs and fear had sent her into a hysterical fugue. "I was told I acted . . . that my language was . . . atrocious."

Lt. Crandall's laugh was sardonic. "Ya think?"

Mel bristled. "I wasn't guilty. They called me an accessory when I had no idea what Maxwell was up to. When you tried to handcuff me, I panicked."

Holding out his left arm, he displayed the scar. "You resisted arrest. I had no choice."

A younger version of the man seated beside her had trapped Mel face down in an alley. A piece of broken glass had lain within reach. She flinched at the pain she'd inflicted and looked away. "I repeat. I was innocent. I spent time in prison for a crime I didn't commit."

"The clerk identified you."

"Of course, he did. Drake pulled a gun. I came out of the bathroom and tried to stop him."

"The only reason that clerk isn't dead is because Maxwell's gun jammed. Probably hadn't taken time to clean it from his last murder," the cop said.

The unfairness of his words hit her like a blast of arctic air. She'd had no idea she'd taken a ride with a cold-blooded killer. She itched to slap the man who wouldn't listen to reason. Thinking of Luke she held back. Striking a cop would be a huge mistake. She gritted her teeth and dug her nails into her palms. "My lawyer advised me to take the plea."

Their mutual amazement culminated into stunned silence. The dashboard lights immersed the car's interior in a soft, eerie glow. Her temporary jailer gazed out the windshield, revealing a masculine profile enhanced by the dark stubble framing his jaw. She understood now where Matt got his good looks.

Oh, for crying out loud. Why would she notice this now?

As the lieutenant stared straight ahead, his voice held gruff disbelief. "What were the odds of this happening?"

When she didn't reply, he turned sharply in her direction and answered for her. "I'd say the odds were nil. Did you plan this?"

A burst of hysterical laughter escaped her lips and she slapped her thigh. "Did I plan this? Well, gosh, you found me out. I called my realtor and said, 'Oh, by the way, when you're looking for houses, see if you can find the police officer who arrested me way back when. I think living next door to him would be a hoot.'" Amazed at his illogical thinking, she shook her head. "Are you nuts?"

"What I am is a cop, and you're pushing your luck."

"You've obviously made up your mind about me."

"Damn straight I have."

Her gaze slanted toward the parking lot. Nausea overcame her and she clutched her stomach. If only the earth would split open and swallow her whole.

The lieutenant's eyes narrowed. "What's wrong? What's happening? Are you sick?"

"The boys," she whispered. "Practice must be over. They're headed this way."

"I'll handle this." He opened the door. "Stay here."

"I will not." She wasn't about to take orders from this man.

"We're not finished, Mrs. Norris. *Stay here.*" Without a word or a look back he stepped out of the car.

She strained to see him talking with the boys. In the dark, the vehicle's headlights captured their profiles. Oh, God, what was he telling them? Suddenly, Luke and Matt gave each other high fives and darted back toward the gym.

The big oaf slid into the car again to face her obviously bewildered expression. "What did you say to them? Where do they think they're going? Luke has homework."

"Well, aren't you a regular PTO mom. The coach told them he'd order pizza and they could watch films. Under the circumstances, I thought it was a stellar idea. I told them we'd pick them up in an hour."

"Fine." She folded her arms. "Now if you're through with your insults, I think we've both had enough of our reunion."

Lt. Crandall fastened his seatbelt and put the car into gear.

"What are you doing?"

He didn't answer, merely drove toward the edge of the high school parking lot. A few minutes later, they entered the gas station on the corner. She withdrew her wallet to pay, but he ignored her. He exited the car, dug a plastic gas container out of the trunk and disappeared into a well-lit convenience store.

When he returned she responded inanely with, "Thank you."

His jaw clenched. "Don't thank me. After all the meals you've provided for Matt, I figure I owe you." Lt. Crandall took a deep breath, and for a moment the situation seemed as difficult for him as it was for her.

"Look, I don't know how to put this without screwing it up any further. By all accounts you're not the same person you were. That's great. I'm sorry I insulted you. I'm truly relieved you've turned your life around."

Grateful he'd admitted that much, she nodded.

"But given our past, I think it's fair to say we could never be friends."

She lowered her head as a wall of frustration ballooned inside her. He obviously knew how to put people behind bars, but understood nothing about them paying their debt to society. Her husband had taught her so much, and in that moment, she felt grief anew.

"Now we have a situation that involves our boys," the cop added, searching her face. "So my question to you is, what are we going to do to split them apart?"

Melanie Norris's stoic expression dissolved into one of despair. "You'd punish our children for something I did fifteen years ago? What kind of monster are you?"

Her indignation took him off guard. What did she expect? For them to ignore the past and become the best of buddies? "You don't exactly come with sterling references, lady, and I'm not about to sacrifice my kid."

Glancing away from him, she drew her hands into fists in her lap. For a time she didn't speak. At last she returned his gaze. "I'd probably do the same thing if I were you."

Hell. A quiet, logical response was the last thing he'd expected. Reconciling the proud, beautiful woman sitting next to him to the hellion of yesterday was nearly impossible. It was like watching an actress perform two roles.

Then it occurred to him. Maybe she was. He'd met all kinds in his line of work. People who could look you in the eye, tell you they didn't pull the trigger, while holding the murder weapon in their hand. On the other hand, he could also cite numerous examples of people who against all odds had turned their lives around.

A throbbing ache resonated behind his left eye. Of one thing he was certain, Matt wasn't going to be part of the equation while Joe made up his mind. He switched on the ignition. "I'm glad we understand each other. I'll take you back to your car."

Chapter Three

At home in his darkened den, Joe sat, arms crossed, feet propped upon his desk, surrounded by a growing stack of paperwork and unopened mail. Why did he feel like the proverbial heel in this misadventure? Obviously, the boys had been confused when both parents showed up and took them home in separate vehicles. The kids liked each other, and from what Coach Hood had said, Melanie had raised an exceptional son.

Hold everything. When had he stopped thinking of her as Mrs. Norris and transitioned to Melanie?

Joe glanced across the room at his liquor cabinet, but Jim Beam failed to call to him tonight. Besides, if more robberies occurred, he needed his wits about him. He lifted his feet off the desk, then rose and sauntered to the den's side window. A full moon illuminated the sky, and a silhouette in the upstairs window next door caught Joe's gaze.

Not what he wanted to see right now, the woman stood brushing her hair. Captivated, he watched until the ghostly vision moved away.

Jesus, she was beautiful.

If he wasn't careful, he'd be arrested for voyeurism. What a career-ending headline that would make. *Police lieutenant nailed as Peeping Tom.* He'd joined Coach Hood's ranks in thinking about the woman, and officially gone insane.

Joe studied the ragged scar on his forearm. Seeing her again after all these years had been a shock, that's all. After he became accustomed to the idea of her living next door, she'd be no more, no less to him than the rest of his neighbors.

Joe turned the mini-blind wand, double-checked the locks and climbed the stairs. Matt's bedroom door was closed, but light glowed from the crack beneath it.

He knocked.

"Yeah?"

"It's after eleven, Matt." Joe opened the door to find the boy absorbed in something on his computer. A short sound played from the speaker, and by the way his son's gaze darted toward the screen, Joe assumed it had to be some kind of instant message. "Is your homework done?"

"I finished it at school."

Narrowing his gaze, Joe said, "Heads up. Starting tomorrow, I'll be logging in to see your grades."

Matt mumbled something unintelligible under his breath.

"What was that?"

"I said, 'yes, sir.'" Matt looked up, but not happily.

"Right answer. Good night, son. Lights out in ten."

This time as Joe shut the door, he made no effort to glean the boy's muttered response. He had enough on his mind trying to understand his inexplicable attraction to the off-limits Melanie Norris.

Fluffing her pillow for the twentieth time hadn't helped. Mel couldn't sleep. And if she didn't fall asleep she'd be a zombie tomorrow. *Damn* Officer Joe Crandall or Lieutenant or whatever his stuffy title was nowadays. He'd taken her happy new life and reduced it to rubble. And damn her scarred, impetuous youth. Now Luke and Matt would bear the brunt of her actions as well.

She sat upright, drew her knees to her chest and hugged them. On the way home tonight, she'd tried to speak to Luke about curbing his friendship with Matt. But the kid was so pumped about practice, she let him talk. His sullen moods were less frequent these days. Luke was likeable and made friends easily. Still, a special bond already existed between him and the kid next door, and the separation wouldn't be easy.

Carl had urged her to tell Luke about her past, claiming that children needed to understand that parents weren't perfect. Because he hadn't insisted, she never had.

Tears welled. She ordered them back. Crying hadn't solved her problems fifteen years ago, it hadn't eased Carl's pain and suffering and it wasn't likely to help her now.

Mel straightened and slid out of bed. If sleep wouldn't come, at least she had options. She eased into her robe and slippers, took a quick peek in at Luke, then wandered downstairs to the basement.

Immediately the smell of damp earth filled her senses, the soft glow of grow lights bid her welcome and her heartache lessened. Portable space heaters and humidifiers provided the climate for the tiny seedlings breaking through the dirt beneath their protective plastic. The moisture felt good on her skin. And because she doted on these baby plants, and believed it helped, she switched on classical music. She'd even been known to talk to them, much to her son's laughter and dismay.

How could he understand? Watching life spring into existence had long filled the void that had gotten her through some desolate times.

Smiling, Mel set to work checking the soil's pH for what she hoped would be an outstanding array of Dragon Wing begonias. They'd be the perfect complement to the northern red oak growing out front. Already, she and Luke had spent hours trimming, then digging up the dead Juniper bushes surrounding the property. If the weather stayed decent, they'd repaint the trim and the shutters soon.

She stopped, suddenly amazed. With tonight's turn of events, why wasn't she frantic, packing her bags?

The point was, she wasn't. For years, she'd held her head high. She no longer knew how to act or feel like an ex-convict. And Lieutenant Crandall's biased reminder wasn't going to make her act like one now. Until the warden's phone call, where she'd learned of Drake Maxwell's impending release, she'd all but erased her troubled youth from her mind.

You are what you believe you are, sweetheart.

Along with his generosity, Mel treasured her husband's memory. *Thanks, Carl.*

Moving toward the narrow flight of steps, she left the music on. Then switching off the basement's overhead light, she climbed the stairs and breathed easier.

A truly evil man had been the factor behind the move to Colorado Springs. The relocation had been emotional as well as exhausting. Joe Crandall might be an ogre, but Mel was fairly certain he wasn't bad. Let him do his worst. She and Luke would survive. No one was forcing them from their home ever again.

Chapter Four

"Hey, Max, you asleep?"

Drake Maxwell stared at a crack in the wall that had begun as a tiny fissure and now ran more than a foot long. He slept on a flimsy fireproof mattress, on a bed bolted to the wall in a never darkened eight-by-ten cell, in a place that reeked of cigarette smoke, piss and disinfectant. He had no money. Everything he owned in this world was in a cardboard box next to the crapper in the corner. Even his dumps were supervised.

Hell, no, he wasn't asleep. He hadn't slept in fifteen years.

"What do you want, Garcia?"

"Just wondered if you're excited, man? One more day."

Garcia was a pesky little fucker. Into feelings and all that. Up for parole in six months, he never let anyone on the block forget it.

"Yeah, man, I'm excited."

"You don't sound it, *hombre*, you sound pissed." From overhead, Drake listened to the familiar sound of Garcia shifting positions. "What's the first thing you're gonna do when you get out?"

Warning bells went off in Drake's brain. Garcia rambled incessantly, but he usually rambled about himself. He was half-afraid of his murderous roomie and never asked anything specific or personal.

Drake hadn't caught Garcia cozying up to the guards—or *the man* as the cons called them—but then Garcia wasn't someone Drake paid attention to anyway. Had the warden, knowing there wouldn't be a parole officer to baby-sit his ass, put his cellmate up to this late-night chat?

Cautiously Drake replied with, "Get me a job. What do you think I'm gonna do?"

Garcia's giggle resembled a teenage girl's. "I know what I'd do. I'd get me a woman."

Melanie Daniel's face flashed in Drake's mind. Tightening his hands into fists and folding his arms over his chest, he ground his back teeth together. He'd get him a woman, all right.

"You staying around these parts?" Garcia persisted.

The warning bells turned into full-fledged sirens. With the little cash he'd made in the pen, he'd paid a guard with a gambling problem for information on Melanie's whereabouts. Had the fat prick squealed?

Drake needed to think. More importantly, he had to talk . . . fast. "My brother owns a construction company outside of L.A. He's promised me work."

Garcia paused, seeming to absorb the information. "That's cool, bro. Just wanted you to know you have choices."

Drake narrowed his gaze. "What kind of choices?"

"Do you remember a con named Denny Ramirez?"

So many inmates had come and gone during Drake's sentence; his mind went momentarily blank. Then he remembered. Ramirez had shared an adjoining cell. He'd been quiet, a leader. He'd also been smart enough to keep his head down, his mouth shut, and do his time.

"Car thief, right?"

"Yeah, busted for running a chop shop ring. Denny's my cousin. He's got himself a new gig on the outside."

"What kind of gig?"

"He'd cut off my legs if I told, man. But Denny wanted me to let you in on it because, get this, you gave him the idea."

Drake smirked. There wasn't a con in the place who didn't talk smack about what he'd do differently to avoid getting caught. Kin or no kin, cons didn't take kindly to people rolling on them. Years ago, Drake had put a man in the infirmary for doing just that. Drake had ended up in solitary, but the payback had been worth it. His reputation had spread and no one had dared snitch on him again.

"Anyways," Garcia said, "Denny said to look him up if you're interested. He's living in the Springs."

Drake shook his head. No way was he going anywhere near Colorado Springs. That's where life had gone south. "Got other plans."

"That's cool, bro."

"You gonna participate in this so-called gig when you get out?"

"Nah, Denny don't want no parolees," Garcia said. "He wants people who don't have to check in, dudes who can move around."

Much as he wanted no part in it, Drake found the scheme worth noting. What had he said to spark an idea? Not that it mattered, he was done. He'd committed the robberies when he was too young to access his trust. He was well over twenty-five now. He'd claim his inheritance and plant his ass on a beach somewhere, after achieving his longtime goal, of course.

Drake felt his lips curve upward. He rarely grinned anymore. Fifteen years in this hole didn't give a man much to smile about.

He'd smile again, he promised himself. When he plunged a knife into the heart of the backstabbing bitch that put him in here, he'd be downright giddy.

Chapter Five

Without a word, Joe observed morning roll call, nodded to Chris, then made a quick exit toward his office. Last night should've been his night to catch up on sleep. Thanks to Melanie Norris's startling re-introduction into his life, the REM cycles never happened.

In the hallway he passed the department secretary, who in a singsong voice said, "You have a visitor," as she ambled on by. Joe slowed his pace and paused in the doorway.

Bruce Bennett, the El Paso County District Attorney sat in Joe's office poring over paperwork.

"Shouldn't you be out campaigning somewhere?" Joe asked.

An unsmiling Bruce looked up from his task and handed Joe the file request form he'd sent over to the D.A.'s office that morning. "Maybe. Thought I'd save the taxpayers' money and play department shrink instead."

Joe felt his gut lurch. Along with Drake Maxwell's case file, he'd requested Melanie's. He didn't give a rat's ass about Maxwell, but he'd already run a NCIC check on her and come up with nothing. Involving the District Attorney hadn't been part of his plan.

Bruce removed a thick Pendaflex folder from his briefcase followed by a much smaller one. "Here's the information you requested, Lieutenant."

"Thanks." Joe moved farther into the room. "I hope you weren't counting on a tip. I wasn't expecting such a high-paid runner."

Ignoring Joe's sarcasm, the D.A. said, "When I told Sgt. Sandoval to alert you about Maxwell, I knew you'd be concerned, I didn't think you'd become obsessed. What's with you, Joe? Maxwell's getting out. You're not a rookie. It's a done deal."

"Just couldn't remember the facts of the case, that's all."

Bruce shook his head. "Don't take up politics, my friend. You're a terrible liar."

"Thanks for bringing these by. Give Marianne and the kids my love."

"You asshole." Bruce jabbed an index finger on the convict's file. "Why the interest in these old cases?"

Christ. Joe had known better than to go digging. Bruce was right. The details of his first major bust were all but seared into his brain. He was searching for clues. Big ones, as to why Melanie Norris had suddenly appeared in the Springs, his neighbor no less, with Drake Maxwell on the verge of being released.

Was it possible, after all these years, that the two were set on revenge?

Taking a deep breath, Joe closed the door. He glanced about the room. "Shrink, huh? I don't even have a couch."

Bruce lifted a shoulder. "That's why you'll only get the mail-order version of my psych experience. C'mon, Joe. Between you and me. What's going on?"

Bruce Bennett was a bulldog of a prosecutor, but honest as any man Joe had ever known. For some reason it mattered that he spare Melanie's reputation if at all possible. With the D.A.'s promise assured, Joe recited the bizarre happenings of yesterday.

For several long seconds, his colleague didn't speak. When at last he did, Bruce said, "So that's why you ordered her file. I wondered. Statistically speaking, I'd say you've been hit by lightning."

"About as probable," Joe admitted.

"You think she's out for revenge?"

"The thought occurred to me. If she were, though, you'd think she'd do it in a less conspicuous way than moving next door. Honest to God, Bruce, she was as shocked as I was."

The D.A. opened Melanie's smaller file and perused it slowly. "I recall this now. We were after Maxwell, and she was our link to put him away. Correct me if any of these facts are wrong, but this states your partner apprehended Maxwell while you ran after Melanie. It was Clyde Rogers' testimony that put Maxwell behind bars, not yours."

"That's how I remember things. Still, people fixate on the damndest things."

"They do, indeed." Bruce frowned. "Melanie Daniels accepted a five-year plea, but as anticipated, she received parole after nine months. According to her case file, Maxwell threatened retaliation after she testified against him."

"So the revenge theory seems less plausible," Joe said. "You think she's running?"

"If she is, she didn't run very far." Bruce continued turning pages. His gaze settled on something, then widened. Frowning, he glanced at Joe. "Impeccable prison record, no parole violations."

"Do I hear a *but* in there?"

"How old did you say her son is?"

"Same age as mine. Fifteen. Why?"

"You have a go." Bruce slid the file across the desk. "My wife accuses me of being a judgmental schmuck. Maybe I'm taking these words out of context."

"Comes with the territory." Joe read the parole board's benign report, followed by a much more damning statement provided in her parole officer's handwritten scrawl.

Melanie Daniels Norris may not have committed a crime in the last several years, but she was certainly no innocent. Along with disgust, an odd sense of disappointment clutched at Joe's chest. "The parole officer claims she exchanged sexual favors with a corrections officer."

Bruce met Joe's stare. "And as a result bore the man's child."

"Mel, take line two. Chloe, these arrangements were due at the Cliff House *yesterday.*"

As predicted Mel was a zombie at work, but store owner Aaron Meyers was too absorbed in running two floral design businesses to let her dig her grave and rest in peace. With Thanksgiving a couple weeks away, customers were already planning December's holiday season as well.

Mel answered, "Pinnacle Creations," and took a large order from one of Aaron's wealthy customers. "That was Elaine Preston," she hollered over the ringing phones and five jabbering co-workers. "Her husband wants custom wreaths designed for his major clients."

Aaron gasped. "Of course, she can't let us survive Thanksgiving first. How many?"

"Twenty-five," Mel replied, wincing, "by December first."

"Talk about multi-tasking," Aaron said. "All right, girlfriend. This is your project. Call the south shop. If they don't have what you need, call the supplier. Do what you have to do."

Store manager Karlee Stanfield hung up from another line and glanced from him to Mel. "Aaron, isn't it a little soon? Do you want me to ask one of the others—"

"No. Melanie can handle this." Leaving no room for debate, Aaron moved onto the next assignment.

Mel gave Karlee what must've been a panicked look.

"He's right, Mel. You can," the manager said. "But I'm here if you need me."

Watching her coworkers go about their own creative frenzies, Mel phoned the south store, then pulled several supply catalogs from the shelf.

On shaky legs, she'd walked into the exclusive shop a month ago and asked for a job. Her horticulture background had helped, but there was always the prejudicial application where she was required by law to list her felony conviction. The storeowner had studied the form for a good while before saying, "When can you start?"

When she replied, "Tomorrow," he'd said, "I need you today." Mel immediately liked Aaron. She loved his entrepreneurial spirit, his creative flare and willingness to let her experiment with color, fragrances and design. He'd never said a word about her past, paid her a fair wage, and was tolerant of her single-mother status.

In short, Aaron was as opposite from Lt. Joe Crandall as a sparrow from a scorpion. What was she going to do if the lieutenant insisted on separating

Chapter Six

Joe had numerous character flaws. Indecisiveness wasn't one of them. Yet, as he entered Warden Simon Rivers' office to wait, the soundness and ethics of coming here weighed heavily on Joe's mind.

Particularly since the warden Joe had come to talk to most likely had never heard of Drake Maxwell.

The East Cañon Complex where Joe now stood housed seven prisons, from minimum to close security, high-risk offenders. Maxwell had been incarcerated in the Colorado State Penitentiary, a prison ranked level V. No big surprise there. But the man Joe had come to see supervised the Arrowhead Correctional Center, a level III facility.

Two years previously, however, before it closed, Simon had been warden of the Colorado Women's Correctional Facility, the prison where Melanie Daniels had done time.

So what was Joe doing here? His job, he told himself, or at least what was necessary. Maxwell was a book already read, Melanie Daniels Norris an unfinished novel.

Warden Rivers had been detained, his secretary explained. To pass the time, Joe peered out the window of the top man's office, finding nothing aesthetic about miles of razor wire, guard towers and cinderblock fencing. From the northwest, a storm was rolling in, and with clouds the color of charcoal, and not a patch of blue sky to be seen, snow threatened.

Beneath Joe's jacket, his shoulder holster lay conspicuously empty. He missed the 9 mm Glock he'd locked in his trunk. Inside the prison, he'd be required to turn the gun over to security. Call him paranoid, but he trusted his weapon to no one.

The door opened, and a winded man with a graying crew cut and wire-rimmed glasses entered. "Lieutenant Crandall? Simon Rivers." He extended his hand. "I apologize. My meeting ran long."

Simon had an intelligent face and a grip that inspired Joe to believe if anyone could help him, this man could. "I appreciate you seeing me on such short notice."

"Not a problem. Why don't we sit down?" Simon looped his trench coat on a tree rack beside the Colorado State flag and dropped into a chair behind his desk.

Joe took the proffered seat.

"Frankly, your phone call intrigued me. Information about a former convict. Is this pertaining to a case you're working on?"

Here came a sticking point. If the information Joe sought wasn't relevant to an active case, the prison head was under no obligation to talk to him.

"It's a closed case, generating new interest," Joe said, hedging. "It's not pertaining to a male convict, Warden. It concerns a female inmate. How long were you warden at the women's correctional facility?"

"Seven years. But before that time, I worked as a corrections officer for nearly twenty-four."

Excellent. Chances were Simon had known both Melanie Daniels and her prison guard lover. "I'm hoping you can shed some light on a few things."

The warden leaned forward. Linking his hands together, he rested his forearms on his desk. "I'll provide whatever information I can. I'm bound by confidentiality, you understand. What's the convict's name?"

"Melanie Daniels."

Simon didn't even blink, but the color leached from his face. Joe was an expert in reading people under interrogation. And although Simon didn't flinch or change facial expressions, Joe suspected the man's heart rate and blood pressure had just elevated.

"She was a prisoner in the women's facility fifteen years ago, Warden."

"I know who Melanie Daniels is, Lieutenant." Simon rose from his chair. "This meeting is over."

Maintaining a calm he didn't feel, Joe remained in his seat. This certainly wasn't the reaction he'd expected from a colleague. "Mind if I ask why?"

"Confidentiality issues. I made myself clear."

"I merely gave you her name. I never asked a question."

Simon glared at him. "Melanie Daniels was incarcerated in the Colorado Women's Correctional Facility for a period of nine months. She was an exemplary prisoner who served an abbreviated sentence and then was released. I'll see you out."

Joe tamped down his frustration. He'd come for answers, but this wasn't his turf. If the warden wanted him gone, he didn't exactly have choices. Preparing to abide by the man's request, Joe took one final gamble. "Her married name is Norris now. She recently lost her husband."

Simon took his hand from the knob. He turned, pinning Joe with a look that made it clear his allegiance ran elsewhere. "What's this about, Lieutenant? Is Mrs. Norris all right?"

"She's fine, Warden. I have a personal stake in coming here. I'd appreciate it if you'd talk to me."

Some of the color returned to Simon's face. "Give me a second." Opening the door, he said to his secretary, "Elizabeth, no phone calls. No interruptions from anyone."

"Yes, Warden Rivers."

He shut the door, slowly returning to the executive chair.

On the credenza behind him sat family pictures. The walls held diplomas, awards, and a picture of the man with the governor.

Simon took so long to speak, Joe resisted checking his watch.

"When you say personal," the warden finally asked, "what do you mean?"

"I was her arresting officer."

"I don't follow."

"She moved in next door."

The warden squeezed his eyes shut. "Well, I'll be damned." Two seconds later, though, his expression hardened. "But the fact that you made an arrest doesn't entitle you—"

"Do you have children, Warden?"

"Three grown boys. What has that got to do with anything?"

"Mrs. Norris has a son the same age as mine." Joe held out his hands. "They're spending every waking hour together. I realize I've exceeded my authority. But if it was your son, and a woman with a questionable past had the power to influence him, what would you do?"

Simon stood and strode to the window. Shoving his hands in his pockets, he jingled the coins within and stared out into the prison yard. "I wouldn't be too happy."

"I'm not here to hurt her, Warden. I give you my word."

For a time Simon faced the window. At last he pivoted, the struggle at violating not only Melanie's confidence, but her civil rights, deepening the lines in his face. "What I told you before was true. Melanie *was* exemplary. I was a lieutenant when she was processed, although I never interacted with her. It was common knowledge, however, that we had a youngster on our hands, and she was having a rough go of it."

Surprised at how much he didn't want to know this part, Joe leaned forward. Ignoring what he knew of Melanie Norris now, he focused on what she had been. "How rough?"

"Young, pretty girl, new to the system. You know the drill. Some women behind bars are predators, vicious. Oftentimes more so than men."

Joe set his jaw. Years of law enforcement played through his mind as he considered what Melanie might've gone through behind these walls. No doubt about it, at times the job sucked.

"Naturally she got into scrapes at first," the warden said. "Ended up in the infirmary once with eyes swollen shut and a broken rib. Turned out, though, that Melanie was tough. She also had something most inmates don't. Brains. She formed an alliance with one of the leaders on the block, taught her to read, helped her earn her G.E.D. That smart move put Melanie under the woman's protection."

Joe discovered he'd been holding his breath. As the air left his lungs, he gained a greater respect for the term *sigh of relief.*

"From that point she kept mostly to herself, spending much of her time in the prison's greenhouse. From there, you know the rest. Her first hearing came around and she was paroled."

"Why do you suppose she stayed in Cañon City?" Joe asked.

"The way I heard it, she had nowhere else to go."

"Family?"

"Mother's dead. Hasn't spoken to her father in years."

Joe filed her family history away for later. Odd, the warden hadn't mentioned a pregnancy. "How'd she make ends meet after her release?"

"She went to work as a nanny."

"A nanny," Joe repeated.

"For one of the correction officers. A man by the name of Carl Norris."

"Her dead husband?"

"One and the same."

Simon moved away from the window and returned to his chair.

Joe shook his head. "Warden, I don't know how to say this tactfully, so I won't even try. A report I read from her parole officer claims she had an affair with a corrections officer during her sentence and became pregnant."

The warden studied Joe, the accusation heavy between them. "I remember the parole officer. A weasel of a man who tried to force parolees into having sex with him. He later lost his job and was sued after harassing dozens of women.

"Naturally, the rumors flew like buckshot when Carl hired her, even kept him from being promoted. It's human nature to think the worst."

"Did Carl work on Melanie's block?"

"No. But they knew each other. Did they have an affair? I never believed it."

"She *is* a beautiful woman," Joe pointed out. "Like the parole officer, it wouldn't be the first time a man used his position—"

"Not Carl," Simon replied heatedly. "Carl Norris was one of my best friends. He was a man of principle. I assure you he wasn't soft on the convicts who needed to be here. Nor was he cavalier about his marriage. As the saying goes, 'desperate times called for desperate measures.' Melanie didn't belong in prison. We recognized that soon after she got here. She was a kid. Misguided, but she was a kid.

"Then as fate would have it," the warden went on, "days before her parole, Carl's wife died in a collision on 115."

God, no, Joe thought.

"When others wouldn't even think of it, Carl gave Mel a chance. It wasn't like he had a helluva lot of choice, he had a six-week-old baby boy to consider."

Several moments lapsed before the statement sunk in. When it did, Joe felt like he'd been sucker-punched. Melanie hadn't been pregnant. Perhaps she'd rejected the parole officer's advances, and taking his revenge, he altered his report. "Luke. She's not his biological mother."

Warden Rivers speared Joe with a look that said he'd made the connection. It also hinted at how deep Simon's feelings ran. "And now you know. Melanie Norris lived in this town for quite a few years. People liked her, respected her. She's not the big bad wolf, Lieutenant. What's more, she may not have given birth to Luke, but I've never heard it said by anyone that she's not that boy's mother in every other way."

Chapter Seven

With exactly seven minutes to get to practice, Luke leaned his crutches against an adjacent locker, then balancing on one foot, twirled his locker combination and yanked on the flimsy metal door. He lifted his hoodie off the loop, grabbed his English lit and crammed his Geometry text back inside. Technically, he could slack off because he was injured, but he wasn't about to be late. Luke might not be on the court today, but he planned to *own* it in the near future.

Through the double door windows at the end of the hallway, he saw it had started to snow and he groaned. Maneuvering on crutches had turned out to be a royal pain. That and English lit class. Holy snap, Mrs. Carson had it out for him. The woman had to be some kind of evil teacher *spy*. How else could she know when Luke was caught up in his other courses? And why had she made it her goal in life to load him up with even more? Add basketball to his schedule and he could forget about free time.

And adults thought they had it rough.

Something tickled the back of his neck and he swatted at it. When it happened again, he knew it wasn't something, but some*body*. Expecting one of his teammates, Luke pivoted to tackle the freak, and *whoa!* He caught his breath.

The body behind Luke wasn't a freak. She was a girl—a very *cute* girl.

She wore a heavy coat, but there was no missing the curves in her legs. Luke swallowed hard. *Nice long legs.*

"Nice to meet you, Luke Norris," she said, eyeing his crutches and tossing her straight blond hair over her shoulder. "I'm Jen. I've seen you practicing. Just wanted to stop by and tell you it sucks about your ankle."

Luke managed to say thanks without his voice cracking.

"Mind if I ask you a question?"

Too tongue-tied to answer, he simply stared at her and nodded.

Her brows drew together and her mouth twisted into a frown. "Did you get held back? I mean, you're kind of big for a sophomore."

Nice of her to stop by and call me a loser. Luke slammed his locker and reached for his sticks. "No, I'm just . . . Look, I gotta get to practice."

"I know. I'm on the cheerleading squad, and we're practicing in the auxiliary gym." She wrinkled her nose. "Sorry if I embarrassed you. But by the way you play, my friends and I thought you were older."

Luke didn't need a mirror to know that his face had turned beet red, one of the side effects of being so pale. Way to stress to impress, when his complexion gave him away faster than a road flare.

"So," she said, "want to walk over to the gym with me?"

She wanted to walk with *him?* Luke wanted to say, *who wouldn't?* But it was as if when he'd slammed his locker, he'd forgotten his tongue inside. When he didn't answer, it was Jen's turn to turn red. She stepped back. "Oh, I get it. You're going out with someone."

Luke all but choked. *Going out with someone?* "No! I mean, I'm *not*. I mean, sure, I'll walk with you."

"Sweet," she said. "Let's do it."

Luke slid his arms through the straps of his backpack, then with Jen walking beside him, he hobbled ahead of her to get the door. Now might be a great time to show her he could complete a sentence. "So, uh, is this your first year cheerleading?"

As they stepped outside, fresh, powdery snow stuck to everything, including her pretty face. *Sheesh, stop gawking, Norris.*

Wiping snowflakes away, Jen laughed and smiled back at him. "No, I've been at it for a while. This is my senior year."

Mel swung her Corolla into a parking space, switched off the radio and took her anger out on the unseen broadcaster. The wisecracking jerk had been right about one thing. The blizzard meteorologists had predicted would miss El Paso County had settled in like an uninvited guest with no plans to leave. As temperatures dropped and the streets turned to ice, Mel endured a storm of her own. She entered the lobby of the Police Operations Center, brushed off her coat, stomped her feet and shoved the wet hair out of her eyes.

With cars drifting into snow banks, she had no business being anywhere but at home. Unfortunately, Lt. Crandall had made her his business, and like the frost adhering to the windows, fury gripped her soul.

Simon had told Joe *everything*. For long moments afterward, Mel had held her breath and felt the blood rushing through her ears as the warden related his morning discussion with her next door nemesis.

"Under the circumstances, I thought he should know," Simon had said after apologizing profusely at what Mel perceived as a gross betrayal. "He appears to be a decent guy, Melanie, and having a cop for a neighbor might be just what you need."

Lt. Crandall was the last thing she needed and she intended to tell him so. Too angry to be nervous, she'd barged into the operations center without thinking things through. Yet, as armed men and women wearing badges sauntered past, she felt her fifteen-year-old humiliation to the core.

"Ma'am, have you been helped?"

She pivoted to find a uniformed officer whose badge read, C. Sandoval, addressing her.

A youthful face belied his age, but the gray at his temples and the three stripes on his sleeve promised he wasn't a rookie.

"I'm here to see Lt. Crandall." As she spoke, the words came out a dry, strangled rasp. Mel cleared her throat.

The man who'd intruded on her deepest, darkest secrets chose that moment to appear. Mel drew her hands into fists inside her coat pockets. Looking every inch the professional and in charge, he wore a long-sleeved white cotton shirt and tailored black pants. And as gold reflected off the badge on his belt, she wasn't sure what was more intimidating, the breadth of his shoulders or the gun tucked in his holster.

Concern etched his features as he strode toward her. "The city's on accident alert, Mrs. Norris. What are you doing here?"

What am I doing here? Mel wanted to scream, "*You idiot,*" but the insult lodged in her throat. The man had breached his authority, invaded her privacy. How dare he act as if he didn't know why she was here, or worse, that she was wrong to confront him?

He nodded to the sergeant who with one glance made a silent exit.

"You heard from Warden Rivers," Joe said.

"Are you surprised? Not only was he my husband's boss, he's a close personal friend."

Joe shook his head. "I wanted to tell you myself, that's all. C'mon. Let's talk."

Once again, he was giving her orders. Even so, she could hardly tell him what she thought of him in the lobby. Struggling with how she *really* wanted to handle the situation, she followed.

Stonily, Mel waited while he used an access card to open the steel door he'd just come through. She walked beside him, passing cubicles of law enforcement personnel until they came to a small office at the far side of the corridor.

He stood aside for her to enter, then pointed to a chair. "Would you like to sit down?"

She glanced toward the window. Outside, the snow continued to fall and she knew a moment's panic. She had a couple of hours before she had to pick up Luke, but if the coach cancelled practice, what then? "No. What I have to say won't take long."

"Fine. But I'm going to. I've had a long day." He sat in the chair behind his desk.

Mel met his stare with an equal challenge. "I should say. Looking into my past so *thoroughly* must take a lot out of a man."

"You're angry."

"Furious."

"You have every right to be." His matter-of-fact tone set her teeth on edge, her heart to pounding, enraging her further.

"I told you my past was none of your business. If I alerted your supervisor—"

"You'd have my badge."

Mel opened her mouth, but words failed her. She hadn't considered how deeply the ramifications of his conduct ran.

"My guess is my commander's in his office. If you like, we can go see him now."

"Your career means so little to you?"

The lieutenant rose from the chair and walked to the door. "On the contrary, my career means everything. My son means more. You wouldn't answer my questions. I had to know." He extended his arm. "Shall we?"

When she made no move to accompany him, he said, "I'm busy, Mrs. Norris. It's treacherous outside. You should get home. What's it going to be?"

Shooting him was out of the question. Suddenly, all she wanted to be was gone. She brushed by him. "Keep your job, you pompous jerk. But I warn you, stay the hell out of my personal business."

"And if your boyfriend shows up, should I look the other way?"

Mel gasped. The cop was beyond cruel. He played on her deepest fear. "In fifteen years you haven't changed. You're still one mean son of a bitch."

Lt. Crandall moved so close she could smell his aftershave, glimpse the muscle ticking in his jaw and the makings of a five o'clock shadow.

She wasn't about to retreat.

"Maybe so, Melanie. But if Drake Maxwell gets wind of your location, I'll be the best friend you've got."

Feeling like he'd butchered Mary's little lamb, Joe escorted Melanie out of the building. When she'd stared up at him with huge, fear-filled eyes, he'd wanted to pull her close and kiss her senseless.

No one deserved to be that afraid. So what had he done? Terrified her even more by reminding her of Drake Maxwell's impending release from prison.

Joe watched for a moment as she cleared the snow off her car, then ordered patrol to make sure she got home. He would've offered to drive her, but figured she'd sooner scratch his eyes out than be anywhere in his vicinity. He did manage one compromise before she left. He insisted on picking up the boys from practice. With Luke's bum ankle, and in this weather, no way could the slender Melanie Norris maneuver someone of Luke's stature into her car.

Looking back, Joe should've seen that the kid didn't resemble her in the slightest. Fair skinned and blond, Luke was far different from his stepmother's auburn hair and golden coloring. When Luke grew to be a man, he'd bear the physique of a Viking warrior.

What was it about her that brought out the antagonistic asshole inside Joe? She had every right to demand an apology. He had indeed crossed a line by going to such lengths to discover her past.

Melanie deserved better from him.

Simon Rivers had explained that for years Maxwell had touted his plans for revenge to anyone who would listen. Then, in the last few years, he'd grown moody and silent. When asked about the change, he'd shrug, claim some ridiculous notion like he'd found Jesus, or that he'd put Melanie Daniels behind him.

Not many in positions of authority bought the convict's story, and because of Melanie's marriage to Carl Norris, she now fell under the protection of the Department of Corrections. Before Carl had died, he'd asked the warden to look out for his family, to protect Melanie from the man who'd threatened her life.

Simon Rivers had been the idea man behind the Norris's move to Colorado Springs. The Springs, he'd explained, was close enough that if Melanie needed him, he could get to her, and, ideally, the last place Maxwell would look since it was where the crime had been committed.

Because Melanie had taken her husband's last name, the plan was secret, furtive and logical. With only one hitch, Simon never thought to check out the neighbors.

Joe secured his weapon, then reached for his trench coat. With snow falling and an apology due, a long night lay ahead of him. Exactly how did one apologize to the woman he'd sent to prison, who'd then turned her life around and moved in next door? This was a new one for the manuals, one that would never be found in print. Joe shrugged into his coat and grimaced. For one thing, no one would ever, ever believe it.

Mel shoved boxes aside, the single-car garage she used for storage a combination of clutter, cobwebs and dust. Surveying the area, she paused to rub her arms to ward off the chill in the non-insulated space. She should've rented a storage unit, but with plans to sell the majority of items come spring, she'd chosen to keep the stuff nearby.

When she caught sight of the box she wanted, dread filled her. Years had passed since Carl had packed it away. In an old microwave container, it sat harmless. Once removed however, whether she used it or not, Mel could be opening the proverbial Pandora's Box. Steeling her disenfranchised nerves, she wrapped her arms around an old microwave box marked with her husband's name, then backtracked through the maze she'd created and hurried into the kitchen.

What a fool she'd been. Simon had assured her that in Colorado Springs she and Luke would make a new start; that Drake Maxwell had recanted on his plans for revenge. So, if that were true, why had Lt. Crandall brought up the subject, and why had Simon been adamant that she and Luke keep a low profile?

Fear prickled her spine. She'd discovered the truth. They suspected Drake would come for her.

Mel checked her watch. Practice was over, and most likely the lieutenant had reached the high school by now. Frantic to get this job done, she grabbed a steak knife from the kitchen drawer and sawed through the worn packing tape. Her hands shook as she removed a heavy oaken carrier, then trembled further when she felt for the key Carl had taped to the bottom.

Odd, in the garage she'd been freezing. In the kitchen, sweat trickled from her brow. As she unlocked the box, her heart sank. No longer could she claim to be a law-abiding citizen. By opening it, she'd committed a crime that, if discovered, could send her back to prison. Tucked in gray foam, Carl's Smith and Wesson .357 Magnum lay exactly as he'd placed it fifteen years before.

"You mean more to me than a chunk of steel," he'd told her. An honorable man, her husband had respected the law that felons couldn't keep handguns in their possession. Without a backward glance, he'd locked the powerful weapon away and pulled her close. "We'll keep it for Luke, give it to him when he's older."

The day after their marriage Carl had taken the gun and left it at a friend's for safekeeping, who, when Carl passed away, promptly returned it to Mel.

Tears welled. "Dear God, Carl, forgive me." She couldn't save it for Luke. If Drake Maxwell came anywhere near her or her son, she wouldn't hesitate to pull the trigger.

The phone rang, and she nearly jabbed herself with the knife. Shaking, she tossed it away from her. It was as though every law enforcement agency in the country had just witnessed her duplicitous act.

Swallowing hard, she answered the phone.

"Hey, Mom, it's me Luke."

Why her son felt the need to identify himself, as if anyone else in the world called her Mom, she would never know. It did, however, lessen the tension and brought a smile to her face. "Hey, baby, where are you?"

"We're through with practice and Matt and Lt. Crandall invited me to dinner. Can I go?"

Mel's smile faded. With Carl so sick, Luke had chosen to stay by his father's side and hadn't hung out with friends. Frankly, with the move to Colorado Springs, he seemed happier than ever. She'd wanted Luke and Matt to remain close, but with Joe's underhanded interference, she wasn't so sure anymore.

Still, Matt couldn't help who he was related to, and in her haste to retrieve Carl's gun, she'd completely overlooked dinner. Luke had to eat, and with nothing prepared, Mel wasn't thrilled about going out in this weather.

"Mom?"

"I'm here." She overheard the interfering cop say something in the background. "Lt. Crandall says he'll grab something for you, too, if you want."

She gritted her teeth. "Tell him 'no, thank you.' You can go, Luke. But not too late, okay?"

"No sweat. Later, Mom."

No sweat? Mel wiped her damp forehead. *Easy for you to say.*

She hung up, relocked the box and carried it to her upstairs bedroom. She tucked it on the far side of her closet, then positioned two shoe boxes in front of it for added measure. Convinced the oaken chest was hidden at all angles, she shut the closet door, then scanned the room for a hiding place for the key. She finally taped it to the left hand corner of her nightstand drawer.

Her illicit act accomplished, she dropped to the window seat and pulled back the sheers. As white blanketed the city, Mel's stomach knotted in grief and despair. She hugged herself tightly. What did the future hold for her and her son?

Chapter Eight

All Drake wanted when he caught the taxi at Los Angeles' Ontario Airport was to escape the crowds, check out the newest rides cruising traffic and get lost in the California terrain. Instead, he'd gotten stuck in gridlock and in the backseat of a nonstop-talking cabby.

Now, if the pony-tailed loser didn't shut the fuck up, Drake was going to ram the guy's head into the steering wheel and do it for him. He sure hadn't gotten the message from Drake's one-word replies.

Several times he'd caught the dude staring from the rearview mirror. Finally, gabby came right out with it. "You from around here, man?"

"Nah, just got out of the pen." Maybe that would keep his trap shut.

"No shit." The driver, sporting a string of tattoos on every visible part of his body, adjusted his rearview mirror. "I got a cousin in Folsom."

What was that supposed to do, make them related or something? Drake tamped down his annoyance.

"What were you in for?"

Drake tore his gaze away from the window, met the dude's dark eyes in the mirror. "Murder."

"Huh," the cabby replied. "Is that right?" He jerked his head back toward the road.

Drake smirked. Worked every time. Two days out of prison, and he knew how the dinosaurs felt when they'd slid into the La Brea Tar Pits. It had taken him hours to board one of the flights leaving Denver. With no valid driver's license or passport, and only a Colorado Department of Corrections letter of release, he'd been escorted to a shit-can room off the concourse where some suits with badges badgered him to make sure he wasn't on some kind of no-fly list.

Pissed as hell that no one had warned him, and that his brother had wired very little money, Drake had finally managed to catch a plane west.

Everywhere he looked he took in the unfamiliar. Where were the Riverside pasturelands of his youth? Once home to thousands of dairy cows, the area had evolved into nothing but tract housing. From the window, he caught sight of the foothills. LA's smog often masked their visibility, but it was December, and the Santa Ana winds must've sent the pollution packing. His bearings out of whack, anger merged with uncertainty. Fifteen years. Fifteen irreplaceable years stolen from his life.

The driver made yet another unrecognizable turn. Clutching the armrest,

Drake leaned forward. When he'd left years ago, Maxwell Construction had been located in a low-rent part of the city, made up mostly of warehouses and rundown buildings.

"You sure you know where you're going?"

"3820 Marauder Drive," the cabby said.

"You ever heard of Maxwell Construction?"

"Who hasn't? They got it going on all over Southern California."

Well, well, well. Drake settled back in his seat. If the cabby recognized the company by name, and knew what he was talking about, that meant Drake's trust was intact. What's more, with the money untapped, it'd grown larger.

"Step on it," he said.

Ten minutes later, the driver pulled alongside a curb. Drake didn't know what to gape at more, the shock of the cab fare or the transition of Maxwell Construction.

The company, housed in an impressive two-story adobe structure, was set back several feet behind a massive sign and a landscape of grass, cactus, hedges and palm trees. Certainly not the real estate he'd known in his childhood.

Dumbfounded, he grabbed his gym bag and slid out of the cab.

All around him Hispanic workers mowed lawns or pruned hedges. For most, the scent would have smelled like cut grass and fertilizer. Drake inhaled freedom.

Inside the lobby, however, his high came crashing down. Behind a marbled counter, an uptight bitch with red lips and claws looked him up and down. "You're here to see whom?"

He'd been preparing a biting reply when another woman carrying files rounded the corner, took one look at him and dropped the entire load.

Drake stared into the enormous blue eyes of Marcy Davidson, now Marcy Maxwell, his sister-in-law. They'd had some good times in the shed behind her house in their early teens. Her nervous display in front of an employee chapped his ass. "Yeah, Marce, it's me. Do I get a welcome home kiss?"

She skittered back, straight into the arms of her husband.

Adam Maxwell greeted Drake with the same stunned reaction. *Some reception committee.*

In their youth, people had said the Maxwell brothers looked similar. Based on his waistline, Adam hadn't missed a meal *ever*, but Marcy still had a pert little ass. Seeing what flab did to a man, Drake was glad he'd spent his prison years in the weight room, pumping iron.

"What are you doing here?" Adam finally blurted. "I told you I'd send a driver when you got into town."

"I missed you too, brother. I lost your number so I came on over." Drake glanced around. "Nice place. You want to handle our business in front of these people or what?"

His sister-in-law's face had gone ashen. Adam whispered something only she could hear. Whatever he said had the effect of someone granted a stay of execution. Leaving the scattered files where they lay, Marcy made a beeline away from the area.

"Hey, Marce," Drake called after her. "Good seeing you. We'll catch up later."

By Adam's flaring nostrils, he was ready to snort fire. "Let's go to my office."

Drake winked at the equally startled receptionist. She shifted her gaze from his, back to the computer screen. Ah. Even the staff knew all about him. Good to know.

Walking with Adam down a fancy corridor, Drake stared at the various construction jobs displayed on the walls and all but drooled. Hospitals, schools, manufacturing facilities. No wonder these people were scared. They were about to lose part of a goldmine.

Adam motioned Drake into a large corner office, shut the door and rounded on him. "How dare you talk to my wife like that? And just look at you. Couldn't you have gotten a hotel room, showered and shaved before you came?"

Drake narrowed his gaze. His sandy blond hair was plastered to his head and he'd been wearing the same clothes for the last two days. "With all that money you sent me? And I'll talk to your *wife* any damned way I please."

Dropping his bag, Drake left Adam where he stood and ambled to an oversized desk. It dwarfed most of the other furniture in the room. "What's this, your need to compensate?"

Adam's frown said he wasn't amused.

A framed picture of a couple of school-aged kids Drake had never met sat on the polished cherry wood surface. No one had cared enough to send a birth announcement. "These yours?"

His brother closed the distance between them and yanked the picture out of Drake's hands. Placing the frame facedown, he said, "My instructions were plain. The minute you reached L.A. you were to call and I'd send my driver. Not that I'm surprised, but why would you ignore something so simple? And why would you come *here* of all places?"

So the very important man doesn't want to lay claim to his ex-con brother. "Because I wasn't about to be put on your leash, and I imagine the last place you'd tell your *driver* was to bring me here."

Adam looked like he'd swallowed something sour. Moving to his desk, he sat behind it, while Drake continued to circle the up-scale room. This office was plush—statues, awards, a leather sectional, conference table and chairs—hell, it even included a wet bar.

"Looks like you made a bundle with our parents' money. So why don't you save all that hot air for some exercise equipment and let's get down to business."

"What *business?*"

"My inheritance."

The anger seeped from Adam's beefy face, replaced with unmitigated shock. "Your what?"

"My inheritance. I'm here to collect."

"You've got your nerve. Our mother's estate was settled years ago. Your inheritance? Not only did we spend your share, but a great deal of our own, on that high-powered lawyer who saved you from life in prison."

Drake strolled to the bar, took out a glass and poured two fingers of Chivas Regal. He swallowed the scotch in one single gulp. It burned all the way down, reminding him that he was alive. Fifteen years in prison, a man wasn't sure. He poured another and drained the second as well.

"My God," Adam stammered. "It's nine-thirty in the morning."

Raising his glass, Drake said, "So it is. When the bottle's empty, I tear this place apart. Starting with you, Adam. My money, I want it."

Adam lifted his hands from behind the desk and held them, palms up. "Don't you get it? The last time I came to see you in Cañon City I tried to explain, but you were too incensed to listen. Mother revoked your trust, Drake. She disowned you. She left you *nothing.*"

Memories of his childhood flashed in his brain. His mother had doted on Adam and his younger sister Kristina, while Eileen Maxwell called Drake a disappointment.

Still, Adam was right. At Drake's trial she'd spared no expense. To cut him off without a dime? She wouldn't. Rage tore at his insides. "You're lying."

Adam withdrew a file from the lower right side of his desk, dropped it on the smooth cherry finish, then said defiantly, "It's all here in black and white. That is if pushing dope with those drug-addict friends of yours didn't deter your ability to read."

For a man who appeared to be smart, pushing Drake was a very stupid thing to do. He poured another glass of scotch.

"I've never understood," Adam went on. "You had everything. Education, money, looks, and some even say, charm. You threw it all into the sewer, then dove in after it. When you teamed up with that Rander character, that pretty much sealed your fate, didn't it—"

"Why are you bringing up all this shit?" Drake said, through gritted teeth.

"Speaking of the sewer rat," Adam continued, "he came to see me last month. Asked for a job. I might have considered it, but he refused the company drug test."

Drake set the tumbler upon the desk. "You're almost out of time, Adam. All I care about is my money, which so far is in *your* checkbook."

Sighing, his brother rose, rounded his desk and negotiated the sectional.

Standing between the sofa and Drake, Adam pulled a picture away from the wall, exposing the safe behind it.

Drake stood in the center of the room, clenching his hands into fists and tasting his excitement.

"Ever think of making things right?" Adam keyed in numbers on an electronic pad.

"Such as?"

"I meant what I said. If I would give a second chance to someone like Rander, the least I could do is make the same offer to my brother. You could come to work for Maxwell Construction, earn your way up, maybe even find your way back into the family."

Drake studied his surroundings. "Would I get this office?"

Adam's hand remained on the latch and he shook his head slowly. "Not even close. Weekly drug tests, entry level position, but I pay a decent wage. Prove yourself. You'll make a nice living."

And Drake thought he'd met con-men in prison. It had to be killing Adam to give up Drake's share of the money. "As much as letting my skin turn to leather and crawling around in dirt appeals to me, I'll pass. Why should I do that when I'm a rich man?"

Adam's face turned purple. "Have you no shame at all? When you shot and killed that clerk, you might as well have murdered our mother. That lawyer pled you down, all right. At the expense of our father's reputation. Sexual abuse, Drake? A dead man can't defend himself. People who Mother had known forever would cross the street rather than talk to her."

Rage and bile rose in unison. His lawyer had done what he had to do, and still Drake had been put away for fifteen years. What was wrong with his asshole brother? All Drake wanted was his inheritance and to forget these people ever existed. He was a fraction from ripping Adam to shreds. "I've had guilt shoved up my ass my entire life. It didn't work then, and it's sure not working now, so save it." Drake moved toward the sofa. "My money, Adam, you're out of time."

"And I told you, you don't have any coming." Shaking his head, he pushed down on the lever, opened the safe and withdrew a manila package.

He tossed it to Drake, who caught it one handed. "What's this?"

"My emergency fund. You won't work for it, so it's fifty thousand dollars to get out of our lives. *Permanently*. And there's no point in contacting Krissy. We're both in agreement. We hoped you'd changed, but clearly you haven't. We don't owe you a dime, and I'm telling you, once and for all, there's nothing for you here."

Drake snapped. His vision blurred. Blindly, he sideswiped a crystal lamp on an end table. As it shattered on the floor, he roared, "I'll kill every last one of you!"

Rounding the sofa to get to his brother, Drake suddenly skidded to a stop. In a million years, he'd never seen this coming. Where had the pacifist

Adam Maxwell come up with a gun?

Heart ramming inside his chest, Drake drew his hands up.

"Do you think I haven't dreaded this scene every day for the past fifteen years?" Adam said, the small-caliber weapon trembling in his hand. "Or that I would leave my family defenseless? Look over the door."

With sweat clinging to his brow, Drake glanced back, still almost missing the tiny surveillance camera built in to the ceiling. It had never occurred to him to check. Locating them in the joint had been second nature, but in a construction company?

"We're also being recorded," Adam said. He trained the gun on Drake, watched him warily and moved back toward the desk. "And with the threat you just made and the damage done to my office, I could have you arrested. Then my emergency fund stays in my vault."

"You built this company using *my* money," Drake said, from between his teeth, all while taking small steps in Adam's direction. "And you and I both know you don't have the balls to pull that trigger."

Adam cocked the hammer, then moved his free hand down the side of his desk. "You're partially right. I wouldn't ever want another human being's death on my conscience. But I will defend myself and my family. I've pushed the panic alarm, Drake. You have two choices. Stay here, come any closer and I will kill you. Or leave now with the only money I have to give you, because the police are on their way."

"This isn't over," Drake said. But rather than face the cops, he headed to the door.

"Oh, yes, it is," Adam called after him. "For once in your life, accept that you alone are responsible for your actions!"

Scrambling down the hallway and out into the bright sunshine, Drake stashed the measly payoff into his gym bag. He didn't stop running until he'd dropped into a seat on a city bus. One way or another, he would get what was coming to him. And every morning when Adam Maxwell looked in the mirror, he'd be wise to picture a dead man.

Not only Adam, but Kristina—she was in on this, too. No matter what, those two suck-ups would pay. Drake had hated his parents ramming their perfection down his throat. They'd called him lazy and unfocused, when the plain truth was, he just didn't give a damn. At first he'd been indifferent. Later, he'd grown defiant. And if anything went wrong, he got the blame. Some things never changed.

You alone are responsible.

Now that was a crock of shit. Drake had fifteen years to think about what had happened. Melanie had shoved over a display case containing floor-to-ceiling cases of beer. The impact had knocked him out cold. He'd never stood a chance. He'd awoken to cops entering the convenience store. Her testimony had sent him to prison.

With the bus doors hissing closed and the wheels droning beneath him, he pondered a question. What meant more to him—fifteen stolen years or his stolen inheritance?

Damned, fucking both, he decided.

Drake stared at the bag in his hands. So Jason Rander had come asking Adam for a job and been turned away. And they'd called Adam gifted?

How stupid of Adam to mention it. How incredibly careless and stupid.

Drake had business to conduct, and although he couldn't leave California just yet, he hightailed it away from Riverside and took the Metrolink train northwest to L.A. Without his long-anticipated trust fund, he was forced into areas where even an ex-con felt unsafe. The streets near the Coliseum where he'd chosen to lie low were nothing more than a larger version of prison.

In the pen, a pinched cigarette could set off a gang riot. On the streets, carrying around fifty grand could set off a war.

California might have been smoke-free, inside and out, but it wasn't hooker-free or gun-free and every ethnicity on the planet seemed to hang out here. When he wasn't skulking in a back alley and lying low from the cops, he was buying a pre-paid cell phone, fake IDs, new threads and a used Jeep Wrangler. Which brought him to a more-immediate problem, the piss-pour amount Adam had given Drake was running through his hands like a sieve.

Some of the boys he ran with in the old days finally agreed to see him, and when they did, their tips about Jason Rander led Drake to a warehouse in Santa Monica.

For once, he saw eye to eye with his greedy sibling. Adam had been smart not to hire the loser. Rander's collapsed veins and rotted teeth gave him away. Unfortunately, Adam hadn't used an equal amount of brains when it came to dealing with Drake. And because of that costly mistake, he made Rander an offer no junkie could refuse.

The moment he learned of Adam's death, Drake would contact his sister. And here came the juicy part. If she didn't pay up, he'd let her know who he planned to go after next. Picturing his little sister's panic-stricken face, he almost smiled. If Krissy wanted to protect her family, she'd start doleing out the cash.

There was only one flaw to the whole scenario. To get what Drake promised, Rander would be anxious to carry out the deal. And when that happened, Drake needed to be miles and miles across the state line.

He pulled out a map and planned his route. What a businessman he'd turned out to be. He infinitely preferred to go it solo, although he'd found it never hurt to access his networks. Look how easily he'd dug up Rander. With Adam all but a thing of the past, Drake moved onto his next order of business. Melanie Daniels.

He just had to find her.

Chapter Nine

Days after his debacle with Melanie, Joe still hadn't made a move to apologize, nor could he seem to get the woman out of his head. He'd done everything but, shoveling her drive after the first major snowstorm, recanting on his decision to separate the boys, carpooling whenever he could, and generally touting a good neighbor policy from afar.

But to walk up to the ex-con and say, "I'm sorry, I invaded your privacy," or "I might have been a *tad* out of line," didn't seem to be part of his vernacular, any more than saying "thank you," appeared to be part of Melanie's.

How their kids could be attached at the hip, while the parents did their best to avoid one another was beyond him, but if Melanie wanted it that way, so be it.

That didn't mean he wouldn't try to protect her. He'd researched Maxwell's movements since his release, and had traced the convict's return to California as DOC officials had predicted.

Joe arrived home that evening, the same way he'd left in the morning—in the dark. He pulled into the garage, noting his neighbor did not, and an uneasy feeling washed over him. Parking outside, whether a woman had been threatened or not, was a damn risky venture, leaving not only her, but her personal property exposed as well.

Upon closer inspection, his discomfort shifted to annoyance. She'd left the trunk open, her front door ajar, and Joe felt his blood pressure soar. Her car was chockfull of groceries, explaining the still-open trunk. He grabbed the remaining bags, slammed the lid shut and walked into her house. He didn't bother to knock. He had a point to make, and announcing his presence wasn't part of the plan.

The ready lecture never happened. On the contrary, what occurred when he strode into her kitchen was a complete loss of words. Bent over in her pantry stocking canned goods, Melanie displayed one of the finest asses he'd seen in a very long time. Leaning against the door jamb, he allowed himself a fleeting fantasy. That was, until she dropped a can and it rolled in his direction.

Determined not to startle her when she came to retrieve it, Joe cleared his throat.

She shot upright, banging her head in the process. She clutched her chest and whirled on him. "What in the hell are you doing here?"

At the unexpected impact, he suffered a pang of guilt. He placed the bags on the counter. "Being a good neighbor. Lucky for you."

She eyed the groceries and winced as she rubbed her head. "How is giving me a heart attack or a concussion lucky?"

Maintaining his position by the counter, he said, "Why would you of all people, leave your front door open?"

She glared at him. "Because as much as this may surprise you, Lieutenant, I can't walk through walls. I'm unloading my groceries, you—"

This time he did walk toward her. "Ah-ah-ah. I already get that I'm a son of a bitch from our last time together. You didn't leave your door unlocked, Melanie, you left it wide open. I could have been anybody."

She swallowed, calling attention to the creamy column of her throat. Of all the cons he'd arrested over the course of his career, why had the one who was by far the most attractive moved in next door?

"You're absolutely right," she replied. "I forget with all the luxuries afforded me, I should've had the butler do it."

"Cute. Luke could've helped. He'll be home any minute."

"And starving." She shrugged. "Oh, I'm sorry, honey. Dinner? You'll have to wait. We have plenty of food, but it's *in the car.*"

"You coddle these boys way too much, Melanie. They can fend for themselves on occasion."

"Think what you want. But if my father had coddled me, I might never have hit the streets. And I have to coddle Matt." She shot Joe another look of disdain. "You're never around to do it."

"You really are a condescending—"

"Ah, ah, ah." She held up a hand.

Touché. Joe stepped back, ashamed that she'd gotten to him. Not many could, but when it came to his kids, his guilt was relentless. "You could park in the garage."

"Sure, if I want to get high centered on boxes. It's stacked with things from our move."

"So get a storage unit."

"I plan to," she shot back. "But for now, I don't know what needs to stay or what needs to go. But I know one thing that does." She waggled her fingers. "Good-bye, Lieutenant."

"Joe."

"What?"

"Call me Joe. We live next door to each other."

"You could move," she muttered.

He laughed, he couldn't help it. Melanie Norris had a comeback for everything, and he had to give her an A+ for not backing down from him. "Do you ever plan to be nice?"

She coughed. "I beg your pardon."

"You know, be civil? You wave to me, I wave to you, say thank you when I shovel your walk. It's called civility. And you're welcome, by the way."

She cocked her head. "I guess that depends on you. Do you ever plan to apologize?"

Propping a hip against the counter, Joe folded his arms. What was with him? Why couldn't he say he was sorry for visiting the warden and be done with it? Joe supposed largely because he wasn't. In his line of work, men and women didn't wait around for surprises.

Dispatch chose that moment to intrude. Reading a page ordering him to headquarters, he sighed. "Looks like you get your wish. I'm outta here."

"Will you be gone long?"

"I could be gone thirty minutes or several hours. Do you care?"

"About you? Not in the least."

"That's what I figured."

"But I do worry about Matt."

"Matt knows what's expected of him. He'll set the alarm and be fine at home."

Melanie moved to the counter and began unloading the rest of her groceries. "Would you think it condescending or coddling of me if I asked if he could stay here?"

Hearing nothing but concern in her voice, Joe resisted a comeback. Damn it. He should be thanking her, not sparring with her. He lifted his head sheepishly. "Frankly? I'd appreciate the help."

The look of understanding she returned hit him all the way to his gut. He'd started to move through the doorway when he thought to pause. "About that apology?"

Melanie stopped rummaging.

"I can't apologize for the background check. You wouldn't talk to me. I had to know."

She stiffened and Joe rushed on. "But I *am* sorry I hurt you in the process."

Half an apology. As Joe traversed their yards, Mel clung to the porch column and wondered what had just transpired in her kitchen. In a way, she should be congratulating herself. She suspected many never got that much from the unflappable Lieutenant Crandall.

To her dismay, she'd learned at recent high school events that her neighbor was respected by men, sought-after by women, and, that most, if they'd found him in their kitchen carrying in groceries, would've expressed their gratitude far differently than by telling him to get out.

Mel shuddered against the cold, annoyed that she too felt drawn to the six-foot-two-inch shell that made up the cop. The only thing saving her from herself was the knowledge that beneath the appealing exterior beat the heart of the man who'd slipped cold cuffs on her and walked her through booking while she'd pleaded and begged.

Luke didn't know. And until she was ready to tell him about her past—on her terms, she'd damned well keep her distance from Lieutenant Crandall. Already she'd gambled, encouraging her son's friendship with Matt. Even so, Matt had never let on that he knew anything about her background, something she ought to thank his father for. Nevertheless, becoming chummy with the man who sent her to prison wasn't high on her to-do list.

Joe's Crown Victoria pulled out of his drive the same time Josh Rearson's souped up Charger careened down Serendipity to drop off the boys. The Charger jumped the curb and jerked to a halt on the sidewalk.

Mel vaulted down the steps, but Joe's rapid exit from the Crown Victoria beat her to it. Leaving his car running, he crossed to the driver-side window where he had a one on one with the desperately nodding kid behind the wheel. Joe's angry stance guaranteed Josh wouldn't be driving their sons anywhere again, anytime soon.

Obviously humiliated, Luke and Matt sauntered past Mel as she held open the door for them. No doubt, a police lieutenant's words carried ten times the weight hers did with the high school senior.

As Josh drove away, this time at a snail-like pace, and Joe hit his lights speeding off in the opposite direction, Mel smiled. Maybe there were some advantages to a cop living next door after all.

By one-forty in the morning, however, she wasn't smiling. Joe still hadn't arrived home. She knew this because she'd called. And when he didn't answer, she paced beside the bay window in her bedroom, pausing every so often to look out at the darkened house beside hers.

Maybe it was the sirens that had screamed throughout the night, or the fact that his son slept under her roof, but she was wide awake and willing Joe to show.

Unbelievable. She detested Joe Crandall. She tried to shake her concern by revisiting their earlier conversation. Condescending? After everything she'd been involved in by seventeen, she had no right to judge anybody. As for coddling, she and Carl had raised a boy using love *and* discipline. Along with the ruler she owed the cop, maybe she'd buy him a dictionary. That was, if he ever came home.

Where was he?

Restless, she checked the view from her window again, then slipped into her robe. On tiptoe, she moved down the hall. Luke and Matt had carried up an old futon from the garage and stuffed it in Luke's tiny bedroom.

From the doorway, she noted the cluttered room smelled of sweaty socks and teenage boys. Luke obviously treasured Matt's friendship. He'd given up his bed and taken the futon. Although he slept, his lanky legs hung off the odd-shaped couch. Tears welled as she remembered the blond, freckled-face little guy who'd easily fit on the futon just a few short years earlier.

Carl had bought it when Mel had first come to work for him. He hadn't had a lot of money to spend. His wife's funeral had come at a time when he was still paying the hospital bills from Luke's birth.

Mel hugged her middle. Those had been terrible, difficult times. Carl had been so consumed with grief, she'd been almost afraid of him. It had taken him months to say more than a few words to her. She'd made up for the loneliness by making his tiny son her whole life.

Emptiness encircled her heart. In three years Luke would be off to college. More than once she'd worried what she would do then.

At three-fifteen, Mel returned to the window and began another vigil. Shortly afterward, headlights shone on the quiet residential street, and when the lieutenant's car turned into his drive, she relaxed her shoulders. To her surprise, he didn't enter his garage. He parked in the driveway, got out of the car and focused on her bedroom window.

Caught, she nearly pulled away, but an almost-magnetic force held her in place. *Do you ever plan to be nice?* She lifted her hand in a hesitant wave.

With what appeared to be equal deliberation, he returned her greeting.

The tightness eased from her chest. Assured Joe was all right, she let the curtain fall.

Chapter Ten

The next morning, Joe attacked the buzzing clock with his fist, then draped an arm over his eyes. It couldn't be six already. What a night. He needed to contact the Commander, the coroner, Public Relations, Internal Affairs, the list went on. Per policy he'd placed Sam Ortega on paid administrative leave pending investigation.

This wasn't the first time he'd had to suspend one of his officers. Still, one never knew what to say to a distraught cop for doing his job. "Your shield and your gun," might've been police procedure, but to Joe it sounded a lot like "you're guilty, now prove your innocence."

He planted his bare feet on the cold wood floor and buried his face in his hands, feeling a headache behind his eyes and a jaw in desperate need of a shave. Later. He had the morning off. With any luck he could spend it comatose after dropping Matt off at school.

Matt.

Joe groaned. The kid had spent the night at the neighbor's. Hell. Joe tugged on jeans, grabbed the flannel shirt he'd strung over the bedpost and went into the can to do his business.

Ten minutes later, hands in his pockets, he stood freezing his ass off at Melanie's front door. Hopefully, she was asleep and the boys were ready. Seeing her in that window last night had had a strange effect on him. She'd never admit it, but he'd bet a month's paycheck she'd waited up for him. Joe wasn't sure how he felt about that.

Noting he could see his breath, he rang the bell. The approaching holidays, while joyous for many, were a time of despair for others, and arguably one of the most dangerous seasons for law enforcement. He'd been focused on last night's tragedy when the door opened.

"You didn't get the message."

At Melanie's soft statement of fact, he turned. She stood in the doorway, dressed like she hadn't lost a minute of sleep. As he examined her from head to toe, he suspected she'd chosen the high heels, the simple black skirt and camisole to show professionalism. On her the look fell flat. What her ensemble needed was another body, preferably one without his neighbor's spectacular figure.

"What message?" he asked.

Extending her arm, she held the door wide. He strode in, catching a whiff of perfume.

"You're staring," she said, as she closed the door.

"You look good," he replied.

"I left a message on your machine saying that I would take the boys this morning so you could sleep in."

Joe closed his eyes. He could've really used that information, along with a few additional hours in bed to escape last night. "I didn't check. People usually leave messages on my cell."

"I'm sorry, I didn't know."

"Not your fault." He glanced toward the kitchen. "Is that coffee I smell?"

"Yes." She didn't move. After a moment, she sighed. "Come with me. I'll get you a cup."

In spite of her reluctant hospitality, he followed her into a spotless kitchen. The curtains were open, and sunshine permeated the room. Unlike his kitchen, hers was warm and inviting. Walking toward the table, he chose a spot nearest the window. With warmth radiating his back, his mood lifted—until he spied the front page of *The Gazette*.

Before Melanie placed the aromatic brew in front of him, Joe grabbed the paper and read the headline, *Police shoot and kill father of five year old*, plastered on the page.

What could he say? Sensationalism sold newspapers, and, technically, the words were correct. But why did editors have to word it so that cop-haters fed off it?

Tensing with resentment, uninvited memories of the eight-hour standoff that had ended in tragedy flooded his brain. A methamphetamine dealer had taken his kid hostage. Joe and a CBI negotiator had failed to convince the man to give himself up and let the boy go. When the situation turned deadly, SWAT team member and marksman Sam Ortega took the shot. The dealer died, the child lived and Hazmat moved in to do the impossible cleanup job when a meth lab was involved.

Joe tossed the rag away from him.

Melanie set Joe's coffee before him and withdrew to the kitchen sink. "Is that where you were last night?"

He nodded.

"Your job is awful, Joe."

"My job is necessary, Melanie."

"And there's people you can talk to if—"

"If it comes to that," he replied.

She looked at him, he looked at her, and that's all they had to say to each other. Joe drained the coffee, wishing she'd offer him another. She didn't.

He wanted to thank her for waiting up last night, but suspected if he mentioned it, she'd deny it had anything to do with him, and their tenuous truce would shatter. He rose. "Thanks for the coffee." Then because he couldn't resist, he added, "You really do look nice."

Somewhere between the living room and kitchen, she'd slipped on a blazer, probably to counter his prying eyes. "I'm working the display area and I'll be in front of customers today," she said, glancing anywhere but at him.

Lucky customers, Joe thought. "I appreciate you looking after Matt. It was one less worry on my mind. Are you going to the game tonight?"

She met his gaze, and, suddenly, the stoic Melanie Norris wasn't so stoic.

"You are going, right?"

"Of course."

"Good. Get there early. We're playing Palmer. They're number one in the city. The parking will be insane."

She nodded, but as she strode to the table and picked up his cup, he detected the tremor.

Ah, hell. The game. She was nervous about going. An inner voice warned, *Don't do it, Crandall.* Even so, he found himself saying, "You could go with me."

She placed the cup in the sink and whirled in his direction, obviously floored at the idea. "Excuse me?"

Her reaction made him grin. "I said you could go with me. People do it all the time. A few have even survived." That comment earned him a ghost of a smile. He decided to try for an all-out chuckle. "I'll provide references if you like."

It worked. She laughed. Still, she didn't accept or decline. She walked him to the door.

"If I decide to take you up on your very obliging offer," she asked, opening it, "what time would we leave?"

He lifted a brow. "Six-thirty."

"All right. I'll be ready."

As Joe jogged down the steps he started to count. Exactly how much time did he have before she changed her mind?

"Joe?"

Three seconds. That had to be a record. He pivoted.

"About tonight?" Melanie bent over the railing twining her fingers. "You might want to have those references ready."

At precisely six-thirty, Joe rang the bell. Up until then Mel had been pacing. What was she, crazy? Why hadn't she picked up the phone and cancelled. The only reason she hadn't was of her overwhelming desire not to fight the crowd or go to a strange place alone.

She counted to ten before opening the door, then as she did, caught her breath.

She should have cancelled, damn it. Joe looked amazing, dressed in a brown leather jacket, T-shirt and jeans. This morning's bristles were gone, and so too were the bags under his eyes. And whatever cologne he had on, she could've basked in it in all night.

Wondering how bad it would look to come down with a last-minute migraine, she wiped a clammy palm on her jeans.

"Ready?" he asked.

Hardly. Her feet felt like they were encased in cement. Her fear of Joe Crandall existed on so many levels she couldn't begin to sort them all out. And yet, he must never know. To do so would place her at a complete disadvantage. "Sorry. I thought I was supposed to come to your place."

"Then you're late."

Ignoring his chronic need to one-up her, she grabbed her purse and locked the front door. Joe placed a hand at the small of her back and guided her down the steps.

Okay. Why was he being nice?

Worse, why did she like it?

Keenly aware of him, and the strength he possessed, Mel's mind drifted back to the night of her arrest. He'd thrown her to the ground as though she weighed no more than a sack of potatoes. That memory did nothing to improve her mood, and she flinched.

"You okay?"

"Fine," she said. But she wasn't. If they lived next door to each other for the next hundred years, it would boil down to how they met.

Nearing their property line, she stopped. A newer model Ford Mustang sat in his drive. She caught his gaze. "Yours?"

"At least until Matt starts driving. I thought you might prefer riding in something other than the City's finest."

Her discomfort rose to a new level. He was obviously focused on the past, too. They rode in silence, arriving as he'd predicted, to a parking lot jammed to capacity. They didn't talk on their way to the gym, and even their footsteps echoed with tension.

Inside an auditorium three times the size of Cañon City's, Joe appeared to know everyone, while Mel endured their stares like a micro-organism under glass.

Tonight, Coronado faced its 5A rival, the Palmer Terrors. The team was full of athletic, scholarship-bound kids, who made three-point shots, free-throws and lay ups look easy. Joe had said they were number one in the city, and suddenly Mel hoped Luke wouldn't play. His ankle wasn't a hundred percent and this wasn't the time to test it.

Coronado took the floor, the band played *Hit Me with your Best Shot*, and the home crowd went wild.

"Melanie," Joe yelled to be heard over the commotion. "Meet Noah Washington. His son Chet's our leading scorer."

Nervousness forgotten, a genuine smile overtook her. She shook the man's hand. "I'm so happy to meet you," she hollered. "My son idolizes your son, Mr. Washington. I hear Duke's recruiting Chet."

Noah grinned. "And it's going straight to my boy's head, Miz Norris. From what I hear, your boy's the real deal, too. We were sure sorry to learn about his daddy."

A lump formed in Mel's throat. No one in Colorado Springs had known Carl, and it was easy to forget he'd existed. She thanked the man, then focused on Joe. He too wore a sympathetic look. She'd never seen this side of him, and a protective voice inside her whispered, *Careful, Mel, guard up.*

Midway down the aisle, a group shouted from the stands. Joe's warm breath tickled her ear as he motioned. "Up there."

With every second, her hesitation grew. He had been nice enough to provide transportation. Surely that was as far as the invitation extended. Fortunately, Coach Hood's girlfriend Connie waved and pointed to the empty space beside her. Relieved, Mel climbed the bleachers and sat next to Connie, while Joe sat in front of Mel, next to a bald spectator Joe appeared to know well.

She happily chatted with Connie, and all seemed resolved, until during the national anthem, a striking blonde made her way up the stands. Mel remembered the woman from tryouts, mainly because compared to the rest of the moms with boys on the team, the blonde stood out like a model for Victoria's Secret.

Every male head in the vicinity followed her progress, including Joe's. The model-mom obviously worked out and was proud of her body. With a coat draped over her arm, in December no less, she wore a low cut top over tight-fitting capris.

Mel tried not to stare or feel overly self-conscious, but it was a battle not won. Particularly when the removal of her own GOR-TEX jacket left her sitting in plain denim and jeans.

"Her name's Lydia Ryerson," Connie said close to Mel's ear. "On her third husband, I think. Rumor has it, Lydia's nominated Joe as number four." Connie stiffened and sat back. "Look out. Here she comes."

And she did. Choosing the spot next to Joe. As people shuffled to make room for Lydia, an absurd bout of jealousy hit Mel squarely between the eyes. Her face went hot, and although she did her best to ignore them, with Luke and Matt sitting the bench, and Connie talking with a group behind her, Mel found it hard not to hone in on the couple's conversation.

"Was my cooking that bad?" Lydia asked. "I wondered why you hadn't called."

Joe appeared absorbed in the game. "No, it was great. I've been busy, that's all."

"I know. I've been watching the news. You poor man. If there's anything I can do for you . . . or Matt." The little hussy placed a manicured hand on Joe's upper thigh.

Mel jerked her head toward the game. Chet Washington fouled. The crowd groaned. Palmer went to the free-throw line.

Joe took off his jacket, bumping Mel's knee in the process. Annoyed that she could possibly care who touched whom, she moved closer to Connie who busily chewed her thumbnail.

The game progressed and Mel did her best to ignore the pair until Lydia cried, "Joe! Oh my God. That scar? Where'd you get it?"

The blood drained from Mel's face. If only she could fall through the bleachers. She set her gaze on the cop's rolled-up sleeve and the damage she'd inflicted fifteen years before. The puckered flesh of Joe's forearm stood out like an angry snake on his otherwise perfect skin.

Whatever he said to Lydia, he did so quietly.

Lydia, however, was nowhere discreet. "Well, if that happened during an arrest, I'd like to see the other guy," unaware the *other guy* sat close enough to count the roots of her bleached-blond head. "I bet he didn't walk straight for weeks."

Mel shot to her feet.

Connie broke away from her conversation. "Melanie?"

She glanced down. She was too big to fall through the bleachers. As the past closed in on her, she said, "I'm going for popcorn."

With Lydia Ryerson pawing him, Joe watched Melanie bolt from the stands. Well, hell, she'd heard. Grabbing his jacket, he removed Lydia's hand from his thigh. For someone else he might've practiced diplomacy. Tact with Lydia hadn't worked. "You'd have better luck with someone else," he said.

Disregarding her look of shock, he jogged down the bleachers and through the gymnasium doors.

Melanie didn't walk toward the concession stand. She walked to a pay phone, reached for the phone book and started thumbing.

Joe headed her way. When he got close enough to be heard, he said, "The last time I checked you could buy popcorn at the concession stand. No need to order out."

Her lips formed a thin line as she shoved the directory back into its slot. "I'm not going for popcorn and you know it. I'm calling a cab."

"For?"

"A ride home." She hesitated as the gym doors flew open and people made their way out of the gym for half time. "What was I thinking going anywhere with you?"

"Were you going to tell me?"

"I'm sure you didn't reach lieutenant without good reason. You would've figured it out."

"Classy move, Norris." Joe shook his head. "You're upset because Lydia mentioned my scar."

A group of kids bypassed them, whooping and hollering and making it difficult to hear. Melanie picked up the phone. "Can't pull anything over on you. I'm sorry I put you to so much trouble. Enjoy the game."

The woman was impossible. Joe grabbed the phone, hung it up and reached for her hand. Against her objections, he led her through the exit and into the frigid night air.

"What are you doing?" she asked, clutching her arms from the cold.

"Trying to find out why you're such a coward."

"What is it with you and name calling?"

He made a mental note to curb the verbal jabs. "People mention my scar. It happens. And not once have I ever said, 'Melanie Daniels did this to me.' I tell them it happened during an arrest. *Period*."

She jutted her chin. "You're missing the point. You wouldn't have that scar if it weren't for me. Can we go inside, please? It's freezing out here."

It was cold, but, no, he wasn't budging. Joe slipped off his jacket and wrapped it around her shoulders. She glanced up, wearing a look of surprise.

"We're going to hash this out once and for all. Okay. I admit checking into your past wasn't the right thing to do. But it's done. And the night of your arrest I was doing my *job*."

Melanie stepped back. He invaded her space. He wasn't about to let her retreat. "You married a prison guard. You're friends with a warden, so I know your problem isn't with authority. So I want to know, what's the real reason you hate my guts?"

"I don't hate you." She turned from him and huddled deeper inside his coat. "Not anymore."

The comment was almost a whisper, but at her admission, relief shot through him. Hate was a strong emotion. He could chip away at dislike. "Speak up. I didn't catch what you said."

She faced him, ramrod straight. "I said I don't hate you. But we could rethink it."

"Funny. Talk to me, Melanie. What is it with you?"

Her breath came out in a crystallized huff. She looked out over the crowded parking lot and her shoulders fell. "Luke doesn't know."

"*What* doesn't Luke know?"

Pain shadowed her face as she lowered her head. "He knows I'm his stepmother and that's as far as it goes. He doesn't know about my arrest, Maxwell or the time I spent in prison."

Suddenly, the skies parted and a revelation occurred. Where Joe failed miserably in the home and hearth department, Melanie Norris prided herself on being the consummate parent. Luke was all she had in this world. "And you think I'd tell him, is that it?"

She met Joe's steady gaze. "I don't know you well enough to know what you'd do."

"Maybe you should get to know me." Sensing progress between them,

Joe moved closer. "For one thing, it's up to you to tell your son. I give you my word, he'll never hear it from me."

"Thank you." She all but melted in relief.

Too bad Joe didn't have it in him to leave well enough alone. "That doesn't mean I agree with how you're handling the situation."

"Of course not." She crossed her arms.

"That pedestal you've put yourself on, it's gonna hurt like hell when you fall off. Luke needs to know."

"You think I don't know that?" She squeezed her eyes shut. "It must be *awesome* to be so all knowing and perfect."

Perfect? That term hardly fit him the night he'd gotten between his stepfather and his mother. When the old man went after her, Joe had resorted to using his fists instead of his brains. He'd knocked the vicious drunk into a stupor. In the end, he might have done both Joe and his mother a favor. His stepfather pressed charges. Joe's mom left an abusive marriage, and a judge ordered Joe to enlist in the army or face jail. Law enforcement came later.

Emitting a humorless laugh, he said, "I think you and I both can discount the all-knowing and perfect statements."

"You want the truth?" She fidgeted with the zipper on his coat. "All right. I'm afraid."

He hesitated. "You're afraid of the unknown. Your son loves you. Nothing will change that."

"And if it does?"

"I don't follow."

"If Matt gets angry at you, you have an impenetrable bond. It's called blood. Plus, he loves *and* admires you." Melanie sighed. "Of course, if I tell Luke about my past he'll still love me. I've raised him."

"You think he'll stop admiring you?"

"As insecure and as vain as that sounds, yes."

The parent inside him ached for her. "You really sell yourself short. Have you ever looked at yourself in the mirror? How many wardens do you think go to such lengths to protect an ex-con?"

She shook her head. "Simon did that for Carl."

"Originally, maybe. But later on . . . remember, I spent some time with the man. He arranged that move for *you*. That job of yours?"

"What about it?"

"How long did it take the shop owner to hire you?"

Again, she shook her head. "That's different. I had a portfolio. I'm highly qualified—"

"How long?"

She let out a long-suffering huff. "Aaron hired me on the spot."

"Exactly." As for Joe, he felt a satisfied smile coming on. "The warden, your employer, Matt. I think my son would walk over hot coals for you. And don't forget Coach Hood."

Melanie broke out in laughter. "Now that's stretching things. You're saying Coach Hood admires me."

"The first day we met, he warned me away from you."

"Yep. Sounds like admiration, all right."

"Darn straight it was. Rick was afraid we'd like each other . . ."

They stood near the gym doors, where an overhead safety light illuminated the area. Whether it was from the cold or something else, Melanie's cheeks flushed.

Fighting a husky edge to his voice, Joe said, "As for Luke, that kid adores you. And even if—when—you tell him, he'll feel the same. Admiration isn't optional."

Tears sprang to her eyes. It was the first time Joe had seen that happen. Melanie Norris wasn't a simpering female. At least around him, she held her emotions firmly in check.

"Thanks, Joe." She smiled and searched his face. Then laughing she added, "So which one of us is going to have Coach Hood committed?"

"I don't know. Putting him away's kind of rash, don't you think?" Joe inched closer. "Before we do something like that maybe we should at least disprove his theory."

Her smile faltered, but she stood her ground. When Melanie didn't lay him out flat, Joe pulled her into his arms. And at a high school basketball game, and under the romantic glow of safety lights, he lowered his head. There, he'd put their relationship on an entirely different level, meeting her first in a tentative, then lingering kiss.

Chapter Eleven

After midnight, and days after leaving L.A., Drake's next order of business brought him to Cañon City. As much as it pissed him off to drive past the lit up concrete buildings and chain-linked fences topped with razor wire, this time he planned to go nowhere near the correctional facility.

He drove toward the Royal Gorge Bridge, but before traveling that far, he turned south, occasionally stopping to look at his handwritten notes. He'd overheard customers when he bought his cell phone talking about GPS devices, but he'd never considered buying one. Fucking people ought to learn to read a map. Now in the dark, he wished he'd sprung for one.

He finally got his bearings, circled a tiny house in an older neighborhood and eyed the parked cars in the driveway and along the street.

Evidently Jesse Ropes hadn't lied. The corrections officer often boasted to the cons behind bars that he played poker on Tuesday nights with a group of guards from the surrounding prisons. In addition to Ropes' fat stomach, he had a big mouth. He also bragged that with all of his earnings, it was only a matter of time until he could leave his day job. Many of the prisoners had told him he was full of shit, but Drake had taken it all in. Ropes had a gambling addiction. And when Drake discovered someone had a vice, he used it to his advantage.

He parked the Jeep behind a copse of cottonwoods and sat alone in the darkness, listening to the empty sounds of the freezing night. It was a weeknight and he wondered how long the guards would play. By one in the morning, he got his answer. The first man sauntered out, followed by another, then more. One dude staggered, and their loud voices pierced the air.

Good, they'd been drinking. Drake had the advantage of being stone-cold sober. Tugging on gloves and zipping up his winter coat, he stepped from the Jeep and kept to the shadows. Not so much, though, that he couldn't see that Ropes' yard was a dump. An engine block sat under a barren tree, and trash had collected under the raised, disintegrating wooden porch. The grass had long ago been choked out by weeds. What little survived crackled like straw beneath Drake's feet. At last Ropes came out of the house with another guy, and they walked out to the drive. Drake moved to the side of the porch.

"How much you win tonight?" Ropes asked.

"Me? I'm up five hundred."

Ropes shook his head. "I'm down, Gordy. Say, you wouldn't—"

"No, I wouldn't," the man called Gordy replied. "You gotta know when to say when, Jesse. Maybe you should hang it up before you get in too deep."

Ropes laughed. "I can quit anytime I want, man. I'm just in a slump right now. Hell, I've won more than I've ever lost."

"Keep telling yourself that," Gordy said. "From what I hear you're not simply gambling with friends anymore. You're in with the wrong people, *man.*"

To get closer, Drake shifted positions. His coat rustled.

Ropes' fat head shot up. "You hear somethin'?"

Drake went flat against the side of the house.

"Probably a creditor," Gordy said, laughing and sliding into his car. "Relax, Jesse, it was the wind. Take my advice, if you can't walk away, get help." Gordy started the car and drove off.

Drake stepped from the shadows. "Good advice. You gonna take it?"

Ropes jumped back, his eyes narrowing. "Who's there?"

Drake climbed onto the porch, directly under the light.

"Maxwell?" The guard's eyes grew wide. "What the hell are you doing here?"

Why was that question everyone's standard greeting where he was concerned? A warped, beat-up wooden rocker sat on the front deck. Drake took a seat. "Did you think I'd forget? I'm one of those creditors come to collect. You got information for me?"

Understanding dawned on Rope's ugly snout. He strode closer to the porch. "You want dirt on the girl who committed the crime with you."

"Damn, Ropes, you're a bloody genius."

"I would've gotten in touch," he said, shrugging. "I—I just didn't know how."

"Well, isn't it lucky for you that I happened by." The little puke had pocketed a thousand bucks of Drake's money, thinking after he got out of the pen, he'd never hear from him again.

Pulling his shoulders back and sucking in his gut, Ropes puffed himself out like he had with the prisoners. Joining Drake on the porch, he said, "Look, I asked around. Someone said she'd lived here in Cañon City the whole time."

"No shit." Finally. Drake's hopes soared.

"Yeah, but he said she moved a while back. Husband died."

Leaning forward in the rocker, Drake clenched his teeth. "So . . . where'd she go?"

"No one seems to know."

His renewed optimism plummeted. "Did she take her old man's name?"

Ropes' eyes shifted. "What do you plan to do to her if you catch up to her?"

"What do you think I'm gonna do to her? Take her out to lunch, talk over old times." Drake stood. As in anytime he conjured up an image of Melanie Daniels, anger took center. He'd had a helluva week, and walking back streets and freezing his ass off were not how he'd planned to spend his time. "What I *do* with her is none of your business." He advanced on Ropes, who despite the cold night, dripped with sweat. "I asked you a question, Ropes. "What's her married name?"

"I don't know it, Maxwell," he said, licking his cowardly lips. "I tried to find out a couple of times from people who knew something about the women's prison and I got slapped down."

"What do you mean *slapped down?*"

"I was told to leave it be."

"For asking about an ex-con? Give me a break."

"Hey, she made friends, all right? Apparently she married someone within the system."

"So what's her freakin' married name?"

"I don't know." Ropes moved away. "And another thing. I'm not gonna lose my job or my pension trying to find out."

"You're not, huh? How much do you owe these creditors of yours?"

"None of your damned business. Look, you paid me a thousand bucks. I'll write you a check."

Drake laughed. "Like that'd never bounce. Besides, I'm a businessman now." He closed in on the little turd. "It's no longer a grand. With interest, it just went up to fifteen-hundred."

"You're crazy. Look at this place. Do I look like I have that kind of money?"

"Get it or I'll ring up the warden. I'll tell him about your little problem, how you took money from a con. How long will you have a job then?"

Ropes' gaze darted toward the front door. He obviously wanted to get inside to call for help or to get his hands on a weapon. Drake stood between the guard and the door. Ropes wasn't going anywhere.

"I'm telling you when it comes to Melanie Norris, no one will talk to me."

"*Norris.* I thought you said you didn't know her name." Placing a foot on the seat of the rocker, Drake yanked out one of the spindles supporting the back. Gripping it, he waved it back and forth, inches away from the guard's terrified face. Ropes stumbled backwards. "What else aren't you telling me, Ropes?"

"Swear to God, man, that's all I know," he blustered. "Her name's Norris . . . and she's got a kid."

"A kid now." Drake grabbed the overgrown piece of shit by the collar, slammed him up against the house and pressed the spindle against his throat. Drake was sick and tired of being fucked around. He needed the guard. Otherwise, he'd end him this moment. Pressing hard enough to make Ropes struggle for breath, Drake said, "I've been around liars all my life. And you're not even *close* to being good at it. Tell me or I'll beat it out of you."

"You want me to make something up?" Ropes rasped. "Cause that's what it'll be. I can't help you."

Drake was losing it. The little cocksucker knew where Melanie was, he could feel it.

"I'm telling you I learned quick the lady was off limits."

"Lady?" Rage and frustration attacked Drake from the inside out. He pressed harder. Ropes' eyes bulged. "One last chance, Ropes, tell me."

He gasped. "Ah, man. If anyone finds out . . . someone mentioned Pueblo. And . . . and . . . she works with flowers. Swear to God, Maxwell, that's all I know."

Drake eased the pressure from Rope's throat, and that's when the guard got stupid. He tackled Drake, and the two crashed down the battered steps and into the front yard. With the spindle in his right hand and the guard on top of him, Drake whacked the right side of the bastard's skull. The guard cried out, his arms flew up and he clutched his head. Drake drove a fist into Rope's gut, then slammed it beneath his chin.

Drake was strong; adrenaline made him stronger. The man, well over two hundred pounds landed with a thud, nearly a foot away.

He lay on his back, groaning. Drake climbed to his feet.

Ropes opened his eyes and must have sensed what was coming. With Drake standing over him, Ropes gagged, "Help," apparently no longer able to scream.

Drake lifted the spindle overhead. He hammered it down time after time after time, until Ropes stopped lifting his hands to defend himself, and blood bubbled from his mouth.

Then with uncontained fury, Drake threw the broken-off piece of wood as far as he was physically able.

Dogs started barking and lights switched on. But, with no other choice, he was forced to take a chance. He couldn't leave Rope's fat ass outside for immediate discovery.

Glad he'd worn gloves, Drake yanked the corpse up and over his shoulder. Then he carried the body into a musty living room littered with empty beer bottles and burnt-out cigarette stubs. Rounding the vacated poker tables and chairs, he entered a grimy kitchen.

And there, he dumped Ropes on his torn-up linoleum.

Drenched, with blood pounding in his ears, Drake slipped out the back door where the barking increased from random to frenetic. He scanned his inky surroundings, then glanced down at his brand new coat covered with blood. *Shit.*

He had no time to worry about the bloodstains now. With sirens joining the mutts in their nonstop racket, he underwent a terrifying case of déjà vu. And like the first time he'd killed a man, Drake ran.

Chapter Twelve

"Lt. Crandall, line three," the department secretary's voice said over the intercom.

Joe picked up the phone. "Crandall."

"Hi, Joe, it's me."

He flinched. With his job, running a household, the callouts, basketball practices and life, he'd simply hadn't had time to add *argue with ex-wife* to the list.

"Morning, Karen. What can I do for you?"

"Call me back for one thing." The statement was a jab, but it was laced with uncharacteristic humor.

"God, I'm sorry, I've been busy."

"That's what Matty said. Listen." There was a pause in the conversation. "I owe you an apology."

Joe glanced out his office window to make sure this wasn't the Second Coming. "An apology?"

"Yes. I've made no secret that I felt Matt would be better off with me."

You sure haven't.

"But when I saw his last progress report . . ." She paused again. "Did you get him a tutor?"

Damn. The progress reports. He'd meant to keep logging on to the school computers to follow Matt's grades, but after the first two weeks when he'd shown improvement, Joe'd slacked off. "No," he said carefully. "No tutor. Matt's been hitting the books since it's basketball season and he wants to play."

"Well, an A in history and a B in English, Joe, whatever you're doing, I couldn't have done better myself."

Never had he had such a pleasant conversation with his ex.

"How's Trish?" he asked, his gaze drifting to an outdated picture of his little girl.

"Growing up way too fast. She misses you. That's the other reason for my call. I wanted to discuss Christmas. Are you expecting Madelyn and Alfred for the holidays?"

"Not this year," Joe said. "Alfred has a conference in Miami in February. I imagine Mom will go with him. We'll arrange to see them then. Why do you ask?"

"I was thinking of bringing Matt to Chicago for winter break."

It was stipulated in the divorce decree, so Joe had little to say in the matter.

"He's not crazy about coming. Matt sounds really happy."

"And that surprises you?" The first trace of testiness entered Joe's voice.

"Frankly? Yes. If you're spending time with him, then I'm ecstatic."

He conceded the statement. For too much of Matt's and Trish's childhood, he'd been their father in name only. After last night's dismal defeat against Palmer, he and Melanie had taken the boys out for pizza. He'd never seen Matt as animated. Karen was right. Matt was making a fine transition, and Joe had enjoyed their time together, as well.

"So what do you think?" Karen asked.

She'd been talking. "About?"

"About Trish and me coming to the Springs for Christmas?"

With his schedule, Joe hadn't even thought about the approaching holidays.

"Trish wants to go skiing. I thought we could make it a family thing."

"Family?"

"We could rent a condo in Breckenridge, separate bedrooms for you and me, of course, and hang out. What do you think?"

Over the phone, it sounded ideal. His kids loved to ski, and he could use some vacation time as well. "What about Mark?"

After another perceptible lull in the conversation, Karen said, "I gave him back his ring. We're taking a timeout."

A timeout engagement? "I see," Joe replied, not really understanding, but not interested enough to pry further.

"Mark wants to move up the date and I'm not certain. I—I miss you," she said.

Joe gripped the phone. Too bad it had taken ripping a family apart and relocating to another city clear across the country for her to realize it.

"Joe?"

"What do you want me to say? Of course, I want to see my daughter. And if you take the kids skiing, great. I'll come up during the day. But the nights. . ." He left the words unsaid.

His ex was a dark-haired beauty who could play seductress. If she really was uncertain whether she should marry Mark Bryant, the emergency room physician she'd left Joe for, he wasn't going to be her guinea pig while she made up her mind.

"You don't want to see me," she finished for him.

"Not particularly."

Her sigh was audible. "You were never home, Joe, and I can't undo what I did. But don't take it out on the kids, okay?"

"Why would I hurt my kids?" Even contemplating the thought caused his heart to ache.

"I'd like for us at least to appear to be friends when I get there."

She had a point. "Go ahead and book the flight."

She hesitated. "I already did. We get in the evening of the twenty-third. It'll be too late to drive up to Breckenridge. Would you like Trish and me to book a hotel, or can we stay at the house?"

Holding the phone away from him, Joe stared at it. Karen had launched this plan long before she'd placed the call. For a moment, he contemplated making a room reservation in her name. But Trish would want to stay with her mom, and what kind of father expected his daughter to stay in a hotel when her old bedroom was readily available?

Sort of. A bedroom existed, but Trish's furniture resided in Chicago. He'd never replaced it. Moreover, her bedroom doubled as storage. Joe picked up a pen, scribbled *shopping*, then tossed the pen across the desk. He'd been meaning to get her room ready. Hell. He'd been meaning to do a lot of things. "No hotel room," he said. "Of course, you'll stay at the house."

"Thanks, hon . . . Joe," Karen amended. "I'll send you an e-mail of our itinerary."

"You do that." He hung up without a goodbye. What was she up to? His thoughts turned to Melanie and the kiss they'd shared last night.

Why was it when a guy thought he might be on the right track, life derailed him and sent him hurtling in a different direction?

Chapter Thirteen

Drake entered a roadside motel room and tossed his bag onto a tattered piss-colored bedspread. Cheap furniture, threadbare carpet, the place stunk of nicotine, neglect and old age. But it was the Ritz compared to the places he'd crashed in West L.A.

What had been going through his head when he offed the guard? The asshole sure couldn't help Drake dead. Knowing he should get away from the murder scene as quickly as possible, and taking advantage of Rope's leads, Drake had left Cañon City. From there he'd taken US 50 West and driven forty miles to Pueblo, Colorado.

To his knowledge, he'd made no mistakes. But shit, the stuff these forensic dudes had come up with these days. Drake's ruined gloves and coat had protected him when he'd handled the body. But with blood on both items, he'd traveled several miles east of I-25, until he found an abandoned campground, lit a fire and burned them.

With one of his recently purchased fake IDs, he'd checked into this flea trap and stripped naked. As he checked over his injuries, he wondered if the scratches on his neck and chest had come from the guard, or were they the result of their rumble off the porch? And what primarily concerned him was whether the cops could tell one from the other.

He frowned at his reflection in the mirror. His fifty thousand was down to twenty-six grand. Now, thanks to bloody Ropes, Drake had to spend more on winter clothes.

Whoever found the body was in for a gruesome surprise. All he could hope for was the fuzz would believe it was a leg breaker who'd had no success in finalizing a bad debt.

In any case, Drake wasn't too worried. He'd told anyone who'd asked that he was returning to California upon his release. Now, all he had to do was wait until visiting hours of the East Cañon Correctional Facility in Cañon City, and put a new plan into motion.

He dozed until later that morning, then, faking a Hispanic accent, called the prison and asked for Ramon Garcia. His former cellmate was a trustee and had phone privileges, or at least he had before Drake left the joint.

"Who are you holding for?" some hard-nose said as he came on the line.

Drake stressed the accent. "Ramon Garcia. This is his cousin. He's expecting me today and I can't be there. I need to let him know."

"I'll relay the message," the guard said.

Damn. "That's cool. But I wanted to tell Ramon why I can't be there. It's his uncle. He's sick, ya know? He's not gonna make it. Let me break it to him, will ya?"

The guard hesitated, but finally came back with, "Hang on."

Five minutes later, Garcia answered the phone. "H'lo."

"Garcia, this is Max."

"Max? Where you at?"

From his Pueblo motel room, he exhaled slowly. "Riverside. Ramon, listen. Remember that venture you told me about?"

"Yeah, but you said—"

"I know what I said, but this working construction's the shits. You gotta get me out of here, Garcia. You got a number for me?"

"*Nada,* man, sorry. My contact would kill me. Leave your number. I'll have him call you."

Shuddering at the thought of Colorado Springs, Drake asked, "Is he in the same place we talked about?"

"That's where he was the last time I talked to him. But who knows, he might've split. Look, this ain't my time for privileges. The man's breathing down my neck. How can I reach you?"

Drake wanted to press his ex-cellmate for information to speed things along, but clearly he was afraid of Denny Ramirez. Risking the prison's recording system, Drake gave out his cell number. No way could he risk hanging around Pueblo. This close to Cañon City, Pueblo wasn't small, but it wasn't a metropolis area either. And if he was a suspect in Rope's death . . .

He'd head to Denver to await Ramirez's phone call. In a city that size, Drake could turn invisible and wait for the heat to die down.

"Got your number, bro. Go work on your tan. He'll call you," Garcia said.

Drake nearly squeezed the life out of his cell phone, before he pressed end. That had been the plan, to lie on a warm beach and soak up the rays. Who would have thought he'd still be freezing his ass off in Colorado.

The only thing that made him calm down was Ropes' three solid leads. Melanie's last name was Norris now, she had a kid and she was living here in Pueblo. All possible ways for Drake to find her. Ropes also said something about her working with flowers. That could mean a whole slew of things, from peddling for a landscape company to setting up funeral arrangements.

Drake stuffed his meager belongings in his bag, then started for the door. But before opening it, he doubled back to the nightstand beside the bed and ripped off the Pueblo phone directory. While he was stuck in Denver, he'd let his fingers do the walking. He'd find the pretty little bitch that set him up if it was the last thing he did.

He'd start with the flower shops.

Chapter Fourteen

"This is stupid," Matt said. "Why does American history have to be so screwed up? Why all these amendments? Why couldn't Franklin and Jefferson get it right the first time?"

Standing beside her kitchen counter, Mel laughed. "Maybe because they didn't have a crystal ball, Matt. Remember, back in the late 1700s, the issues didn't pertain to women's rights or gay rights, but *human* rights. Slavery was the issue. Taxation without representation," she added. "Imagine a government imposing a tax simply because it felt like it. That's what King George was doing, particularly to the Colonies. So I bet Mr. Franklin and Mr. Jefferson had a few other things on their minds, including the fear of hanging from a very long branch."

Matt closed his book. "Yeah, well, it still bites having to know all this worthless stuff. How come you're not a teacher, Mrs. Norris?"

Luke entered the kitchen. He'd been on the phone with a girl, and Mel was dying for details. "Yeah, Mom, how come? You'd be great at it."

Caught between two staring boys, she turned toward the sink. "Never crossed my mind," she lied. "Who was on the phone?"

"Nobody." Luke moved to the refrigerator. "Dad always wanted you to go to school. Why didn't you?" Luke took out a gallon of milk and started to drink it straight from the container.

"I thought about it," she said, taking the milk from his grasp and lifting an eyebrow. "But then there was you, the commute, and your dad got sick."

Luke frowned. "So what's stopping you now? Didn't you tell me your mom was a teacher?"

Mel swallowed hard. Her son was growing up and becoming far too insightful. "Yeah, she was. Hey, how about I make shakes, and you take a novel approach and drink it from a glass?"

Both boys readily agreed, saving Mel from any more rapid-fire questions.

Her refrigerator-freezer was out of ice cream, so she went into the garage where she kept the stand-alone unit. *So what's stopping you now?* She loved working with kids. Some she'd even tutored at the elementary age. But she'd never accepted a dime, even though many parents had offered to pay. Convicted felons couldn't hold teaching licenses.

Funny, when it came to politics she read everything she could to stay current. What was she, a Republican, Democrat, Independent? It didn't matter. Ex-cons couldn't vote.

She sighed deeply. When she'd hitchhiked and ended up with Drake Maxwell all those years ago, she'd screwed up her entire life.

She located the vanilla ice cream, wandered back toward the kitchen and discovered Luke and Matt talking about something other than schoolwork. Mel eased closer to the door.

"Do you want Coach Hood to kill you? Skiing?" Luke screeched. "If you break one leg, Coach'll break the other one."

Matt laughed. "It'll be winter break. He can't have contact with the players anyway, and this means a lot to my mom."

"I guess," Luke replied. "You miss her?"

"Yeah, you know. I talk to her a lot, and I never thought I would, but I even miss my brat sister."

Luke laughed. "How old is she?"

"Eleven."

"How come your parents split up?"

Luke wasn't the only one who was curious. Mel hung on every word.

"I don't know," Matt said. "My mom was crying a lot, and dad seemed mad all the time."

"Did they do a lot of yelling?"

"Nah. It was the cold shoulder stuff, that kind of thing. You know what's weird?"

"What?"

"My mom said my dad was going skiing with us, and she sounded excited."

"Sweet. Maybe they're getting back together."

"That's what I was thinking," Matt said.

Mel clutched the ice cream, barely feeling the cold. Were Joe and his ex-wife planning to reconcile? The thought left her numb. Last night, she'd returned his kiss with as much enthusiasm as he. What was wrong with her? Did she have dolt plastered to her forehead? She took a long breath, squared her shoulders and re-entered the kitchen.

The doorbell rang and her heart lurched.

Placing his hands on either side of his head, Matt leaned back and groaned. "That'll be my dad. I completely forgot."

Luke rose from the table. "I'll get it."

"Forgot?" Still reeling, Mel placed the carton on the counter.

Matt shot to his feet and shoved books into his backpack. "The first night we don't have practice, and my ol' man expects me to spend it cleaning out my kid sister's bedroom."

Joe strode into the kitchen. "I heard the ol' man comment, and you're right. I do expect you to pull your weight. C'mon, Matt, hurry it up. I could get called out tonight."

Studying Joe from her peripheral vision, Mel noted the circles shadowing his eyes. With his coat looped over his shoulder, his tie askew, he looked like a man who'd spent eight hours under pressure.

Stop it, Mel. This is absurd. You can't care for him.

He joined her near the kitchen sink. "How was your day?"

"Fine. I was making the boys milkshakes." Pouring the thick concoction into glasses, she raised an eyebrow. "Want me to skip it?"

"No. But the moment they're finished, we need to get a move on."

"Sweet." Matt reached for his drink. "C'mon, Norris. Let's catch something on the tube."

As Luke and Matt dashed from the kitchen, Mel fought the urge to call them back. Their presence offered a buffer between her and the playboy next door.

"Actually, this gives me a chance to thank you." Joe moved closer, evidently unaware of the route her mind had taken.

"For?"

"My ex-wife called, ecstatic about Matt's grades. Even went so far as to ask if I'd gotten him a tutor." Joe leaned against the counter and crossed his arms. "I had. Only I didn't know it. You've been helping him, haven't you?"

So Matt was right. Joe and his ex had been talking. Mel needed to get a grip on reality. If they did get back together, wouldn't that be best for their children?

"Matt's been doing all the work," she said, stiffening. "All I've been doing is encouraging him to focus."

"Simon mentioned you taught one of the prisoners to read. It didn't take much to put two and two together. You're obviously a bright woman."

"Yeah?" Mel replaced the lid on the ice cream. "If I'm so smart why didn't I see what Maxwell was up to from the very beginning?" *And why did I kiss you last night?* "Excuse me. My ice cream's melting."

Before she snapped, and let him know what was *really* on her mind, she brushed by him. Re-entering the garage she stored the ice cream in the freezer.

Unfortunately, Joe followed. Closing the door to the kitchen behind him, he said, "Is Maxwell the reason for your lousy mood?" In seconds, he'd gone from father and neighbor to a cop on heightened alert. "Did something happen?"

She might be upset, but not enough to let him worry. "No, nothing like that."

He relaxed visibly. Surrounded by boxes and way too much privacy, the longing within her awakened and her mind wound back to last night. Even now she wanted Joe to ignore her off-limit vibes and crush his lips to hers. And by the heat in his eyes, if she didn't do something fast, he most definitely would.

No, he wouldn't, damn it. She sidestepped him and reopened the kitchen door.

Oh, God. This was insane. She was *jealous*. The fact that she was capable of such an irrational emotion irked her further. She wanted to ask about the boys' conversation, to know that the kiss they'd shared last night had meant something. Most of all, she wanted an iron-clad guarantee she hadn't risked her heart to a man who planned to use her and wouldn't return her feelings.

The boys' loud guffaws carried from the living room. Joe glanced at his watch, then narrowed his gaze and shrugged. "Well, something's eating you, so we'll get out of your hair."

"Fine." Instantly she regretted her surly tone, but the damage was done.

"Have I done something?" he asked.

"Why did you kiss me last night?"

Joe held up his hands. "I don't know. After our talk I thought I felt a connection. I obviously misinterpreted. Matt," Joe hollered.

"Ah, Dad," the kid called from the other room.

"Time to go. Now!"

Mel extended a hand. "Joe, wait."

But the man who'd showed such compassion last night wasn't listening. He walked out without another word.

Chapter Fifteen

Never let anger control you. Anytime you feel like lashing out, hit this.

Joe's breath came hard and fast as his gloves slammed into the bag. A former commander's sage advice never failed. With every jab, uppercut, grunt and groan, his mind began to clear.

What an idiot. Never again.

From manpower shortages to the robberies, the one thing that had felt right all day had been Melanie's kiss. And by the way she'd responded, he'd been sure she felt the same. He tore into the bag and vowed from now on to trust his instincts. He would fight this attraction and get over it. Hell, he hadn't known her that long. Not *this* Melanie.

The doorbell rang and Joe glanced at the clock on the basement wall. Who would be stopping by at this hour? He shucked off the gloves, ran a towel over his sweating body and fumbled into his clothes. On the other side of the door, he expected law enforcement, but one never knew. To be on the safe side, he grabbed his Glock.

Upstairs, he checked the peephole. Finding no one there, weapon in hand, he stepped out in the freezing night, his breath ghostly white, adrenaline racing. His late night caller had already made it to her property line. "Melanie," he shouted.

She pivoted and returned to his porch. But at the sight of his gun, she drew back.

"Are you all right?" he asked.

Her eyes never leaving the Glock, she nodded. "I . . . thought you'd gone to bed. If you have a minute, I'd like to talk to you." She lifted her chin. "I mean, if this isn't a bad time."

Renewing his promise to himself to keep his distance, Joe held open the storm door and waved her inside.

Mel had been inside Joe's house before. That time, however, she hadn't been focused on details. Bachelors obviously lived here. A layer of dust covered the entryway table, a withered coleus sat neglected in its clay pot and a stack of junk mail lay unopened.

She couldn't let Joe believe she'd been angry about their kiss. On the contrary, it meant more than she'd ever imagined. As far as her earlier behavior, she hadn't quite figured that out for herself. She'd waited for Luke to fall asleep, then left him a note and came over.

"You wanted to talk to me?" Joe asked.

Clearing her throat, she faced him. Evidently, he'd been working out. He looked different in a T-shirt and sweats, tougher if that were possible. Every muscle in his body appeared rock hard and galvanized. Infinitely more intimidating.

"I wanted to explain about this afternoon."

At his set jaw, she thought about leaving. He wasn't about to make this easy on her. "Well?"

The last time she'd stopped in to see him, he'd invited her into the den. Tonight, he wasn't near as accommodating. "Could we sit down?"

Unsmiling, he extended his arm.

Mel entered his den. Like the last time she'd been here, she took stock of a room full of clocks. She wanted to ask about them. But, also, as in the last time she'd been here, tension prohibited small talk.

Joe sat, but Mel chose to pace. "Today was a bad day," she began. "The holiday rush, misplaced orders, customers wanting their orders yesterday—"

"I couldn't possibly understand the stress that you're under."

She stopped walking. Oh for crying out loud. This wasn't working. This man had real issues to contend with. *She* thought she sounded pathetic.

Joe rose from the couch. "I'm sorry you had a bad day. Why don't you sleep on it and see if you don't feel better tomorrow. Good night, Melanie."

Well, that had to be the politest dismissal she'd ever received. Without an ounce of finesse, she blurted, "Are you and your ex-wife getting back together?"

"Where'd you get an idea like that?"

Grinding her back teeth together, she strove to recover an ounce of her pride. "From Matt. Your ex-wife's coming to town, you're taking her skiing. You cleaned out your daughter's bedroom tonight."

"For Trish and her mother." Joe frowned. "I have to buy furniture this weekend for my daughter. Karen's not sleeping with me."

Mel stared back at him. This wasn't happening. Why not put up a billboard advertising her feelings?

Joe obviously read the sign. His lean, angular face lit up in a knowing smile. "You were angry this afternoon because you were jealous?"

"What? No!"

"That story about having a bad day, you made it up?"

"I did not. I had a tough day." Mel might as well have been standing next to a furnace her face was so hot. "For the record, I couldn't care less what you do. But I *hate* being used."

Joe took a step toward her. "So if Karen and I were getting back together, you'd be okay with it?"

You conceited jerk. Mel took a step back. "More than okay. What I'm not okay with is you kissing me if you're thinking of someone else. Or maybe because you wear that badge you think you're entitled. Who knows? Maybe you've been leading on poor Lydia, too."

Hands on his hips, Joe tossed back his head and roared with laughter. "*Poor* Lydia. That's a first. Thanks to her ex-husbands, she has more money than both of us."

"You're missing my point, Joe Crandall." Mel bristled. "Oh, what's the use? I'm leaving."

She brushed by him, but wrapping a hand around her bicep, Joe stopped her. "My marriage ended long before I signed the divorce papers, Mel."

Swept up by his touch, his low sultry voice and his use of her nickname, she felt a surge of relief. "It did?"

"It did. Why didn't you just ask me?"

She turned to face him. "I guess I just did."

Joe pulled her into his arms. Using the pads of his thumbs, he rewarded the tight muscles at the base of her skull with a magical massage. "I don't kiss a woman if I'm thinking of someone else. If you want to know something about me, all you have to do is ask."

She wanted to quip something clever, to say she wasn't in the least bit curious. But he was so *close*, and thanks to the strong fingers easing away her tightness, all that emerged was a low, satisfied growl. Worse, it came out so sensual it would have made an adult-film producer proud.

Joe's gaze took on a predatory gleam.

Tormented from last night's kiss, and willing it to happen again, Mel acquiesced.

He took control of her mouth the way he took charge of everything. Urging her lips apart, long-abandoned sensations wound their way through her. Giving in to his taste of salty and sweet, she felt her inhibitions dissolve. His hand moved to her breast. It had been years since she'd been with a healthy, virile male. She lifted her arms in a blatant ploy to give him permission. Her attraction to him was more powerful than any of the illicit drugs she'd once sought. And as their bodies came together, it was Joe's turn to groan.

Until from every corner of the room, his collection of clocks went off, broadcasting the hour with every chime, peal and clang. And along with these noises, she heard a series of coughs.

Persistent coughs.

Shoving away from Joe, Mel put her hand to her heart. Oh dear God, if Matt had witnessed any of this. . .

As for Matt's father, *he* started to laugh.

"I think Matt's awake," she whispered, at a loss to understand what Joe found so funny. "I think he's sick. Didn't you hear him—"

"Cough?"

"Yes," she said, her frustration growing. "You should go check on him. And I should go." She reached for her coat.

Shaking his head and still laughing, Joe took her hand and led her away from the couch. "Matt's fine. He crashed early."

She glanced around. "Then who else is here?"

Joe motioned to the wall behind his desk.

She turned to see family pictures, diplomas, framed accommodations, some photos a younger Joe Crandall in uniform, and, of course, one of his myriad time pieces. "I don't understand."

"My clock—it coughs instead of cuckoos."

"Why?"

"It's broken."

"Then you should fix it."

"I don't think so."

Okay, why would anyone be so happy to own a dysfunctional clock?

"I appreciate the advice, but if I had a choice to get rid of any of the clocks in this room, that cuckoo would stay. It was a gift from my mom. She . . . er . . . sort of made it."

Mel stared at the wall behind her. Despite the cuckoo's health problem, the clock itself was exquisite. It appeared hand painted, with intricate Hansel and Gretel-like figurines standing beyond a cottage façade, each on opposite sides of the cottage door. "Wow. She's talented."

Joe closed one eye and twisted his mouth in a way that said otherwise. "All right. She didn't exactly make them. Her husband's the real artisan. They live in Bavaria, Germany. When Alfred creates something he considers flawed, he sells them to the commercial dealers in the Black Forest. Or if my mom insists, he lets her have a go at it." Joe rolled his eyes.

Mel smiled, even as she thought of her own mom. How she wished she had something to hand down to Luke. To this day, she tasted bile when she thought of the trucker who'd left her with nothing. "I'd never let go of that clock, either." She waved a hand around the room. "And these others?"

Joe grinned. They came from her, too. Don't be surprised if you get one for Christmas."

Mel laughed and joined him on the sofa.

"Alfred," she ventured to guess, "I take it he's not your biological father?"

Joe nodded. "My real dad died young. Vietnam. My mom—her name's Madelyn—later remarried. She, my older sister Kate and I ended up in Galveston, where my mom remarried a barge inspector. Hard worker, good provider, bad disposition."

With Joe choosing to talk, Mel chose to listen. Carefully. Reciting what she was sure was the abridged version of his upbringing, he explained his mother's marriage, how it had ended and Joe's part in it. At the time, Kate attended The University of Houston. Madelyn moved out soon after and settled near Kate. As for Joe, he joined the army. After stints at US bases and a tour overseas, he was stationed at Fort Carson. He went to school on the

G.I. bill, got his degree at C.U. Boulder where he met his former wife, Karen.

However, his run-in with the court system had fared far better than Mel's. Intrigued with law enforcement, he'd chosen it for a career.

Shaking away memories of her own awful experience, she asked, "What happened to your sister?"

"Married, with three kids in Atlanta. She and her husband own an insurance franchise."

"And where did your mother meet Alfred?" Mel grinned.

Clearly ecstatic that his mom was happy, Joe grinned back. "She was a conference planner. She and Alfred met at a clock convention."

"Why, of course," Mel said, laughing. Pleased that they'd talked things out, she could have listened to him all night. Nevertheless, her responsible side took over. "I should be going."

"I could light a fire, pour us a couple of glasses of wine . . ."

"As much as I'd like that," she said, eyeing the cuckoo, then winking, I feel a cough coming on. Besides, Simon wanted me to return his call, and even though he said he'd be up late, I think eleven-thirty might be pushing it."

"He wants you to call? Why?"

"Simon insisted I keep a post office box in Cañon City. He brings my mail up every other week. That way I stay hard to trace."

Joe shook his head. "Simon brings your mail up every other week because he wants to see you."

"Carl's former *boss* made a promise to Carl. Besides, Simon's a sports nut. The boys have a game on Saturday. Plain and simple, he wants to be there."

"If you say so. Sure you won't have that glass of wine?"

Joe could be very persuasive, and she thought about kissing him again. But knowing where that would lead, she stood. "Positive."

Joe rose with her and walked with her to the door. When she turned to say goodnight, she noticed he'd grabbed his leather jacket from a hook near the door.

"Going somewhere?"

"I'm walking you home, Mrs. Norris."

She might have argued that she could be inside her place in less than thirty seconds, but she'd missed the I'll-walk-you-home phase in high school. It felt nice having Lieutenant Crandall by her side. That was until he reached up into his closet and came away with the gun he'd met her with earlier. A guilty reminder of her own bedroom shelf where she'd hidden Carl's .357 Magnum. Unlike her, he had a right to possess a firearm. She did not.

Last night at the basketball game, Joe had said Mel wasn't a criminal. But she was. She slept with an illegal weapon not three feet away from her bed. Something was happening between them, she could feel it. But how would he react if he knew? Mel teetered at the thought of telling him.

"Melanie? You okay?"

Staring at the gun in his hand, she stuck to the truth. "I'm afraid of those things."

He quickly stuffed it inside his coat pocket, held the door open for her as they stepped into the cold night.

You should tell him, Mel. Get it out in the open. If she didn't, Lord knew he had an abominable way of discovering the truth anyway. More and more she saw him as a human being. He loved his son and the rest of his family deeply. She suspected he even cared for her. *But he's still a cop,* an inner voice whispered. *Remember what happened before.*

And she did remember. As Joe walked her home, the topic stayed buried. This was one secret she just couldn't share.

Saturday morning, Joe scanned the headlines, while waiting for the furniture stores to open. Nothing he saw compelled him to read further until the caption, *Prison guard found dead* drew him in.

> Jesse T. Ropes, a former Colorado Springs resident and currently employed as a corrections officer at the East Cañon Correctional Complex, was found dead at his Cañon City home. Police were called to the west-side neighborhood on Wednesday in the early morning hours when a rash of dog barking led a neighbor to complain.
>
> Finding nothing unusual, police left the area.
>
> On Wednesday afternoon, law enforcement was again summoned to the neighborhood, this time to do a welfare check on Mr. Ropes, when the officer failed to call in or report to work. Finding him deceased, it is estimated he died between midnight and the predawn hours. Authorities have declined to list an official cause of death, pending autopsy and further investigation.

Joe drained the rest of his coffee. Huh. *Found dead.*

If Ropes had been discovered in the prison, the words would be self-explanatory. It would mean that an inmate had gotten hold of something sharp and stuck it into one of Ropes' vital organs.

But at home?

Joe drummed his fingers. Drake Maxwell had been housed at the East Cañon Complex. Still, Joe had been assured that the ex-con had returned to California. So the fact the guard worked where Maxwell did time was merely coincidence. *Wasn't it?*

With all the coincidences he'd witnessed of late, why couldn't Joe buy this one?

Found dead. What the hell did that mean? *And what about those barking dogs?*

Joe dialed information, then phoned the Cañon City Police Department and asked for the detective division. The cop on the other end of the line sounded like he'd barely gone through puberty.

Joe identified himself and said, "I read an article about a correction officer's death in our local newspaper this morning. What can you tell me about it?"

A perceptible silence filled the line. "Meaning no disrespect, Lieutenant, but I need to clear this with a superior and verify your identity before I talk to you."

Joe's intuition cycled into dread. The police wanted the details kept out of the media. That could only mean one thing. *Found dead* meant murder. Joe gave the detective the precinct's number. "Tell Dispatch I said to give you my home and cell number. I'll be waiting." He hung up the phone.

Fifteen minutes later, when the Cañon City P.D. still hadn't returned his call, Joe withdrew Warden Simon River's business card from his wallet. What were the chances Simon would confide in Joe about Ropes' death? On a one to ten scale, and based on their recent history, that probability most assuredly fell in the negatives.

Then Joe remembered the warden's planned visit with Melanie today. Joe hadn't forgotten the warden's protective stance when it came to the Norris's. Plus, Joe was only half kidding when he suggested the warden had feelings for her. Simon's visit was too darn convenient to overlook.

Joe dialed Melanie's number. She answered on the first ring.

"Did I wake you?" he asked.

"You're kidding, right? How come my phone only rings when I'm walking out the door? I thought you were going furniture shopping today."

"On my way." The sound of her voice put a smile on his face. "I could use your help. What do you know about mattresses?"

"They're flat," she said dryly. "Otherwise, not a thing. You're on your own. I have to work until three. Why don't you take Matt?"

"He's no fun. His back is killing him from all the heavy lifting. He wants to rest up for the game. Say, are you still expecting the warden today?"

"He's coming for dinner."

"Really? Dinner." Joe wanted that information. If the Cañon City P.D. viewed his phone call as outside interference, he might never hear from them. Could he confide in the warden without alarming Mel or making her suspicious? "What are you making?"

"Pot roast, mashed potatoes, creamed gravy . . ."

"Stop. You're making my mouth water. I know the warden likes you. I didn't realize your feelings were reciprocal. He must be pretty special to warrant such a feast."

She laughed. "Jealous?"

"Green." Joe grinned, noting her jab was payback for his accusation on

Thursday. "So if there's really nothing between you two, maybe you could invite me to join you for dinner."

"*Why?*"

"If I have to go to the game by myself, the least you can do is feed me."

"Before I came along, Joe Crandall, you always went to the game by yourself. What are you up to?"

"I have no idea what you're talking about."

"Why would you want to have dinner with Simon and me?"

"One, Matt tells me you're a great cook. Two, maybe I want to size up my competition."

The laughter was back. "Who says he's competition? And what makes you think *you* stand a chance?"

"Ouch, Mel, that hurt. I kind of liked kissing you Thursday night. I was hoping to do it again sometime. So would Simon mind?"

"You're serious."

"Completely."

She hesitated, and Joe knew she was waiting for him to say 'never mind.' She was out of luck. And then it occurred to him. He didn't make an ass out of himself for just any woman.

She sighed. "Honestly? I wouldn't think so, then again, Joe, maybe it's not—"

"Let's find out. If Simon objects too strenuously, I'll take the hint and leave. What do you say?"

"Oh, all right, five o'clock."

"Great. See you then. Sure you won't come help me shop for mattresses?"

He received her answer by way of dead air.

"Mel, what you do to a place."

Pleased that Simon noticed, Mel stood in the doorway as he surveyed her recently faux-painted living room. One of the specialty wreaths a customer had ordered had turned out so well, she'd made one for herself. It hung over the fireplace. As for the hearth, she'd trimmed it with white freeze-dried gardenias interlaced with gold leaf pinecones, eucalyptus and salal. Between work, school, basketball practice and life, she and Luke had decorated the tree. His childhood ornaments hung on the branches, the scent of pine filled the air and the house she'd been so reluctant to buy indeed seemed like home.

Simon touched the leaf of a spider plant hanging next to the sofa. "Imagine what you could do on a greater budget."

Holding her hands out, she laughed. "Probably grow more plants."

He grinned and said, "Where's Luke?"

Her smile faded. "He wanted to be here, Simon. But the coach requires the players to be at the gym early. Luke really wants to see you. You understand, don't you?"

"Of course, I do. I'll see him tonight." He linked his hands behind his back and rocked on the balls of his feet. "Something smells good."

"I hope so. Dinner's not quite ready. Would you like something to drink?"

"Beer if you have it. I want to hear what's been going on in your life."

They sat on the sofa and chatted amiably, for the most part sharing information they already knew. The warden appeared antsy and out of his element, and for the first time ever, she considered Joe's idiotic statement that Simon might be attracted to her. Lord knew she was nervous, but for an entirely different reason.

Their awkward silence was broken only when Simon cleared his throat. "What about Colorado Springs? Do you like it?"

"It's definitely bigger, but I'm finding my way around. Luke seems happy and we love the house. All in all, it's been a good move . . . thanks to you."

"I'd have done anything for Carl, you know that." Simon's brows knit together. "I'd like to think you and I have become friends as well."

"Without a doubt." She smiled uneasily. Who knew? Without the warden's assistance, she might've been in Drake Maxwell's clutches even now.

"If I have one regret," Simon went on, "it's that I let you down. If I had any idea that cop lived next door . . ."

Oh, God. He was going to bring up Joe.

"When that police lieutenant came to my office, Mel, he was as determined as any man I've ever met. You understand I had no choice but to tell him, don't you? And, of course, about Maxwell."

Shaking her head, she said, "It all worked out. It's over now."

"I have to say I don't care for his machinations. He's probably the type who uses them to advance his career. But since I can't be here, I suppose Crandall's the next best thing."

She arched a brow. Next time Joe provoked her beyond reason, she'd refer to him as *the next best thing*. Envisioning the reaction she'd get from that remark, she smirked. "Joe's not a bad guy when you get to know him."

The warden's eyes narrowed. "You call him Joe now?"

Immediately, she felt a charge in the atmosphere. She rose from the couch. "Our boys have become great friends. Lt. Crandall asked me to call him Joe."

"You see him frequently then?" Simon stood as well.

"Luke and Matt play on the same team. Of course, I see Joe."

"Melanie, I think you should stay away from him. To be honest, I'm not certain he's all that good a cop. Personally, I don't like him very much."

The timer went off on the stove. Never had she been so ready for an interruption. Joe should be here by now. Maybe he wouldn't show. Or maybe he hadn't planned on coming in the first place. Perhaps he'd only finagled a dinner invitation to annoy her. *Please, God.* One could only hope.

They walked into the kitchen where Simon's gaze fell to the extra place setting on the table. "I thought Luke couldn't be here."

The doorbell rang, and she jumped. Pressing a hand to her chest, Mel turned to the warden and sighed. "He can't, Simon. Please. Sit down. That man you don't like very much is joining us for dinner."

Much to Mel's surprise and annoyance, Joe kissed her cheek when he walked through the door. Simon's eyes grew wide and a flush made its way up his neck.

Gazing between them uncertainly, she said, "I believe you two know each other."

"Warden," Joe greeted him.

"Lieutenant."

"I hope you don't mind me joining you," Joe said. "Melanie was nice enough to ask."

She turned a shocked gaze to his.

He winked. "And I'm very grateful."

She flashed the big jerk her best behave-yourself-look. "Let's eat so we're not late to the game."

But it wasn't to be. Over dinner, as Simon and Joe stared at each other, Mel quite simply wanted to die. Their remarks had been hostile from the start. The pot roast she'd slow cooked to perfection tasted like cardboard in her mouth.

"You been busy, Warden?"

She looked from one man to the other. Okay, this was better. Asking about each other's jobs had to be a safe topic.

"Very," Simon replied. "Mel, this is a fantastic meal. I read about the robberies, Lieutenant. If you and your team can't apprehend the culprits, perhaps you should ask for state or federal assistance."

Joe's mouth formed a tight line. "We'll get 'em. It's just a matter of time."

"Simon." Mel placed a hand on his arm. "Out of forty-five boys, and as young as Luke and Matt are, they both made Varsity."

"That's wonderful, Mel." Simon refocused on Joe. "How many robberies have there been now, Lieutenant? Six?"

"Five," he replied.

Oh, dear God. Joe's clamped jaw reminded her of an electrical wire set to snap. Helplessly, she studied the men as they engaged in a bizarre verbal battle. "Joe, please," she murmured under her breath.

He turned to her. "The warden's right, Mel. If the robberies go unsolved, it could hurt my career. How about those unexplained budget overruns, Warden? There's been talk of embezzlement."

A practiced political smile formed on Simon's lips, but his eyes shone with hostility. "Indeed. We're investigating the matter."

Mel threw down her napkin and glared between the men. "This is your idea of a pleasant dinner? What's wrong with you two?" She unleashed her anger on Joe. "You just had to come, didn't you? Fine. Sit there and insult each other. But I'm not going to sit here and watch it."

Mel's rapid footfalls sounded on the stairs, followed by the very loud bang of an overhead door.

"That was the rudest display I've ever witnessed," the warden said. "I can't believe you intruded on my time with Melanie."

"I had to," Joe said. "I need information."

"So you bulldozed your way in here? Next time, pick up the phone."

"Does she know how you feel about her, Warden?"

"Does she know how *you* feel, Lieutenant?"

"She has an idea. Are you aware that a corrections officer by the name of Jesse Ropes was murdered in Cañon City?"

Simon nodded. "It's been the talk for days. But it didn't happen at a prison facility or in your jurisdiction, so why your concern?"

"Because Ropes worked at the Colorado State Pen, the same place Maxwell was incarcerated."

"So?" Simon wiped his mouth and tossed his napkin on his plate. "Maxwell's gone."

"Are you positive? Have the police any leads?"

Simon sighed and placed his elbows on the table. "Ropes had a gambling problem, a big one. The police suspect his creditors got to him. That or . . ." A look formed over the warden's face as though his next thoughts were repugnant to him.

"Or?" Joe pressed.

"The night of Ropes' murder, he held a poker party. Ten corrections officers were in attendance. Jesse Ropes wasn't especially liked, and the men in attendance haven't been fully cleared of any involvement."

Armed with these different and more probable scenarios, the tightness that had lodged in Joe's chest all day lessened. It also explained Warden River's reluctance to talk.

"Drake Maxwell's not in Colorado. I personally sent a man to watch him board a plane."

"He could've come back."

"For what reason?"

"Don't give me that. He could've discovered Melanie's whereabouts."

"Then he'd have to be psychic. You've seen the lengths I've gone to keep things quiet. With the exception of you, I've told no one her location."

"What about Luke?" Joe asked. "Has he been in touch with his former classmates?"

"Mel only recently bought him a cell phone. And even if he used it to keep in touch with old friends, I don't think Maxwell knows she has a son. How would he make the connection?"

"Guards talk to the convicts, Warden. Surely Maxwell knows something."

"Correctional officers keep their mouths shut, particularly about their families. It's ingrained in them from the day they accept employment. If they don't, they don't work for the DOC." Simon pushed back his chair. "It seems you ruined our dinner for nothing."

Having gotten what he'd come for, Joe stood. He was, however, unimpressed by River's arrogance. No matter how much confidentiality was stressed, there was always a weak link in the system. "It appears I owe you and Melanie an apology. Will you do one thing for me?"

"I don't know why I should, but if it'll make you leave, gladly."

"Find out if Ropes knew Maxwell . . . for Melanie's sake."

"It'll be a waste of time, but I guess I can do that much."

"Great." Joe handed Simon his card. "I'll let myself out. Enjoy the game."

"You're not going?"

Joe shook his head, regretting the way he'd manipulated Melanie to come by the information. But if it meant keeping her safe, he'd do it again. The realization of how much she'd come to mean to him stunned him. "Not tonight. I think Mel's stomached about as much of me as she can stand."

Chapter Sixteen

Simon had been cool after dinner, courteous during the game, then pensive on the drive home from Coronado. Mel wanted to talk to him, to explain Joe's reprehensible behavior that afternoon, but simply had no understanding of why he'd gone to such lengths to humiliate her or embarrass Simon.

He drew to the curb, cut the engine, and suddenly she didn't want to explain anything. She gazed out the window at her quiet little house and wanted to be inside, the whole episode forgotten.

"Your son's a superstar, Melanie. I wish Carl could've seen him play." Simon made the statement without smiling.

"Thank you. Every time Luke steps on the court, I wish the same thing."

Her husband's longtime friend leaned back against the headrest. He looked tired, older. "Do you trust me, Mel?"

At a loss to understand such a ludicrous statement, she said, "Excuse me?"

"Do you think I'd ever steer you in the wrong direction?"

"Would I have gone through all of this if I did?"

He shook his head. "Then hear me out. Part of my job as warden is dealing with statistics. I see men and women returned to the system more often than those who go straight. On average it happens in months, not years, oftentimes weeks."

Her throat went dry, the subject too close, and not at all to her liking. She'd beaten the statistics, hadn't she? She gripped the armrest. "Why are you telling me this?"

"When Carl got sick, and he and I hatched this plan, we discussed these numbers. We agreed that Maxwell was the type who, once on the outside, would resort to his old habits."

Hope surged within her. "You think he'll commit a crime and go back to prison?"

The warden shrugged. "He had every opportunity growing up. Maxwell wasn't a kid who came from nothing and acted out of desperation. From the beginning, he felt like the world owed him something. Yes. I think he'll end up back in the system."

"Well, that's a good thing, isn't it?" She wanted to cry out in relief.

"Absolutely. If you keep your head down."

Frustration tightened her chest. "What do you think I've been doing? I've done everything you've asked. Left my home, my friends—"

"Do you have any idea how many people you talked to tonight?"

The more games she'd attended, the more people she'd gotten to know. "Five, ten, maybe? They're the players' parents, Simon."

"I don't care if they're cloistered nuns. You need to keep a low profile. Unfortunately, your son is going to bring you unwanted attention."

"What are you talking about?"

"When I said superstar, I didn't mean it as idle praise. Luke came off the bench and scored twelve points in one quarter. If that coach doesn't make him a starter, he's a foolish man. If the papers don't make something of this boy, then they're blind."

Mel held up her hands. "What has this got to do with Drake Maxwell?"

"Nothing, if he goes back to prison soon like we anticipate. It's if he doesn't that concerns me. Each day that he's out gives him more opportunity to find you. Luke's a sophomore. Right now, hundreds of college scouts are taking notes. Soon they'll be tracking this kid, taking pictures, writing reports—"

"Of Luke, not me," she said, her voice rising.

"They'll want quotes from the parents, personal interest stuff. When they hear about this fatherless boy, living with his stepmother, the press will gobble him up."

"Are you suggesting I make him quit?"

Simon brushed a hand through his short military-cut hair. "God, no."

"Then what would you have me do?"

"Be more standoffish. If someone wants to include you in the photograph, become camera shy."

Mel glanced out the window. In other words, remain in prison. She'd been so proud tonight, reveling in the praise of her son, and in talking to people who genuinely seemed to like her as well.

"And for God's sake stay away from Crandall," Simon added.

Mel twisted to meet his gaze. "I thought you liked the idea that a cop lived next door."

"I did. Until I realized you were forming an attachment to him. You looked for him the entire night, do you realize that? Tell me something. Are you sleeping with him?"

Her pulse quickened and heat shot to her face. "How dare you ask me that? I couldn't believe he would miss his son's game, that's all. Not that it's any of your business, but we do not have that kind of a relationship."

"Finally, something that makes sense. If you're thinking there could be something more between you, prepare to be disappointed."

To hell with self-control, she made her fury visible. "Not that I'm looking for anything permanent, but why is that?"

"The divorce rate for cops is astronomical. Same for alcoholism, domestic violence, nervous breakdowns. The stress they're under, do you think they turn it off in the driveway?" Simon studied her. "Of course not. They bring it home to their families."

She wasn't a total fool. Every word he described was true. She'd had a taste of that lifestyle being married to Carl.

The interior of Simon's Explorer became deathly still. Finally, he said, "Lt. Crandall already has one strike against him. He's divorced." Staring up at the ceiling, the warden blew out a long breath. "He's a *walk away*, Melanie."

If Simon had punched her, he couldn't have inflicted more pain. "What did you say?"

"You heard me."

She hadn't heard the term since prison. The term *walk away* was used to describe a man who took advantage of a woman. Women who fell for *walk aways* were the stupidest life forms imaginable. During her indoctrination into the Department of Corrections, both the officers and the inmates had referred to her *walk away* as Drake Maxwell. In other words, he'd set her up, left her to rot, and *she'd* let it happen.

"I've met Joe Crandall's type before," Simon continued. "His career will always come first.

"It's too early even to be having this conversation," Mel said, looking away and aching that so much of what Simon said was true. "You're worried about nothing."

"But that's just it. I'm very concerned. Carl left you in my care. At first it was my duty. Now . . ." It was Simon's turn to look away.

Like her, he'd lost a spouse. But it had been years. He'd raised his children alone and never remarried.

"Perhaps I made a mistake in insisting you come here. Perhaps you should return to Cañon City."

If she'd been in better spirits, she might've laughed. Still, there was nothing humorous about his tone or this heart-wrenching topic. "But I'm known there. That was your whole point in suggesting that Luke and I leave. People could point us out."

"Yes, but if you come back, you'd no longer be alone."

"You're not making any sense."

Simon reached for her hand. "I thought my feelings were simply because I admired you. They're not, Melanie, I swear it. I'd planned to wait a respectable time. I swear to God, I did. Luke can play ball in Cañon City. Sure, it's small, but he'll get exposure no matter where he plays. And you said it yourself, he's fond of me."

Mel pulled back her hand and pressed a palm to her mouth. This couldn't be happening.

"Becoming a warden's wife has certain advantages." Simon's voice became embarrassingly pleading. "You'd never want for anything. Drake Maxwell wouldn't dare approach you if you were under my protection."

Nausea engulfed her. These people had *taken care* of her most of her adult life. Did he think that because she'd loved Carl Norris's infant son and married the corrections officer as a young girl, she wanted a repeat performance?

Under my protection. You'd never want for anything.

Did he think he could buy her?

For the first time in her life, she felt free. Even with Joe's sudden interest and his off-the-chart kiss, she loved having full say over the decisions she made.

If she'd learned anything in prison, she'd learned survival. She'd be a fool to alienate the warden. She had to preserve their friendship. "I'm sorry, Simon. I'm not in love with you. I'm not in love with anyone." And although it sickened her to lie, she added, "I'm honored that you've asked. You have a long drive ahead of you, and it's getting late. I'd like to go inside now."

"I've offended you."

She shook her head. "Never. I don't want to talk about this anymore. I'll take your advice. I'll try not to be as *outgoing*."

Frowning, he watched her. "Does that apply to Crandall as well?"

He's a walk away, Melanie. She lowered her head. Giving Joe up so new in their relationship would be painful. But too much of what Simon had said made sense. "Yes, it applies to Joe as well."

"I'll see you inside."

Two nights ago, Joe had said the same thing and she'd welcomed his advances. Tonight, she couldn't bear a man's company. "There's no need. Good night, Simon." Before he could argue, she opened the car door and walked into the night.

The warden sat waiting until she reached the porch. A vehicle made its way down Serendipity Lane. Mel turned, expecting her son.

But it wasn't Luke. Most likely it was one of the neighbors, a dark Taurus she'd seen coming and going for days.

Mel inserted the key in the lock, stepped inside and leaned against the door. Closing her eyes, she clenched her fists. How long was she willing to play victim? She was through being taken care of, damn it. No more.

Her gaze traveled to the stairway and what lay beyond. Illegal or not, the gun hidden away in her closet ensured she'd be able to defend herself. If Drake Maxwell came for her, she'd be the last person he ever came for.

Chapter Seventeen

In a noisy, smoke-filled tavern across town, Drake scanned the booths for Denny Ramirez, hoping to remember what the guy looked like. It'd taken the ex-con three days to return Drake's phone call, and if not for the tip on Melanie, he might have said "fuck this" and left Colorado altogether.

Looking over his shoulder was becoming a habit. He flinched when he heard sirens, he watched for squad cars, but the cops never burst in. What's more, no one seemed to pay him any mind, which made him rest easier.

Last night in another dumpy hotel room, he'd watched a Denver television station. Not one mention of Ropes' death had made it to Colorado's largest metropolitan area. Guess the state's capital had enough crimes of its own to report. So far, anyway. He'd never take his freedom for granted again.

Shit. He had to find a place to lay low.

In the back booth next to the john, Drake saw a Hispanic man drinking beer. Drake made eye contact and the dude nodded. His hair was shorter than Drake remembered and Ramirez had grown a goatee.

He stood and gripped Drake's hand in the familiar fashion they'd used in the pen. "Max, thanks for comin'."

Drake slid into the opposite booth. A waitress came and gave him an eyeful of her cleavage. He took a leisurely look down her blouse, but ignored further invitation. Pointing to Ramirez's drink, Drake said, "I'll have what he's having."

Both men studied the sway of her hips as she sauntered away. Turning to Drake, Ramirez said, "You look fit, *amigo.*"

Yeah, boredom and prison could do that to you. On the inside he'd bench pressed two-twenty. Now, he missed his regular workouts. When he finally got settled, he'd join a gym. "Your cousin mentioned a venture. I want in."

"Let's eat, then we'll talk." Apparently, Ramirez was in no hurry. But Drake's nerves felt like a skittering metal ball in a pin-ball machine. He wanted in on the plan. It wouldn't be long before he was out of options, and as much as things cost these days, out of money.

The steak dinner helped, but not much. The waiting was making him want to smash something. He felt the same pressure building as he had with Ropes. "Garcia said you wanted to see me. Well, I'm here. Quit wasting my time."

"Fair enough." Ramirez shoved his plate aside and lowered his voice. "I got a team of six players. All cons, none on parole, and all able to move around at my say so. If you got an old lady you're attached to, don't waste *my* time."

Drake's mind meandered to the hooker he'd picked up on Colfax. She'd hinted about coming with him when he left town. He'd retrieved the money he paid her, then left her asleep in a Denver hotel room. "I ain't attached to nobody."

Ramirez lifted a brow. "You gay, man?"

Drake shook his head. Guess if he was going to be living around a bunch of men, Ramirez wanted it out in the open.

"The way you was ogling that waitress I didn't think so. But I'm glad to hear it. The heat's on in the Springs, so we're givin' it a rest. The way I see it, we're good for one more job here. After that, we leave the state."

Drake thought of the Pueblo phone directory he'd left in his Jeep. He'd made it half-way down the list so far. Once he found Melanie and eliminated her, Ramirez's venture would be perfect.

"Another thing, I need you to stay out of trouble. If you're into anything else, don't lay it on my doorstep." The con's dark eyes narrowed. "No crimes other than our hits. Got any secrets, Max?"

Picturing Ropes' lifeless body, Drake said, "I just got out of the joint. Who's had time?"

"To work for me, you better keep it that way. I need men I can trust, or at least those quiet enough to get rich.

"I got some ground rules, so hear me out. One, I'm in charge. I give the orders. No one crosses me. You never bring a woman or drugs to the house. You park your vehicle in an apartment complex down the street, then walk. We meet at my sister's place. She lives in a nice neighborhood, man. We don't want no one ratting us out to the cops. My sister ain't home much, but when she is, she's off limits, understand?"

Drake nodded.

"No drinking or drugs during a job. I need people with clear heads. And if I let you in on this, forget about having my boot up your ass, you talk to anyone, you're dead."

Adrenaline shot through Drake's veins. Denny Ramirez's reputation with a switchblade was legendary. Drake had no doubt the former con meant what he said. "I can live with your terms."

Ramirez stood and picked up the bill.

Outside the tavern, music and laughter filled the night as people, obviously regulars, came and went. Veering away from passersby, Ramirez slapped Drake on the back and returned to his affable self. "This thing is working, Max. The way I see it, we're kind of like a union."

"A union." Drake scoffed. "What? I get a pension and benefits?"

"Better. You get someone watching your back. This city's shitting, Max. They never see us coming. Get this, we even made the nightly news. They're calling us the Chaos Bandits."

Drake shook his head. Sounded like a damned video game. "When do I meet the others?"

"How about now?"

Nearing their cars, Drake shoved his hands in his coat pockets as the gang leader paused again. "You don't like people, Max, and that's cool. For what I have in mind, you'll work alone. But to distract the cops, I need every man on my team, so play nice. My boys have already proved themselves. You haven't. If any one of them says you're out, you're out."

Drake slid into the Jeep. He followed the gang leader's car out of the tavern's parking lot. *Play nice.* Drake drew his mouth into a sneer. He'd do what he could to fit in. As for playing nice? He'd given that up a long time ago.

Chapter Eighteen

In the Op Center's largest conference room, Joe sat as a representative of the CSPD among people from two other agencies, the El Paso County Sheriff's Office and the Colorado State Patrol. The three law enforcement bureaus had joined forces to stop the orchestrated robberies and the individuals responsible. So far only one store owner had been injured, but it was only a matter of time.

Now some media wise-guy had given these criminals a nickname, and it'd stuck. Just what law enforcement needed—for these lowlifes to think of themselves as celebrities. The sensationalism had also fueled the ire of the mayor, city council and county commissioners, which meant if the outbreaks weren't stopped, and soon, they'd be howling for badges.

The meeting today was to strategize how the unencumbered agencies could provide backup and resources to their activated law-enforcement counterparts when the 911 calls went down.

With the city and county growing at inordinate rates, statistics had shown the criminal element encompassed only ten percent of the population. Unfortunately, they tended to find each other, then band together like lint on a sweater.

At first Joe clung to every syllable, but as the sheriff's commander rehashed locations on a PowerPoint presentation of the MOs, getaway routes and times that Joe had seared into his brain, his thoughts turned to Ropes' murder, Drake Maxwell, and naturally, to Mel.

How had he come to care for her in such a short time? More importantly, sharing a past like they had, why should he want her at all?

Since dinner Saturday night, he'd done his best to give her space, because she needed it, and because he could use the time to sort out his feelings as well.

He hadn't dated much since the divorce, but with the few women he had spent time with, he'd never made even a hint of a suggestive remark. Maybe because he was half-afraid they'd take him up on his offer. Mel had been fun to tease, and seemed as reticent as he about their relationship. Until Thursday night, that was. If she made love the way she kissed. . . Joe rubbed his forehead. Is that what he wanted?

"Lt. Crandall, do you agree with Lt. Fowler that the lull in the Chaos Bandits' activities indicates they've left town?"

Good thing the commander repeated the question, because Joe sure as

Chapter Nineteen

Drake settled in with the ex-cons. Well, about as well as he'd settled in with anyone. When you've been in prison you make do. As he'd suspected would happen, Ramirez was kicking his ass. From the moment Drake joined the team, he'd been surrounded by nonstop planning and bullshitting. Early mornings, late evenings, Ramirez concentrated on dividing these men who thought they were bad-asses into teams. From there, he trained them to disorient, strike fast and hit the least suspecting.

With the exception of Ramirez, Drake didn't see one he couldn't take. And after seeing the gang leader's smarts, and what he had planned for the future, Drake wanted in on this deal. In a few short months, this crew had raked in some serious bread.

There was one small problem. Ramirez watched everybody—especially Drake. Maybe it was because the gang leader had bought Drake's lie that he was flat-assed broke, or maybe it was simply because, in or out of the joint, cons don't trust easily. Whatever the reasons, he had found himself *invited* to camp out in Ramirez's sister's basement—which might have worked for Ramirez, but not necessarily for his younger sister.

Not much shocked Drake anymore, but that's what occurred the moment he met her. She'd entered her eastside Colorado Springs home two nights ago, taken one look at the diverse group of thugs sitting around her dining room table, said something to her brother in Spanish, and the chill factor in the room had plummeted to sub-zero.

Ramirez shrugged, said something back to her in Spanish, to which she'd grabbed her suitcase, glared at them all and disappeared into the back of the house.

Unless you crossed him, Ramirez was very good at keeping his cool. That night, however, he'd met every con's gaze with a snarl and a warning look. And who could blame him? Maria Ramirez was a sweet piece of meat, with a gorgeous face, long legs and shimmering black hair down her back.

From that time on, the house had been filled with her perfume and the smell of her spicy cooking, which to a con who'd spent fifteen years in the joint, was like tossing a single piece of prime rib to a pack of wild dogs.

This morning, however, Drake had other business on his mind. Ramirez had left early, and Drake saw it as the perfect opportunity to take advantage. He'd had the stolen Pueblo phone book in his possession for several days now, and he'd managed to work his way through the Ks. So far, the people he'd talked to at the floral shops were either morons or crazy suspicious. But the end result was still the same—no one had ever heard of Melanie Norris.

Now that he was on the outside, he realized another thing the bitch had cost him. Namely, he couldn't keep up. Just like the GPS device he considered totally worthless and alien, he felt the same about computers. He'd go crazy if he ever had to spend any length of time behind one.

So if he was going to find her, he needed someone with a grasp of technology.

Tucking the phone directory inside his coat, he slipped on gloves and walked out the front door. Outside, the sky was blue, but the day was brisk and he could see his breath as he strode to the apartment complex where he parked his Jeep. Next to the complex was a coffee house where the cons met up, and there was one team member he was anxious to see.

Ramirez called the guy "Breakneck," when his name was actually something unoriginal like Mike Brown. Breakneck had something to do with the guy's typing speed and accessing of information. From what Drake had learned, Brown had been in and out of the pen since he was eighteen years old. Now in his late thirties, he'd been convicted of everything from dope dealing to grand theft auto. But the last time Brown had gone back to prison, he'd said he was done. He'd then enrolled in the slammer's vocational training program to learn computers. Now he fixed them part-time for a struggling electronics shop, and when he wasn't there, Ramirez gave *Breakneck* a cut for researching the hits.

Sure enough, the moment Drake entered the cafe, he saw the dude, fingers flying, in one of the booths near the johns. Drake ordered two cups of coffee, sauntered through the semi-crowded restaurant, placed the extra coffee in front of Brown and slid into a seat across from him.

Brown's stubby fingers paused on the keyboard. The man with a really *bad* goatee eyed the coffee, stared back through black-rimmed glasses, with an obvious look of suspicion.

Drake took no offense. It was an expression most men in the pen wore when they wanted to stay alive.

"What's up, Max?" he said.

"How'd you like to make some money?"

Brown started typing again. "You know the rules. No business outside of our hits."

"Nothing crooked about it," Drake said. "There's five-hundred now, and five-hundred when you finish the deal."

"Where'd you get a grand? You haven't helped us with a job yet."

Brown grilling Drake about where he got his money pissed the hell out of him, but with forty or so witnesses, he unclamped his jaw and tamped down his temper. "Where I got it is my business. Look, my old lady disappeared." He forced the next words. "I'm still hung up on her. Someone said she had my kid. I gotta know for sure, one way or the other. Nothing illegal about it."

Brown folded his arms and his eyebrows shot up. "She live here?"

"Pueblo." Drake pulled out the rolled up phone book from the lining of his jacket. She works with flowers, so I was trying the floral shops. I've scratched off how far I got." He shrugged. "With all we've got going on with Ramirez, I'm not getting very far."

When Brown picked up his coffee, Drake took it as a good sign. "There's probably a faster way to do it," Brown said. "Does Ramirez know what you're doing?"

"No."

"Good. Let's keep it between us."

Why didn't I think of that? Drake extracted the bills from his pocket.

"I don't hack government agencies, Max. I got enough problems with my IP address, and hacking those places carries a sentence of five to ten. I'll do my best, but I ain't going back on the inside." Brown paused. "By the way, say I don't find her, do I . . . I mean, there's some work involved . . . keep the five hundred?"

Drake leaned back, looked the dude in the eye and resisted laughing out loud. Under the table, he tightened his grip, imagining the feel of the spindle that he'd used to crush Rope's windpipe. But Brown could do what Drake couldn't, so slowly he uncurled his fingers. Covering the money with his palm, he slid it across the table. "Tell you what. Ramirez wants to leave the Springs by New Year's. If you find my chick by Christmas, I'll include a bonus."

Brown's eyes narrowed and made with the familiar suspicion again. "Seriously?"

Drake forced something he hoped was a smile. "Absolutely." And if Brown kept Drake's money without results, his nickname of Breakneck would be Broken Neck.

"Okay, Max. You got yourself a deal. Here's what I need . . ."

Ten minutes later, Drake wiped the grin off his face as he rounded the corner toward the hideout. Good thing he did, too, because Ramirez sat in his low-rider in the driveway with the motor running. "Where you been, Max?"

Who was this guy, his mother? In that instant, it didn't matter how good the highfalutin spic was with a blade, Drake had his fists, which he was about to use on the gang leader's face. "I went for coffee."

"Dressed like that?"

He glanced down. He wore jeans and a jacket over a flannel shirt, almost identical to what Ramirez wore. Returning a what-the-fuck look, Drake replied, "Yeah. "

"Get in, Max."

Warily, he did what he was told, then for the first time considered that Brown might have pocketed the money and ratted Drake out anyway.

He'd kill the son of a bitch. Holding his breath, Drake said, "Want to tell me where we're going?"

Ramirez backed into the street and put the car into drive. "You look like shit, *amigo*. You need some new clothes."

Later that afternoon, when they sat in Maria's kitchen again, Drake ran his hand over the back of his neck and winced at the noticeable lack of hair. Turned out Brown wasn't doomed to die anytime soon after all.

Ramirez joined Drake at the table and plopped down a heavy binder. "Why are you frowning, *amigo*? I did you a favor. You no longer look like shit. As a matter of fact, you clean up real nice."

Nice? He frigging looked great.

When he'd walked into the swanky men's clothing store with a pocketful of Ramirez' cash, the store manager had eyed Drake like a bum. But then he plopped down two grand on a suit, and a couple of dress pants and shirts later, the stiff dick had found religion and treated him like a god.

Dressed in his new threads, he'd left the store. People on the street had said excuse me, actually met his gaze and smiled. Not that he'd smiled back. For a moment, he'd glanced over his shoulder to see if there was somebody else behind him. Nope, they'd been looking at him. *Respect. It was about fucking time.*

Now Ramirez opened a binder full of Brown's research. "Based on what I've gone over here, I've nixed some of the previous plans. Take a look at the ones I've highlighted in yellow."

Drake pulled the papers close, but he was like a boy stuck in a wet dream. This couldn't have turned out better if he'd written the script. If the cops were on to him for Ropes' murder, they were matching his description to the long-haired dude who'd left prison, not some guy dressed like a model for *GQ*.

"So, Max, what do you think?"

What did he think? He'd turned into a natural born delegator, that's what. In California, with Rander panting to earn drug money, Adam was as good as dead. And in Colorado, Brown was working to find Melanie. Now that he'd handed off his dirty work, Drake could relax into the plan.

Ramirez's notes looked promising, but without seeing them in real life, it was still too big a risk. "Looks good on paper," Drake said. "But we'd be crazy not to scope these out in person."

Ramirez gave Drake a sly look. "You see any of my other men wearing fancy threads? I told you when you signed up for this gig, you'd work alone."

Drake didn't think this day could get any better. But it did, including a finale he never saw coming. Maria walked over to the table set a beer in front of her brother and handed one to Drake. His gaze traveled from her breasts to her pouting lips and finally to her eyes. Dark, curious . . . interested.

Guess I do clean up real nice.

Before her brother noticed and slit him from ear to ear, Drake returned his attention to the hits. At last, things were going his way. As for little sister, he'd get him some of that. *Later.*

Chapter Twenty

"Mel, there's someone out front to see you."

Mel lifted a brow and paused in her work on an alstroemeria arrangement. Taking a quick whiff of the fragrant orange and yellow petals, she tucked a flyaway strand behind her ear, then followed Aaron through the connecting doorway.

An attractive older woman stood at the counter bedecked in a mid-length mink and very authentic-looking jewelry. Perplexed, Mel glanced from the visitor to Aaron.

The store owner beamed. "Melanie Norris, this is Elaine Preston. She's the customer you made the wreaths for."

Mel joined in Aaron's excitement. "Oh, hi."

"Hello, Melanie." Elaine extended a gloved hand. "I had to stop by to tell you how pleased my husband was with your work. His clients are raving. Last year I gave them fruitcakes." The woman rolled her eyes. "Let's just say I'm *still* the butt of all jokes at our parties."

The three broke out in laughter.

"When Aaron told me a member of his staff had made the wreaths, and each one so unique, I wanted to stop by and thank you personally."

Mel felt herself blush. "I loved doing them, Mrs. Preston. It was a new experience. Thank *you*."

Elaine removed an envelope from her mink coat pocket. "I hope you'll let me show my appreciation by giving you a little something extra."

"Oh, no, ma'am. I couldn't. Aaron paid me, I assure you."

The older woman's smile faded, indicating not many said no to her.

Aaron intervened. "You worked hard on a tight deadline, Mel. I have no objection."

"Wonderful. It's settled then." Aaron's customer pressed the envelope into Mel's hand. "Enjoy your holidays," she said, and left through the chiming front door.

Staring after her, Mel asked, "Was she wearing tennis shoes with that mink?"

"I believe she was," Aaron supplied. "Well, girlfriend, aren't you going to open it?"

"Should I?"

"No. Keep me standing here, dying of suspense."

She grinned, retrieved a letter opener near the cash register and ripped through the seal. A hundred dollar bill lay inside. Her eyes widened, and she turned to her boss. "Technically, Aaron, this money belongs to you. After all, I was working for you when I made those wreaths."

"I made a comfortable profit. The money's yours, Mel. It's Christmas. Have fun with it."

Wow, she loved this job.

"There's something else I want to discuss with you," he said. "It looks like I'll need a new manager here in the near future."

"Oh?" Mel made no effort to hide her disappointment. Karlee Stanfield had been an ally as well as a good manager. "Is Karlee okay?"

"The Air Force has transferred her husband to Japan. Can you believe it?" Aaron sighed dramatically. "After all I've done for her, she wants to join him. So, as a heads up, I'll be starting the interview process as soon as possible."

"Thanks for letting me know." How could Aaron sound so upbeat? Karlee was one of those rare finds who maintained authority, but still managed to create fun. Who knew what her replacement would be like?

Up until now, Mel's work environment had been ideal. Her personal life might be a cesspool, but she loved coming to work every day.

"Unless I could get someone like you to interview for the position," Aaron said.

She'd been so wrapped up in her dismal thoughts it took a moment for his comment to register. She looked up to find the blue-eyed blond smiling. "Me?" Mel gasped. "Aaron, really?"

"Mel, *really*." He laughed. "Karlee and I discussed it this morning. No one knows plants the way you do. The other employees love you, and you're quickly learning the business. Why would I hire someone who might not work out when I already have you?"

She didn't want to squelch her chances, but she had to be honest. Her boss had given her a chance when others might not. "I've never managed a store, Aaron. Not only do I not have a degree, I have no college credits." *None.* Damn. What was she doing, trying to talk him out of a promotion?

"I reviewed your application, remember? You may not be college educated, but you're no Neanderthal either. Heck, I've seen the stuff you bring to work. You read books with titles I can't pronounce."

Mel stared at him speechless.

"And about college," he continued. "Don't you think it's time you remedied that?"

Recalling her conversation with Luke a few nights ago, her heart sank. He'd mentioned the same thing. *What's stopping you now?* "I suppose the main issue is money," she said.

"Managing the shop requires hard work, longer hours. With me running between two stores, I can't be everywhere. You'll supervise, schedule the staff and deliveries, and close much of the time. In exchange, I'll increase your salary and add benefits, including tuition assistance."

Mel couldn't take her eyes off of Aaron. "You'll help pay for my college?"

"For As and Bs, of course."

Oh my God. With Luke playing sports, she didn't pick him up until after eight anyway, and in a few months he'd be driving. She could do this.

With all of the "do this, Melanie" and "don't do this, Melanie's" she'd heard for years, Aaron was offering her nothing short of a lifeline.

Returning his goofy, lopsided grin, she said, "You are the most generous man I know. I think I love you."

"Well, I *know* I love you." Then tilting his head, he seemed to think about it. "In the most-platonic employer/employee-related non-sexual harassing fashion, of course. So, what do you say? Do you accept?"

"Are you kidding me?" She flew into his arms, and he swung her around. "I accept, I accept."

The bell over the door chimed. Beaming, Mel glanced over her shoulder. Aaron cleared his throat and set her down.

Joe stood in the doorway, unsmiling. "Don't let me interrupt."

Seeing Melanie wrapped in a stranger's embrace, Joe had obviously intruded on a happy moment. Whatever she'd accepted was clearly a big deal, and of her own volition. After Simon's phone call, his *I asked Melanie to marry me* had resonated through Joe's brain the rest of the day. All he could hope for was that she wouldn't rush into anything.

Now this.

Who was *this* guy?

The man with short spiked blond hair eased her to the floor and quickly approached. "Happy holidays, sir. Aaron Meyers, owner of Pinnacle Creations. How may we help you?"

Joe was known to have a firm grip, but this guy had one of iron. Odd in contrast to his rail thin countenance and long tapered fingers.

"We're not always so demonstrative. We're celebrating. Melanie's agreed to become my store manager."

The words *store manager* took seconds too long. The words *agreed to become* felt like a defendant awaiting a not guilty verdict.

Store manager. Joe blinked, then moved farther into the store. "Is that right?" His gaze traveled from Aaron's face to his beautiful next door neighbor. Melanie stood behind the cash register, pretending to be skimming paperwork when Joe knew damned well she was hanging on every word. "Congratulations," he said.

"Thanks," she replied. She didn't look up.

"Is there something we can help you find?" Aaron asked.

As Joe directed his attention to the store owner, Joe caught her sneaking a peek. He hadn't seen her in two days. Forty-eight hours. By giving her space, whatever Simon had said to discourage their relationship, had taken root and was working.

Appreciating the long blue sweater that outlined her curves, he could also see she'd put in a long day. Her auburn hair fell free of her barrette. Joe wanted to take her in his arms, explain that he'd acted in her best interest. As if the independent Melanie Norris would tolerate or appreciate that. Instead of giving her space, why hadn't he picked up the goddamned phone?

"I'm looking for something for a friend. Something in the way of an apology," Joe explained.

"Ah, I see," Aaron said. "I take it this gift is for a *lady* friend? Roses perhaps?"

"Yes, she's a lady, and I hope we're still friends. But roses?" Joe shook his head. "Knowing this particular woman, she probably grows her own."

Aaron frowned, and although Melanie wouldn't acknowledge Joe, her mouth had begun a curve upward.

Progress, he thought. His iceberg was melting.

He moved to a display case containing odd-shaped, earth tone platters, bowls and vases. They didn't do much for him, but Karen had come home with stuff like this many times. He pointed to one he actually liked, a ceramic vase with a rose pattern etched into its side. "This looks nice. How about something like this?"

"Very nice," Aaron agreed. "I see you're a gentleman with taste. These are very popular, and part of the Theresa Alder Collection. They're handmade and hand-painted, and we import them from Italy. Shall I wrap it for you?"

Behind the counter, Melanie's expression had taken on one of total amusement. Joe also noted the subtle shake of her head. What was she trying to say—she didn't like it? "I don't know. Maybe I should get a woman's perspective. Excuse me, ma'am? Is this something you'd like to own?"

She stared back at him with wide-eyed innocence. "Me? Well, yes, sir. What woman wouldn't love to own a Theresa Alder collector's piece? I have to ask, though. Is the gentleman really experiencing three-hundred-dollars worth of remorse?"

Joe nearly choked on the price. For a vase? Careful not to drop it, he returned it to the shelf. He wanted to say he was sorry, not crazy.

Melanie laughed and finally took mercy on him. Coming from behind the cash register, she moved into the showroom. "Aaron, I apologize. This man's not a serious customer. This is my next door neighbor, Joe Crandall." Then to Joe, she said, "Pinnacle Creations, well, let's just say, caters to people who never think twice about a water bill or putting their kids through college."

Aaron's confusion morphed into happy understanding. "I wondered what was going on here. So you're Melanie's cop?"

"Am I?" Joe turned to face her.

Her face the color of the nearby poinsettias, she fixed her boss with an incredulous look. "Aaron, when have I ever said that?"

"Okay, she's never said that."

"I can't imagine getting that lucky," Joe replied.

Melanie strode behind the counter again, shaking her head. Even embarrassed, she radiated the happiness of the moment. It was a great look on her. Joe planned to keep her that way.

"So," she asked. "Why are you here? *Really.*"

Ordinarily, he'd prefer to have this conversation out of anyone else's earshot. But he couldn't very well ask the shop owner to leave his own store. Plus, this Aaron guy seemed to be taking an inordinate interest in them. What's more, he appeared to be rooting for Joe.

"I *really* came to apologize . . . and hopefully take you to dinner," Joe said.

Aaron all but beamed, then fairly bounced to the front door and flipped the sign over. "Sounds good to me. Instead of standing around saying, 'I'm sorry to each other,' and as dead as the shop is for once, I think we should take it as a sign and close this place down."

Melanie glanced at her watch. "Aaron, we're open for another twenty minutes. It's the holidays."

"See why I promoted her?" he said to Joe. "She's more conscientious than . . . well, me." To Melanie, Aaron said, "When you assume your new responsibilities, free time will be a luxury. You'll be *begging* me for time off. So tonight, go. Celebrate. You've earned it. Besides, will you look at the man?" Aaron fanned himself. "If you don't say yes, *I* will."

Mel reluctantly let Joe help her on with her coat and left the shop with him. What had just happened here? She'd been promoted, then high-jacked. For days now she'd been taking Simon's advice to lay low. But the truth was she missed Joe more than she thought possible. *He's a walk away, Melanie.* The words simply wouldn't let go. In the shop she'd almost whispered to Aaron, 'stay out of this.' But her boss had amazing intuition. Maybe in his own way, he knew what he was doing.

Joe put his hand on her elbow, she pulled away. She wasn't quite ready to forgive him. Not yet. When Carl was alive she hadn't known this topsy-turvy kind of emotion. Her days had been comfortable, predictable. A wave of guilt wound through her. Passionless. Joe Crandall had the opposite effect on her. *Damn him.* "Do you want to know what upset me the most on Saturday?"

"Do we have to talk about it here? I'm sure the list is pretty long."

"That you would miss your son's game," she said, ignoring that he always had an answer for everything. "How could you do that?"

"What if I told you I didn't?"

Oh, you are too much. Stuffing her hands in her pockets, she cocked her head to one side. "Joe."

"I watched from the boys' locker room. I'd already upset you enough. Why drag it out?"

"Matt got to play," she said, testing him.

"For most of the third quarter until he got in foul trouble. I promise, I saw him. He did well. There's times I'm on the job and can't be there. But I'd never miss Matt's game on purpose."

She followed Joe's gaze as he scanned the empty parking lot. With the exception of Aaron's Jaguar, her Corolla and Joe's Crown Victoria, no others remained.

"Look," Joe said. "I talked to Rick earlier. Asked him for a favor."

Here it came again. What was Joe up to? "I'm listening."

"I asked him to give the kids a lift home after practice. He did one better than that. He's taking them to a game at Mitchell. Coronado's playing them next week, and Rick wants to scope out the competition."

"Will they be late?"

"Home before ten," Joe said. "I didn't think you'd mind. The boys were thrilled to be hanging out with their coach. And it couldn't have worked out better for me. I wanted to talk to you—explain about Saturday and what's really going on."

Joe had gotten to know her well. She didn't object in the least to Luke spending time with Rick Hood. With Carl no longer in Luke's life, he needed positive male role models. But the last comment Joe made didn't come from a man offering an apology. His expression had turned deadly serious.

Her heart tripped. "Is it Maxwell?"

"It's possible."

Turning from him, she started walking. What the hell did that mean? No way was she standing around an empty parking lot when Drake Maxwell could be lurking. Thank God she hadn't told Joe about Carl's gun. She wanted to go home, load it and keep it ready.

"Melanie." Joe caught up with her near her Corolla. "This is exactly why I didn't tell you on Saturday. There's no need to panic. I won't lie to you. We don't know where he is. That doesn't mean he knows where to find you."

Her shoulders fell. Joe pulled her close, wrapping her in arms that felt like steel bands. She'd give anything to possess an ounce of that strength. Leaning into him, she whispered, "Oh god, Joe." *We don't know where he is.*

"Let me take you to dinner. I'll tell you everything I know. There's been a development. No more secrets."

Summoning what was left of her depleted inner strength, she said, "Some place quiet. No crowds."

They took Joe's car to a little Italian bistro up the road. It was in a strip mall, and Mel had eaten there once with her co-workers. During the lunch hour, the place was packed. The winter night told a completely different story. She and Joe were the only customers. Cops generally sit with their backs to the wall, and Joe was no exception. Somehow, knowing he watched over her made her feel better. Or maybe it was the eggplant parmigiana, or the glass of wine.

She listened as he softened his baritone voice. In the dim of the quiet restaurant, with its red and white checkered table cloths and the Italian music turned low, she fantasized for a moment what it would be like for him to whisper sweet nothings or make plans for later between them. Instead he told her about a newspaper article, a dead corrections officer and the uncooperative Cañon City Police. From there, he explained why he'd arranged the little tête-a-tête with Simon, and with nothing to go on but bad vibes and morbid curiosity, Joe wasn't about to scare her.

Little by little, her brain and her heart accepted his explanation, and she dismissed Simon's claim. For Joe to go to such lengths didn't strike her as a *walk away*. As a matter of fact, efforts of this magnitude were proof that Simon hadn't a clue what he was talking about.

Joe reached for her hand across the table. This time, she didn't draw back. She held it, smoothed her fingers over a callus, and for the first time in two days, she felt happy. Though wouldn't it have been nice for him to whisper sweet nothings or to plan something for later?

She shook off the notion and stuck to real life. "What happens now? I become a sitting duck?"

"Far from it. First of all, from what Simon's told me, the police have several suspects in Ropes' murder. Drake Maxwell wasn't even on their radar until I tipped them off. In other words, we may be worrying for nothing. Second, Maxwell threatened his family. He went to them asking for money, they turned him down. For all we know, he's still in California plotting against them."

"How horrible that I'm hoping he's still there," Mel said, freeing her hand from Joe's and checking her watch. A good hour and a half remained before Luke came home.

"It's not horrible to want to stay safe," Joe said. "Adam Maxwell has taken precautions. He's no fool. Neither are you. But I do have some advice for you."

"Of course you do." Mel smiled.

Joe grinned back. "You should keep your guard up even if no one's after you. Put all that crap you have in the garage in storage. You've got some place that gives you privacy, use it. And get an alarm."

"I'll have you know, it's not crap," she said. Even so, every word he suggested made sense. An alarm system would also blow her budget. "Glad I'm about to get a raise."

"I'll say. Next time you're buying. Dessert?"

She shook her head. "Even if Maxwell's nowhere in the vicinity, he's still

Mel rummaged through Joe's bathroom, the one downstairs, then reluctantly searched Matt's bath upstairs. Joe's son was a typical teen. Nearly tripping over his basketball shoes, she could barely find the floor. The bathroom obviously doubled as Matt's hamper. Soap scum caked the sink, while miscellaneous toiletries lay beside it. She had no trouble locating the hydrogen peroxide and bandages. They were the only two items inside the medicine chest.

She left the bathroom, encountering as she went, more family pictures in the hallway. Focusing on the striking brunette and an equally pretty little girl, Mel saw firsthand that Trish was the image of her mother. Matt wore his typical grin, Joe his charismatic smile. What Mel couldn't take her gaze off was Joe's ex-wife's hand resting possessively on his shoulder.

In a few days Karen Crandall would arrive. Matt wanted them to be a family again.

He's a walk away, Melanie.

She squared her shoulders, banishing once again Simon's constantly intruding words. Joe had risked his life to protect hers. She entered the master bedroom as he flipped off his cell.

"Did they get him?"

"Not yet, Mel. We will."

She sat beside him on the bed and tried to pry the blood-soaked towel from his head. When he shook off her offer to help, she spoke to him as she would a child. "I need to see how bad it is. Don't be a baby. Let's go into the bathroom before you bleed on everything."

"This wasn't the way I envisioned getting you into my bedroom," he said grimacing.

In spite of his surly behavior, she couldn't resist. She met his lips. In that moment, the big bad Joe Crandall looked like a five year old, missing his teddy bear. But in the next second the look he returned was far from childlike.

Inhaling the scent of sandalwood, Mel followed him through the bathroom door. With no thought to her presence, he stripped off his shirt, sat on the toilet lid, reapplied the towel and waited for her help.

She'd patched up Carl numerous times, yet he'd never affected her like this. Even injured, Joe was miles ahead of ordinary. Admiring his tanned, bare-chested physique, a lump formed in her throat as she stood rooted to the floor.

He shot her a frown. "I need to get to the office. Could you hurry it up, please?"

Chagrined, Mel snapped out of her trance. A fleeing suspect obviously took precedence over his sex drive. She ran her hands under water, draped a clean towel around his neck, then stepped between his thighs. Lifting the formerly white towel from his hairline, she discovered an angry wet gap welled with blood.

Annoyed that her own libido wasn't worried about the APB, she tossed the now crimson towel into the sink and inspected what looked like a one-inch gash. There was nothing sexy about a man bleeding in his bathroom, but she'd never been so close to such raw masculinity before. Just for a moment she fantasized about the bed in the outer room and ran a curious finger over Joe's glistening skin. Then ordering restraint, she quashed her untimely thoughts, and pushed his hair away from the injury.

He stiffened and she yanked her hand back. "What's wrong? Did I hurt you?"

"God, no." Holding the clean towel to his head, his breathing grew ragged.

She made an effort to see where his preoccupation lay, and when she did, her face grew hot. She'd been cruising the same lustful road as he, but as her breasts tightened under his inspection, she lashed out, "I'm up here, Joe."

He pulled his lecherous gaze away from her chest and his mouth formed a smile. "I know. But you should see the view from down here."

That's all it took to jerk her back to reality. She twisted the cap, covered his eyes and in a voice that belied her sincerity, said, "Brace yourself. This is going to sting."

"Just get it over with."

She poured the antiseptic, his smug smile disappeared and he clenched his teeth.

But as the blood continued to gush, her revenge was short-lived. "I gotta tell you, it's quite a gash. You may need stitches."

"No time. Do the best that you can."

His issuance of orders like she was one of his staff didn't set well, but then on top of the peroxide, the injury probably hurt like hell.

Glancing at her watch, she said, "The boys will be home any minute."

"Good. That way you can tell Luke to pack a bag. You're staying here tonight."

His concern redeemed him somewhat, but she still had a parental obligation. "What? And how am I supposed to explain that to Luke?"

"Simple. We had a prowler. I have an alarm system. Luke can sleep with Matt in his room. You'll take the guest room—break in my new furniture."

She applied a new towel to the wound. "I don't know, Joe."

"I'm going downtown, and I can't be worried about your safety—"

The house alarm beeped once, signaling that Matt had come home.

She went ramrod straight. "Luke. He'll go home to an empty house. He'll be worried." Quickly, she draped three layers of gauze, then placed a bandage over Joe's bleeding scalp.

"Dad, where are you?"

"Up here," Joe shouted.

"Do you know where Mrs. Norris is? Her car's out front and—"

Mel glanced up to find both boys in the doorway, looking in on what could only be construed as a provocative situation. As she met Luke's gaze, his entire body tensed and his face flushed with anger. "*Mom?*"

Matt's open-mouthed look of horror mirrored his friend's displeasure. "What's going on?"

Indicating the newly applied bandage, Mel said, "Your dad tried to stop a prowler. The guy nearly ran over him."

"Are you okay?" Matt's voiced rose in panic.

"I'm fine. Thanks for the assistance." Joe's manner was nonchalant as he eased back against the commode tank and Melanie returned to the sink.

But Luke was having none of their explanation. He glared between the two. "Yeah, right." Turning, he stormed away.

Mel's heart vaulted to her throat as she rushed after him. "Luke, just a minute."

He'd already made it down the stairs.

"Luke Norris! Stop right now!"

In Joe's entryway, the teen rounded on her. "I'm going home."

"You can't."

"What?"

"Lt. Crandall wants us to stay here tonight."

Luke glowered at her. "I don't give a rip what he—"

"Luke!" Seeking an explanation that would make sense, she said, "The intruder was scoping our house. The Crandalls have an alarm. First thing tomorrow, I'll have one installed."

The boy tightened his hands into fists. "I don't need an alarm, I have a baseball bat." Luke glanced toward the top of the stairs. "Are you coming or staying with him?"

Mel blinked at the hostility she heard in Luke's voice. "Sweetheart, nothing was going on. Besides, I thought you liked Lt. Crandall."

"I did until he made it clear he has the hots for my mom. That's just weird. Matt's my best friend." Luke lowered his voice. "And what about Dad?"

Her shoulders fell. "What about your dad? Baby, he's gone."

"Have you forgotten him already?" Misery mottled the kid's handsome face.

Luke's sorrow matched her own. She searched his eyes. "I think of him every day. How can I not when you could be his reflection?"

Seconds passed and some of the tension between them lessened. Using it as momentum, Mel said, "I'm sorry you misunderstood what you saw. But nothing happened. Understand something. You are my number one priority. But Lt. Crandall got hurt protecting me."

"I don't want to be here," Luke said. "I want to go home."

"All right. Let's go."

Doubtless confused, and angry as well, Matt had disappeared into his room. But Joe hovered at the top of the stairs. He'd exchanged bloody and torn clothes for a clean pullover top and jeans, and the bandage loomed white against his skin.

She ached at the expression she saw on his face. He'd probably overheard the majority of the conversation. Still, their budding relationship was a topic that was bound to come up sooner or later.

Placing her hand on the banister, she silently implored him with her gaze. *Luke doesn't understand.* "We're leaving," she said.

"All right." Joe descended the stairs. "I'll station a unit outside your house." He focused on Luke. "Your mom didn't panic. You should be proud of her, Luke."

Glaring, he maintained a stony silence.

Joe's cell phone rang. He answered, "Crandall," then narrowed his gaze. "Good work. Put him in B. I'm on my way." He turned to Mel. "They got him."

She squeezed her eyes closed. "Thank, God."

Joe reached for his coat in the entryway closet.

"Should you drive? Joe, your head."

"I don't have much choice."

Luke studied the floor. "Maybe my mom should drive you. You could have a concussion. I'll stay here with Matt."

"You're okay with that?" Joe asked.

Mel's heart warmed, first for Luke in showing such grownup understanding, then for Joe in showing such compassion. Her next door neighbor was definitely a contradiction. Beastly one moment, thoughtful the next.

"I'm sure." Luke glanced at her. "I had one once, remember?"

"I remember. You were in junior high." She smiled.

Looking toward Joe, Luke rolled his eyes. "Every time I'd get to sleep she'd wake me up."

Joe nodded. "Moms do that. It's in a rule book somewhere."

"You'll be back soon?" The teenager's voice reverted to suspicion.

"As soon as possible. I won't let anything happen to your mom. Tell Matt to set the alarm. You boys call me if there's a problem."

As Luke trudged up the stairs, all while watching Joe help Mel on with her coat, she whispered over her shoulder, "Is it Maxwell?"

"We'll know soon enough. But who else could it be?"

With no answer to that, she simply remained silent.

"Let's go." Joe opened the door for her. "Time to get a bad guy off the streets and out of our lives."

Chapter Twenty-two

The moment they arrived at the Police Operations Center, Joe went for an update and Mel fell into protective custody. Not the kind she experienced fifteen years earlier. This time a uniformed officer escorted her to Lieutenant Crandall's office, treating her as though she were royalty, offering her magazines, coffee, tea or something else. She opted for hot chocolate. She'd heard Joe's stories about cops who simply reheated a half-empty pot, and soon it had the consistency of sludge. Which might have explained why he liked her coffee so much.

"How long will he be gone?" Mel said to the officer in the doorway.

"I really can't say, ma'am. But the L.T. generally gets straight to the point. If he has anything to say about it, the interview will go quickly and you'll be out of here."

"You call him L.T.?"

"Short for Lieutenant, and, yeah, most of us do. He's a good guy."

A good guy. Fifteen years earlier, she would have vehemently argued the point. Now she found herself nodding in agreement.

Fifteen years. She gripped a mug so worn she could no longer read the letters and moved to Joe's window. It overlooked Nevada, a thoroughfare that ran north and south. At one time, before the construction of I-25, it had been the city's main corridor between Denver and Pueblo. Now it was a gateway to the interstate, to downtown businesses, Penrose Hospital and to myriad cross streets.

How she wished she was on Nevada right now driving away from this place.

Is it Maxwell? Who else could it be?

He'd seemed so nice, so ordinary when he'd picked her up on that lonely stretch of highway fifteen years ago. She'd learned firsthand that hitchhiking wasn't the optimum mode of transportation that day. But with darkness approaching, and Mel bruised, limping and bleeding, he'd offered to help and she'd risked trusting him.

Drake Maxwell had been cute, he drove a Corvette, and at least he was younger than the last pervert who'd picked her up and tried to rape her. The pawing trucker, trying to kiss her, squeezing her breasts and going for her crotch, had left her frantic, and she'd left him possibly blind in one eye.

That scene, years afterward, would be only one of her nightmares. Mel sipped her hot chocolate and shuddered.

Fast forward past the robbery to the trial, when in exchange for a reduced sentence that would never go to trial, she'd agreed to testify against Drake. Her lawyer, a court-appointed public defender, had said, "Look him in the eye, Melanie. Maxwell's lawyers have convinced the district attorney that you were complicit. This is your only chance to earn that judge and jury's sympathy."

And face Drake she had, with all the bravado she could muster. As she recounted what she recalled to the judge and the jury, he'd sat at the defense table sneering, tearing her from limb to limb with his gaze. Then she'd stepped down from the witness box, and he'd lunged for her. The only things that saved her from his attack had been the bolted-down table, Drake's handcuffs and leg restraints, and the deputies rushing forward.

"You're dead, bitch," he'd roared. "You're fucking dead!"

The crowd had become so shocked, so unsettled, the judge had cleared the courtroom. Heart in her throat, shaking uncontrollably, she'd been whisked back to the county jail.

Even now, Mel's knees went weak at the memory. She clutched the warm cup with both hands. Would Joe make her face Maxwell again? Would she have to relive that terror? She stared down at the traffic coming and going. How she wished she was on Nevada right now, driving away from this place. How she wished she was driving toward home.

On the spare bed in his friend's room, Luke lay with his eyes closed. If he didn't crash soon, tomorrow's practice would kick his behind. He'd tried to count sheep, but with no luck so far, he opened them to stare at the digital clock on the dresser. Their folks had been gone for forty minutes now.

He'd noticed in recent days the way the cop looked at his mom, but hadn't given it much thought. Although, after all that he'd witnessed tonight, he could no longer ignore it.

"Luke, you awake," Matt asked.

"Yeah. What's up?"

"Do you think there's something going on between your mom and my dad?"

Flipping onto his side, Luke moaned. So much for crashing. "How the heck would I know, Crandall? Go to sleep."

"I think there's something goin' on, ya know?"

"Maybe."

"Are you okay with that?"

"Hell, no," Luke grumbled.

"Why? I like your mom. You got something against my dad?"

Luke hesitated. Lt. Crandall was okay. He was tough on Matt, but then his own dad had been strict with him on occasion. Luke's throat constricted. He'd never known his real mom. And now, like the casket that had disappeared into the ground, his memory of his father was fading. Luke didn't want that. *Not ever.*

"Well, do you, Norris?"

"What?"

"Have something against my ol' man?"

Luke sighed. Matt was his best friend. It was time to tread lightly. But no matter what, Luke couldn't lie. How could a kid with two living parents understand what he was going through? "The only thing I have against your dad is he's not my father." Luke inhaled a shuddering breath. "No man ever will be."

Before heading into Interrogation, Joe met with Brooks Morris to pick up the pursuing officer's arrest report. He found the white-haired, barrel-chested police officer hard at work, tongue slightly protruding as he scribbled the details.

"Wouldn't your laptop be faster?" Joe asked.

"Might if I didn't type with two fingers. Here ya go, Lieutenant."

Joe took the clipboard, had already started walking, when he glanced down to decipher the officer's scrawl. It was the suspect's name that made Joe stop and pivot. "Who the hell is Stanley T. Givens?"

Brooks's brows drew together. "The driver of the Taurus, sir.

Joe skimmed the rest of the report as the pounding in his head returned with a sledgehammer-like vengeance. He paused outside Interrogation to gather whatever was left of his wits. Inside were Detectives Jackson and Reese who'd been instructed to issue Miranda, ensuring not one civil right was violated.

As he reached the one-way mirror, Joe stared at the man seated between the two detectives, and his parched throat dried altogether. His last hope had been that Givens was an alias for Drake Maxwell. But this scrawny dude with his pock-marked face was too young to be Maxwell, and to be blunt, too damned ugly. The Drake Maxwell Joe remembered had been solidly built and decent looking, hence his ability to influence a young Melanie Daniels.

Who the hell was Givens? And why had he been sitting alone in a vehicle scoping out the neighborhood? More importantly, why had he risked turning Joe into road kill?

Joe's insides churned. Had Maxwell paid someone to enact his revenge? Or was Joe losing his objectivity where Melanie was concerned? After all, he'd had little to go on when he read about the murder of the Cañon City corrections officer.

He tapped on the glass and Detective Jackson rose from the table and stepped into the hallway. "What've you got?" Joe asked.

"Not much, L.T. We're running his prints now. Driver's license identifies him as one Stanley T. Givens, Kansas City, Missouri. License matches his registration, and, FYI, he hates to be called Stanley."

Joe smirked. "So what do we call him?"

The seasoned detective rolled his eyes. "My man's name is Stan. He's uncomfortable as hell. Chain smoker. Check out the nicotine stains on his fingers."

At least something was going right. The lowlife had an addiction. Joe would use it against him. "Why'd he run?"

"Claims he never saw you. Says he got an emergency phone call, looked up, saw some guy in the street waving a gun and laid on the gas."

Jackson scrubbed a jaw in need of a shave. "When we informed him you were a cop, that's when he started crying for his lawyer."

"You call a public defender yet?"

"No."

"Hold off. When you get his priors, bring them to me. For now I'd like to see Mr. Givens alone."

Jackson shrugged and tapped the glass. "You're the boss." A moment later Detective Reese joined them in the hallway outside Interrogation Room B.

Joe entered the closet-sized room containing a rectangular table and chairs and found Givens tapping his foot and shredding a Styrofoam container. Mason was right. The smell of tobacco clung to the suspect's clothes. By now, their guest had to be experiencing severe nicotine withdrawal.

"Evenin', Stanley," Joe said, dropping into the plastic chair across from him. "I hope you enjoyed your visit with my men. I would have been here earlier, but I was outside enjoying a smoke."

Ugly glanced up. With one look at Joe, the jerking of his leg intensified and his eyes nearly bulged out of their sockets.

"You okay, Stanley? You look like you've seen a ghost." Joe touched the bandage on his forehead. "Or is this darn thing bleeding again?" He stretched his sore legs in front of him and folded his arms. At any other time, Joe might've enjoyed grilling the guy. But with Mel anxious and waiting, he wanted to return to her as soon as possible. When Givens simply returned to his shredding, Joe's patience snapped. "You recognize me, don't you? I'm the police officer who ordered you to stop. Instead, you accelerated and kept on going."

"The name's Stan and that's not what happened." Givens glowered at Joe. "Like I told those two dicks before you, I want a lawyer."

"No problem. The *detectives* are placing the call." Joe shrugged. "But don't blame me if the poor bastard doesn't show."

Givens, who'd thoroughly destroyed the first cup, picked up a second and crushed it. "What's that supposed to mean?"

"Lot of crazy drivers out there. Could be your attorney was the victim of a hit and run."

Ugly shook his head. "I know what you people are trying to do and it's not gonna work. Until my lawyer gets here, I have nothing to say."

Joe resisted the impulse to grab Givens by the collar and extract the answers from his windpipe. All right. He didn't want to talk? Joe would play this joker one step at a time. He stood and faced the one-way mirror. "You know what, Stanley? It's good you don't have anything to say. Leaves me with the floor." Joe turned and zeroed in on the man's cratered face. "From what the detectives tell me, you were simply an innocent bystander with a hearing problem. You had no idea a man was right in front of you shouting 'Stop, police'. Is that correct?"

Givens folded his arms, leaned back and glared.

"Still, I gotta wonder why you were parked in a dark, secluded spot in the first place. I mean, who were you watching?"

"Am I getting a lawyer in this century?"

Planting his hands on the table, Joe said, "You bet you are, Stan. Any minute now. Along with the D.A. who'll tell you what you're facing. Could be anywhere from assault on a police officer to attempted murder. Depends on how generous I'm feeling."

Givens returned Joe's hostile stare, but a nerve twitched near his left eye.

"And to tell you the truth, Stan*ley*, the way my head's coming unglued right now, and with your attitude, I'm not feeling too generous."

Even Given's Adam's apple was ugly. Joe watched it bob up and down. "I thought you were a loon," Givens said. "Somebody out to highjack my car. You can't be too careful these days. You got nothing on me."

An officer entered Interrogation with the suspect's rap sheet, handed it to Joe, then left. Joe perused the report, and suddenly Given's presence on Serendipity made sense.

"Says here, you're a private dick," Joe said, flipping through the pages. "Just barely. Trespassing, breaking and entering, assault on a woman. How's a guy like you keep a license?"

Exposing dingy, crooked teeth, Givens quipped, "Maybe I know the right people."

Keep your cool, Joe. Blocking out Melanie's image, he focused on nailing the asshole. "You like to watch women?"

"Doesn't everybody?"

"Do you know the woman whose house you've been watching?"

"Who says I was watching anybody? Like I told the detectives, I got lost, pulled over and made a phone call."

This guy was an amateur. Anxious to get the piece of shit out of his sight, Joe said, "So you know the right people, huh? Somehow I doubt it. But you know what, Stanley, *I* do. And besides connections, I'm beginning to think this bump on my head screwed up my thinking."

Given's rheumy green eyes drew into slits. "What do you mean?"

"I mean, I don't think you missed me at all. I'm beginning to think you clipped my ass."

Sweat beaded Given's forehead. "I never touched you. You can't lie."

Joe glanced around. "Who's here to stop me? I'm feeling worse by the second." Joe returned to the chair. "So here's what we're going to do, Mr. Ace Private Eye. Get rid of the 'I want a lawyer' shit, answer my goddamn questions, and I make these charges go away.

"Keep up this 'I know my rights crap,' and that license you've never lost is history, and I'll see to it that Stan the man becomes Stan the bitch on the inside of a cell."

A lot of Joe's strategy was bluff, and a competent P.I. would know it. An experienced P.I. would keep his mouth shut until his attorney arrived and bailed his ass out. And unfortunately, if it came down to committing perjury, Joe would give up the ruse. Even so, he'd bet his badge that Mr. Handsome (not) was close to unraveling.

"What do you want to know?" he finally asked.

"Who hired you?"

Givens sighed. "Janice Walford."

"Who's she?"

"Luke Norris's maternal grandmother."

What the . . .? From all the answers Joe expected, this wasn't one of them. Keeping his expression neutral, he tamped down his surprise. "I'm listening."

"She hired me when her old man told her not to, which is why I wasn't too crazy about getting caught. He doesn't know she's paying me."

With such impeccable ethics and credentials, Joe couldn't imagine why. "By old man, you mean her husband, Luke's grandfather?"

"That's right. Old Lady Walford didn't appreciate the Norris dame taking off with their grandson and not telling them a thing about it. Mr. Walford seemed worried, but Mrs. Walford, she just seemed maniacally pissed."

"Melanie Norris says you've been hanging around the neighborhood for a while."

Givens shrugged. "Cush job, one-hundred-fifty bucks a day, and I didn't have anything pressing to get home to."

"That's all there is to it?"

"That's all there is to it. Walford told me to find her grandson and not to come back without results."

It seemed to Joe that one phone call from Melanie could've made this whole miserable situation go away. On the bright side, it didn't involve Drake Maxwell, which brought Joe back to one critical question.

"How did you find Melanie Norris?"

"Department of Motor Vehicles."

Anxiety lessening, Joe leaned back in his chair. "If I drop these charges, I don't want to see you again, understand?"

"I'll leave town tonight."

"I suggest you re-itemize your bill for Mrs. Walford, deduct a couple of days, because I *will* be contacting her," Joe said.

Beaten down, the shady P.I. leaned forward. "You can't blame a guy for making a living. What about my stuff, my car?"

"I'll see that your effects are returned to you." Joe stood. "As for your car, it's in Impound. Call a cab."

"Impound will take my entire fee. Give me a break."

"I gave you a break, Stanley. A big one. Sit tight. You still have paperwork to fill out." At the doorway, Joe turned. "I meant what I said. Stay out of my neighborhood and away from the Norris's."

Chapter Twenty-three

"Why wouldn't you tell them, Mel? These people are concerned about their grandson."

Speechless, Mel stared at Joe as he recounted the events that had transpired in the last two hours. Maxwell hadn't been outside her house; her watcher had been a private detective hired by Luke's maternal grandmother, Janice Walford.

Mel held out her hands. "I know this sounds bad, but with everything going on... Carl's death, Maxwell, the move, getting Luke enrolled in school, finding a job... these people simply slipped my mind. First thing tomorrow, I'll call them and set things right."

Joe reached for her jacket looped over the back of his chair. He held it out to her. "I'd do it *first* thing."

Her stomach in knots, she lifted her gaze, hoping to see a glimmer of understanding on his face. Instead, fatigue outlined his features, made only worse by the bandage covering the gash he'd sustained because of her.

"Peter and Janice Walford may be Luke's grandparents, but they've hardly been a part of his life. Throughout the years, their visits became less and less frequent. Oh, they sent Luke token birthday or Christmas presents, but it isn't like he really knows them.

"When Carl got sick, I called them to let them know what was happening. Not one response, no flowers at the funeral, not even a card. So here's a question for you. Why would I think to call them when I'm running for my life?"

Joe's expression morphed into something less critical. "I suppose you wouldn't."

"You're angry."

He shook his head. "I'm tired. More than that, I'm relieved you're okay."

Holding her coat to her chest like a security blanket, Mel stepped toward him. "And I'm worried about you. Thanks to me, you now have a scar on your arm and a bump on your head. What's next? You only have so many body parts."

Joe relieved her by taking her into his arms. "Good thing my uninjured body parts like being around you. You can make it up to me by finishing what we never got started tonight. Let's go home."

He opened the door to a janitor pushing a cleaning cart, making his rounds. He nodded to the man, switched off the lights to his office, waited for her to exit, then closed the door behind them.

Her mind garbled, Melanie focused on the Walfords and what she would say to them in the morning. Even so, as Joe took her elbow, she found his warm presence comforting. Near midnight, they made their way through the bright lobby to the outside and started toward the dimly lit parking lot.

A police cruiser eased onto Rio Grande, followed by a yellow taxi, and that's when the lone man leaning against the red brick building stepped forward. He crushed out a cigarette and started for the cab, pausing when he saw them walking. "Lieutenant. Hold up."

Joe tightened his grip around her bicep and pulled her close. Instinctively, Mel knew this was the man who'd been watching her.

Joe stepped in front of her, nearly blocking her view. "I warned you, Givens."

The man kept his arms up as if in surrender. In his left hand, however, he held a folded paper. "I mean her no harm."

"Back off." Joe drew his jacket aside, displaying his weapon.

Mel breathed in fear. "No, Joe," she whispered.

Holding his hands out where Joe could see them, the stranger said, "I'm unarmed, Lieutenant. I'll keep my word as soon as I finish the job."

"Your job *is* finished," Joe shot back.

The rest of the events happened in slow motion. The man called Givens sidestepped Joe and thrust the document toward her. Joe shoved the man, he landed on his butt, but not before Mel found the papers in her hands.

Scrambling to his feet, Givens backed away and retreated toward the waiting cab. Then in an authoritative timber at odds to his cowardly behavior and sloppy looks, he raised his voice. "Melanie Norris. You've been served."

Son of a bitch. Joe parked Melanie's car in her driveway and dared a glance at a woman so despondent that despite his head injury, he'd elected to drive.

Switching off the ignition, he asked, "Are you all right?"

Wiping at tears, she scoffed. "What do you think? No, I'm not all right. Custody? Joe, these people don't even know Luke." She buried her face in her hands.

Joe clenched his jaw. He'd seen Mel upset, angry and tormented, and valiantly she'd fought back tears. But this? The thought she might lose her son had opened the floodgates.

And yeah, the Walfords might not know Luke, but how much of that was their fault, and how much was because Mel hadn't made them feel welcome? Their daughter was gone, their son-in-law remarried, now dead. In law enforcement, a cop learned fast that when it came to family dynamics, there were always two sides to every story.

Still, to see Melanie devastated was more than he could handle.

"You want me to wake Luke?" he asked. "It's pretty late."

She lowered her head and chipped at her fingernail polish. "No, let him sleep."

The air Joe inhaled did nothing to clear the weight from his chest. He had to ask. "Do the Walfords know about your past?"

"I'm certain Carl never told them, but that doesn't mean no one else did."

"Did you adopt Luke after Abby died?"

Turning from the passenger seat, she faced him fully. "Yes, Joe, I did. I did something right for a change. Luke Norris is *my* son."

"Of that I had no doubt." Joe placed a hand over her heart. "In here. But legally, I had to make certain."

"Surely, Luke has a say in this, doesn't he? He's already been through so much."

In that moment, her turmoil must've surmounted her pride. She reached for him and Joe thanked his badge he was there. Running his fingers through her hair, he held her while she cried. Finally, when she seemed to have expended every possible tear, he broached the subject he'd been considering. "I know a good lawyer, if you think it will help."

She shuffled back to her side of the car. Leaning back against the headrest, she wiped her damp eyes. "I see no alternative. I absolutely will fight this."

"It's settled then. I'll give her a call." Drawing Melanie's hand to his lips, he kissed it even as she attempted to smile. "There's nothing you can do until morning. Get some rest. We'll make sense of this mess tomorrow."

Luke jammed the key into the lock of his house and raced into the kitchen. Inhaling the familiar smell of home, he had twenty minutes to get ready for school. Matt's dad was driving, and though Matt couldn't care less if he went to school *ever*, Luke liked to get there early.

He strode to the cabinet by the sink, grabbed his favorite glass his mom called a pitcher and made his standard breakfast of a bagel and chocolate milk. After he'd finally nodded off, sleep had worked wonders, and he felt much better than he had last night. Maybe his mom was telling the truth when she said there was nothing going on between her and the cop next door. Luke had woken up to learn that she'd stayed at their house last night.

The cell phone in his pocket vibrated and his stomach flip-flopped. He pulled it out, hoping the caller was from one person in particular. The text read *Meet me for lunch in the commons. Luv, Jen.* Heat fanned his face and he rolled his eyes.

Love? Yeah, right. Luke had no illusions that the hottest senior girl in school loved a goofy-looking sophomore like him.

Still, being seen with Jennifer Franchini was pretty sick.

He'd been getting dirty looks from some of the older guys. Not that any of them had the balls to say anything. Luke was a head taller than most, on varsity, and now the team had his back. Even so, he'd never start anything, preferring to handle it on the court. But if any of them made him their problem, he'd say, "Bring it on."

His mom would freak if she knew he'd been locking lips with a girl almost eighteen, but, hey, what his mom didn't know . . .

Luke downed his milk and headed for the stairs. As much as he'd fought this move, he had to admit it had turned out okay. Reaching the top of the stairway, he peered into his mom's bedroom. The bathroom door was closed and the shower was running.

He shook his head. Lt. Crandall had said to let her sleep; she'd had a late night, which only proved the cop didn't know her at all. She sometimes worked late on her flowers, then got up with the crazy chickens.

He put on his favorite baggy jeans, a Miami Heat sweatshirt, inspected his overly long face and grimaced. Jen said he was cute, but he thought he resembled a blond version of Frankenstein.

Last night, his mom had called him the image of his dad. Remembering the big man, he'd loved and adored, Luke found it difficult to swallow. He took a final glance in the mirror. Maybe his wasn't a bad face after all.

He'd already started working on his mom to buy him a car. Bumming rides everywhere or having parents on scene was getting lame.

Today, maybe he'd buy Jen lunch, pay her back for all the gas she'd used. Trouble was, he'd blown all his money last night paying for both of them to get into the game at Mitchell.

Leaving his bedroom, he eyed his mom's purse on the nightstand and willed her to hurry up with her shower. What was she doing in there? Building an ark? He glanced at his watch.

Out of time, he entered her bedroom, rummaged through her billfold and found a measly three dollars in change.

He wanted to impress Jen, not show her he was a total loser.

His gaze fell to the dresser. His mom sometimes stashed money inside, still he'd never taken any without telling her. But this was an emergency. Okay, not an emergency-emergency. Technically, he'd call Jen a *semi-*emergency.

He opened the drawer and breathed in the smell of cedar. Among the junk collection he found what he needed, an envelope containing sixty dollars. *Sweet.* He removed a twenty then to curb his guilt, scribbled an IOU.

Hey, it wasn't stealing if you left a note.

He moved to shut the drawer when a folded paper caught his eye, more precisely a word. *Summons.*

Twisting his mouth into a frown, he'd watched enough *Law and Order* to know a summons meant trouble. Weird. His mom wasn't the type to keep secrets.

Lt. Crandall's horn sounded, and Luke pulled back an unsteady hand. But he wasn't leaving the house without knowing if she was okay. He picked up the document and read the caption. *State of Missouri vs. Melanie Norris. Request for Child Custody Evaluation. Petition for Legal Guardianship.*

Missouri? Luke scanned the paper until he discovered a name that he knew. Walford. His real mom's parents. His heart began a war dance in his chest. What the . . .? His grandparents wanted him to live with them? What did they think he was, some kind of baby?

The shower turned off. Lt. Crandall's horn blared longer, more urgent this time.

With sweaty hands, Luke tossed the summons back into the drawer then reconsidered. Stuffing the additional forty dollars in his back pocket, he wadded up the IOU and tossed his attempt at honesty into the wastebasket beside the dresser. He ground his teeth, while confusion muddled his thinking. *Screw you, Mom. You should have told me.* Move for a second time? No freaking way. He'd take off before he'd let anyone uproot him again.

Chapter Twenty-four

"Chico, wake up."

Through a haze and someone's shaking, fifteen years of prison life slammed into Drake's dreams. He grabbed his assailant and flung the bastard away from him and onto his back.

An instant later, as his eyes adjusted, he remembered where he was and saw that lying on the mattress beneath him was Maria. Ramirez's younger sister stared up at him, startled and surprised. Drake, however, studied her as if she were a cross between an amoeba and a succulent meal. Then, remembering she paid the mortgage on the place and he was hiding out in her basement, he reluctantly rolled off of her. His mouth dryer than a piece of cotton, his head screaming from too many shots of tequila, he asked, "What are you doing down here?"

Her eyes flashed with something that looked like anger. Slowly, she lifted herself up on her elbows in the cold, unfinished basement. Behind her brother's back they'd been giving each other come-do-me-looks for days. If she was afraid of him, she sure as hell didn't show it. "I came to say goodbye."

It was then that Drake saw the uniform, a blue skirt, white blouse and an emblem with a pair of wings on her left breast.

He zoned in on that breast and his mouth watered. "Goodbye?"

"Yes, I'm leaving in a couple of hours. I fly International and my hub's in Dallas. I need to be back in Texas this afternoon."

"But you have a house here?"

"I like it here. It's home." Her dark eyes met his in a challenge.

He liked the way the bitch stood up to him. Her job gave her independence. It also explained why she was always gone.

"You've been staring at me," she said, making no effort to rise from his makeshift bed.

"You've been staring back," he replied.

"Touché, *chico.*"

Narrowing his gaze, he asked, "Why do you call me *chico?*"

"You called me a chick the other day. If I'm a *chica* then you're a *chico.*"

Her perfume was driving him crazy. Her long dark hair was pulled up in some exotic style. She looked like an Egyptian queen, with black eyes, bronze satin skin and lips so soft they would take nothing to devour.

That didn't mean he was willing to wreck a good deal or risk Ramirez's blade in the process. So even though she'd approached him, he held back. "Where's your brother?"

She arched a brow. "You drank him under the table, remember? Denny's passed out."

Something like electricity jolted through Drake, a conduit transmitting her "I'm-available" signals. He reached for the first button of her blouse. "Is that right?" He'd been dreaming of taking her for days. It had almost been too easy.

When she simply held his gaze, he moved to the next button then the next, freeing her shirt and exposing the next-to-nothing bra underneath.

Close to exploding, he bent to explore the satin tops of her breasts. She arched against him as his hand drifted to the hem of her skirt and he tugged upward.

Shit. The hooker he'd taken a few weeks ago hadn't prepared him near enough for this woman. He was about to come. His fingers slid into her heat and in between gasps she said, "If Denny finds you doing this, he'll cut out your liver."

Drake lifted his mouth from her breast and saw the taunt on her lips, the laughter in her eyes. A siren. His kind of woman. He made sure it hurt her as his fingers went deeper. "You gonna tell him?"

A hiss escaped her lips as she shifted. She panted, then set her jaw. "That depends on what kind of lover you make. Is that the best you can do? I'm not into timid men."

In that case. He treated her breasts to his brutal attention then buried his mouth against hers.

Running her hands through his hair and digging her long claws into his neck, she returned his kiss. Finally, as much as he liked the rough foreplay, he was ready for action. "Take off your clothes."

For the first time she paused, seeming to consider what she was doing.

"Take off your clothes or I'll rip them off you." Drake grabbed her skirt, bunched the fabric and prepared to shred. This wasn't like fifteen years before when he'd picked up a hysterical Melanie Daniels and he'd been a sap weighed down by a conscience. Not so today. Women didn't tell him no, not that he'd ever had to ask. Brother or not, Maria had come on to him, and he'd wanted inside her.

The exercise down memory lane turned out to be moot. Maria rose from the mattress and looked him up and down. Then performing a rapid strip tease, she stood before him naked, revealing a flat stomach, small hips and round perfect tits.

Drake shucked off his shorts. He was rock hard and waiting as her gaze raked over his sculpted body. Her eyes widened and she gave him a smile of approval. "Very nice, *chico*."

He reached for her, and she fell into his arms. With one quick thrust he entered her. Beginning a series of slow rhythmic motions, he said, "You gonna tell your brother?"

She closed her eyes, leaned her head back and gave a throaty laugh. "And miss this? God, no, *chico*. Not in this lifetime."

Chapter Twenty-five

Dressed for work, her eyes swollen from last night's crying jag, Mel removed the address book from the nightstand, turned the page to the "W's", and traced her finger to the name Walford.

She'd stayed in the shower way too long, allowing the hot spray to soothe the stress from her body, when actually her goal had been to avoid her son. Terrified she'd dissolve into tears again if she saw him, she'd contributed to her utility bill.

She would love to call in sick today. For the most part she wasn't lying. She *was* sick. Heartsick. She hadn't felt this grief-stricken since her mother died.

Missing work was out of the question, however. With nonstop orders, a December wedding on the books and several holiday parties to fill, she couldn't desert the man who'd showed such faith in her. She squeezed her eyes closed. Had her promotion to shop manager occurred only last night? What had happened in the hours afterward felt like a lifetime ago.

She steeled herself for the confrontation at hand and punched in the ten-digit number. Why would Peter and Janice do this to her? And why hadn't Joe phoned with information on his lawyer? She'd legally adopted Luke, and he was at an age where she thought he had a say. These people couldn't take him away from her, could they?

She wanted to be reasonable and not alienate them if possible. They were Luke's family, but it had been she who'd insisted they spend quality time with their grandson. Surely, they recognized that.

The connection went through and a small, childish voice answered on the Kansas City, Missouri end. "Hello?"

Mel caught her breath. Was this Abby's brother's little girl? She'd grown up so fast. "Is this the Walford residence?"

"Uh-huh."

The child couldn't be more than three or four and Mel smiled. "Is your grandma home?"

"Uh-uh."

Her breath came out in a whoosh. "May I speak with your grandpa then?"

"Grandpaaaa!"

Avoiding a high-pitched squeal loud enough to burst her eardrum, Mel held the phone away from her ear. Well, that answered that question.

A full minute passed before she heard someone shuffling toward the phone. "Who is it, Tracy girl?"

"I don't know."

"Well, you know better than to talk to strangers. Hello?"

"Peter?" Mel clutched the chenille bedspread beneath her. "Hi. It's Melanie Norris."

Silence followed, then, "Melanie? Good gracious, where are you? Is Luke okay?"

She swallowed hard. "He's fine. I'm so sorry I worried you. We moved to Colorado Springs." In the shower, she'd been rehearsing what she would say and the words spewed forth. "With Carl's passing we needed a change. I needed a job. Luke wanted to play ball at a bigger school. . ." *I moved to hide from Drake Maxwell.*

The older man on the opposite end chuckled. "Well, thank goodness. When we learned you sold your house and left no forwarding address, we were a mite concerned. Wait till I tell Janice. Higher strung woman I've never known. Colorado Springs, huh? That's just great. How's my grandson?"

Mel pictured the white-haired soybean farmer with skin the consistency of leather. He certainly didn't sound like someone intent on suing her.

"He's fantastic. He loves it here," Mel said, placing emphasis on the word *love*. "He's made new friends and he's on the varsity basketball team."

"Varsity? You're kidding me. He's barely out of junior high."

Biting back a caustic remark, Mel said, "He's a sophomore in high school."

"He is? Well, I'll be darned, where does the time go? Now that we know where you are, we'll get out there real soon."

Now that we know where you are. She caught the censure in his words. Nevertheless, the Walfords had made empty promises before. When Luke was small, she and Carl had taken him several times to Kansas City. Naturally, the grandparents had made a big deal over Luke when he got there, but as far as reciprocating, it didn't happen much.

Now they wanted custody?

"Peter?" Mel began. "I'm confused. Last night I was served some papers."

"What kind of papers?"

"A summons. Hold on, let me grab it."

On the way to her dresser, she noted a wadded-up piece of paper on the floor next to her tiny trashcan. Making the decision to pick it up later, she withdrew the summons, returned to sit on the bed and read him the caption.

"I don't understand." The tremors in the old man's voice became more pronounced. "Who would do this to you?"

Mel nearly dropped the phone. "*You*, Peter. The summons came from you and Janice. It states you're suing me for custody."

Apparently Peter *did* lose his grip on the phone then. It clattered loudly as it hit the floor. She waited, picturing him struggling to pick it up. "Melanie," he said breathlessly. "I don't know a thing about any of this. You better start at the beginning."

As Mel relayed the events of yesterday, including the private eye who'd been following her, Peter's sighs and "oh, no's" became audible.

"Why would you hire a detective?" she asked. "Have I ever given you reason to think I would harm Luke?"

Peter became strangely quiet. "I suppose Jan got the idea from me. You see, years ago I hired a P.I. to investigate you."

Mel's throat burned from shock and humiliation, and it hurt to swallow. "All these years you've known about me?"

"I'm afraid so. You were raising my daughter's child, taking her place."

"Exactly *what* do you know?"

"I know about your time in prison. More importantly, I know about the events that led you there." Peter's voice grew shakier. "I know that after your mother's death, your father's remarriage upset you."

Upset her? Is that what the detective had told him? Mel couldn't find the words to speak. Eric Daniels had always been a selfish bastard, but it became readily apparent in the final months of her mother's fight for her life when her father left them alone for days on end.

On Mel's seventeenth birthday, she'd confronted him. "She's terminal, Melanie. Get over it. We're not the ones who are dying. She's accepted her fate; it's time you did, too. Go ahead if you want, but I'm not gonna crawl in the casket beside her."

Furious, Mel had drawn her hand back. He'd stayed her by grabbing her wrist. "Don't do it, kid. I'll land you on your ass."

Hours after her funeral, he'd introduced Mel to a woman young enough to be her sister, and announced she would become Mel's stepmother. The next day Mel hit the streets.

"We were talking about Luke." She set her back teeth, banishing the horrible memory. "Why are you seeking custody?"

"I'm not," Peter replied. "I happen to think my grandson's in excellent hands. As for Janice, there's something about my wife you don't know."

Moments later, Mel wiped away fresh tears, but they were no longer ones of despair. She was late for work, but it didn't matter. Her relief mixed with trepidation, she hung up the phone. How many of these bullets was she supposed to dodge before she could just live her life?

Joe replayed Melanie's message three times, finally concluding he'd heard it right. "Cancel lawyer, late for work, explain later. Thanks!" Her voice tinged with excitement had unsurprisingly made him feel a thousand times better. Picturing her smiling rather than despondent, he couldn't wait to find out what had led to the change. But even if no crises occurred in the meantime, his day was committed to meetings and interviewing new recruits.

God. What had transpired in the last two hours? Melanie Norris had more turbulence in her life than the space shuttle. Joe touched the bandage on his forehead and winced. If he planned to go along for the ride, the least he could do was invest in a shoulder harness. He dialed his lawyer and cancelled Mel's consultation.

Now to work on the boys. Luke continued in his sullen mood this morning when Joe drove him to school. Odd, because he'd appeared over his anger last night when Joe and Mel left the house.

Teenagers. He wouldn't trade places with them for the world. He was still worried about Maxwell, and the Cañon City Police had an unsolved murder on their hands, but so far there was no sighting of the infamous ex-con. Maybe they were worried for nothing, and maybe, just maybe, life would slow to a saner pace.

His phone rang and his secretary reminded him he was late for a meeting at the El Paso County Criminal Justice Center. Joe grabbed his jacket. A saner pace. What had he been drinking?

Chapter Twenty-six

"If we head south on Academy, that might work. If we go north, depending upon the time of day and traffic, we might as well turn ourselves in to the cops," Drake said to Ramirez as they sat outside Liberty National Bank, freezing their asses off because the gang leader wouldn't turn on the engine.

Ramirez, who normally was the talkative one of the bunch, simply nodded and added Drake's comment to a map he was sketching. Finally, he said, "You're sure wearing a sappy look, *amigo*. How come? You drank as much as I did last night. I feel like someone ripped my head off and stuffed it down the john."

Drake adjusted his sunglasses and kept watch on their quarry, a medium-sized bank with a good-sized parking lot and easy access and egress. If the security was lax and their getaway route workable, they might have a potential target.

He didn't feel good; he felt *great*. But to let Ramirez know he'd banged his sister right under his passed-out nose would bring pain. Immense pain. Considering that image, Drake urged the smirk from his face and ordered his happy dick to play dead.

"You see Maria this morning?" Ramirez asked.

Drake's pulse quickened, but he kept his head turned toward the bank. Was this some kind of test? Had Ramirez gone down to the laundry room, maybe seen her leaving the basement?

Drake plotted his lie. "No."

Ramirez shook his head. "Damn, I wanted to talk to her before she took off. She's amazing, don't you think?"

What was up with the twenty questions? What did he want Drake to say? He looked sideways at the gang leader, making note of his hands on the wheel. Before, Ramirez's reputation had been a highly touted rumor. A few nights earlier, though, one of the cons had mouthed off, and Ramirez had whipped out a switchblade before the man could blink. Drake's own piece was tucked in his sports coat. Should he reach for it? Off Ramirez before the prick ended him?

Feeling a test coming on, Drake decided to see if he made the grade. "Yeah, she's sweet. But you made it clear she's off limits." Before he broke out in a sweat, which would be a clear giveaway while they sat in this meat locker, he asked, "We gonna sit here and talk about a chick I can't have, or we gonna case this bank?"

Ramirez's eyes narrowed and he studied Drake for what seemed an excessive amount of time. "You're smart, *hombre*. Real smart." He took the keys out of the ignition. "Let's do it."

Chapter Twenty-seven

Mel answered the door, surprising Joe by flinging herself into his arms. In front of the boys, she generally met him with a simple hello. Suddenly, though, he remembered the schedule change, and that the kids were at practice. Surrounded by the smell of pine and holiday decorations, and not one to miss an opportunity, Joe tossed the package he'd brought to the couch. Drawing her against him, he kissed her. And as her body molded to his, he received the guarantee she felt as good as she looked.

Joe was the one to come up for air. "I'm glad to see you, too." She smiled and his heart took up river dancing. "I guess it's safe to say you have good news."

"Great news." Her gaze dropped to the floor. "At least for me. For the Walfords, not so good. Can I get you something to drink?"

"Got a cold beer?"

"Coming right up."

From the kitchen she called, "How's your head?"

"I'll live." Joe retrieved the package from the couch and followed her inside. Myriad plants on the counters and windowsill breathed life into the place, while the tangy aroma of barbecue simmering in the crock pot stirred his hunger pangs. Considering the frozen pizza he and Matt would share later on tonight, he envied her time-management skills.

She took a beer from the fridge and twisted the cap from the bottle. In exchange for the beer, he handed her the gift he'd tucked behind his back.

"What's this?"

"The apology gift I never got to give you."

"Joe." She shook her head and tore through the wrapping of the book he'd purchased on his way home from work. As she read the caption, *One Thousand Useless Facts*, she met his gaze and laughed. "Are you trying to tell me something?"

"I wasn't sure what genre so I settled for trivia. Start reading. There'll be a quiz later."

"Let's make it a competition." She winked. "That is, if that bump on your head didn't affect your I.Q."

"Funny." Joe nodded to the book. "It's not a Theresa Alder," he said, referring to the expensive vase she'd discouraged him from buying last night.

"It's better." She gave him a peck on the cheek. "I'll memorize it and try out for *Jeopardy*. Thank you."

Wishing for more than that little peck, Joe took a swig of beer and sat down. "So the Walfords. What happened?"

She joined him at the table. "I learned this morning they've known all along about my background. Shortly after Carl and I married, they had me investigated."

Joe paused in drinking his beer. "Really?"

"Yep. What's more, Peter Walford approves of me."

"Meaning Janice doesn't?"

Mel shrugged. "She always ran hot and cold around me. I assumed because of Abby. Today I learned differently."

"Go on," Joe said.

"Janice is bipolar. And according to Peter, they've been having trouble regulating her meds. When she couldn't get hold of Luke or me, she blew the situation out of proportion."

Bipolar. Joe lifted a brow.

"You know what it is," she said simply.

He nodded. He'd arrested people with the mental disorder. An individual with manic tendencies had no sense of propriety, no concept of right and wrong, and often thought he was invincible. Bipolar patients could be treated, but, unfortunately, when a person experienced the highs that went along with the disorder, they resisted taking their medication.

"Anyway, Peter knew about the private detective and nixed the idea. As for Janice contacting an attorney and filing suit, she forged his signature. Peter told me he would remedy the situation immediately."

"And all these years you never guessed?"

"Like I said, we didn't see them often. They'd schedule a trip, cancel, invite us out, then renege. It all makes sense now." Melanie placed her chin in her hand and she sighed. "Now if only the rest of my life would."

"I don't know. I think things are falling into place—your promotion, the boys are doing okay, and then . . . there's you and me."

"That's just it. You and me." She held his stare. "Do you think it's crazy for me to be attracted to you?"

His mouth twisted upward. No doubt she was talking about their past, but no woman had ever worded it quite that way. "Gee, thanks."

"You know what I mean."

He did. "I'm no expert on affairs of the heart. I just know I like what's happening between us. If it had to make sense, I'm not sure people would ever end up together."

She lifted an eyebrow. "Is that what we are? Together?"

"That's the way I see things."

A determined sheen transfixed her gaze, one Joe'd seen before. Melanie was either a woman interested in lovemaking, or a cadet graduating the academy. Pretty sure she wasn't the latter, he needed no more encouragement than that. He rose from his chair. Rounding the table, he gathered her in his arms, gratified that when he kissed her, she kissed him back.

With their bodies pressed tightly together, they stood in the kitchen. And with the timing right, and all indications a go, Joe eased his hand up under her sweater. Finding her warm and malleable to his touch, he whispered, "What do you say we go upstairs?"

The sighs and slight moans he'd found encouraging died instantly, replaced by a groan. She beat her forehead against his chest as he tightened his arms around her. "Don't tell me."

"Practice ends early tonight."

Practice. He'd come to hate that word. Quashing his own teenager-like libido, he cursed the actual two causing his pain and let go. Moving away from her, he ran a frustrated hand through his hair. "Why can't those coaches stick to a schedule? And when did those boys start running our lives? Shouldn't it be the other way around?"

Mel gave him a total look of sympathy and returned to his arms. Her breathy kisses against his collar only sent more agony his way. "It's only for a few more months. They'll be driving soon. As for our first time together, you wouldn't want to rush, would you?"

"I could live with it."

Laughing, she started to pull away. "I'll just bet you could."

"As it stands right now, I'll be collecting my pension by the time I make love to you." He held her at arm's length. "How much time do we have?"

"What?"

"How much time?"

Her gaze traveled to the clock on the wall. "Thirty minutes tops. Joe?"

He drew her close, returning his hands to the hem of her turtleneck sweater. Tugging upward, he left her gaping and standing in her kitchen in a shimmering peach bra. "Joe?"

"Relax. I have no intention of taking you here." He glanced at the table and remembered an earlier fantasy. "Not that I wouldn't like to."

"Joe!"

He liked that he'd shocked her. He also liked that he read no hesitation, only a lust-filled gaze that matched his own. Breathing in the smell of citrus, he nibbled his way down the column of her throat. Alternating between kisses and love bites, he found the spot behind her ear especially sensitive, and concentrated there for a while. And when Mel collapsed into a set of full-fledged sighs, he smiled in satisfaction.

"You like that?"

"You're getting warmer," she said breathlessly.

"What about this?" His hand grazed her breasts, the warm, flat plain of her stomach, then settled on the button of her jeans. Granting him permission via a wet, don't-stop kiss, he unsnapped the button of her jeans. Her breath hitched as his hand went lower. "How much time?"

She threw her head back. "Not enough . . . but who cares?"

"That's my girl." Giving her pleasure affected him as well, and when his own urges demanded equal time, he ordered them back.

It didn't take long to learn the rhythms that rocked her. Her soft mews became louder. Still, he granted her no release. Not until he took her to the edge.

For silent moments they stood, entrenched in each other's arms, Mel panting, Joe stunned at the forgotten emotions now swamping him.

She chuckled against his chest. "I know it was good for me, the question is what about you?"

"It was great for me." Placing his forehead against hers, he said, "I'm not a total jackass. When you wear a pager, you make the most of your time."

She left his arms, but rewarded him with a smile. Fastening her jeans, she reached for her top. "Well, you made the most of mine. Then she looked at the clock and it was back to business as usual. "If I invite you to dinner, can you pick up the boys?"

The smell of barbecue had been almost as tempting as her. "You got it." On his way out, he kissed her. "Besides, now that I know the plan is to starve me sexually, the least you can do is feed me."

Joe flipped the collar of his jacket to ward off the cold, then tried to conceal a satisfied grin as he jogged up the high school steps. He'd seduced a beautiful woman, she'd invited Matt and him to dinner, and if he was lucky, he might not get called out tonight.

Two of Matt's teammates met Joe at the top of the stairs, one he instantly recognized as team captain Chet Washington. "Hi, Mr. Crandall," the black six-foot-four post player greeted him. "Matt's still in the locker room if you're looking for him."

"Thanks." Noting their damp hair, flushed faces and the fact they appeared to be dragging, he asked, "Tough practice?"

A look passed between the two, followed by Chet saying, "The worst. I'll say one thing for Coach. He doesn't play favorites. He gets mad at one of us, we all die."

"Someone get on his bad side?" Joe asked, hoping the troublemaker wasn't Matt.

"Someone didn't show," Chet said.

"Or bother to call," snarled Chet's sidekick.

"So to remind the rest of us not to pull something similar," Chet explained, "we spent practice running suicides."

Joe winced. Suicides were a brutal conditioning drill designed to increase endurance and speed. "Two more days, guys, and you'll be out for winter break."

"Can't be soon enough for me, Mr. Crandall," Chet said. "See you later."

Joe walked away, approving of the team's vote to make Washington captain. The soon-to-be-graduate was a leader, looked Joe in the eye and called him mister, perhaps unaware that he was a cop. No big surprise. He doubted Matt went around broadcasting the information. It wasn't a topic that made a kid popular or got him invited to parties.

Joe pulled open the heavy steel door and sauntered onto the gymnasium court. The only people in sight were Rick Hood and his assistant coaches. The trio wore somber expressions, and at Joe's entrance, Rick waved him over.

"Heard you're missing a player," Joe said.

"Yeah. Any idea where he could be?" Rick replied.

"I was told Matt's in the locker room."

"It's not Matt," Rick said. "My missing player's Luke Norris."

Joe's stomach dropped at the same time Matt and a few of his teammates exited the locker room.

His son nodded to his friends, then eyed the adults the way a prisoner viewed the backseat of a squad car. Nearing six foot, the boy seemed suddenly smaller. His usually long strides became shorter as he approached. "Hi, Dad."

"Where's Luke?" Joe asked.

Matt rolled his eyes and broached the subject head on. "I'll tell you the same thing I told Coach, 'I don't know.' Luke didn't say a thing about missing practice when I saw him this morning."

"You call his cell?" Joe asked.

"Only about a dozen times." Matt glanced down at his shoes. "He doesn't answer."

"Luke Norris has eight hours to explain to me why he should still be part of this team," Rick said. Then refocusing on Matt, he added, "I cut older players to give you boys this opportunity. If I find out you're lying, Matt, you're off the team, too."

Matt's face turned the color of beets and the father in Joe took over. "He says he doesn't know." Placing his arm around Matt's shoulders, and wondering how the hell he was going to break this to Melanie, Joe said, "C'mon, son. Let's go."

Chapter Twenty-eight

Joe took so long to pick up the boys Mel's heightened arousal evaporated into worry. So much so that when she spotted him coming up the walk toward her house, a hard knot had formed in the pit of her stomach. She stepped out on the porch. A snowflake brushed her cheek and she wiped it away. "What took you so long? Where are the boys? I had dinner on the table twenty minutes ago."

The look he gave her sent utter panic right down to her foundation. He took her hand and led her inside to the couch. "Why don't we sit for a minute."

Her heart lurched. "I don't want to sit down. What's happened? Where are the boys?"

"Sit down," he repeated. "Matt's in his room, checking his e-mail."

This really beat all. Fear did a mind-meld with exasperation. To make dinner extra special, she'd included dessert. For what? So Matt could check his *e-mail?* Curbing an impulse to tell Joe what she thought of his son's manners, and worse tolerating them, she said, "So where's Luke?"

"Matt's checking his e-mail in hopes there's a message from him."

She cocked her head. "What?"

"Luke didn't show up for practice."

Suddenly, she understood why Joe was so anxious to get her off her feet. With him following, she bolted from the couch and ran into the kitchen. She picked up the phone and pressed speed dial, only to reach Luke's voice mail.

Keeping her voice steady when she wanted to scream, she said, "Luke, call me *right now.* Why weren't you at practice? If this is about last night, we need to talk. Call me. Better yet, come home!"

Her beautifully decorated table, her home-cooked meal lay abandoned. She wanted to rip off the table cloth and let her prized ceramic bisque plates fall to the floor. Frantic, she paced the length of the kitchen. Luke. Where was he?

"Melanie," Joe said from the doorway.

She pivoted, then stared at the man as panic sent rational thinking into exile. "I know he was upset, but I thought he'd calmed down. I can't believe this." Her throat ached from the hysteria taking hold. "Luke wouldn't miss practice, Joe. He *wouldn't*. Do you think Maxwell—"

Joe crossed the room and grabbed her shoulders. "No. And neither do

147

you. Think. If Luke had been acting normally, I might consider it, but he's having some emotional issues. *Calm down.*"

Right now, those words weren't part of her vocabulary. She wrenched out of his grasp. She strode into the living room, opened the closet and reached for her jacket.

"Where do think you're going?"

"To find my son."

"And where do you plan to look?"

Clutching her coat to her chin, she lowered her head and squeezed her eyes shut. Damn his irrefutable logic. Did he honestly think she could sit by and do nothing while Luke was missing?

"Melanie, look at me."

She opened her eyes to find Joe just inches away. The top buttons on his shirt were open, revealing a smattering of dark hair over his solid chest. She lifted her gaze to his eyes, a beautiful deep brown and full of concern. He'd given her such pleasure, she'd been so happy— she longed to go back in time to an hour before. So much had happened between them. They'd begun their relationship at odds; who would believe she'd turn to him in her darkest moments.

Without a word, he pulled her against him, and for a moment she caved, leaned into his strength and allowed him to absorb some of her agony.

"It's going to be okay," he said. "Trust me."

Seconds later, she withdrew from his embrace.

"Can you think of anywhere Luke might go?" Joe asked.

"I don't know. He's made a lot of new friends. I mentioned that girl he's been talking to on his cell phone."

"It's a start," Joe said. "Matt will be here soon. I'm sure he knows her name. Do you mind if I look in Luke's room?"

"No. I'll go with you."

Joe squeezed her hand. "Now we're talking. Let's focus on what we *can* control."

Upstairs in Luke's room, Mel leaned against the door jamb, knowing if she didn't, her legs would fail to support her. Joe rifled through her son's inner sanctum, probably the way he did a crime scene. He opened drawers, examined papers and sifted through clothing. He searched behind pictures, behind furniture and under Luke's mattress. Shaking his head, each time he found nothing substantial, he moved to the closet, felt inside pockets and shoes then ran a hand over the upper shelf.

Her stomach roiled as he went about these tasks. Naturally, she wanted a clue to Luke's whereabouts. What she didn't want was the knowledge she'd badly misjudged her son.

When Joe's silence became unbearable, she asked, "Exactly what are you looking for?"

"Notes from friends, receipts that will tell us his hangouts, that sort of thing." He continued his search of the closet.

"Drugs?"

Glancing over his shoulder, Joe held her gaze. "We'd be fools not to consider it, Mel."

She hugged herself tightly. "I'll bet you're wondering how I of all people can be this naïve."

He lifted a brow. "I don't wonder at all. You of all people have tried your damndest to protect your son."

She swallowed hard and lifted her gaze to the ceiling. "You seem to have done all right."

"You think?" He closed the closet door and sat down at Luke's computer.

She blinked at the sarcasm filling his voice. "You're saying you haven't?"

He squinted as he moved the mouse over the desktop icons. "When Matt turned thirteen, his mom and I discovered he'd developed a fondness for alcohol and smoking."

"Matt? No way. At thirteen?"

Joe nodded. "Karen and I were in the midst of our divorce. Matt was angry about the breakup and hanging out with a new crowd in school."

"What did you do?"

"Put the fear of God in him." Joe clicked on the screen and a Word document popped up. "It's not fun being a cop's son and trying to fit in."

"I would guess not. What happened to his friends?"

"I put the fear of God in them, too. As it turned out, we didn't see much of them after that."

"I can't imagine why," Mel said wryly.

Joe leaned back and folded his arms. "Well, the good news is, there's not one sign that Luke's on drugs, and as of two nights ago, he was doing his homework."

Mel closed the distance to look over Joe's shoulder. "*Death of a Salesman.* Yeah, I've seen him reading it."

"I hated that play," Joe said.

"It's a classic," she argued.

"Maybe so. But why do classics carry the theme, 'Life's a bitch and then you die?'"

She chuckled.

"Sorry. In your present frame of mind, I should probably keep my opinions to myself."

"Please don't. Right now, your opinions are all that's keeping me sane." She wrapped her arms around his neck and placed a soft kiss against his cheek, needing not only his strength, but the comfort in having him here. "Do you see anything else?"

Joe closed the document and opened up Luke's e-mail program. A small box flashed, requiring a password.

"Any ideas?"

Frowning, she said, "He's only had this address for a couple of weeks. I didn't think to ask."

He stood and grasped her hand. "For what it's worth, Mel, Matt's had his e-mail several years, and I still don't know his password. We're parents, not perfect."

"Thank you for that." She pulled back, feeling slightly better, but no closer to finding her son. "What now?"

"Got any recent pictures?"

"Of course. Why?"

He hesitated. "If Luke doesn't come home soon, I'll distribute them tonight at third shift briefing."

She tasted bile. "Oh, no."

"Having every cop in the city looking for your son's not a bad thing."

"When you put it that way." She blew out a frustrated breath. "Come with me. I have some current pictures in my bedroom."

In the hallway, she paused. She had a perfect view from her bedroom window, and the tiny snowflake she'd felt earlier had morphed into several. Her self-control disintegrated as she fell into the cop's open arms. "Oh, Joe, where could he be?"

"Oh, my God. When the killer jumped out of the pantry with that butcher knife, I almost peed my pants," Jennifer Franchini said.

Luke grinned, the first smile he'd managed in hours. After dark, the high school cheerleader clung to him.

"Weren't you scared, Luke?"

"Nah." In truth, he hadn't watched much of the movie. While she munched on popcorn, he'd glanced at his watch, surreptitiously using the day-glo feature, and wishing he was at practice. He needed to get over it. If his grandparents had their way, he'd be living in Podunk, Missouri. He doubted they even had a basketball program.

When they'd arrived earlier, the Tinseltown lot had been empty. It had been cold, but not freezing. After eight, the place was packed, the temperature had dropped and snow was sticking to cars and to windows. He drew himself into his jacket and tried not to worry about where he'd spend the next several hours.

"You're awfully quiet," Jen said. "You're not still thinking about that fight with your mom, are you?"

He stared straight ahead. He'd out-and-out lied to Jen, telling her nothing about his grandparents demanding custody, or that he hadn't been home in hours. What kind of loser got shipped off to his grandparents at almost sixteen years old?

"Luke? You gotta cheer up. I fight with my folks all the time." Jen grinned up at him. "What's she gonna do, kick you out?"

Before he had time to dwell on the subject, a voice from behind them said, "Well, lookie here."

He and Jen turned to face three guys wearing letterman jackets. Luke had seen them before, and although he didn't know any of them personally, he did recognize Gavin Mitchell, a senior at Coronado and the high school's first-string quarterback.

"Hi, Jenny," one of the boys next to Gavin said in a mocking voice.

Jen grabbed Luke's arm. "Bobby, Leo," she replied. It didn't escape Luke's notice she didn't say hi to Gavin, or that he hadn't taken his eyes off her for a second.

The kid named Bobby asked, "Is this your new boyfriend, Jenny?" A kid who appeared to have more muscles than brains, he leered at Jen.

"He might be," she said.

"Sort of robbing the cradle there, aren't ya, babe?" Leo asked.

From their expressions and circling patterns, this wasn't a friendly encounter. Luke wasn't scared *yet*, but he damned sure wasn't comfortable.

"Shut up, Leo," Gavin said. His gaze remained focused on Jen, and she appeared particularly fixated on him as well.

"Probably likes him because he's a big shot basketball player," Bobby chimed in. He placed his hands over his heart. "Oh, but wait, he's not anymore. The way we hear things, he skipped practice tonight."

Jen glanced at Luke and he shifted uneasily.

"You think Ol' Man Hood's gonna put up with that shit?"

"I thought you told me practice was cancelled," she said quietly.

Luke shrugged.

Bobby laughed. "So guess what? He ain't no big shot basketball player, Jen, he's just a *pussy*."

"Knock it off, Bobby. Let's go," Gavin said.

"Did you quit the team?" Jenny asked.

Luke's face grew hot. "What if I did?"

"You lied to me?"

Words were useless now. The quarterback's boys were in his face. Gavin threw his arms up and walked several feet away.

"I can't *stand* liars." She frowned at Luke, then her gaze traveled after the quarterback. "Gavin, wait up."

Luke was hardly surprised when the moonfaced kid wrapped his arms around her and they started talking. This, of course, left Luke to deal with Bobby and Leo.

"Ah, the poor little sophomore," Bobby taunted. "Kicked off the team and lost his girl in one night."

"You kind of cut in on our buddy's turf," Leo said, stepping even nearer. "The minute Jenny and Gavin have problems, you horn in on his action." Leo shoved him.

Luke held up his hands. "I don't want to fight."

"Really, you don't?" Leo pushed him again.

Bobby's sucker punch to his mouth had Luke reeling. Somehow he found the presence of mind to duck when Leo's fist came flying.

Luke tackled Bobby, slamming the dumbass into the wall. "I *said* I don't want to fight."

A crowd had gathered. Jen and Gavin returned to the side show. A patrol car approached and Gavin said, "Cool it."

"C'mon, Luke," Jen said. "I brought you. The least I can do is take you home."

Luke wiped blood from his lip, as pride and embarrassment got the best of him. Besides, he couldn't go home. He glared at Jen. "No way. Forget you."

"Forget you," Bobby mimicked. "You're ours, Norris. We're gonna kick your ass."

The cop flashed his spotlight, the crowd dispersed and the kids held up their hands like nothing was going on.

Luke took advantage of the cop's presence and slipped back into the theater. He tasted blood and became queasy from the smell of popcorn and hot dogs. Sensing that Bobby and Leo might follow, he bought time, seeking out the farthest men's room in the complex. Hopefully, if they came looking for him, they'd look in the closer bathrooms first.

Inside his hiding place, Luke's heart pounded as he struggled to catch his breath. A man eyed him suspiciously before he left, most likely because he caught Luke spitting blood into the sink.

Damn. The old guy would probably report him. Luke couldn't go crawling home, but he couldn't handle these two creeps alone, either. He pulled out his cell and surveyed the long list of missed calls.

Along with his mom, Matt had called several times.

Matt.

Luke texted his friend. *At Tinseltown South. In trouble. Hurry.*

With Mel removing photo albums from a cedar chest in front of her bed, Joe entered the room he'd envisioned from his den's picture window. He'd done a remarkable job imagining it in his mind's eye. A floral patterned window seat complemented a solid maroon bedspread, while plants of all kinds meshed with the décor. Like Mel, the place was feminine and immaculate, and her special scent filled the air.

Unlike Luke's room, she hadn't given Joe permission to search her things. As unobtrusively as possible, he clasped his hands behind his back and moved from space to space looking for clues. Hints that could drive a boy away from what Joe had come to believe was a loving home.

Unfortunately, those thoughts emerged from a man besotted. Life lessons as a cop warned that appearances weren't always what they seemed.

Occasionally, she glanced out the window, then continued slipping photographs out of the albums. When Joe wasn't focused on her, he concentrated on his surroundings, in particular, a framed charcoal etching of Melanie, Luke and her late husband. As expected, Carl Norris had been a big man. Luke appeared to be no more than five or six in the likeness, but the resemblance to his father was uncanny.

In the lower right hand corner of the sketch, Joe read the initials, *M.N.* Coming around to face her, he asked, "You drew this?"

She nodded. "From a snapshot a friend took of us."

He shook his head. "Why am I surprised? You're talented."

He moved to a group of knickknacks on the dresser, some apparently made when Luke was in elementary school. The keepsakes were similar to those his kids had made for Karen and Joe. Next his gaze meandered to a waste basket a few feet away and a wadded-up piece of trash beside it. In Joe's cluttered existence, the item would have been easily overlooked. In Mel's house, it stood out like a chalk outline of a body at a crime scene.

He bent to retrieve it, then glanced up with a smile. "This place is the pits."

His attempt at humor had no effect on her. Photographs in hand, she strode to him. "I meant to take care of that earlier. Do you think these are enough?"

Disregarding her outstretched palm, Joe unfolded the note. "Does Luke often write you IOUs?"

"What?" She placed the pictures on the dresser, took the message with Luke's hurried scrawl and studied the content. Obviously onto something Joe wasn't privy to, Mel opened the top bureau drawer.

She withdrew a bank envelope, then gasped when she opened it.

"Mel?"

"I had sixty dollars in here this morning."

"You're sure?"

"Positive. I went to the bank yesterday. Why would Luke write me an IOU for twenty then take the whole thing?"

"Has he ever done this before?" Joe asked.

"Never. He always asks before he takes money." She rummaged further in the drawer.

When her hand fell upon the Walford's summons, their gazes collided.

Joe reached around Mel and picked it up. "Was this in the drawer this morning?"

"Yes." She groaned. "You don't think . . ."

"Yeah, I do. Luke needed money. You were in the shower. He writes out an IOU, then discovers his grandparents' petition."

"But why not just ask me about it?"

"Who knows what's going through the kid's head right now? He's lost his father. He spotted you with another man." Joe held up the petition. "Now this."

"Oh, please. Surely Luke knows I wouldn't give him up without a fight."

"Does he?"

She shoved the summons inside and slammed the drawer. "I've got to find him."

Joe caught her arm. "Slow down. Now that we know why, we know how to fix it. I'll check with Matt to see if he's had any luck coming up with Luke's whereabouts."

"I'll come with you."

With Mel leading the way, Joe rushed down the stairs and into the snowy night. As they neared his driveway, light streamed from his open garage. Upon closer inspection, they found Joe's Crown Victoria parked inside. It was his prized yellow Mustang that was missing.

Chapter Twenty-nine

"Calm down, Joe."

Inside his son's room, Joe no longer sat at Matt's computer. The boy had left in a hurry, leaving his Facebook account logged on. Messages had been flying back and forth regarding her son.

Joe paced the length of the teenager's lived-in room. Mel sat on his unmade bed, not so much because she was tired, more to stay out of Joe's angry way.

"Calm down? When I get my hands on that kid— He took my car." Joe pivoted. "Matt can't take my car. He's driving around with a learner's permit. He doesn't have a bloody *license*."

Mel suppressed a smile. An hour earlier it had been Joe telling *her* to calm down. "I'll bet you ten dollars he went after Luke."

"I was right next door," Joe bellowed. "Why the hell didn't he come get me?"

Mel stood, placing her hands on her hips. "I don't know. Probably the same reason Luke didn't ask *me* about the summons. They're fifteen."

He glared at her and stormed out of the room. She followed. "Joe? Joe, where are you going?"

He made his way downstairs into the kitchen where he picked up the phone, then punched in several numbers. "Norma, Lt. Crandall. I need to report a BOLO for a 2001 yellow Ford Mustang, license TX3798. Avoid force at all costs," he said. "Got that? *At all costs*. The car thief's my son."

The moment Luke saw the yellow Mustang pull up to the curb outside Tinseltown, he stopped looking over his shoulder and gulped with relief. He braced for the lecture he was sure to receive, telling himself Lt. Crandall's reprimand was far better than being beaten to a pulp by Gavin's goons.

With snow sticking to the ground, Luke pushed through the theater doors, slid into the car, then gave the driver behind the wheel an incredulous look.

"Not that I'm not happy to see you, Crandall," Luke said. "But just what the hell are you doing?"

Matt took his hands off the wheel and held his palms out. "You said hurry. I hurried."

"When I said that, I meant to get your dad or my mom or a *licensed* driver." Luke shook his head. "And with it snowing? We are so screwed."

Matt pulled into the stream of traffic, exiting the theater parking lot. "They can't kill us both. The way I see it, they're so mad at you, that when I get you back in one piece, they'll be so relieved, they won't even remember I took the car."

Luke rolled his eyes. "What have you been smokin'?"

Matt laughed. "So who messed up your face, and why'd you ditch practice?"

Leaving none of the events out of his miserable day, Luke told his friend about the summons, his grandparents' petition for custody and that he'd been so pissed off he'd taken off without thinking things through.

"Can your grandparents do that?" Matt asked.

"I don't know," Luke said. "But if they can't, why didn't my mom say something? Why keep it from me? Maybe the fact she's not my real mom gives them some kind of say so."

Taking his eyes off the road, Matt glanced at him. "That sucks. I guess I don't have to tell you Coach was pissed."

"Tell him to get in line."

"Maybe if you talk to your grandparents, let them know how much you like it here, they'll reconsider," Matt said.

"Maybe."

Matt merged onto I-25 and Luke squinted, blinded by the snow and headlights of oncoming traffic. Tightness lodged in his chest as he blinked back tears. He'd cried at his dad's funeral, he'd been unable to hold his emotions in check. Those were the feelings overwhelming him now. "Matt?"

"What?"

"What if my mom didn't say anything because she *wants* me to live with them?"

Obviously uncomfortable with the topic, but too scared to take his eyes off the interstate due to the bad weather and heavier traffic, Matt's brow furrowed. "That's crazy, man. She loves you."

"I always thought so, too, until today," Luke replied.

A trucker in the left-hand lane whizzed by, his tires sending backsplash onto the windshield. Matt's fists tightened around the steering wheel. Sensing his friend's growing agitation, Luke sat up straighter and joined him in watching the road.

Flashing red and blue lights, along with a quick burst of sound, interrupted their intense concentration. From behind them, a patrol car's loud speaker and a cop's baritone voice boomed, "Pull over."

Matt groaned, but immediately obeyed. He veered his father's Mustang to the northbound shoulder of the interstate. Leaning his head back against the headrest as the cop got out of the patrol car, he said, "Remember when you said we were screwed?"

"Yeah?" Luke replied, as every drop of spit dried from his mouth.

"And I said they can't kill us both?" Matt asked.

Luke glanced over his shoulder. The cop was heading their way. "I remember that, too."

"I lied."

The only thing Mel could think of to take Joe's mind off Matt's astonishing behavior was to remind Joe of his stomach. Near ten p.m., neither of them had eaten since lunch, and her tender, slow-cooked brisket sat cold and ignored.

While waiting for news of the boys, she made coffee and sandwiches. Joe wolfed them down, saying nothing about their taste, then sat staring into his coffee cup.

She left him alone with his thoughts, storing the leftovers in plastic containers.

Oddly, she wasn't as frantic as she had been in the hours before. Of course, she was desperate for Luke to come home, but a sort of transference had occurred when Joe had become the parent to worry.

One of them had to remain calm.

The food put away, she'd begun to wipe off the counter when Joe's cell phone rang. The nerves she'd succeeded in calming exploded.

"Crandall," Joe said. "You did?" Straightening, he kept the phone to his ear, placed his elbows on the table, lowered his head and massaged his right temple. "No. Don't take them downtown. Bring them to my house. Yeah. Appreciate it. Tell Wilkerson thanks, also. See you in a few minutes."

Mel turned from the counter, awaiting his explanation.

Joe flipped the phone shut and rose from the table. The weight seemed to fall from his shoulders. His dress shirt was wrinkled, his sleeves rolled up to his forearms. He looked tired and yet relieved. "Two patrolmen are on their way. One's driving my car. The other's bringing the boys."

As the air left her lungs, she tossed the dishcloth into the sink. "I'll get my coat."

"No. I want you to stay here."

"I don't *think* so."

"You'll try to baby them, and now's not the time. They're in a shitload of trouble and I'm going to make sure they know how deep. More importantly, this all started when Luke saw us together. He doesn't need any more reminders right now."

Mel's first thought was to argue, then to remind Joe that it was his son who took the car, not hers. But that was unfair. Matt had rushed to help his friend. She was forever grateful, and in spite of Joe's slight to her parenting, he did have a point.

He gathered her against him. "Will you trust me to handle this?"

Reluctantly, she nodded, taking comfort in the security she felt in his arms.

"I'll send him home as soon as possible." He set her away from him. "And when I do, Melanie, it's time. You need to have that talk with him. I mean a *real* discussion."

She drew an unsteady breath and turned away from him.

"Mel?"

"Of course, I'll talk to him. Luke needs to know I would never give him up. Never."

"The fact Walford didn't approve of his wife's actions worked in your favor. This time. The truth would be better coming from you."

Mel lifted her hair and rolled her shoulders. The muscles in her neck bore the tension of the last few days. What was he, a mind reader? She'd been thinking the same thing. What Joe didn't understand was tonight she'd had a taste of what it would feel like to lose her son. She never wanted to experience anything like it again.

Joe's eyes narrowed.

She hated the disappointment she read on his face. "Shouldn't you get going? They should be here any minute."

He arched a brow and strode from the room.

She saw him out, then slumped to the couch. *You climb so high on that pedestal, it's gonna hurt like hell when you fall off.* Intrinsically, she knew Joe was right. But the real reason she hadn't told Luke? She wasn't ready to fall.

Joe opened the door to a snowy gust of wind, two defeated teenagers and the two police officers beside them. Gardner and Wilkerson were experts in scenarios like these, escorting kids to their parents, making sure they were aware of how close they'd come to the justice system and juvenile hall. Their faces unsmiling, their bulk magnified by Kevlar vests, the cops maintained the demeanor of granite. "Lt. Crandall, this boy claims to be your son," Wilkerson said. "The other boy here says he lives next door. Is that correct?"

Joe's gaze raked over the miscreants. "That's correct."

Matt shifted nervously, avoiding Joe's scrutiny and lifting his eyes to the sky.

"Do you wish to press charges, sir?" Gardner asked, handing Joe back his car keys.

"Not at this time," Joe said, shoving them in his pant pocket. "By the time I get through with them, they might actually prefer jail."

At that comment, Luke raised his head. The left side of his face was bruised, his bottom lip puffy and oozing. "It's my fault, Lt. Crandall. Matt only came because I asked him to."

"Will there be anything else, Lieutenant?" Wilkerson asked.

"No." Joe glanced at his watch. "About time for dinner, isn't it?"

Gardner smiled. "I was just thinking the same thing, sir. Goodnight."

Joe shut the door and ordered the boys to take a seat on the couch in the den. Acting as judge and jury, Joe explained what their punishment entailed. In slack-jawed amazement, they stared, but knew better than to protest what they obviously construed as a grossly unfair sentence.

"Any questions?" he asked.

Together they replied, "No, sir."

"Good." Joe walked to his desk and picked up the cordless phone. He handed it to Luke.

Puzzled, the boy stared at him. "Sir?"

"You need to call your coach. Tell him you'll be at practice tomorrow."

Luke's Adam's apple bobbed up and down. "I—I don't think I—I—"

"Wait much longer and you'll be off the team. Is that what you want?"

"But I thought I already was—"

"I think your coach will accept that you had extenuating circumstances. If you can be sure of anything in this world, Luke, it's that your mother loves you. After you make that phone call, I suggest you go home and give her the chance to explain."

Luke's gaze darted to Matt, and for the first time they shared a grin. Joe motioned to Matt and he stood. He placed a hand on the scruff of his son's neck and said, "What do you say we give him some privacy?"

Matt nodded.

As the two of them exited, Joe closed the door to the den.

Mel resorted to doing what she always did when she was under stress, working with plants. She headed for the basement. Her Spanish lavender was root-bound and in desperate need of transplant. As she carried it toward the stairs, the lock in the kitchen door turned.

Everything stopped as Luke walked in. Observing his dirty clothes, his battered face, she held back a startled cry, but refrained from voicing concern.

He glanced down at the floor. "Hi, Mom."

She swallowed hard. "Hi, Luke."

She placed the plant on the counter and wiped her clammy palms on her jeans. This was the boy she'd raised from infancy, and yet she felt like she was looking into the eyes of a stranger. "Are you hungry?"

His face turned red and he shrugged. "Starving."

"Would you like to take a shower while I make you something to eat?"

"Aren't you going to yell or something?"

She took a step forward, then hesitated. "Maybe later, okay?" Then all of her fear and heartbreak swirled into one tumultuous emotion and she walked toward him. Taking the big kid in her arms, she hugged him. He hugged her back, and she whispered, "Welcome home, sweetheart."

"I'm sorry, Mom. I—"

Tears clogged her throat. "Go take that shower. We'll talk afterward."

So much for leftovers. Before Luke devoured the remaining portion, Mel took a plate over to Matt. As much as she wanted to stay and thank him for coming to Luke's rescue, she didn't have time. She had a mixed-up teen to contend with, and she intended to make things right between them.

A short time later, Luke scrounged around in the refrigerator, "Are there any more sandwiches?"

She smiled and shook her head. Reaching around him, she said, "Sorry. We have chocolate pudding," then risked mentioning his injury. "It might feel good on that lip." She handed him the dessert in one of her favorite glass dishes, then removed an ice pack from the freezer. "This might help, too."

Then like a turned-on faucet, Luke's words gushed out, and he started to talk. He explained that finding the summons had added to his anger from the night before. "After our fight, and the fact you didn't say anything, I just kind of lost it."

Mel placed a hand over his. "I was only served last night, Luke. I wanted to talk to your grandparents before I involved you, and as it turned out, we have absolutely nothing to worry about."

Dark circles shadowed his eyes. She was about to suggest he go to bed, but he'd opened the lines of communication and wasn't through talking. "Why would Gramps and Gram do this now? 'Cause Dad died? After all this time, they don't trust you?"

Mel caught her breath.

This time. How odd that Luke had chosen Joe's words. *You're a damned coward, Melanie Norris.* She rose from the table and walked to the sink. Beyond the window, the cop's lights were blazing. "You're not the only one who made a mistake, Luke. We all have from time to time. Me more than most people."

"You?" Disbelief seeped into her son's voice. She turned from the window, met his gaze and her long-avoided moment of truth. "Your grandparents were upset because I moved you to Colorado Springs without telling them. Your grandmother hired a private detective to find you, hence the summons you read this morning."

Luke frowned. "You didn't tell them? Why not?"

"Because I've been hiding, Luke."

Luke's eyes went wide, followed by a brow wrinkled in confusion. "*Why?*"

Grief nearly paralyzed her as she realized she couldn't take back the words. She'd gone this far, and Joe was right. If her son heard this from anyone, it needed to come from her. Using the counter for support, she gripped the edge and leaned against it. "I've been in prison, Luke."

His face went chalk white. When he didn't scream or bolt from the table she continued. "That's where I met your father and how I came to love you."

Chapter Thirty

"Drink up, *amigos.* To the holidays." Ramirez raised his beer bottle. Sitting in the crowded, smoky bar with his team, Drake nursed his own bottle, growing more restless by the second.

So far, Brown had come up with nothing on Melanie, and during his check in with Rander in California, the screw-up had said he had it all under control—whatever the hell that meant coming from a heroin addict. Drake couldn't leave Colorado to off his brother right now. With the heist this close, Ramirez would shit. But with Rander most likely doing nothing but shooting up, it appeared Drake would have to take care of Adam himself—and then kill Rander, of course.

Outside Maria's house, the gang wasn't *allowed* to mention the upcoming robbery. But Drake was having a hard time getting Ramirez alone. The way Ramirez saw things, hitting Liberty National Bank was a foregone conclusion, and plans were in motion. Drake had serious concerns. The location and timing felt wrong.

He'd gone back three times to the bank on South Academy, and each time a different scene with a new set of problems presented itself. One, the old geezer of a security guard had been replaced with a younger, more attentive employee. Drake had no problem taking either man out. But he'd chosen the bank because the older man spent most of the time yakking, yawning or scratching his balls.

Then there was the traffic. Apparently their first visits, when they hadn't hit pile ups, were anomalies. He'd recently learned Academy Boulevard was notorious for snarls and gridlock. He'd also found out the airport was nearby, and military personnel took this route to Fort Carson. On top of that, they'd chosen the Friday afternoon before Christmas for the hit, because the bank would be brimming with cash. It would also be rush hour.

Also, twice while they'd been casing the bank, he'd felt someone's eyes on him other than the guard. Did the cops have an idea when and where the Chaos Bandits planned to strike next? Had somebody snitched?

No. Pure and simple, the setup felt wrong.

"Max, you been on the same beer forever," Ramirez said. "You got a problem?"

Drake raised his head to find Ramirez and the other cons studying him. He never voiced his opinions in front of the entire team. "No problem. But I want to talk to you later."

Ramirez nodded. "Tomorrow afternoon. You can come with me to pick up Maria."

Maria. That was another thing stuck in Drake's craw. He'd been with two other women since he'd taken Ramirez's younger sister, and neither had come close to getting Drake off. He may have gotten into her pants, but she'd gotten under his skin.

"She's coming home?" he asked offhandedly.

"For a couple of days, then she's leaving again. South America this time." Ramirez signaled the waitress for another round. "Good thing, too. She'll be gone when we take care of business. I don't want her around."

Drake swallowed the last of his beer. *Holidays. Business.* Ramirez's code words. He was damned smart about controlling his team, a major reason they hadn't been busted. If only Drake could persuade their leader that robbing Liberty National Bank this close to Christmas could work against them and very well land their asses back in prison.

Tomorrow he'd take off on his own, buy another piece from a backstreet gun dealer and search for a better target. He had to convince Ramirez of the need to strike elsewhere, and after December twenty-fourth. Changing the plan wouldn't sit well. Ramirez had mentioned repeatedly he wanted to leave Colorado Springs before New Year's, and with Rope's murder, Drake wanted to split as well. Still, he had unfinished business: Melanie Norris.

Which brought him back to Brown. Drake was losing patience, and it was time to apply pressure. The computer nerd didn't come to the bars with the other cons. So Drake would have to find out the name of the electronics store where Brown worked.

Drake would give him until Christmas day. And if the dick who'd smugly asked if he could keep Drake's money hadn't come through by then, he could forget about unwrapping presents. Drake would be digging a hole for his body.

Chapter Thirty-one

After midnight, Mel and Luke were still talking. They'd moved from the kitchen into the living room and sat on opposite ends of the couch facing each other, Mel's legs tucked beneath her, Luke's long limbs stretched in front of him on the coffee table.

Arms folded, his look pensive, he'd been quiet for some time.

"Disappointed?" she asked.

Lowering the ice pack, he gingerly touched his lip. "Nah, just replaying scenes of my life over in my head."

"And what do you see?"

"I always wondered when you and Dad talked about his job, why you understood it so well." Luke shrugged. "Now I know why. You'd been there.

"It also makes sense why you went ballistic whenever you heard about someone doing drugs." Luke rolled his eyes. "And why *I'd* get a three-day lecture."

She lifted her chin, granting him a wry smile. "If I hadn't been smoking dope the night Maxwell robbed the convenience store, I might have made better choices. If I hadn't been doing drugs, I might never have hitchhiked or let him pick me up in the first place."

"I don't do drugs, Mom," Luke said reassuringly.

Mom. Nothing had changed. Joe had been right, she'd confessed her deepest, darkest secret and her son still loved her.

"There might come a time when you're tempted," she said. "I can't tell you all the scary stuff that's out there. There's coke, heroin, meth—"

"Mom, chill!"

They broke into laughter and he hugged her.

Settling back, Luke sobered. "How weird is it that Lt. Crandall's the guy who arrested you? No wonder the two of you act like you've known each other forever. What's really bizarre is that you can be friends."

"Yes, it is," Mel admitted. "We didn't start out as friends, Luke. He wanted to end yours and Matt's friendship."

Luke scoffed. "He could've tried." Then glancing at his watch, Luke said, "Anyway, we'll be pretty much inseparable over winter break."

"More so than normal?"

"For sure. We've been sentenced to detailing off-duty patrol cars."

Mel blinked. "The *entire* holiday?"

Shrugging, Luke said, "Maybe not the whole time. The only thing saving us is Matt's mom's coming into town. Since he's spending a few days with her, I'll get those days off, too."

Mel grew dizzy at the thought. She'd almost forgotten Joe's ex-wife and daughter's winter excursion. "How many cars are we talking about?"

"No clue. But something tells me we're talking a fleet."

Pride in her son overtook Mel. He could've argued it wasn't his idea for Matt to take Joe's car, but he didn't. Luke was prepared to work beside the kid next door and accept his share of the blame. They'd developed quite an amazing bond.

"That won't leave you with much of a break," she said, eying him sympathetically.

He shook his head. "Nope. And when I'm not cleaning cop cars, I'll be in the gym. Gotta redeem myself somehow. Coach could've kicked me off the team."

"How long are you suspended?"

"First six games in January."

"And Coach Hood will still let you practice?"

Luke stood and stretched. "What do you mean *let me?* He's ordered me to be in the gym till my legs fall off. Long day tomorrow, Mom. I'm going to bed."

"I'm right behind you." She lifted her arms overhead and twined her fingers. "Luke?"

"Yeah?"

"Are we okay?"

Luke leaned down and kissed her cheek. "We're cool, Mom. I love you."

Her eyes filled. "I love you, too, baby."

He walked up the stairs; she sat motionless until his door closed. Then, lowering her head, she felt as though a stone had been removed from her chest. She could only hope Luke would take her warnings to heart and use her as an example before acting on impulse.

Perhaps she should send the Walfords a bouquet as a thank you. Not that she enjoyed Luke's reaction when he discovered the summons. But Janice had forced Mel to admit her past, and she did need to put Luke back in touch with his grandparents. If he hadn't gone looking for money in her dresser drawer, this issue might have stayed unresolved.

Joe had seemed surprised that she would give Luke access to her belongings, but then she'd never had anything to hide. Luke was her family after all, and nothing she owned was off limits to him.

An army of chills ran down her spine. *Until now.*

Mel rose from the couch, strode to the stairs, tempted to run. Tonight, she'd thought she'd rid herself of all secrets. But if Luke was near sleep, she didn't want to disturb him.

Entering her room, she approached her closet, and yanked it open. Her heart pounded at the foolish mistake she'd made. She'd never worried that

Luke might look in her drawers, but what if he went searching for something in here? And with Luke's insecurities, what would he think if she changed the ground rules now?

Mel swallowed hard. When she'd told Luke about Maxwell, she'd seen an expression she'd seen often in Carl. Luke thought he was a man. He now considered it his responsibility to protect her.

She lifted her gaze to the box holding the weapon Carl had bequeathed to Luke. What better way to protect her than with a gun? *You're overreacting,* an inner voice whispered. *He'll never find it.* But a voice bearing the judgmental tone of an executioner taunted, *But what if he does? He's not yet sixteen years old, and it's your job to protect him.*

Mel shuddered as her louder conscience won. As long as Luke lived with her, the gun didn't belong in this house. Still, she couldn't just leave it with anybody. She turned her gaze toward her snow-frosted window, and beyond it the logical choice for Luke. The question was, was it a safe choice for her? She rubbed her wrists, even now remembering the cold pinching steel of Joe's handcuffs.

He wouldn't, came the indignant reassurance of the first inner voice. But this time the harsh and exacting voice remained stubbornly silent.

Moving closer to the window seat, she saw that Joe's bedroom light was on.

She risked a late night call.

He answered on the first ring. "Crandall."

Still wrestling with her decision to tell him, she cleared her throat before saying, "Can't sleep?"

"Just about to turn in. Everything, okay?"

"I told him, Joe. I told Luke about my past."

"How'd he take it?"

"Better than I expected or hoped. It cleared up a lot of things between us. I thought you'd like to know."

"Fantastic, Mel. What a relief to have this off your chest at last."

At least one thing. "Just wanted you to know you were right."

"Once in a while it happens." He chuckled. "I'll bet you sleep like a baby tonight."

Not likely. "Joe?"

"Yes?"

"Are you terribly exhausted?"

"Not if you need me. Something wrong?"

"Do you mind if I come over? It's kind of important."

"It's bad outside, Melanie. I'll come over there."

"No. I'd prefer to do it at your place. I need to show you something. Please?"

He hesitated. "All right. But it's slippery outside, so be careful. I'll be waiting downstairs."

She disconnected. Releasing her pent-up breath, she retrieved the box from the closet, grabbed the key from the nightstand and scribbled a note for Luke. Once he was asleep he was out, but in the event he woke up, she left her whereabouts plainly displayed on the dining room table. After putting on her warmest coat, gloves and boots, she stepped out into frigid conditions. As snow landed on her cheeks and eyelashes, she trudged through the accumulated snow.

Joe had been more than fair with the boys tonight. She, on the other hand, by keeping this gun had willfully and premeditatedly broken the law. It might be foolhardy to confide in him. There was no forgetting his unmoving stance in the past. Still, she'd come to care for him, to trust him. Believing firmly she was making the right decision, she quashed down trepidation and concentrated on doing what was right for her son.

As promised, Joe was waiting downstairs. Standing in the open doorway, his impressive physique formed a silhouette against the interior light and the outside world. Armed with the evidence of her deceit, there was no turning back now. Mel could only pray that her trust hadn't been misplaced.

Joe stared at the woman bundled from head to toe making her way up his walk. She carried a box in her arms, and from where he stood, he could make out the word *microwave*. For a second, he dared to hope that hers was broken, and she was under the misguided impression that he could fix it. But a handyman he wasn't. Nor, by the look on her face, or at this late hour, had she come to ask his advice on a faulty appliance.

He opened the storm door, she stepped inside. Taking the load from her arms, he discovered it lacked the standard bulk of a microwave. Even so, it held some weight.

"Do you want me to take off my boots?" she asked, stomping all over his entry mat and tossing back the coat's hood to reveal an agitated expression.

"Not necessary. What's in the box?"

She held his gaze. "A Smith and Wesson .357 Magnum."

Joe blinked. Every time Melanie had come remotely close to his weapon, she threatened to go comatose. What the hell was she doing with a gun? Especially a gun as powerful as this one?

"I know what you're thinking," she said.

"Do you?"

"I've broken the law."

He shook his head. "Not even close. Let's go into the den." He led her into the other room, set the package on his desk, pulled back the flaps, then lifted an oaken box from the inside. The weapon was housed in an old time carrier, which in itself was in good condition, even containing a built-in bottom drawer full of brass rods, brushes, and other cleaning elements. "Do you have the key?"

Wide-eyed, she nodded and wordlessly handed it to him.

Well, she hadn't lied. After removing the lid, he saw that tucked in the gun box was a beauty of a Magnum revolver insulated by gray foam. He refrained from touching the long-barreled weapon, wondering for the first time if it contained prints, when it was fired last and if Melanie had something to tell him.

His heart sped up as he looked at her. "You said you'd broken the law?"

Eyes welling, she bit her lip. "That gun belonged to Carl." She then proceeded to go off on a near hysterical explanation of how ex-cons couldn't own guns, how her dead husband had understood that, but wanted to save it for Luke. Therefore, he'd left it with a friend who returned it to Mel the day of Carl's funeral.

"Okay," Joe said, resisting taking the trembling woman into his arms until he knew more. "*How* have you broken the law?"

She stared at him. "I kept it. I didn't get rid of it." She paused and visibly swallowed. "The day I went to your office to confront you for talking to Simon, and you brought up Maxwell, I opened that box and consciously made the decision to keep it."

Joe felt the corners of his mouth slide upward. But before she thought he was laughing at her, he vanquished the smile.

"But now that I've had time to think about it, I don't want it. I know I have to give it to Luke, but Carl wanted to wait until he was an adult. I'm thinking thirty-five."

She was such a mom. "When was it fired last?" Joe asked.

"Oh, gosh," she said. "I can't be sure Arnie never fired it, but my guess is that it's been fifteen years or more."

Taking Mel at her word, Joe removed the solid weapon from the container. She was right. The revolver showed no evidence of being fired anytime recently. In fact, to get it primed, he would only need to run a mop or two through the barrel and wipe down the key elements. But no way could Melanie handle it—these things had kick. "So what are you asking me, Mel?"

"Well, for one thing, am I in trouble?"

Joe did grin then. "I wish all ex-cons were as conscientious as you. I don't think when lawmakers enacted that particular legislation, they had you in mind. You're right, you're not supposed to own one. But you're not in trouble. *Yet.* So, let's do something about it. What concerns me more is that you have something lethal, and you don't have the strength, or the first clue how to handle it. A .357 Magnum is known for over-penetration."

She frowned. "Which means?"

"It can go through a human being and cause injury to innocent bystanders, not to mention what it will do to your property."

Her beautiful face went pale. She stared at the Magnum in horror. "Now I really don't want that thing in my house. I was going to give it to Luke, but neither one of us has ever been around guns." She paused. "Does Matt know how to use one?"

Joe nodded. "He's grown up around them. He's also been taught to respect them. He also knows never to touch mine."

"He took your car," Mel reminded him.

"This is different. I can swear on a stack of Bibles that Matt would never handle my weapon without my permission."

The worry lines eased from her face.

"What do you want me to do with it?" Joe asked.

"Keep it. Save it for Luke. Maybe show it to him, tell him about his father's wishes."

"Which were?"

"That Luke take ownership of it when he's a man. Also, could you work with him . . . teach him how to use it? Make sure he knows it's not a toy?"

"That, I'd be happy to do. I'll store it in my vault."

Her whole body slumped in relief as Joe allowed his smile to form fully. He did hold her then. Lifting her chin, he looked into her eyes and murmured, "You're such a worrier." When she looked like she might argue the point, he kissed her, loving the sound of her protests, followed by her laughter against his lips. It didn't last long. As Joe deepened their kiss, Mel wrapped her arms around him. Not only was her coat proving to be a nuisance between them, it was wet. He'd just unzipped it when his cell phone rang.

She stiffened, stepped back and stared at the phone on his desk.

First clocks, now cell phones. Give me a break. Striding to it, Joe returned a helpless shrug, and held up a finger. "Crandall."

He listened as Dispatch alerted him of a house fire, and that a family was suspected inside. "Emergency vehicles and patrol are en route," the operator said. "But as fast as the blaze went up, the arson investigator suspects a heavy accelerant."

Joe knew the area well. The neighboring houses also consisted of townhomes and duplexes, all in dangerously close proximity. "Ask the sergeant to get a detective on scene, and until we know something conclusive, don't talk to the press. I'm on my way."

"You have to go," she said.

He nodded.

"I can't believe I ever called you a monster. You're amazing." She kissed him.

Now who's putting who on a pedestal? "If I recall, you had your reasons. Let's get you home, Mel."

Chapter Thirty-two

Coronado High School's long-awaited winter break arrived, but for Luke and Matt, playing video games, hanging out with friends and sleeping in weren't part of their itinerary.

For the third day in a row, Mel drove them to the Police Operations Center to complete yet another segment of Joe's imposed community service.

"I must've already gone through six bottles of Armor All," Matt said. "Check this out." From the back seat, he thrust his hand out so Luke could see it. "I rubbed so hard I grew a callus."

Luke laughed, but refrained from his typical sarcastic retort. Mel studied him as she drove. Since taking off, and being suspended last week, he'd been pretty subdued. His lip had healed and the angry bruise on his left cheek had faded to a dull yellow.

"I know why they call cops pigs, Mrs. Norris," Matt continued. "You should see all the crap they leave in their cars."

Catching Matt's gaze in the rearview mirror, she gave him a wink. "Maybe you should take that up with your dad."

Matt rolled his eyes. "I'll pass on that one. But I guarantee my ol' man's car never looked like that. I think he told them to make sure they left plenty of sh—junk in their cars so we'd have lots of work to do."

Mel tried, but failed to contain her smile. That sounded *exactly* like something Joe would do. Her cell phone rang as she pulled alongside the CSPD. The boys got out of the car and she waved.

"You dropping off the delinquents?" Joe asked.

"Yep." She looked over her shoulder and had to wait for oncoming traffic. The early morning sun was so bright it hurt her eyes. She fumbled above the visor to locate her sunglasses. "You should be seeing the whites of their eyes any second."

"Good. Cooper tells me they're doing a good job."

"Cooper?"

"The vehicle maintenance supervisor. He's keeping them in line."

"Slave driver."

"You free for lunch?"

"I'm not sure. Why?"

"I thought you might come by and pick me up?"

"What's wrong with your car?" she asked.

"It's out of commission. I'm having it detailed."

"You rat."

"Call me if you can get away. I'll take you some place pricey."

She laughed. "As much as I'd like to break your wallet, this close to Christmas the shop's bound to be swamped. Tell you what, if I'm not there by one, I'm not coming."

"Fair enough."

Mel swung from the curb. Naturally, pressed for time, she hit a yellow light. "Be nice to our boys," she said.

"Oh, yeah," he lied and disconnected.

It probably wasn't a good thing for the brand new manager of Pinnacle Creations to hope the store wasn't booming today. But that's exactly what she wanted. Mel caught a glimpse of her sappy grin and wiped it away. She was in serious trouble. She had it bad for the cop next door.

At ten till one, Joe glanced at his watch and assumed Mel wasn't coming. Too bad, he thought. He'd wanted to see her before Karen and Trish came into town tomorrow night. He wasn't particularly anxious to connect with his ex again, but couldn't wait to see his little girl.

Two sharp raps on the door brought his attention back to work. Bruce Bennett leaned in the doorway. "Don't you eat lunch?"

"Just haven't gotten around to it." A shred of unease tore through Joe. He was fairly sure Mel was a no-show, but if she appeared, the situation could turn ugly. Fifteen years ago, Bruce Bennett had been the prosecutor who'd sent her to prison.

Now that Luke understood how Joe and Mel met, many walls had come down. Nonetheless, Joe wasn't anxious to resurrect them. "What brings you by?"

"The rumor mill, of course, the majority concerning you."

"Wow. You people keep better track of me than my mom."

The D.A. frowned and took a seat. "Someone has to look out for you. Know where I was this morning? In Chief Gallegos' office, along with two city council members. It's starting, Joe. With Archambeau's retirement, someone's on his or her way to commander." Bruce hesitated. "I always believed it was you."

Joe resisted grabbing a Tums. "And now?"

"Chief likes the bad guys to make headlines, not members of his staff."

Bruce may have been a prosecutor, but he was still a lawyer. He made his living using words and subtext. Joe waited for the bottom line.

"Nice scab on your forehead. Ever think of staying out of the street?"

So he knew. Joe wasn't surprised. He clasped his hands behind his head and maintained his poker face. Something told him it was useless, though, because Bruce had stacked the deck.

"Tell me something. That private dick who tried to run you over. . ."

Why wasn't he arraigned, and why didn't he spend one *hour* in the C.J.C?"

Joe shrugged. "Jail's overcrowded. He wasn't a threat to anybody else and he promised to leave town."

That answer didn't sit well with the future attorney general. "The man assaulted a cop. The old Joe Crandall would have hung the guy up by his thumbs."

"As opposed to the new?" Joe tired of guessing games. "Spit it out, Bruce, what's on your mind?"

"Do you know who your competition is?"

"I've heard a few names bandied about. Good people. All qualified."

"Avery Ballard's being considered."

Joe's inside quaked. Ballard was a prima donna, a man who'd risen through the ranks by bringing good people down. He and Joe had butted heads on numerous occasions. Most cops, when assigned to Internal Affairs, took the job reluctantly. They did their stint and got out. Avery Ballard signed up time after time, mainly because he was an asshole. He was book-smart, educated and recently touted a PhD. That didn't make him a good cop—or a decent human being.

After years on the force, Joe had earned his Master's. Still, he'd achieved his real education on the streets, while Avery had hidden behind a desk. "Rotten choice, if you ask me."

"No one's asking. Instead, you're giving the higher ups reason to consider him."

"And how the hell am I doing that?" For the first time, Joe raised his voice.

"She's trouble, Joe, and you're falling for her."

As the D.A. played his hand, Joe clenched his fist. So the entire discussion revolved around Melanie. "I don't know what you're talking about. All right, a P.I. was watching her. I apprehended the son of a bitch and sent him on his way."

"Did it have anything to do with Maxwell?"

"Not a damn thing. You're judging her based on several years ago. Do you know why she's in Colorado Springs?"

"Why don't you tell me?"

"Simon Rivers, the warden of Fremont County Women's Correctional Facility, arranged for the move. For years she was married to a DOC officer who recently died. She's a decent woman, Bruce, who made a mistake when she was seventeen years old." Joe stood. "Yeah, I let a scumbag go to protect her, and if that makes me a lousy candidate for commander, feel free to change your recommendation."

Joe fought hard to keep things in perspective. It wasn't the first time they'd disagreed; it wouldn't be the last.

Bruce lowered his voice and leaned forward in the chair. "Ninety-five percent of the cops in this building want to see you promoted. That doesn't mean a damn thing. Cops are discouraged from fraternizing with convicted felons. If you were a first year patrolman, I'd be warning you off. As a twenty-year veteran of the CSPD, you have to know this. I'm telling you this can ruin your career. Not only will you *not* make commander, you'll never advance, and the likelihood of demotion or termination is even higher."

Joe swallowed hard. He wasn't a rookie. He'd been ensconced in the system so long he could recite the rules—written and unwritten—by heart. If a subordinate had been sitting before him, engaged in a similar situation, he'd be citing the same advice as his colleague.

But damn it, he no longer thought of Mel as an ex-con. His breath caught, and he shuddered at how deep his feelings ran.

Tiny crevices lined Bruce's eyes and gray peppered his temples and sideburns. In all the time Joe had known him, he hadn't gained an ounce. No. He hadn't changed on the outside, but what about the inside? Bruce rose from the chair. "That's all I came to say. Think about it." He strode to the door and yanked it open.

Preparing to knock, Mel stood in the doorway. At the sight of the man who'd introduced her to the penal system, her eyes went wide and she stared between the two.

Joe rounded the desk.

Ever the politician, Bruce was the first to recover. He extended his hand. "Mrs. Norris. We were just talking about you."

She blinked, then glared at the man, but made no attempt to shake his hand.

"My condolences on your loss," the D.A. said, returning his hand to his side. He turned to Joe. I appreciate you filling me in on those facts."

"Come in, Mel," Joe said.

Swallowing visibly, she took a step back. "No, thank you, Lieutenant. I left the shop at a particularly hectic time and I need to get back." She stared at the district attorney. "As it turns out, I've suddenly lost my appetite."

For a moment Joe stood motionless, fighting his immediate reaction to go after her. Fifteen years ago he'd chased Melanie Daniels, and that event had turned to disaster. He glared at the man, who up until now, he'd considered a friend. "*We were just talking about you?*"

"All right. Poor choice of words. But if you think about it, you'll see I did you a favor. That woman or your career, Joe." Bruce shrugged as he walked away.

Mel drained the last of her water bottle and returned to the shop.

"That was the quickest lunch in the history of mankind," Aaron said. "I thought you said you were going out with the hunk?" With Christmas upon them, poinsettias and holiday accessories were selling at record speed. Aaron paused from bringing new plants into the showroom.

"The *hunk*, as you call him, was in a meeting." She shrugged out of her coat, wishing she could shuck her misery with it. "What's next, boss? Did we get the McKenna order taken care of?"

"We did." He refused to be put off. "Do you want to talk about it?"

Her shoulders slumped. Her boss was such a good man. "No." Communicating the fact she'd run into the overly ambitious jerk who'd sent her to prison wasn't something she wanted to share with anybody. To top off that dismal meeting, Joe had seemed embarrassed to see her. "You understand, don't you?"

"Of course. But remember, I'm a pretty good listener. Any chance you can shake off this mood by tonight?"

"Tonight?" She groaned inwardly. Had he scheduled her to close and she'd forgotten?

"Karlee's going-away party." Aaron held up his arms, shuffled his feet and snapped his fingers doing his own unique rendition of a Flamenco dancer. "We're meeting downtown at the Ritz. Karlee's husband's coming with a few of his Air Force buddies." Aaron winked. "You said you wouldn't miss it."

She had, hadn't she? A party. Mel preferred to stay home and wrap Christmas presents. Still, Karlee had been a staunch supporter and was now a good friend.

Several thoughts ran through Mel's head. From last week's episode in her kitchen, to the compassion he'd shown with Luke's gun, to the embarrassing situation today at his office, she could use a distraction. A party. Something like that might be just what she needed to forget Joe Crandall ever existed.

Joe lingered at the basement door and listened to Matt and Luke take turns brutalizing the punching bag. Having just completed the same routine, he wiped sweat from his face and neck.

A going away party. Good for Mel. She deserved to have some fun. It occurred to him that gnashing of his teeth was the polar opposite to his forced sincerity.

He'd picked up the kids from the vehicle maintenance lot and found Luke talking on his cell to his mother. Overhearing his side of the conversation, Joe had gathered Mel was concerned about how Luke would be spending the evening.

"Tell her you'll be with me," Joe had said, tempted to yank the phone out of the kid's hand and explain the whole horrible debacle she'd overheard outside his office.

But what was there to explain?

Melanie had understood precisely what had been discussed just minutes before her arrival.

Joe was bitterly disappointed that their lunch had been disrupted, and at the thought of others enjoying her company, and not him, damn envious. Her demeanor outside his office had made it clear they were back to where they'd started.

He headed upstairs. Maybe he'd shake off the doldrums in the shower. Hell of a choice to make when you got right down to it. Should he fight for the woman he was falling in love with, or the badge he'd worn for twenty-two years?

"Okay, girlfriend," Karlee said. "Let's get you buckled in, what do you say?"

Light-headed, tipsy and in no condition to argue, Mel acquiesced as Karlee fastened her into the backseat of Karlee's car.

"She's really out of it," Chloe Johnson, another Pinnacle employee, said.

"I heard that," Mel replied, pressing a palm to her forehead.

"Open your eyes," Karlee ordered. "If you keep them closed while we're moving, everything will start spinning."

Mel opened one eye. Her tongue felt thick, like it needed to go on a diet. "I know *that*. What'd that bartender put in those drinks anyhow?"

"Alcohol." Chloe giggled and climbed into the passenger side of Karlee's 4-Runner. "So what? You had a good time."

Karlee started the car. "I'll say. This is the best going away party Craig and I've ever been to. Who knew Mel could loosen up like that?"

She grimaced. "Uh, exactly how loose did I get?"

"Not bad. You danced and did a mean karaoke."

Oh, yeah. She'd had fun dancing and loved the karaoke. It was Eighties' Night, and she'd pretended to be one of the Bangles as she belted out *Walk Like an Egyptian*. "That was fun."

As Karlee drove, Mel did her best to keep her eyes open, even if it was one at a time.

Chloe twisted and peered over the passenger seat. "I think your trouble began when you mixed drinks. You started out with wine, then that guy bought you a rum and coke."

"Three rum and cokes," Karlee qualified.

"You're right, that was dumb." Pressing fingertips to her temples, Mel leaned forward. Where the hell was the floor? "I was only trying to be polite. The man's serving our country."

"Oh, you were polite." Karlee rounded a curve, causing Mel's stomach to lurch. "His name is Roger, by the way, and I think he's ready to propose."

"Oh, no." She groaned. "I didn't—"

"No. You danced with him, that's all. But he was relentless about asking for your number."

"Did I give it to him?" Mel squeezed her eyes closed, and as Karlee predicted, the vehicle spun. Instantly, she reopened them.

Somewhere in her alcohol-induced haze, she reflected on Simon's warning to keep a low profile. Some low profile. The way she'd imbibed tonight and lost her inhibitions, she'd risen from nobody to celebrity status.

"I don't know. But he *is* a nice guy. He's Craig's best friend. He's a captain stationed at Peterson," Karlee said.

"Great. An officer." An image of Joe snapped in her brain and she frowned. "Make a note of it, ladies, I'm through with officers."

Karlee took another turn.

Once again, Mel's stomach rolled, but soon the 4-Runner came to a stop in a place that looked vaguely familiar. Mel gazed out the window and urged the world into focus. Then she smiled. "My house. Where did it come from?"

Joe descended the stairs to do one last check before bed and to set the alarm. Matt and Luke were in the living room stretched out on their stomachs, watching some horror flick.

From the entryway, Matt called, "Dad, know what? Luke's never been skiing."

Sensing what was coming next, Joe paused in the doorway. "Maybe we'll take him some time."

With Luke pretending his focus was on the movie, and not on every word, Matt said, "Why can't we take him on Wednesday? We'll be back by Christmas Eve."

Joe hadn't mentioned he wasn't planning on spending the nights. He'd ski during the day, come home in the evenings. He and Karen might not have been suited emotionally, but there'd never been anything wrong with their physical relationship.

"His mom might want him around," Joe argued. "Besides, I know beyond a doubt *your* mom wants to spend time with you."

"Yeah, yeah, yeah," the disgruntled boy said. He returned his attention to the movie, dismissing Joe by turning up the volume.

Joe left the room as a character in the film emitted a blood-curdling scream.

The slam of car doors stopped him from keying in the alarm code. The small rectangular window next to the entry provided a poor vantage point, so he opened the front door. Much as he'd tried not to, he'd checked periodically to see if additional lights were on in Mel's house.

His gaze honed in on two women pulling a third from a dark-colored SUV, and when he realized whom they were hauling, he stepped onto the porch, quickly recognizing a non-threatening situation. Amid giggles and shushes, three soused women stumbled their way up the walk. He considered leaving them to their fun, until the smaller female lost her balance. Mel landed on her ass and every dog in the neighborhood started barking. A light across the street switched on. Knowing Mrs. Kearney, it wouldn't be long before she called him, or worse, 911.

Joe shook his head. He'd wanted Mel to have a good time. It appeared she'd had *too* good a time. Grateful someone had sense enough to take her keys, he made his way next door.

"Help me get her up, Chloe. And be quiet," the tallest of the trio said. "On three . . ."

"Yes, be *quiet,*" Mel slurred in an overloud voice.

Unsuccessfully, her friends tried to bring her to her feet. Flat on her back, she gazed up at them. "You guys are good friends, but you're not very strong."

Fifteen years ago, seeing her in such a state wouldn't have surprised him. Watching the reformed version of Melanie Daniels Norris was almost comical. Still, it was late and noise was a factor. He stepped forward, crossed his arms over his chest and said, "Can I be of assistance?"

Wide-eyed and open-mouthed, the two standing women whirled on him.

The one drunk on her butt brought herself up on her elbows. Shaking her head, she placed a finger to her lips. "Shhh. Don't tell him anything. He's a cop. If he thinks we've been drinking, he'll arrest us."

He gave her a cursory glance. "You *have* been drinking." Then acknowledging the woman who appeared the most sober of the group, he said, "You must be Karlee."

She smiled. "You must be Joe."

He nodded. "Have fun tonight?"

"We had a blast."

"Sorry to see you go."

"Yeah, well, when you're military it's SOP."

Mel glared between the two. "Excuse me! Remember me? Are you guys gonna leave me down here all night or what?"

Joe lifted his eyes to the sky. "Want me to take her off your hands?"

"I don't know, Joe. She's pretty mad at you."

His offer brought Mel up as far as her knees. "That's right. And for your information, Lt. Crandall, we're doing just fine." She tried to stand upright, but failed.

"I can see that." Ignoring her protests, he scooped her into his arms, catching her subtle perfume and the evident whiff of booze. "Anybody got her purse?"

The petite blonde stepped forward. "Right here, along with her coat."

"Dig through her stuff, will you? See if you can find her keys."

Karlee still wasn't certain. "If I let you take her, she's not going to be very happy with me come morning."

"Can you get her upstairs?"

Her friend looked hesitantly at Mel, then toward the house. "Not very likely. In her present condition, she's dead weight."

"Traitor," Mel mumbled, then dropped her head on Joe's shoulder. "Put me down," she added weakly. "How can you take sides with *him?*"

"Be quiet, or I will arrest you," Joe said. But Mel was no longer paying attention. She'd already drifted off and started to snore.

Joe shook his head. "Let's hope tomorrow morning, she doesn't remember a thing. "Give me a hand?"

Chloe carried Mel's purse while Karlee unlocked the front door. Glad Melanie had found such protective friends, Joe nodded his thanks. As the front door swung open, he said, "Thanks, ladies, I can take it from here."

As her friends headed toward their car, he overheard Chloe say, "He can take it from here with me any day."

Joe allowed himself a half smile. But only for a moment. He tightened his hold, and from the glow of her porch light studied Mel's drunken, angelic face. God, he wanted her. Too bad he saw no way of that happening.

Chapter Thirty-three

Drake never got Ramirez alone the night of their celebration. But true to his word, the next afternoon, the gang leader invited Drake to tag along to the Colorado Springs Airport. On their way to pick up Maria, he pled his case. Seated in the passenger side of Ramirez's low rider, Drake explained why the gang leader should rethink the Liberty National Bank heist, and more importantly, the timing.

Staring straight ahead as he drove, Ramirez remained unreadable. "We'll take this up with the others. We work as a team."

A team?

While he and Ramirez took on the federally insured financial institution, the gang would be hitting smaller targets to disrupt the cops. When the 911 calls went down, who the hell did Ramirez think the cops would go after?

The woman who'd screwed his brains out two weeks ago barely gave him a nod when she slid into the car, which did little to improve his mood. But when her brother wasn't looking, she winked. Drake grew hard right then and there. Perhaps later that night, he'd find a way to be alone with her.

Ramirez pulled into the drive and cut the engine. "The others will be here in less than an hour. You'll explain your position then."

Drake remained silent, but later, as he sat with a bunch of loser ex-cons, and Ramirez talked to them like he was a fucking CEO and they were shareholders, Drake knew it was time to blow this place.

"About Christmas Eve," Ramirez began. "Max has some concerns." Eyeing Drake, he said, "Tell them, *amigo*."

Emotionlessly, Drake laid out his observations about why he wanted to scout a new site and extend their deadline.

Most of the men in the room kept their thoughts to themselves. One man, though, a scrawny dude named Sanchez, stared at Drake from across the table. His already unsmiling face drew into a scowl. "Is that right? So a plan we've hatched for weeks just doesn't *feel* right? *Fuck you.* I'm going broke sitting around."

Drake returned the man's glare. Over the past few weeks, he'd formed the impression Sanchez believed himself Ramirez's second in command. That role had changed, however, as soon as Drake came on the scene. Ramirez no longer solicited Sanchez's opinion; what's more, Ramirez and Drake often had private meetings, as in today's trip to the airport.

Evidently, Sanchez had noticed.

"It's not a feeling. The cops have the place marked." Drake nodded to the man next to him. "Mercer came with me when I cased the bank yesterday."

Ramirez acknowledged the burly black man. "Merce?"

"Could be," he admitted. "The guy Max fingered filled out a deposit slip, but I never saw him approach a teller."

"So he's got you spooked, too, *ese*?" Sanchez's stare included the rest of the men at the table. "Before Maxwell showed up, we did just fine. Now he wants to change things. I say we stick to the plan. I also say he's a *gringo* coward who's afraid of going back to the slammer."

Knocking back his chair, Drake grabbed Sanchez by the collar. He jerked him over the tabletop. Men scrambled, while plates, cups and silverware flew everywhere.

Shoving the bastard against the wall, Drake wrapped his hands around the slimy prick's throat. "Damn straight I'm afraid of going back to prison. And it ain't gonna happen because I walked into a trap. *Fifteen* fucking years, Sanchez." Like always, the convenience store robbery flashed in his brain, and he relived Melanie's betrayal. "What'd you do in the joint, you piece of shit, eight months?" Much like he'd done with Ropes, Drake wanted to kill this guy, end his association with these losers.

Something sharp pressed against his ribcage. "Let him go, Max."

This was it. His life was over. But fear for his existence couldn't match his intense anger. Pivoting, he threw Sanchez against the gang leader and made a break for the door. Sanchez screamed, leaving Drake to suspect Ramirez's knife had found the wrong mark.

Now that he'd crossed Ramirez, Drake was a dead man.

Without looking back, he raced for the Jeep, and didn't ease his foot from the gas until he was halfway to Denver.

With each passing mile, however, he regained control. He'd done it again. Out and out lost his mind. If he'd kept his cool, he might've talked Ramirez's gang into waiting to pull the bank job. But now? Drake was on his own, with limited money and *no* connections.

Sweat trickled down his face as he considered his next move. Hiding from the cops would be child's play compared to hiding from Ramirez and his gang. At least the cops had procedures. Ramirez had his own brand of justice, and Drake had violated a cardinal rule by turning on the leader and walking out. His prepaid cell phone rang, startling him and very nearly causing him to swerve into oncoming traffic. He checked the number and recognized Ramirez's number.

Shit! Should he answer? Hear the gang leader confirm that he'd put out a hit, and very soon Drake would be no more than an unidentified body on a slab in the morgue?

The call went to voice mail, but just as quickly rang again.

He pictured Ramirez's taunting face. *Sanchez was right to call you a gringo coward, Max.* It would do no good to show fear. On the contrary, if he answered, it might persuade Ramirez to back away and cut his losses. Belligerently, Drake answered, "*What?*"

"Where you at, Max?"

Watching the northbound road, he scoffed. "Lost, man, no telling."

"Scared?"

Drake swallowed hard. He was friggin' terrified. "What do you want?"

"We got us a job to do, man, and you walked out on me."

Drake squinted against the lights of oncoming traffic.

"The way I see it, you can come back and make things right, or I can send out the word and have you chopped up into little pieces."

Drake sped up to pass a semi. "And how do I know I won't be puréed the moment I return? No thanks, I'll take my chances on the street."

"You're one crazy son of a bitch, Max, but you're a *smart* S.O.B. We had a good plan till you went off half-cocked. The way I look at it, I just need to rein in that crazy streak of yours to make our partnership work."

Partnership. That was a first. Up until now, Ramirez had made it clear his word was law. "You got my attention."

"These other guys, Max, we need them because they're decoys. After we take the bank, they're on their own. I didn't tell you cuz I thought you knew. How many dudes I let sleep in my sister's basement?"

Slowing the Jeep to the speed limit, Drake couldn't dispute the fact.

"You and me, Max, we're the brains of this operation. Find me another bank and we move on your say so. But we've come too far to let this go now. What do you say?"

Drake pulled into a rest stop near Larkspur. He opened the glove box and examined the easy-to-conceal Derringer the arms' dealer had sold him. He leaned back his head as his thoughts swirled into a frenzied panic. Was this a trap? Would Ramirez slit his throat the moment Drake walked in?

"How do I know I can trust you?"

"I could've killed you tonight," Ramirez said. "I stopped Sanchez from following you. The men, they're behind you, Max. We're ready to do this."

"Even Sanchez?" Drake asked.

There was a slight pause in the conversation. "Well, maybe not Sanchez."

"If I come back, I'll end up killing the motherfucker."

"I don't think so. That's another reason you gotta come back," Ramirez said. "I saved you the trouble. Sanchez wouldn't compromise. I need you to help me get rid of the body."

Chapter Thirty-four

Inside one of two cars gracing Coronado's dark, abandoned parking lot, Mel sat waiting for Luke to finish his workout.

Not one other player had shown up for open gym.

Who could blame them? Two days before Christmas, most likely they were with family and friends. Not so for Luke or Coach Hood. Luke wanted to make up for his lapse in judgment. The coach obviously planned to let him.

She glanced at her watch. By now, Karen Crandall's plane had touched down. Had Joe taken one look at his ex-wife and daughter and wondered how he'd ever let them go? Had he and Karen looked longingly into each other's eyes and felt the rekindling of a love gone bad?

Weighed down by depression, Mel sighed. She had to stop this negative thinking. She had no claim on Joe, and after the humiliating scene outside his office, as well as her drunken abandonment of common sense last night, she doubted he would speak to her even in passing.

She remembered Karlee and Chloe bringing her home last night, and vaguely remembered Joe discovering them in her front yard. What she couldn't remember were the events that followed afterward, or why she'd awoken in her bedroom. With her head threatening to split wide open, she'd sat up carefully to find herself minus her clothes, with her jeans and sweater folded neatly on her cedar chest. On the nightstand beside her, two aspirins and a glass of water were waiting, along with Joe's note, "Feel better."

Oh, God. While she lay passed out, he'd undressed her, which had reminded her of the night he'd brought her to climax. Her heart had ached at the unfairness of life, and she'd pressed her fingertips to her temples and resisted a groan.

A knock on the Corolla's passenger window pulled her from her mortification. She unlocked the door and Luke slid in beside her. "Hey, Mom. Headache?"

Mel blinked. Amazingly not. She'd downed the pills and water the moment she spotted them. "No, just tired," she said. Luke obviously hadn't taken the time to shower. She cracked a window. "How about you?"

"Beat. Coach and I played one on one. Holy cow, Mom, he's awesome. I can't tell you how many times he stuffed me."

It was nice to see Luke smile. "Feel like driving?" she asked.

In a few months, Luke officially would have his driver's license. He needed supervised hours to complete the training.

"Sure," he said.

Luke did a good job of negotiating the short distance to their house and Mel relaxed. She had gifts to wrap, among them a tie clasp and cuff links she'd purchased for Simon. After their last dismal encounter, the warden hadn't called much. Mel planned to invite him up for Christmas dinner and hopefully place their friendship back on track.

As Luke veered onto Serendipity, a car pulled into Joe's drive. Suddenly the headache she hadn't felt made itself known. Talk about awful luck. The entire Crandall clan had arrived.

"Cool," Luke said, placing the Corolla into park. "Matt's home."

Cool? Mel did everything but slink down in the seat.

"You coming, Mom?"

Damn.

She gathered her purse. "In a moment, sweetheart. I dropped something."

Matt tore out of the backseat of Joe's Crown Victoria and dashed over to join his friend, while a woman and girl got out of the car. Joe popped the trunk and began unloading luggage. All this Mel noticed through the corner of her eye. No way in hell would she be caught staring.

Intent on giving a friendly wave and making a dash for her front door, she climbed out of the car.

"Mrs. Norris?"

Heart thudding, Mel turned to see a dark-haired woman approach. With Luke and Matt hovering close by, an adolescent girl in tow, the woman extended her hand. "I'm Matt's mom. I've heard so much about you, I wanted to introduce myself."

Stunned, Mel held out her own.

Joe stood in the background, arms loaded with luggage.

"Karen Crandall," the woman said, shaking Mel's hand. "Luke is all Matty talks about."

"Vice versa, Mrs. Crandall. Very nice to meet you."

"Karen, please."

It didn't take daylight to see that Karen was beyond attractive. Joe's ex-wife was a statuesque brunette, had straight white teeth, perfectly applied makeup and not a hair out of place.

She appeared to be sizing Mel up as well. Arching an eyebrow, she said, "No one mentioned that you were gorgeous. This is my daughter Trish."

A thin girl around eleven or so stood close to her mom. With dark hair and eyes, Trish Crandall would grow to be the likeness of her mother.

"Hi, Trish," Mel said.

"Hi," the girl replied. "Mommy, I'm cold. I'm going inside. I want to see my new room."

"Sure, sweetie."

Mel shifted uneasily. With Karen and Trish in Chicago, it was easy to forget Joe's additional responsibilities. Up close and personal, reality hit her squarely between the eyes.

Karen returned her gaze to Mel's as Joe carried the bags into the house. "Joe said you've been helping Matty with his homework. I'm very grateful."

Finding it difficult to speak, Mel also found it hard to dislike this woman. "It's been my pleasure," she said, rediscovering her voice. "Matt's the best friend Luke's ever had."

"You know these two have been plotting." Karen grinned.

"About?"

"Matt's been begging me to let Luke come skiing with us."

"Oh, I don't think so." Mel shook her head, noting Joe had reappeared and made his way toward them. Ignoring her knotting stomach, she said, "This is family time, and it's the holidays."

"Ordinarily I'd agree," Karen said. "But have you ever been trapped with a bored teenager on the slopes? You'd be doing me a huge favor if you'd let Luke come along." She hesitated. "I promise to have him home before Christmas."

Daring a glance at Joe, Mel asked, "But what about Trish?"

Joe met her gaze, then quickly looked away. Mel was surprised at how badly his cold shoulder hurt.

"She'll be fine. She'll be skiing with Joe and me most of the time anyway, and we'll be playing a ton of board games at night."

Joe and me. Ouch. Accepting the fact, Mel nodded. "Joe?"

"If it's okay with Karen, sure," he said.

"Great, then, it's settled. Thank you. Hey, you two," Karen called, then sauntered toward the boys. "Good news."

As Matt and Luke's excited whoops filled the air, Mel endured the loneliness of being the outsider.

Out of Karen's earshot, Joe asked, "How are you feeling?"

Her gaze drifted back to his. No doubt he referred to last night's binge. Heat stung her cheeks. "I'm fine, thanks. I should get inside."

"Mel?"

She stopped, but Joe seemed as tongue-tied as she. For a long moment, they simply stared at each other.

"I'm sorry," he said at last.

The pain on his face nearly undid her. What was he sorry for? That his career had to come first? That his feelings for her had been a lie? That he realized he still cared about his ex-wife? "Enjoy your family," she said, and darted for her front door.

Chapter Thirty-five

After an exhausting day of skiing, Joe led his daughter to a bench outside their cabin to help her remove her snow boots. The other three in their group made the trek from the Chevy Tahoe that Karen had rented to the three-bedroom A-frame cabin nestled among the snowy pines. In truth, the day had been glorious. Sun, fresh powder and almost no wait at the chairlifts.

Luke's athleticism had served him well. He'd caught on to skiing like a pro and had gone from snowplowing to advanced technique in no time.

Wrapping his arms around his daughter, Joe said, "You're a speed demon, you know that? Tomorrow, take it easy on your old man."

She giggled. "Tomorrow, Daddy, we switch to the *black* trails."

Joe narrowed his gaze and tweaked her nose. The girl had no fear. "We'll see."

Removing his ski boots, Joe switched to hiking shoes, then noticed Karen struggling with hers. "Need some help?"

She tugged off her cap, allowing her dark shoulder-length hair to tumble free. "Would you? I'm a little sore." She glanced toward their daughter, who now, free of the heavy footwear, had engaged in a snowball fight with Matt and Luke. "It appears I'm not eleven anymore."

Joe took in her shapely curves. She certainly wasn't.

Amid squeals and yelps of the warring kids, he lifted Karen's leg. Resting her calf on his knee, he unfastened the boot buckles, then pulled. Even in bulky stretch pants he made out her well-defined legs. Karen took pride in her looks and had always stayed in good shape. A divorce and a move to Chicago had proved no exception.

Rotating her ankle, she leaned back and lifted her face to the afternoon sun. "Oh, that feels good."

Joe didn't trust the seductive tone in her voice. She'd fallen a couple of times today. Naturally he'd stopped to help her. What bothered him was that Karen had taught him to ski. He tried to curb his suspicion, cautioning himself that she was simply rusty.

His distrust was cut short by a snowball hitting him in the back. With Karen laughing and looking on, Joe joined in the war zone between his aggressors and soon emerged the snow-covered loser.

Later, when he walked inside, Karen had changed into slacks and a tight-fitting silk pullover. The smell of chicken vegetable soup and cornbread filled the rustic cabin. The kids meandered to the lofts upstairs, challenging one another to a game of Monopoly.

"Hungry?" Karen asked.

"Famished," Joe said. "I'd like to eat before I get a move on."

She stopped spooning the soup into bowls and set the ladle aside. "You were serious."

"What about?"

"About not staying the nights?"

His gaze fell to her breasts which filled out the top spectacularly. "Very."

As she spread honey and butter onto the cornbread, a drop fell to her fingers. She licked it off, then turned her gaze on his. "And if I don't want you to go?"

Years ago, a ploy like this would have had him carrying her to their bed. He smiled, but it lacked humor. "What are you up to, Karen?"

"If we ski all day, when will we have time to talk?"

"Is that what you want to do? Talk?"

"Of course. We have children to discuss."

"I'm listening."

She pursed her lips, a gesture that after thirteen years of marriage he was well acquainted with. "Do you ever . . ."

"Ever?"

"Why are you making this so difficult?"

He clenched his jaw. One would think after four years he could let this all go. Still he'd never forget how he'd felt when he'd followed her to the Antlers Doubletree and discovered her taking an elevator up to a room with the rich Dr. Bryant. Had she thought about Joe's comfort? Hell no. But past was past, and they did have children together.

He took a seat on the bar stool. "What is it you want to say, Karen?"

She joined him at an adjoining stool. "I made a mistake."

Joe was suddenly void of all appetite.

"You know that saying, 'the grass is always greener'? Well, it's true. You and I had a good thing, and I blew it. I'd hoped this ski trip might be a way for us to rediscover each other."

"What about Mark?" Joe asked.

A flush fell over her face and she lowered her head. "I think the grass will *always* be greener for him."

Ah. The truth. Guess it was time for Joe to be honest as well. "You're one of the sexiest women I've ever known. It'd be a lie to say I don't desire you. But I'm not in love with you anymore, K."

"I see." She looked to the ceiling and blew out a breath. "Is there someone else?"

He thought of Mel and the passion she ignited in him, but hesitated to share that with Karen. "I want there to be, but no. We've got too many barriers between us."

She gave him a sympathetic smile. "We're a hopeless pair, aren't we?" Wrapping her arms around his neck, she placed a soft kiss on his cheek. "No more games, Joe, I promise. I respect you too much to toy with your feelings."

"I appreciate that, K." He hugged her back.

"These barriers . . . "

"Yeah?"

"Just make sure they really exist. Life's too short."

Later, as Joe drove the winding route from Breckenridge to Colorado Springs, Karen's advice weighed on him. Was she right? Was there a way for Mel and him to be together? Solutions weren't exactly forthcoming. She would be forever an ex-con, and he a cop who had no intention of ending his career.

"Melanie, are you sure about this?"

Mel pushed a plate of sugar cookies across the table to Lenora Sims. "Absolutely not, but it's Christmas. I say 'eat hearty.'"

Lenora frowned. "You know what I mean. This is an extremely good offer. Do you have any idea how rare this is, or what a profit you'd make?"

Mel cringed. What was wrong with her? Lenora Sims, the woman who'd gotten Mel into this house in the first place, had brought her an offer. The full purchase price of what Mel should have actually paid for her house on Serendipity. Lenora had done Mel an amazing favor by going down in price so she and Luke could live here. And now, out of the blue, a former homeowner had seen it, liked what Mel had done to the place, and wanted it back.

She rubbed the back of her neck, pressing hard on the never-ending knots that had taken up residence in her body. Is that how Lenora saw Mel now? An interloper? She'd signed the contract in good faith. Luke loved it here, while she. . . The knots cramped up with a vengeance.

Wouldn't it be ideal if she could find another place in the school district and get away from Joe? Maybe even fit all the stuff she'd finally moved into storage? Still, the idea of packing, moving, renovating, buying another alarm system—when she'd just installed one—she was not putting herself through it again. Joe, or no Joe, she'd meant it when she said no one was forcing her from her home again.

She thought of her plants heartily taking off in the basement, how much work and pride she'd put into converting it. In Cañon City, Carl had built her a greenhouse. It was a labor of love and three times the size of her new home's lower level. She'd even occasionally made money from the enterprise. She rarely thought of the place anymore.

Why? Because she had a new life here, and this was her home.

"You're right," Mel said. "It's an excellent offer. But my answer is no. I can't uproot Luke again."

Lenora nodded slowly. "I thought you might say that. But you *were* worried about money for his college. So tell you what I'm going to do. I'm going to leave this contract with you, as well as some MLS listings of some lovely houses you could trade up to if you made this deal." Lenora grinned. "I wouldn't be doing my job if I didn't apply *some* kind of pressure."

"I'll look at them," Mel said. "But don't get your hopes up. I'll make you a promise, though. If I ever do move again, you'll be the first person I call. And if anyone needs a realtor, I'll refer them to you."

"Well, that's all I can ask, isn't it?"

Leaving the contract and listings on the table, Mel showed Lenora to the door. What Mel hadn't mentioned was that she loved living on a street named Serendipity. The very idea had filled her with hope that she was finally headed in the right direction.

She swallowed over a lump in her throat. But while serendipity meant fate, it didn't guarantee happiness. She tried not to think of Joe in Breckenridge with his stunning ex-wife, or the sensations he'd brought out in Mel by a look or a touch. She discovered the feat nearly impossible. Could one die from this all-encompassing sadness?

Not if she didn't let it. She'd survived much in this lifetime. For Luke's sake, she'd survive this heartache as well. She returned to the kitchen, placed the sugar cookies in a tin for her son, then picked up the MLS listing.

The doorbell rang, and she tossed it aside.

Standing at Melanie's door, Joe stuffed his hands into his pockets and waited for her to answer. He'd been checking his mail when an older woman drove off. He figured the least he could do was give Mel an update on Luke's day on the slopes.

Now that he'd made his decision to keep his distance, the plan was to tell her quickly and leave. But the moment she opened the door, his good intentions went into hiding. Amid the soft glow of lights, wearing a plaid flannel shirt and jeans, her hair carelessly piled atop of her head, she had the appearance of someone spending an evening alone.

She'd never looked better.

Subtle scents of pine and vanilla greeted him, which was just as well, because she did not. "Busy?" he asked.

Their eyes met and his damn heart rate increased.

"I—Not really," she said, frowning, a look more of confusion than displeasure. "What are you doing here?"

"I needed to stop by work. Thought I'd check in on you as well. Luke's having fun, by the way."

She smiled. "I know. He called a couple of hours ago. Thanks for inviting him."

"No problem." *So much for the update. All right. You've seen her. Get the hell out.* "Think I could get a cup of coffee?"

Wariness crossed her face, but she stood aside and opened the door for him. He entered the house, feeling the awkwardness of the first few times he'd been here. They'd seemed to have taken several steps backward; yet, seeing the keypad that led to her new alarm system filled him with satisfaction.

He followed Mel into the kitchen, watching her lithe movements to the coffeemaker until a set of documents on the table distracted him. He recognized them as computer printouts of homes for sale. With both their sons in basketball, they knew many of the same people. "Somebody moving?"

She turned from the sink. "Oh. Sorry, I meant to put those away."

That comment merely fueled Joe's interest. He didn't intend to snoop in her private affairs, but a comment like that was as good as a dare. Another look down revealed a contract. "Mel? What is this?"

"It's nothing." She took the contract from the table and stuffed it in a drawer. "Nobody's moving. I received an offer on my house."

"I didn't know it was for sale."

"It's not." Shrugging, she held her hands up. "It came out of the blue."

"Out of the blue."

"Yes, you know, random."

"Somebody drove past your house, and of all the houses in this neighborhood that *are* for sale, picked out one that isn't and made you an offer?"

She put her hand on her hip. "Why are you grilling me? I just told you it's not for sale." She cocked her head. "But now that I think about it, I guess it wasn't truly random. A man who used to live in Colorado Springs is moving back and wants to repurchase it."

"Gilman?"

"I don't know," Mel said, staring at Joe in exasperation. She pulled the contract out of the drawer and handed it to him. "See for yourself." She returned to the counter that held the coffeemaker.

"Gilman took crappy care of his yard."

As Joe raised his head to view her profile, she lifted a brow, forming something between a smirk and a smile. "Well, that settles it. I'm definitely not selling to him now."

"This is a nice offer, Mel," Joe said, scanning the particulars.

She spooned coffee into the filter. "I know, and it would probably solve everything, but this is my home now, and I'm not interested. So don't waste your breath."

He approached her, leaning his backside against the counter so he could read her face. "Is that what you think? That your moving would solve our problems?" He folded his arms. "Because you're wrong. Okay, originally, yeah, I wanted you gone. But not now. The day you saw Bruce in my office, I never got the chance to explain. I never apologized."

"You didn't have to. One look at that bastard's smug face, I knew he'd come to warn you away from me." Melanie poured water into the reservoir, then shuddered. "It was as if there'd been a time warp and Bennett was Sylvester all over again."

"Say again?"

She sighed. "It was a game I played when I was in lockup. The first time that pompous assistant district attorney came to see me he was wearing this fancy black pinstriped suit. He was so arrogant and overbearing, and I was this know-nothing little *nobody*, that I felt I had to protect myself. I compared him to Sylvester the Cat, while me, I was Tweety Bird." Her gaze stayed on the coffeemaker as it began its drip.

"When I sat across from him in his office on Vermijo, and he insisted I take the plea agreement instead of going to trial, he made it sound like I had no choice. He knew my mom couldn't come to my rescue, and my dad had said sayōnara. As for my public defender?" Mel scoffed. "He was about as effective as that little white-haired lady with the bun and the glasses who goes about her business, never suspecting that poor Tweety's about to be eaten."

At the painful edge to Mel's voice, Joe lowered his head. Fifteen years, and another perspective, certainly could shed light on things. It was hard to believe Melanie had been only two years older than Matt when Joe chased her down that back alley after the robbery. Sure, she'd been on drugs, and twice as wild, but she was right. With no parental guidance, Bruce probably thought prison would scare her straight.

Looking at her now, who knew? He might have done her a favor, not that Joe would ever tell Melanie that. She'd turned out so responsible, level headed, sexy, beautiful.

"You have every right to despise both of us," Joe said quietly. "But here's a tip for you."

She lifted her head to look at him.

"Tweety Bird outsmarted Sylvester the Cat every time."

"Thank you for that." Mel smiled sadly. "But can I share something with you?"

"Any time."

"When it comes to how I feel about you, despise isn't the right word. As for our past, you've more than wiped the slate clean."

The kitchen filled with the aromatic smell of coffee, but as she started to pour him a cup, Joe placed his palm over the rim. "You know how I feel about you, don't you?"

"I have an idea."

"I'm pretty sure I'm in love with you, Melanie."

She swiped at a tear. "Don't do this."

He moved so close she backed away from the counter. And as their gazes locked in a battle no one could win, Joe understood at last. So this was heartache. He'd thought he'd known. Nothing in his past had prepared him for this. Karen was the mother of his children, and he'd loved her. But not like he loved this woman. Melanie, with her intense, intelligent, compassionate viewpoints, was everything he wanted in a partner. And because of one lousy mistake she'd made as a girl, she was forever off limits to him? Twenty-two years of law enforcement swirled in his brain: the good times, the awful times, the successes, the failures.

He was ready to roar, screw this job!

Her eyes were shimmering pools, the color of Tennessee whiskey. "You've been right to keep your distance, Joe." Her smile finally made it to her eyes. "What we've had these few short months has been nice, but if you think about it, I'm just a blip on your radar."

He narrowed his gaze. Was she out of her mind? For fifteen years, thanks to the scar on his arm, he'd thought of this woman. If he were a mystical kind of guy, he'd say she'd been brought to him by some cosmic force. But superstition had nothing to do with it. Now that he knew what she was about, he wanted her in his life.

"A blip on my radar." Joe shook his head. "Just so we're clear, you may find it easy to forget me, but I will *never* forget you." As tears filled her eyes, he echoed the same careful tone, she'd used with him. "And, baby, I don't want to."

Mel had made mistakes in her life. No doubt, taking Joe into her bed was one more. But for right now his presence was perfect—and needed. Throughout the night the sex between them had been slow and giving one minute, desperate and fierce, the next. In short, as she'd always known it would be, spectacular.

They'd never gotten around to drinking their coffee, they'd switched to white wine instead, and as she lay facing him now, her chin in her hand, her elbow supporting her body, she watched him watch her.

Day-old stubble covered his jaw and chin, making him appear in the glow of a vanilla-scented candle, the essence of dangerous. But looks could deceive. Joe Crandall was a very good man.

With only a sheet between them, she traced her nail lightly over a bicep that felt like iron, guiding it down until she reached the puckered flesh of the scar she'd inflicted. "Did it hurt, Joe?"

He shook his head as gooseflesh rose on his arm where she'd touched him. "It's been so long ago, I honestly can't remember."

Slanting her gaze, she replied, "Liar. How many stitches did you need?"

"I didn't count. I wish you wouldn't think about this, Mel." Then a teasing glint matched his smile. "Some men tattoo a woman's name on their body, you gave me this scar. Besides it's one of several now. Comes with the job."

"Not funny." Enjoying the scent of a men's cologne he called Aramis, she went to work learning the places of the others. Joe had once had shoulder surgery, he had a scar where his appendix had been, and he'd suffered visible trauma to his left hip and right knee. I'll feel bad about it forever," she said.

"I won't. Every time I look at it, I'll proudly acknowledge that the little hellion who did it turned out to be a remarkable woman. By the way, I sure hope you're through exploring down there. Come here, you." Pulling her on top of him, he brought her close for another kiss, where Mel did her best to show Joe what he meant to her.

Afterwards, Mel drifted off to sleep, smiling.

Morning, however, had a way of forcing reality. She opened her eyes, immediately missing Joe's touch and the comforting arms that had held her all night. He stood by the window seat, staring down at his phone.

She rose up on her elbows. "Problem?"

He shook his head. "Just got a text. Sorry, didn't mean to wake you. Go back to sleep."

Even in the early dawn, she could see the downturn of his mouth. Ready to take his advice, she turned onto her side, but already she felt the distance of the last few days.

"Joe? What is it? Can I help?"

He lifted his head to look at her. "Honey, I wish you could. It's a message from Chief Gallegos. I've been asked to appear in front of an oral review board today.

Wide awake now, she sat up, propped her back against the headboard and tugged the blankets over her breasts. As she sucked in air, all she could think of was that damned Bruce Bennett. *We were just talking about you, Mrs. Norris.* She released her breath and swallowed. "Does it have something to do with me?"

"I'm being considered for a promotion."

Suddenly, her stomach knotted and she couldn't find air. As if the gulley separating them wasn't already wide enough, the prospect of a future with him grew even bleaker. "That's terrific, Joe. Congratulations."

He rounded the bed. She moved over to make room. "It's not a done deal," he said, sitting beside her. "I'm up against another lieutenant with equally impressive credentials and backing."

"If they have any sense, they'll choose you. You've worked hard. I know how much this means to you."

"Melanie—"

"I know what you're going to say."

"You do." Peppered with sarcasm, his tone wasn't a question.

"We can't see each other anymore."

"I was going to say, 'It'll be tough.'"

Her throat hurt now, but as she'd fought to do since he'd walked in the door, she kept the damn tears at bay. "If you want this promotion, Joe, and you do, we'll end this thing right now. An association with me will hurt your career."

"How do you know?"

The shock in his voice only confirmed what she'd put together in the last few minutes. That day in his office, Bennett hadn't come to complain she was bad news. The D.A. had come to warn Joe he risked a promotion by his involvement with her.

Shaking her head at not seeing it, she inhaled before answering, "It's reasonable to assume that the police department and the Department of Corrections have similar policies."

"I imagine they do."

Her throat burned so badly now, it threatened to close. It was time to broach a subject she'd rarely shared. But she had to impress upon him how foolish he'd be to pursue her. "When Carl and I had been married a year, he was up for promotion. We were thrilled. It would mean more money, more desirable shifts, and put him on the fast track for further advancement. That was the first time he was overlooked."

"The first time?"

"We learned his supervisors had blackballed him because of me and my criminal conviction." She worked a thread loose on the bedspread. "After everything Carl had done for me, it nearly destroyed me to see him so disappointed. So, I asked for a divorce."

"You thought it was because of you?"

"There was no thinking about it." Mel yanked out the string. "It *was* because of me."

Frowning, Joe's gaze traveled from it to her face. "Obviously, the divorce never happened."

"Carl refused, and that was the end to it."

"Sounds like he was a terrific man. Wish I could be more like him."

"You already are." Overwhelmed with the need to touch him, Mel stopped herself. "But that's the last thing I want from you. If Carl hadn't gotten sick, he would have come to resent me. I couldn't bear that from you."

"I've wanted to talk to you about this. Turns out you already knew."

Still, she hadn't seen coming. After all she'd been through in this life, how could she have been so naïve? Maybe because he'd achieved a high rank already, she thought him immune.

"I don't deal in fantasy, Joe. You owe it to yourself to earn this promotion. And to get it, we have to stay away from each other." Amazed that she could keep her voice even when she was dying inside, she held his gaze.

It was Joe who looked away. "And if *I* don't want this, Melanie. Do *I* have a goddamned say?"

The tears she'd been holding released in an onslaught. She wiped them away as fast as they poured out. "I've already given you an external scar," she said, staring down at his arm.

"If you care about me, you won't make me responsible for your internal ones."

Chapter Thirty-six

On Christmas Eve, Drake received a text message from Michael Brown, aka "Breakneck", saying he'd found Melanie. Not only did this get Drake one step closer to fulfilling his fifteen-year-old ambition of killing the bitch, it also meant that Brown wouldn't die anytime soon.

As he drove his Jeep toward Brown's part-time computer repair job, Drake smiled. The first real smile he could remember. By helping Ramirez dispose of Sanchez's body, Drake had gone from bottom-feeder of the organization to managing partner. And now that he knew the gang leader's entire scheme, Drake had a new admiration for the ex-con who'd shared the adjoining cell.

Ramirez had no intention of splitting the bank proceeds with the others. While the gang provided a diversion by hitting gas stations and liquor stores around the city, Ramirez and Drake would be taking the bank. There was one more thing that made Drake happy. Ramirez finally agreed they'd scope out a different institution than Liberty National Bank.

The plan would involve several stolen cars and a meeting place. Only when the gang leader and Drake completed their part of the heist, they'd be no-shows at the appointed rendezvous. With the cops chasing their tails, and no honor among thieves, he and Ramirez would head south with the loot. They'd get away from the murders they'd committed, then catch a plane to South America, compliments of Maria's flight passes.

Hard to believe Drake had fallen for her. Eventually, they'd have to tell her brother, because she planned to join Drake often. He'd enjoy a good lay and a great lifestyle.

For now, though, there was still Melanie Norris to take care of.

Drake slowed his vehicle before turning into the shopping center off Union, having had no trouble finding Brown's place of employment. Every storefront held "for lease" signs in the window, except for the mom-and-pop operation Brown worked for. Drake glanced at his watch. Brown was set to get off in ten minutes, which left Drake time to handle another project weighing on his mind. He parked next to Brown's piece of shit El Camino, stretched out his legs and shoved his hands in his jean pocket. After removing his prepaid cell phone, he located his contact information from his wallet, punched in the ten-digit numbers and waited for the call to go through.

"Yeah?" A female voice that sounded like its owner had a two-pack-a-

day habit answered.

Drake held the phone away from his ear, compared it with the handwritten note and found it correct. It had been a couple of weeks since he'd checked in with the junkie, Rander. Drake wanted an update on his brother's disposal.

"I'm looking for Rander," Drake said. "He around?"

"He ain't here," she said. "Who's this? Oh, wait, I see him. He's downstairs. Hold on."

Drake ground his back teeth, listening to what sounded like a window sliding up, followed by hacking and the woman's grating voice. "Jay. Get your ass up here. Somebody's on the phone."

Damn. Drake could read the signs already. Rander had been doing squat toward getting rid of Adam. Drake listened as Rander squabbled with the bimbo before he came on the line. "Hello."

"Rander. Don't you fucking say my name. Do you know who this is?"

"I do. Hey, I was going to call you later. Where are you?"

"Out of the country. Listen to me. Get out of there, away from that hacking dog, and call me back. You talk about our deal in front of anybody, they'll have to fish your body out of the river."

Drake disconnected, seething at the imbeciles he had to deal with.

Five minutes later, his phone rang.

"Maxwell, it's me. I swear I'm alone, and I ain't told nobody, man."

"Any news on our project?"

"Nah, bad news. Your brother's one paranoid stiff." Rander coughed. "Sorry. Bad choice of words, eh? I've been following him, but your bro's never alone. He's always hanging with some big MF."

"Did I ask for excuses? If you can't help me get my hands on my money, fuck off. I'll get somebody who can."

"Whoa. Harsh, dude. Who says I'm not doing it? But, you know, it might move things along if you sent me some dough beforehand."

"What, so you can piss it up your veins? No way. Deal's off. I got me a guy who's eager to earn the five grand I promised you. And I can't pay him until I get my hands on my inheritance, so—"

"Maxwell, no. Wait. I'll handle it. Swear, man. Don't be going and hiring nobody else."

Drake gritted his teeth and lifted his gaze to the ceiling. "You've got one week. If Adam isn't dead by then, I hire my other contact."

Drake snapped the phone shut. *What a fucking loser.* Why couldn't he find somebody reliable?

Just then, the lights in the repair shop went off, and Brown walked out. Five seconds later, he sat beside Drake in the Jeep, rubbing his hands over the dashboard's heating vent. "Took some time," Brown said, "but I tracked her down. You'd never have found her in Pueblo. She works right here in the Springs, in a shop called Pinnacle Creations."

Drake gripped the steering wheel. "But I remember seeing that name in the Pueblo phonebook."

"Yeah, that's what screwed me up, too," Brown said. "But when I called the south shop, they said she worked up north. That's when everything fell into place." Brown grinned. "Get ready to pay me that bonus. You said before Christmas. The broad you're sweet on is Pinnacle's store manager. When I called, they'd told me she'd gone to the bank."

"Bank." Drake squinted, never taking his eyes off Brown. "Which one? Did they say?"

"Nope."

Flexing his fingers, Drake prepared to yank out Brown's brain via his greasy ponytail.

Brown saved himself by adding, "So I waited, called back and pretended to be a telemarketer. Place was a madhouse, phones ringing and shit. I get their delivery girl this time, a real chatterbox—turned out to be the owner's niece. I asked if they were happy with their current bank, and she said she thought so."

Drake, who couldn't care less about the details, repeated, "Did she say which one?"

"Yeah, she did, Max." Brown held out his greedy palm. "But I'll take my money first."

Drake smirked. Maybe there was something to this shit called holiday spirit, because he didn't even feel like wasting the guy anymore. Drake pulled out the bills and waited while Brown counted the money.

Satisfied, Brown said, "Assurance Bank."

Processing the information, Drake hesitated. "The first time you called the store and asked for Melanie, and they'd said she'd gone to the bank . . ."

"Yeah?"

"Do you remember what time that was?"

"Sure do. I'd just left work. Five o'clock on the nose."

Chapter Thirty-seven

To the surprise of law enforcement, the holidays came and went with no known interruption from the Chaos Bandits. With the exception of the normal increase in drinking and driving, domestic violence and small time illegal activity, the crime rate stayed relatively low.

As for Joe's oral examination before the board, and his potential promotion, that had gone well, too. The scuttlebutt rumored he was the division's next commander. He refused to let it consume him, however. His superiors would make their decision when they made their decision.

Now that Joe had come to an understanding with Karen, he'd enjoyed their Christmas together, also. Matt had gotten several new video games, a new cell phone and gym shoes, Trish, an I-pod, some too-grownup outfits Joe wasn't sure about, and a new bike awaited her in Chicago.

It also hadn't escaped Joe's notice that Simon had dropped by at the Norris's on the twenty-fifth. And later when Joe drove Matt and Luke to open gym, those two jokesters seemed in great spirits.

But this morning when Joe dropped Karen and Trish at the airport, and he'd kissed his little girl good-bye, it had been Joe who'd suffered the aftereffects of the season.

Arms crossed, he leaned against the briefing room wall and observed Chris Sandoval conducting morning roll call. Cops sat at rectangular tables surrounding the podium in which the sergeant stood. Rookies and veterans alike, the men and women in this room placed their lives on the line as soon as they walked out the precinct door. And they did it for not enough thanks and certainly not enough pay.

"Anything else?" Chris asked.

Officer Bobby Newel shook his head, then met the several pairs of eyes in the room. "Guess that'd be me. Me and Gomez had a situation last night in the E.R. A prisoner got the drop on us. Pulled a blade out of his drawers."

The room erupted in murmurs, and Chris held up his hands for silence. "Did you pat down the individual?"

Newel stared at his hands. "Yes, sir. Obviously, not well enough. He was coming off meth, and we had him face down on the table so the doc could examine him. Doc told us to uncuff him. We thought the guy was comatose, but he came up swinging. He must have had the knife tucked between his balls."

No one laughed and certainly no one ridiculed. This was a mistake every cop faced at various times in his career.

"I just wanted to share so no one makes the mistake we did," Newel said.

"Appreciate you mentioning it." Joe moved away from the wall. "You could've kept the incident quiet, Bobby. Search these people, ladies and gentlemen. They can and will get the jump on you if you give them the opportunity."

Joe left the briefing, not pausing as he normally did to confer with his second in command. Talk wasn't on his agenda these days. Hell, nothing was. With Mel out of his life, the only thing he wanted was his career back on track. He'd given up someone special to earn this promotion; the sacrifice had damn well better be worth it.

Melanie. Why hadn't he just stayed away? Did he have to make love to her? *I'll be just a blip on your radar.* Maybe she was right. She wasn't the only woman on the planet. He had no doubt he'd get over her—eventually. *Keep your mind on your business, Crandall.*

In the early morning hours, cops had apprehended the man suspected of torching his house several days before Christmas, risking his children and murdering his wife. Joe drove the short distance to the courthouse to sit in on the McPherson arraignment.

Joe jogged up the courthouse steps and met Marianne Bennett in passing.

"Joe?" A prominent Colorado Springs neurosurgeon, and also the wife of the district attorney, she shortened her strides. "Oh my gosh, it is you, isn't it?"

He kissed her cheek and gave her a quick hug. "Afraid so. Warts and all."

"Where?" She looked him up and down, grinning. "Good grief, how long has it been?"

"Long time," Joe replied. Ordinarily being polite to the redhead, who combined caring and intelligence in a nice little package, wouldn't have been a challenge. Not so today. "What are you doing here?"

"I was summoned for jury duty."

"You?" He laughed. "I bet there wasn't a public defender within a ten-mile radius who wanted you on his panel."

Marianne held out her palms. "Hence, why I'm standing on the outside while the other prospective jurors are still on the inside." She screwed up her mouth. "I feel so unwanted."

"If you say so," Joe said.

Her expression turned serious. "Bruce mentioned he'd seen you a couple of times in the last few months." She placed a hand on Joe's arm. "For what it's worth, he's really behind you in this commander business."

Joe focused on the city auditorium across the street. "I know he is."

"He also mentioned you're involved with a woman."

At the mention of Melanie, anger curdled Joe's insides. "Past tense. Next time you two discuss my personal life, tell Bruce that, will you?"

Marianne sighed. "He said you were upset. You're like a brother to Bruce, you know that. You two came through the ranks together. Believe it or not, he thinks the system is grossly unfair, and that the woman you care for genuinely seems like a good person."

Before he rudely brought up the point that the woman had a name, Joe said, "Hey, good or bad, it's the system. We work within it. Good to see you, Marianne." Hugging her briefly, he said, "Better luck next time with jury duty."

"Ha ha," Marianne said, and waved good-bye.

Joe walked into the courthouse, bypassing the metal detectors. He had the record, the credentials, votes of confidence from peers and subordinates and the support of the district attorney. Combined, these factors all but guaranteed him the next level in law enforcement.

He was one lucky cop.

Images of Melanie flashed through his brain as Joe entered Division Room Four. So with so much going for him, why wasn't he smiling?

On the west side of town, things weren't going much better for Mel. With Aaron visiting family in New York, she cleared the shelves of Christmas, Hanukah and seasonal items and prepared to mark them down. The best way to overcome heartbreak, she reasoned, was to throw herself into the things going right, namely, Luke and Pinnacle Creations.

According to Aaron, they had thirty days to reduce inventory, then gear up for Valentine's Day. Thanks to holidays and special occasions, the floral industry never ended. Unlike relationships.

Mel shook her head, trying her best to banish the thoughts that kept popping up from nowhere. Praying for customers to enter the shop and keep her mind occupied, she dusted the glass partitions. She and Joe had barely had time to repair their relationship before it ended.

Still, she'd made the right decision. Mel had been down this path with Carl before. He'd sacrificed his career for Mel. She couldn't ask it of Joe.

Just because it was over, however, didn't erase the memory of his kiss. Even now she craved his touch. In the lovemaking department, he'd been wonderfully considerate—putting her needs first. Even to the point of carrying protection in his wallet.

Mel splayed a palm over her stomach. What would it be like to have a baby? During her marriage, birth-control had never been an issue. Carl's illness had left him sterile.

She sprayed the shelf with glass cleaner. Would Carl have liked Joe? She suspected he would have. The two were alike in a lot of ways. But in one important way, oh so different.

She let out a groan just as Chloe came in from the storeroom.

"What's wrong?"

"Nothing." Mel's face went hot. "I broke a nail."

"Uh-huh." Her co-worker stared at her. "Well, it's just you and me. I did like you said and sent everybody home." Chloe glanced around. "Who would've thought after last week's rush it would be so slow?"

Mel came to her feet and dusted off her knees. "Gives us time to whip this place into shape."

Chloe saluted. "Aye, aye, Captain. Ready when you are. So which nail did you break?"

"Excuse me?"

"You said you broke a nail. Which one?"

Placing a recently polished hand behind her back, Mel said, "Why do you care?"

"I had a broken nail once. I picked up the phone and called him."

Mel rounded the counter toward the cash register. The day's receipts were abysmal, and she considered locking the little cash they'd collected in the safe to make a larger deposit tomorrow. "What on earth are you talking about?"

"Oh, I think you know exactly what I'm talking about. You're never this out of sorts. You've been thinking about Joe all day. He's really put you in a foul mood."

Ignoring Chloe, Mel reached for the calculator.

"Look, I don't know what happened between you two, but I was there last week. I saw the way he looked at you. If that man's not in love, he's nearing the border. Mel, *call* him."

"Stay out of this, Chloe."

"All right. But I know what's going on here."

Mel's fingers stumbled over the calculator keys, forcing her to start over. "What's that?"

"You're feeling guilty."

"About?"

"About having feelings for someone else. Carl's dead, and you think it's too soon to fall in love."

Mel frowned. Oh, she felt guilt, all right. But not in the way Chloe was thinking. She'd cared deeply for Carl, but she'd never been *in love* with him. She knew now that theirs had been a marriage of convenience and not a union of love. She'd settled. And that was a secret she'd take to her grave. She owed it to Luke for him to believe she'd loved his father with every inch of her being.

"I'm right, aren't I?" Chloe asked.

Mel nodded. "So give it a rest, huh, Chloe?"

"Whatever you say. But maybe in a few months—"

"No." Mel needed to end her friend's delusions once and for all. "Not even in a few months. Joe Crandall is a police lieutenant on his way up, and I'm a—a . . ."

"You're a what?" Chloe frowned.

An ex-con. Oh, God, she'd almost blurted it out.

"Way out of his league." She gave Chloe a pleading look. "It would be foolish for me to believe we could ever be together. So, please, back off."

Stung, her co-worker stared at her. Mel couldn't bear the fact that she'd hurt Chloe. Skinny deposit or not, Aaron didn't like leaving cash in the store overnight, and while she was out, she'd get her emotions under control, then find a way to make it up to Chloe. "I'll be back," Mel said. "I'm going to the bank."

Chapter Thirty-eight

Brown's tip that Melanie managed a shop, and went to the bank on the store's behalf, was the only thing that had kept her alive during the holiday weekend. The Monday after Christmas, however, businesses reopened, and her time was up.

Drake gripped the Jeep's steering wheel as his heart thundered like a racehorse coming down the stretch. Today, whether the bitch had her affairs in order or not, she was leaving this world. The only question was, how was he supposed to survive the next eight hours? His entire day would be the shits. He couldn't afford witnesses, which meant the safest options were to grab her at either the bank when she made a deposit or at her shop after it closed at six p.m. Never mind that the waiting was killing him.

Now that he knew where she worked, he found it nearly impossible to stay away. But if he got near Pinnacle Creations, the urge to walk in and blow her head off would be too great. Already, he was having trouble tearing his gaze from the passenger seat and the map beside him. He ran a hand over the huge red X he'd circled, which planted a bulls-eye on the shop's location. The diagram sat beside him taunting and daring.

It's time. What are you waiting for? What if she gets away? Do it now.

He offset the maddening craving, by picturing himself taking on four of Centennial's guards. In his psyche, he kicked their asses, but in the end, they overpowered him, strapped him to a gurney and jabbed a lethal injection into his veins.

Fear of going back to prison and dying obviously trumped rage. Wiping sweat from his brow, he leaned back in the driver's seat, leveled his breathing, until once again he was just another businessman. Still, as uncomfortable as it was thinking about all of this, it didn't stop him from recognizing that Melanie had done him a favor. Maybe he'd thank her before he dumped her lifeless body and left her for the maggots and magpies. Brown's mention of Assurance Bank had provided Drake with an alternative hit. And by all indications, it was a perfect choice.

According to the map, there were three possible escape routes from Assurance Bank, one with a straight shot to the interstate, the others more convoluted. From what he could tell, though, even if the cops pursued and forced Ramirez and Drake to take side streets, all intersected with I-25.

He spent the morning learning the various routes. But once satisfied he could maneuver them, hours remained before he could set his plans for

Melanie in motion. He returned to the bank. Feeling a strain behind his eyes, he stared once more at the map. Was it his imagination or was that X on the map growing larger and bleeding redder?

It's time. What are you waiting for? What if she gets away? Do it now.

He squeezed his eyes shut, overwhelmed by the impulses ordering him to go to Pinnacle Creations under the guise of *just one look.*

Jesus. Even his own mind was trying to turn on him. He pounded the steering wheel, and screamed, "Shut the fuck up!" Then swallowing, he scanned his position in the bank's outer parking lot to ensure no one had been watching.

Maybe it'd been better when he *couldn't* find her. Had Melanie's betrayal, and too much time to think it over, robbed him of his sanity? If he didn't harness this fury, just as he'd lost it with Ropes and Sanchez, Drake could destroy weeks of careful planning.

Needing a distraction, he whipped out his phone. If anyone could save him from himself, Maria could.

By four o'clock that afternoon, she'd done just that—helped him screw his head back on straight, among other things. He left her at the home of another flight attendant, who was off traveling. Maria herself would be flying out in a couple of hours, and he'd miss her. But, truthfully, with murder the only thing on his mind, she couldn't have picked a better time to split for a while.

Dressed in his tailored slacks, dress shirt and a sports coat, Drake adjusted his sunglasses. He strode from the Jeep and walked inside ready to case the place and inhale the smell of money.

The lobby, displaying the gold-lettered logo, *Your Financial ASSURANCE Comes First,* had the typical bank layout. A look of success, with customer service desks and transaction counters out front, the president and vice presidents behind glass partitions thumbing their noses at the all the have-nots. Drake had seen this set up so much recently, he could visualize it in his sleep.

But who gave a fuck about all of this?

What he wanted to see were the teller cages. Venturing farther inside, he counted six in the lobby, while two tellers worked the drive up. He'd yet to see a guard, which meant that management feared the liability issues that came with one ending up dead, and had instead equipped each station with panic alarms.

He picked up a flyer and pretended to read, while strategizing which teller to approach. As he scanned the six available, he looked for one with a disability, one who was young, or petite, perhaps even pregnant. Drake would watch her hands as he slid a little love note her way, saying that if she went for the alarm or acted unnatural, he'd make her face disappear. Ramirez would stand in the back of the lobby, ready to fire into the ceiling—or worse—should anyone foolishly decide to get brave.

Just then a middle-aged broad, who wore the hoity-toity look of his mother, appeared to notice him and approached. Drake stiffened until he realized by her look of approval, she too believed custom clothes and forty-dollar haircut made the man.

"Good afternoon," she said. "I'm Dorothy Hayward, manager of bank operations. Is there some way I can help you, sir?"

Sir. After being disrespected for fifteen years, he couldn't hear it enough. He smiled, using an expression that felt more natural with each passing day. "Maybe so. Kent Jackson. My wife and I just moved to the Springs, and we've been shopping banks." Getting into the brilliant performance, and as if he'd ever let a woman tell him what to do, Drake shook his head. "But she can't make up her mind and I have accounts to transfer."

The dumb bimbo reacted like a bloodhound catching a scent. "Well, if there's one thing Assurance prides itself on, Mr. Jackson, it's customer service. Would you like to join me at my desk while I explain our programs?"

This time the smile that spread over his face was no act. "Lead the way, Ms. Hayward. That's what I'm here for, to learn the workings of your bank."

While Dorothy rambled on about low interest loans, competitive money markets, online banking and other services he couldn't give a rat's ass about, he crossed one leg over his knee, taking in the security cameras and the two existing exits. He also pinpointed the direction of the vault, while keeping an eye on the customers coming and going.

The bank manager all but gave him a tour, and he suspected she would if he asked. Still, he'd found it—the place he and Ramirez would strike in less than a week. Drake didn't want to arouse suspicion. At five minutes till five, the lobby was about to close. If Melanie had used the drive-thru, then he'd missed her completely. It was time to switch to plan B, and wait for her to leave Pinnacle Creations after hours.

The inner voices were ruthless now, shouting over the windbag's spiel that he'd missed his chance. His right hand, which he'd been resting on his knee, started to shake. He squeezed it tight, ready to blow the manager off, when an exiting bank customer held the door open.

And then she walked in.

Fifteen years of hate slammed into Drake. Dumbstruck, he almost locked gazes with Melanie as she passed by, but at the last moment, he had the presence of mind to turn his head.

"So Mr. Jackson, if there's nothing else?" Dorothy said.

He reached inside his sports coat, ready to chuck it all.

"Mr. Jackson?" Dorothy said louder. "Is there something else?"

Drake came to his feet, as the whore who'd taken everything from him joked with some teller. Tossing the banking pamphlets onto the manager's desk, a low growl made its way up his throat. "Didn't you hear what I said? My ol' lady makes the fucking decisions. Woman's got me by the balls."

Dorothy's face went pasty white. If Drake weren't so livid, he might've laughed. But fifteen years ago, the woman talking to the teller had wiped away his sense of humor. It was time to get it back. Drake walked out of the building to wait.

Chapter Thirty-nine

Her emotions more settled, Mel stopped at Starbucks on her way back from the bank. She ordered two coffee mochas and returned to the shop. This close to rush hour, traffic was wild on I-25, but it didn't matter, she was in no particular hurry.

She drove into the lot, and against store policy parked under a tree, close to the shop. With no customers coming and going, it wasn't like she was taking anyone's space. As she stepped inside, the bell tinkled overhead and Chloe looked up. She'd cleared the remaining shelves and was in a glass-cleaning frenzy.

Mel cleared her throat, to which her friend simply glanced sideways at Mel and returned to her polishing. Mel winced. She deserved the cold shoulder and more. "I brought you a peace offering, Chloe," she said, moving toward her kneeling co-worker. "I was awful to you. I am out of sorts over Joe and I took it out on you. Forgive me?"

Chloe rose and dusted off her knees. Accepting the drink, she said, "If that's what I think it is, I'll forgive you anything. I'm sorry, too, Mel. Your personal life is none of my business."

Relieved the awkwardness was over between them, Mel surveyed the store. "Wow, you made progress while I was gone."

Chloe blew a blond strand out of her eyes and shrugged. "Well, it wasn't like customers were beating down the door. By the way, you forgot your cell phone again."

Mel groaned. In Cañon City, she'd never needed one. She kept forgetting to take it with her when she went out.

Winking, Chloe said, "Lucky for you, I can't mind my own business. Don't worry. I answered it. Luke called. There's some kind of coach's meeting, so practice will be over early. He said it's your turn to pick up."

"What time?"

"Six-thirty."

Thirty minutes from now. "Thanks, Chloe. I'll close up shop if you want to head out."

"You're sure?"

"Positive. After I pick up the guys, I'm going home to soak in a tub."

Chloe gathered her belongings and said, "Sounds grand. See you tomorrow."

Mel saw Chloe to the door, then turned the lock and flipped the closed sign. She'd just drawn the shade when three rapid taps sounded on the glass.

Unlocking the door, she grinned, "What'd you forget?"

But it wasn't her friend. A man sporting the look of Pinnacle Designs' wealthy customers stood at the door.

"Oh. Sorry. I thought you were someone else." Couldn't he read the sign? Ordinarily, she'd let him in, complete a rush order and hope for repeat business. But with little notice that practice had ended early again, she had to get to Coronado. Hiding her irritation, Mel said, "We're closed, sir."

It was then that she settled fully on his features. And when he smiled, she felt the blood drain from her face.

"It's been a while, Melanie."

Before she could respond, he shoved her. She flew backwards, striking the back of her head as she crashed against the counter. Instantly nauseated, she tasted bile. Reeling, she tried to rise from the floor, but as dizziness swamped her, she went down again.

He seemed bigger than she remembered. Prison had transformed a lanky young man into a terrifying wall of muscle. He relocked the door, drew out a small gun and advanced on her. "Closed, huh?" He yanked her upright. Then wrapping her in a python-like crush, he jammed the weapon against her temple. "Not to me, bitch, you're never closed. In fact, I'd say, you're just about to open."

Mel had been harangued by dreams over the years. She willed herself to wake up from this one. But dear God, this wasn't a nightmare. Drake Maxwell had found her.

Chapter Forty

With Mel picking up the boys, Joe used the extra time to go through his backlog of paperwork. A few days off and he was seriously behind. He felt a moment's guilt about reverting to his old ways and neglecting his son.

No doubt Mel would object. But then objections were meant to be one-sided. She certainly hadn't given him any choice when she made the decision to end things between them. And although Joe hated the ruling, it didn't mean he couldn't admit it was a wise one.

Melanie would never take out her frustrations on Matt, Joe knew that much. His son and Luke would stay friends. As for Joe and Mel, they'd become passing acquaintances.

Acquaintances. Joe grabbed a pencil and snapped it in two. When it came to Melanie, an occasional hello was the last thing he wanted.

His cell phone rang, pulling him from his funk. "Crandall."

"Dad, hey. Are you picking up, or is Mrs. Norris?"

"It's Mel's turn, why?"

"She's not here yet."

"Did she know about the coach's meeting?"

"I don't know. Luke left a message with someone from her work."

Great. Who knew what kind of mix-up she'd received second hand. "Who'd Luke leave the message with?"

"Beats me."

"Was it Aaron?"

"I don't know, Dad. *Jesus.*"

"Watch your mouth and answer my question."

Matt let out a huff. "They said she was at the bank. Some lady took the message. Look, she's twenty minutes late, and Riley said he'd give us a ride. Is it cool if we go with him?"

"Sure. But try Mrs. Norris again in case she's on her way. I'm leaving here in a few minutes. See you at home."

At home, a short while later, Joe found Matt taking a frozen pizza out of a box. "Luke at his house?"

The boy nodded.

"You get hold of Mrs. Norris?"

"Not yet."

Joe glanced at his watch. Seven thirty on the nose. Normally, practice ended at eight. She obviously didn't get the message about the coach's meeting. Joe shook his head. If she was out shopping, sticking to the original schedule, and went to the school, she wouldn't be happy that no one was there to meet her.

His first thought was to drive to Coronado and be there when she arrived. He nixed that idea as soon as it formed. She'd made her position clear.

Respecting her wishes, Joe picked up the phone and tried her again.

Chapter Forty-one

Drake turned off the lights and pushed Mel into the rear of the store. The back of her head was splitting. Close to retching, she sought refuge against a floral refrigerator and slumped to the floor.

Watching him pace, she tried to swallow, but fear dried her throat. Her lungs couldn't collect enough air, and despite the cool workroom, sweat soaked her body.

Think, Mel, think.

It was as though the madman had read her thoughts. He stopped pacing, and with a glassy-eyed leer, lowered himself to her level. "Ah, did I hurt you?" Before she could respond, he added, "Did it feel anything like jumping from a semi to escape a trucker who left your bleeding body to rot?"

Oh, God. "Drake, listen to me." The words felt like they'd come from outside her body.

He pressed the gun to her cheek. "No. You listen to *me*. Know what I thought about night after night in that cell? I thought how I'd tried to help you, how for once in my life I gave a damn, and look how you repaid me."

"I *was* grateful." Mel held out her hands. "But you wanted to kill that poor clerk simply for earning a living. I—I had to stop you. What do you want? Money? For me to beg?"

A snarl formed over his lips, and the man she'd once considered stage handsome became a creature grotesque and ugly. "What do I want? Now that's a loaded question. Man, look at you all cleaned up. Fucking *hot*."

She turned away. But from her peripheral vision, she saw him lift his shirt to reveal teardrop prison tattoos and a scar that ran across his torso. He wore three, which if she recalled correctly meant one for every five years he'd been in prison.

He pointed to the scar. "Know what this is?"

She didn't meet his gaze, nor did she answer.

He grabbed her chin and forced her to look at him. "I asked you a question."

Her heart stuttered. "What is it?"

"It's from the *first* time I got shanked. I was in the shower, and a gang introduced me to the system. While they held me down and stuck me, the guards heard me screaming. Know what they did?"

She shook her head desperately.

"*Nothing*," Drake replied. "Know who I blamed?"

"The gang members?" She kept her voice soft as she attempted to reason.

He laughed. "Nice try. *You*. I blamed you."

"Remember how you said your friends called you Mel?" He positioned the gun at her neck. "I've thought about that a lot over the years, *Melanie*. You said we were friends. I took care of you, saved you from being raped, God knows what else."

She flinched.

"Ah, I'm scaring you." He moved the gun downward and stroked the barrel over her breast. "Very nice. Maybe that trucker had the right idea, after all."

She closed her eyes.

"I should have fucked your brains out and left you half-dead for the coyotes and scorpions to finish off."

Opening her eyes, she summoned anger to counteract fear. She couldn't let this bastard win. She ordered her mind to focus. Her car. It was parked out front. The boys. She was overdue to pick them up. Surely they were concerned by now. Her thoughts turned to Joe. Maybe Luke had already called him. Oh, no, Luke. This would destroy him.

Drake reached for her just as her cell phone rang in the display area. It was tucked in a drawer below the cash register.

"What's that?" He glanced toward the front of the store.

"My phone."

"Who's calling you?"

"My husband." Her tongue tripped over the lie.

"You got married again? So soon?"

Her panic deepened. Exactly how much did he know about her?

"Figures. A bitch like you wouldn't wait to find another meal ticket. Too bad. The groom's about to become a widower."

Relieved that he'd bought her lie, Mel said, "I should answer it. If I don't, he'll come looking for me. He may already be on his way."

"If he shows up, he's dead." Drake jerked her to her feet.

She stumbled as he dragged her to the display area. By the time they reached the counter, the phone had stopped ringing. Drake flipped it open. Five voice mails had been left on the phone, the last one from Joe. Her hopes surged. If she could somehow call, talk to him as a wife would a husband, it would tip him off that she was in trouble. "Let me call him back so he doesn't come looking for me."

"Yeah, like I'd ever trust you again." He dropped the phone on the floor, then with the heel of his boot, stomped down on her lifeline. "You won't be leaving hints for anyone. Hope you said good-bye to the hubby this morning 'cause you'll never see him again."

Mel stared at the shattered phone. Frantic, she wracked her brain for a means of escape. Nearby businesses had already closed. Drake and the counter stood between her and the front door. If she made a break for it, and tried for the rear exit she risked a bullet in her back.

She didn't like the wild look and sense of finality in his eyes. Eyeing the clock, she noted the time read seven-thirty-five. *Oh, Joe, forget what I said. I need you.*

Reasoning with Drake was useless, but she had to try. "If you kill me, this time you'll be executed. Do you want that? You're free now. I swear, if you let me go, I won't say a word."

He reached under the counter and grabbed her purse. "After all this time I've waited to get my hands on you, you think I'd let you go now?"

He scanned the room and kicked her inoperable phone under the counter. Then the angry look seeped from his face, replaced by a sneer. "Come here, little girl."

Shaking violently, she said, "No."

Drake took a step toward her, raised his weapon. "Say good-bye, Melanie."

She emitted a blood curdling scream.

Chapter Forty-two

At eight, Joe disregarded his promise to Melanie and circled Coronado's parking lot in search of her Corolla. When he didn't find it, nervous energy pulsed through him. Good God, where was she?

He told himself not to panic. He'd feel ridiculous when she appeared and he'd been frantic for nothing. But as the minutes ticked by, so did his distress. Although he'd always empathized with parents and people searching for loved ones, he had a new appreciation for what they went through.

At ten after eight, his cell phone rang. *Finally.* He released the air from his lungs. But it wasn't Mel. The caller was Matt, and the butterflies in Joe's stomach dropped like stones. "Yeah, Matt, what is it?"

"Dad. Luke's here." Matt's voice was low, agitated. "He's in the kitchen and he's freaking out. His mom's not home, there's no answer on her cell or at the shop. Is she there?"

Willing her car to materialize, Joe scanned the dark parking lot a final time. "No, son, she's not."

"He keeps blabbering about some dude named Maxwell. What's he talking about, Dad?"

Swallowing over the lump in his throat, Matt's mention of the ex-con made Joe's fear tangible. "Someone who may be after her. We don't know for sure. I should've told you. I was respecting her privacy."

Joe's gut clenched. With the Givens' incident turning out to be nothing, along with Mel moving her stuff into storage and getting an alarm, Joe'd grown complacent.

"Matt," he continued. "I'm heading to the shop. You boys stay together and *stay put.* Set the alarm. To be on the safe side, I'm going to order a unit to patrol the neighborhood."

Matt lowered his voice. "You think this Maxwell creep's got her?"

"I don't know what to think," Joe replied. "I don't care how you do it, but keep Luke under control. Beat the hell out of the punching bag, race up the stairs a thousand times, but don't let him fly off half-cocked."

"Okay," Matt said uncertainly.

Hitting his lights, Joe tore out of the high school parking lot. "We're probably overreacting. I'll wager she's just fine."

Joe ordered two squad cars, one to monitor his neighborhood and one for back-up at Melanie's place of employment. He negotiated the twenty minute drive in ten and swung into the parking lot. At the sight of Mel's white Corolla, his heart thundered in his chest.

God, I know I don't pray enough, but this isn't for me. Please, keep her safe.

He drew his Glock as a squad car with flashing lights on silent response raced into the parking lot, along with another cruiser that must've been in the vicinity behind it. He directed the scurrying cops via hand signals, then tried the door. Ready to break the glass if need be, he found it unnecessary. The store stood in pitch black surroundings, and the door was unlocked.

His system on turbo-charge, he entered the store. He signaled one cop to take the showroom, the other to secure the perimeter. Joe raised his weapon and strode to the storeroom. The night was cold; it might as well have been a heat wave. As adrenaline rushed through his system, he forced himself to prepare for what he might find.

When every inch of the interior had been searched, Joe and the cop on the inside rendezvoused. "All clear," Joe said, as he flipped on the store's lights at the same time he released his breath.

"Think this place was robbed, sir?" the officer asked, taking in the large inventory of boxes on the floor. A bottle of glass cleaner lay on the floor with paper towels resting on a nearby shelf.

"More like someone was cleaning," Joe said. Intermingled with floral scents, the place gave off the dissipating smell of ammonia.

The cop on the outside stood in the door. "No cars out back, and we're running the plates on the 2007 white Toyota Corolla out front."

"Unnecessary to run plates," Joe said. "It belongs to one of the employees."

"No windows broken and the rear doors are also secured," the exterior cop added.

Quelling panic and forcing objectivity, Joe said, "Well, something happened here. Front door's unlocked and the woman who manages the place is gone. Keep a look out. And get a technician over here to dust for prints, and have him dust the Corolla while he's at it."

"Yes, sir."

Joe moved through the shop. In the backroom, he found what must've been her station. A card listing a dental appointment for Luke was tacked to a cork bulletin board as well as a picture of Luke and Matt shooting hoops in the driveway.

Joe's stomach convulsed. He returned to the front area, forcing himself to swallow. He pressed a button on the cash register, it swung open. He found it empty, then recalled Matt's comment that the co-worker said Mel had gone to the bank. He lifted the lightweight compartment that held change. Inside was a work schedule listing the store employees' home phone numbers.

Joe removed the list and exited the building. Reluctant to interfere further in what he suspected was a crime scene, he used the glow from a street light to dial the workers who'd been listed on the schedule for today.

Thirty minutes later, he had an idea what had happened in the hours before closing.

A car drove up, a young woman got out of a Mini Cooper, slammed the door and rushed forward. The patrolman stopped her. "Sorry, ma'am. You can't go in there."

She attempted to sidestep the man two times her size. "Joe. Lt. Crandall, it's me, Chloe. From the other night? Karlee's going-away party? Remember?"

A burst of hope shot through him. Joe nodded to the patrolman to let her pass. He met her halfway. "Chloe, thanks for coming."

"When my dad said you'd called from the shop, I came straight over. What's wrong? Have we been robbed?"

"I don't think so. Did you see Melanie this afternoon?"

She gaped at Joe. "Mel? Sure. I was with her a short time before we closed. It was dead, so she'd already sent everybody else home. Why? What's wrong? Where is she?"

Chloe's story confirmed what his phone calls to three other employees had said. She'd given them time off. "You left her alone?"

Chloe frowned. "Well, yeah, I mean, if it's slow the managers send us home. We work in a safe area. Aaron or Karlee closed all the time by themselves. Now that Mel's manager, it's her job. You're scaring me. Where is she?"

"I don't know, Chloe. Try not to worry. Let's see if we can sort out the facts. Let's go over here, shall we?" He led her to his Crown Vic and opened the rear door to get the flustered woman off her feet. Shaking, she wrapped her coat tight, sitting sideways and planted her feet outside the vehicle.

For the first time all evening, Joe felt the cold. Notebook in hand, he squatted to meet her at eye level. "Did anyone enter the store while you were working?"

"Absolutely no one. We were a little shocked. I mean during the holidays it was wall-to-wall customers, now this."

"Did you see anyone hanging around? A stranger, perhaps?"

"No one. I'm sorry."

"Any phone calls for Mel? Did she seem nervous?"

"Nervous?" Avoiding his gaze, Chloe worked at the hole in her jeans. "No, not nervous, if anything, she was upset."

"Upset?" Joe was grasping for clues and his pulse quickened. "Why's that?"

Chloe sighed. "Screw it. She'll kill me for telling you, but she was upset . . . over you."

"Me."

"Yeah, you. Mel's one of the most even-keeled women I know. She's fun and likes to laugh. Today, you would have thought she was the Wicked Witch of the West."

Joe felt lower than the asphalt he stood on. "You're certain it wasn't some other reason?"

Chloe rolled her eyes. "Her words were something like, 'Lt. Crandall's on his way up and he's way out of my league.' And then when I tried to talk to her about it, she told me to back off."

Shit. Having trouble meeting the pretty blonde's gaze, he removed his card and handed it to her. "Thanks. If you think of anything else, give me a call?"

"Sure." She rose from the back seat, then hesitated. "She's not, you know."

"Excuse me?"

"Out of your league. Whatever you did to make her feel that way, I hope you'll rethink your sorry attitude."

Joe's eyes grew moist and he lifted his gaze to the night. "When I see her again, I'll do just that. You got a key so we can lock this place up when we're through?"

"Yeah." Removing a key from her chain, Chloe said, "Tell Mel to call me when you find her. I won't be able to sleep until I know she's safe."

As the perky young woman walked away, a knot formed in Joe's chest. "That makes two of us, Chloe."

Chapter Forty-three

"Are you out of your whacked-out, *gringo* mind?" Ramirez roared.

When Drake had told Ramirez he'd located a new bank to hit, Ramirez had left Drake to it, then disappeared with his latest squeeze. Carrying a six pack into his sister's house, he'd been in a decent mood until Drake announced that he'd brought home a package.

"One of my rules is no women," Ramirez shouted. "The cops will be all over this. My boys will tear her apart. If my sister was here, she'd have my head and *your* nuts. I can't believe you brought the broad here."

"What'd you want me to do, leave her outside? And your sister's not here, she's on a fucking airplane."

Ramirez's eyes narrowed. "I should cut you into little pieces for knowing that. You're out of control, Max. First Sanchez, now this."

"You did Sanchez," Drake argued.

"*You* pushed the mother into me on your crazy rampage. Dude went berserk, turned on me. It was him or me. We're onto some serious money, Max. Don't blow this. You kidnapped the piece. Get her out of here."

"Not yet. I've thought it through, we can use her."

"I ain't into rape, *hombre*. Know what bros in the joint do to cons who take women and children by force?"

"I've heard," Drake said dryly. "You talk like we're going back. She owes me, Ramirez. She sent me up. I almost killed her tonight." Drake held a thumb and forefinger an inch apart. "I came this close, then thought of a better way. If I shot her, she'd get off too easy. She'd never know."

Ramirez shook his head. "Know what, asshole?"

"What she took from me."

"Damn, Max, you're one screwed-up dick. How are you gonna let her *know?*"

"She's gonna do the bank job."

Ramirez reached for a beer. Twisting the cap, he said, "Say what?"

At Ramirez's confusion, Drake did something he didn't know he could do anymore. He out-and-out grinned. "No shit, man, it's doable. I've been worried about security, and all we have is a couple of minutes to do the job. There's no guard at Assurance Bank, the new place I scoped out today. Each teller pushes a panic button, which alerts an alarm company. Melanie will buy us time. She banks at this place. The tellers know her by name. It's perfect because they'll identify her. And by the time she's in custody, we'll be in a different vehicle and long gone.

"With her prison record, the cops will never believe she had nothing to do with it, and she'll be the one doing time."

"So we just tell her she's gonna do the job for us?" Ramirez scoffed. "She'll walk in and scream her bloody head off. She'll yell for help, tell them she's been kidnapped. Max—"

Hadn't this dude ever heard of Patty Hearst? Drake sighed. "Cool it." He walked to the counter and grabbed Melanie's purse. Tossing it on the table, he said, "She'll do the job, and she'll do it willingly. We'll be waiting outside. We get our hands on the dough, take off and leave her behind."

As he voiced his plan, the scheme became better than a horny dude watching porn. He'd dump her on the Interstate just like the trucker had when she was seventeen. Of course, Drake would kill her if he had to, but sending her back to the pen would be the ultimate revenge.

For the first time, the gang leader seemed to consider it. "I don't know, Max," he said, staring down at the handbag. "What makes you so sure this will work?"

"Leverage, man. Leverage. Our soon-to-be partner has a weakness."

Chapter Forty-four

Mel stirred, awaking to pain. Mind-numbing, head-shattering pain. Arms tied behind her back, ankles bound, duct tape over her mouth, she lay face down on a thin sheet covering a mattress.

Oh, God. Her heart beating wildly, she rolled onto her side. Where was she? From the looks and smell, it appeared to be some kind of a basement. A single light bulb illuminated the dark unfinished space.

To her right, she could make out the edge of an appliance, probably a washer or dryer. From overhead she heard voices. Loud, angry, arguing.

Then everything came back to her. She couldn't count herself lucky to be alive—yet. She was Drake Maxwell's prisoner.

As bile forced its way up her throat, she did her best not to retch. With the tape binding her mouth, she could aspirate. The knots binding her hands, cut into her wrists, and her shoulder blades ached from being kept in such an unnatural position.

She had to get out of here. Her gaze caught on four tiny windows near the ceiling. If by some miracle she could get free, could she climb up there, squeeze through one of them and call for help?

The door above her opened and what sounded like an army of footfalls descended into her version of hell.

Too late.

Bile rose in her throat yet again as the army proved to be Drake and another man. They moved close, Drake holding back, the stranger standing directly over her. He shook his head. "Max, Max, Max, what have you done?"

Mel glared up into the pitch-black eyes of a Hispanic man who wore confidence like his T-shirt and jeans. He wasn't as tall as Drake, but he was fit.

Squatting beside her, he said, "Hello, *amiga.* What can I say? You've made a serious enemy. I extend Max my hospitality, and this is how he repays me. He involves me with a woman he plans to let bleed all over my floor."

Mel squeezed her eyes shut. This guy was just as bad as Drake, toying and menacing.

"Open your eyes, *chica.*"

She obeyed to find he'd drawn a switchblade. Eyes wide, she tried to scream, but any sounds emerged muffled and useless as she struggled to get away.

He rolled his eyes. "See, Max, you've scared her to death." Holding the blade between his straight white teeth, he gathered her by the front of her shirt and pulled her upright. Then, in one quick tug, he ripped the tape from her mouth, untied her ankles and cut the bindings from her wrists.

Slowly, she brought her arms forward and rubbed the feeling back into her hands. "Who are you?" she asked.

"My name's not important. What's important is that you're still alive." He nodded over his shoulder. "But Max, he wants to kill you."

Her unwilling gaze drifted to her arch enemy. Drake stood leaning against the stairs, arms crossed, his mouth pulled into a furious scowl.

She rubbed her still-stinging mouth. "He missed his opportunity."

"Don't be a fool, *chica*. He could have killed you at any time and still may. If I'm not here to stand between the two of you, he will get rid of you."

What was this? A criminal's idea of good cop/bad cop? "You want me to thank you, is that it?"

"It would be a start. Who knows what Max has in store?"

"I'll thank you when you let me go."

"Ah, Max, you didn't tell me she was a spitfire." The stranger reached out to stroke her cheek.

Mel jerked away and he laughed. "*Es, muy linda.*"

Whatever the hell that meant. She couldn't just sit by and play victim. It was time to develop a strategy. "I'm thirsty," she said. "And hungry."

"Of course. What do you think, Max? Should we feed her?"

"Let her starve."

His companion shook his head. "See there, so unfriendly. Max, play nice."

Keeping her face neutral, she studied him. Who was in charge here? Drake, or this man? It didn't matter. Fifteen years ago, she'd sat in a sparse room much like this one. A gray-headed detective tried to be a father figure, to persuade her he was on her side, while the younger one tore the truth to shreds. Guess they didn't know she didn't trust her father. She didn't trust cops, and she damn sure didn't trust these guys.

The Hispanic man held out his hand. "Come with me, *chica*, I'll get you something to eat."

Reluctantly, she took his hand and tried to appear grateful. And with that she steeled her will to survive. *All right, you bastards, let the games begin.*

Chapter Forty-five

Joe had no proof he'd stumbled onto a crime scene.

So when analyst Harriet "Harry" Landau responded to the callout, he was glad to have her experienced set of eyes and know-how. To anyone on the street, Harry could be someone's grandmother. To forty-year veterans, she was a skilled professional; to rookies she was an embarrassing pain in the ass who caught what they missed, often reprimanding a FNG (fucking new guy) for botching a crime scene.

Joe had gone over every inch of the shop, but admittedly Mel's disappearance had skewed his objectivity. In a very short while, he might experience one of the toughest conversations he'd ever had as a cop, explaining to a fatherless, teenage boy that he hadn't a clue what had happened to his mother.

Observing no signs of violence, Joe had sent the assisting cops back on patrol.

He clenched and unclenched his fists, then shoved his hands in his coat pocket, visually skimming the area, while Harry dusted the counter, cash register, phones, work areas and knobs for prints.

Even Harry's phenomenal track record didn't leave Joe with much hope. Pinnacle Creations maintained a steady stream of customers. Locating prints that matched the Integrated Automated Fingerprint Information System would be the proverbial needle in the haystack.

Powerless to produce something that wasn't there, he left the crime scene analyst and walked outside, past Mel's car to the group of mail boxes fifty yards away. It wasn't enough to escape the smell of flowers and greenery that were a constant reminder of Mel, but it was a start.

"Joe? Got a minute?" Harry called from the door, then disappeared back inside the shop.

Jogging back, he reentered the business a lot faster than he'd left it. "Harry? Where are you?"

"Down here," came her muffled voice.

He rounded the corner to find the heavyset woman on her stomach, flashlight in hand, shining it into a small crevice beneath the counter.

"What've you got?"

"I don't know. Something." She slid her gloved hand into the space. "Damn these fat fingers. They don't fit." From over her shoulder she glanced up at him. "Yours won't either. See if you can find something long and skinny."

Joe entered the store room. He picked up a broom handle, determining it was too big for the space. *Long and skinny.* He scanned the room. On a back table next to the door was a helium tank with deflated balloons and a cylindrical tube next to it containing sticks. He grabbed one and rushed back to Harry.

"Atta boy." She handed him the flashlight. "Hold this."

With the woman's stretched-out bulk, he did his best to squat beside her between the counter and the wall.

Harry never said please, she rarely said thank you. Rank meant nothing to her. She was a civilian, good at her job. If she smiled, you were on her good side, a frown meant she had little use for you. Over the course of his career, Joe considered it a compliment he'd received more smiles than jeers.

"Come here, you little dickens," she said, huffing from the exertion.

"What does it look like?"

"Whatever it is, it's shiny."

"It's under the cash register. Could it be dropped change?"

"It's not that flat. Shine the light over here."

Grimacing, Harry took the stick and swung back and forth under the area. Several attempts later, she cried, "Gotcha."

As she forced the object via the stick in her direction, Joe stood over her, narrowing his gaze as the remainder of a battered cell phone made its appearance.

"Mind telling me what made you look down there?" he asked, helping the panting woman to her feet.

"Same thing that makes you guys crawl through the sewers. It was there."

She turned the phone in her glove-covered palm. His heart sped up. It had obviously been crushed. It also was identical to the one Luke Norris owned.

"Want me to bag it?" she asked.

"Not yet." He took a pair of tweezers from her kit, pinched the phone between the rubber-tipped ends and placed the phone on the floor. Then raising his foot he came down like he was going to crush it. "Someone stomped on this. He might have touched it."

"Unless he caught Mrs. Norris trying to make a call and told her to drop it," Harry argued.

"You just can't think positive. Check it for prints. Then run it by Lishock, ask him to do a trace on the memory card."

"Got it."

"You're one tenacious woman, Harry. Glad you're on our side."

"Do I get a raise?"

"You get something better, my undying respect. Get me those prints." Joe held the door open for Harry, then locked up the store. He was about to see Harry to her car when his cell phone rang. Waving her on, and watching her move toward her vehicle, he took a breath before answering. "Crandall."

"Lt. Crandall. My name's Clayborn Morrison. I'm Chief of Police for Riverside California Police Department."

Joe pinched the bridge of his nose. This couldn't be good. What can I do for you, Chief?"

I received your name from Mrs. Marcy Maxwell. She asked me to get in touch with you. I'm afraid I have some bad news."

"Marcy Maxwell. Is she any relation to Adam Maxwell?"

"She is. She's Maxwell's wife." The chief hesitated. "Late this afternoon, Maxwell was the victim of a hit and run. He and his body guard, as it turns out, were crossing the street at one of Maxwell's job sites, when a man driving a stolen Ford Excursion struck both men."

Joe closed his eyes, trying to block out the image of flying bodies, and what a vehicle the size of an Excursion could do to two grown men. The driver had wanted to make sure he did permanent damage. Joe thought of his recent conversation with Adam. He'd claimed to have beefed up security. Obviously he had.

"Adam Maxwell died instantly. As for the bodyguard, he's on life support."

Joe swallowed hard. "Did you catch the driver?"

"Not at first. That's when Mrs. Maxwell became hysterical. Said that you'd tried to warn her husband this might happen. She put me in touch with you."

"The man who did this," Joe said, urgently, trying to make sense of it. "You said not at first. What does that mean?" Joe thought of the crooked P.I. Givens and *that* debacle of a goose chase. If Drake Maxwell was in California killing his brother, then who in the hell had Melanie?

"We apprehended the driver not a half hour later. A man by the name of Jason Rander fled Riverside, apparently trying to make it to L.A. When police pursued, he lost control of the Excursion. It swerved into another lane. A semi coming in the other direction hit the Excursion head on. Driver of the semi survived, but the suspect died en route to the hospital.

"I suppose it would be too much to hope he made a deathbed confession?" Joe asked.

"Looks like you caught a break, Lieutenant. Rander told a paramedic that Drake Maxwell hired him to kill his brother."

Joe placed a hand on the back of his neck, rubbed it and squeezed.

"I understand you told Adam Maxwell that his brother might be after him."

"For all the good it did," Joe said. "I also think Drake Maxwell might have killed a corrections officer here in Cañon City, Colorado. It gets worse. Tonight Maxwell may have kidnapped a woman."

The chief responded with a muffled oath. "Do you have any idea where he could be?"

"Not at this time," Joe said. "I'm about to put out an APB. I appreciate the phone call. Will you relay my deepest condolences to Mrs. Maxwell and her family?"

"I will. If it's any consolation, Lieutenant, Mrs. Maxwell said to thank you for trying."

"That's no consolation."

"I wouldn't think so. Anything I can do for you on this end?"

"You can contact your counterpart in Cañon City, tell him what you told me. Perhaps with both our agencies telling them about Drake Maxwell, they'll listen. We think he's around here somewhere."

"Will do. Anything else?"

"Just remind them we're on the same side," Joe said. "And help us get this guy."

Chapter Forty-six

Too bad her captor had chosen a life of crime, because he might've made a decent living as a chef. Mel cleaned her plate of enchiladas, *rellenos* and rice, and drank two glasses of water before a different bodily function set in.

"I have to go to the bathroom," she said.

Drake stood by the back door, glaring. The Hispanic man smiled. "Of course. Down the hall and to your right."

Warily, she rose to her feet. Was he simply going to let her go?

She had her answer before leaving the kitchen. "*Chica*," he said. "Before you get any ideas about leaving the house, be sure to look out the window. Two of my men are watching. For now I have left instructions that no one touches you. Reject my hospitality, and they *will* take turns at your luscious body."

Avoiding the cruel quirk of his lips, she refused to look back and entered the hallway. She had no reason to believe he was lying. Nonetheless, as she paused at the first bedroom window, her heart sank. It was dark and she couldn't see anyone inside, but a lone car was parked in front of the house.

Entering the bathroom, she resisted slamming the door. She dropped her jeans, sat on the toilet and buried her face in her hands.

Joe. Get me out of here.

Afterward, she washed up and pushed back the hair falling into her eyes. One thing she'd figured out while they fed her, Drake was second in command to the man in the kitchen. And she suspected something else. They might be treating her decently for the time being, but they were up to something, or she'd be long dead by now. So, if their plan wasn't rape and murder, what did they want? Did they think she had money?

The bathroom had no window, and as she took in her surroundings, she noted its feminine touches. Peach tones and teal towels, ceramic sea shells on the counter, and a seahorse wallpaper border. Was the criminal in the other room married? Was he committed to his wife, and that was the reason he'd spared Mel from sexual abuse? It didn't matter. For whatever reason he'd left her in one piece, she was thankful. But not stupid.

Gingerly, she opened the medicine chest to see what else she could learn. In it she found feminine products, deodorant and pain relief medications. A nearly empty prescription bottle of Amoxocillin sat on the bottom shelf issued to somebody named Maria Ramirez. It was filled at a

Walmart store in Colorado Springs.

Her gaze slid to the bathroom door. Was that the name of the man in the other room?

Committing *Ramirez* to memory, Mel squatted at the cabinet below the sink. Here someone had stored toilet paper, tampons and sanitary napkins. Again, nothing to suggest this house belonged to a man. Worse, nothing she could use as a weapon to get her out of this miserable place and back to her son.

Mel leaned her head against the cabinet door. She'd been gone several hours. Luke would be frantic by now. She stood, regretting that she'd ever told him about her past. Could he handle it? Would Joe help Luke through it?

Two loud raps shook the door and she jumped.

"What's taking so long?"

Drake. Barely recognizing her haggard reflection in the mirror, Mel raised her voice. "My stomach's upset. Give me a break."

He banged on the door. "Like the one you gave me? Get out of there. It's time for bed."

Perhaps she'd spoken too soon. In no position to argue about sleeping arrangements, she opened the door. Arms crossed and scowling, he leaned against the opposite wall, waiting for her. She followed wordlessly, re-entering the kitchen to find they were alone. A new burst of panic set in when he strode toward the basement. As she had in the bathroom, she scanned the counters for a weapon. When that, too, proved unsuccessful, she envisioned grabbing a chair. She'd slam it over his head the second he looked away. That never happened, unfortunately. He watched her with the unmistakable aggression of a man who wanted her dead. He stood aside for her to go downstairs before him, but at least she'd accomplished something. She'd discovered the location of the phone and estimated the distance to the kitchen's rear entry. Nor had it escaped her notice there wasn't a lock on the basement door.

Unable to resist testing him, she took the first few steps. "Your boss leave you alone?"

"Don't push it, Melanie. If I say you're gone, you're gone."

It was probably good advice that he offered. She breathed in and out and disregarded it. "If you hate me so much, why not just kill me?"

"For a broad with no future," he said from behind her, "you gotta big mouth."

She did indeed. Lowering her head, she bit back her rage. But the risky outburst, and the fact she was still standing, confirmed her thinking. They were keeping her alive for something. For the first time in hours, she felt safe. Qualify that. *Safe—er.*

Downstairs in the cold basement, he led her back to the mattress, covered only by a sheet and the ropes that his so-called partner had cut from her body.

Drake picked up a shortened, useless strand. "Shit."

Maybe it was hysteria taking hold, but she found his predicament funny. She laughed.

Ignoring her, he yanked the sheet from the mattress and ripped the material to shreds.

She knew better than to taunt him again, but she couldn't resist. "You could leave me untied."

The force of his palm across her cheek snapped back her head. "That's what I think of that lousy idea. Now get over here."

She raised a hand to her stinging face. If she got the chance, she *would* kill him.

He shoved her to the mattress, then bound her with the cloth restraints. Now she didn't even have the benefit of the lightweight sheet in the cold, unfinished basement. The bastard grabbed blankets from a nearby chair, lay down beside her and threw them over himself

She, on the other hand, had only the warmth of her jeans and a linen shirt. Suspecting he wanted her to beg, she huddled into a fetal position. He could wait forever. She'd rather—

His cell phone rang. He rolled to his side and grabbed it. "One sound," he said, "and I'll break your ribs."

He'd struck her twice already. Missing his ally, who'd at least provided a buffer between them, she took the threat as gospel and kept quiet.

Drake got up and walked to the far side of the room. His voice became soft, reminding her of when she'd met him years before. That's when she realized the caller was female. In spite of her deep-seated hatred, she was intrigued. Did Drake still have a spot of humanity left in him to care about someone? He hadn't been out of prison long, so when and where had he met the woman on the phone? More importantly, was there some way Mel could use his feelings to her advantage?

From across the room, he murmured something about "naked on a beach," and he laughed. Finally the phone conversation ended with, "Yeah, me, too."

Afterward, he dropped down beside her. "Get an earful?"

"Sorry," Mel said, dripping sarcasm. "I would have left the room but I was all tied up. Didn't take you long to find a woman."

"Never did, babe. It could've been you."

Her mind focused on Drake standing over the traumatized clerk pleading for his life and she wanted to gag. "Sorry, cold-blooded killers do nothing for me."

"So what is your type?" He flipped her onto her back, grabbing her throat with his huge calloused hand. "Tell me about this husband of yours."

As taunting as she'd been with her words, he did the same with his fingers, gripping her neck just hard enough to let her know he could squeeze the life out of her with very little effort.

Her heart raced, but damn her pride, it was greater than her fear. She gritted her teeth. "He's wonderful. What's more, he doesn't even know how to spell Department of Corrections."

Drake laughed as his fingers wound tighter. "Sounds like a loser."

Instinctively she tried to swallow. "I thought you wanted to sleep."

"Not anymore. I want to talk about your old man. Funny, you don't even wear a wedding ring. What's his name?"

"Larry," she croaked.

"Larry," Drake repeated. "Good old, *stupid* Larry."

She rolled her eyes. Her intended insult had backfired. "He's not stupid."

"You're the one who said he couldn't spell. So, you know what's bothering me? How come there's not one picture of good ol' stupid Larry in your wallet?"

God help her. Drake had gone through her things? "We haven't been married long. I've been meaning to put one in."

"Guess that explains it." He pressed his mouth close to her ear. "Know what I did find, though? Tons of photos . . . of a kid."

Luke. Mel felt ill, like her heart was being ripped from her chest.

"You're a lying bitch, you know that." Increasing the grip he had on her throat, he forced his weight onto her. "There is no husband. It's you and your brat."

She wanted to spit in his face. She couldn't think, she couldn't breathe.

"Don't die on me yet, Melanie. This is too much fun. Know what else is great about wallets? They contain so much information. Credit cards, checking accounts, *addresses.*"

She fought against passing out, giving in to the bastard. No matter what, she had to protect Luke. She gasped. "You think you're so clever, that you can get to me through my son. You *idiot.* He doesn't even live here."

Her enemy's gaze drew into slits. "What are you talking about?"

"After my husband died, I couldn't afford to raise him. I sent him to his family in Florida."

The monster, this *devil personified* eased off of her and let go of her throat. Free of his hot breath and unbearable presence, the air returned to her lungs.

He stood, paced the length of the floor, then turned to her and laughed. "You're good, but not good enough. If the boy doesn't live here, why's your heart doing the tango?"

"The idea that you know anything about me makes me want to retch."

He lifted a sandy blond brow, reached into his back pocket and withdrew his phone. A few seconds later, he said, "Ramirez, she says the kid doesn't live here."

Even from her place on the floor Mel could hear the other party bellow.

"She's lying," Drake said. "She's scared shitless. But we gotta have the kid."

Mel held her breath as her tormentor's cocky gaze collided with hers. "Tell Mercer and Skinny to head over to 39 Serendipity Lane and pick him up."

No, no, no. This wasn't happening. She ordered herself to calm down. In the back of her mind she knew Joe would never leave Luke alone. Joe didn't have it in him to make her son vulnerable.

"And if the kid's not there?" Drake laughed. "We'll do what I should've done in the first place."

Chapter Forty-seven

Later that evening, when Joe turned onto Serendipity, he was angry enough to hit someone. And the person he wanted to hit hardest was himself. He'd dropped the ball on this one. By putting his career first and honoring Melanie's request to stay away, he might've very well gotten her killed.

He stared at the white knuckles gripping the steering wheel. A police officer had to be mentally prepared to handle worst-case scenarios. But in this case, it was the first time he'd allowed himself to seriously consider that Maxwell had truly abducted her. If that were the case, and by the looks of the battered cell phone he had, Melanie's chances for survival were close to nil.

What in the hell was Joe going to tell Luke? No matter how many times Joe'd criticized Mel's overprotective nature and argued that Luke was almost a man, beneath his six foot-two-inch stature, lurked a boy.

Joe's throat threatened to close from sorrow and guilt. If something happened to Melanie, Luke wasn't the only one who would feel her loss. Damn this helpless feeling. Joe would be on this twenty-four/seven until he found her.

As he neared his house, he narrowed his gaze at the car parked at the curb. A new rush of fear set in, until he recognized the vehicle as Rick Hood's beat up gold Camaro.

Joe pulled into the garage. He could use some of Rick's positive thinking about now. Every bad experience Joe had known as a cop was crushing him.

He strode into the house and stopped at the door to the den. Luke sat on the couch, covering his right eye with an ice bag, while the coach sat at his side.

Rick rose from the couch and nodded to Joe. "We should talk in the hallway."

Joe followed the former basketball star into the entryway, trying to comprehend what he was seeing. "Where's Matt?"

"Here."

Joe turned to see his son standing at the top of the stairs holding a bloody wash cloth over his nose. About to lose what was left of his remaining self-control, Joe said, "Somebody better start talking."

"They got in a fight," Rick explained.

Keeping his head back, Matt negotiated the stairs. "Luke wanted to go look for his mom. You told me to keep him here. I did my best, Dad, but he's not exactly a *girl*. When I tried, it came to blows. We kind of lost it from there."

Luke stood at the door to the den. "When I drew blood that was all it took. I mean, Matt's my best friend. But seeing all that red made me calm down. We couldn't get hold of you, so we called Coach."

To Rick, Joe said, "I appreciate you coming over." To Matt, Joe added, "I shouldn't have put you in this position, son. I'm sorry."

Head back, Matt kept the washcloth in place. "No biggie."

"Any news on my mom?" Luke's gaze bored into Joe's.

"Why don't we talk in the den?"

"No. Everybody knows what's going on." Luke's voice cracked. "You gotta tell me, Lieutenant. Did Drake Maxwell kill my mom?"

How could Joe give Luke the facts and still give him hope? "I don't know, Luke. "There's no sign of violence. She's missing. That's all we know."

"It's gotta be Maxwell." Luke's shoulders heaved and tears pooled in his red-rimmed eyes. "I'll kill the son of a bitch."

Joe grasped the teen's shoulders. "I'm not giving up. You're not either."

Luke wiped his face. "The next time you go to your job, I'm coming with you."

"If I were in your position, I'd feel the same way. But one thing your mom would want is for you to be safe. And I'm going to do my best to make sure that happens."

"I can't just *sit* here."

"Your mother's purse wasn't found at the shop, Luke. If Maxwell does have her, it's reasonable to assume he knows your address. I've been in this job a long time. Criminals often show up at a victim's house after the fact to rob it."

"So let's set a trap for him," Matt interjected.

Joe cast Matt a look as if to say 'you're not helping.'

"That's exactly what we're going to do," Joe said. "But without you boys being anywhere in the vicinity."

"They can stay with me," Rick said.

For the first time in hours, Joe felt his worry lessen. He needed his complete focus to remain on Mel. "That would be great."

"No way," Luke argued. "If Maxwell comes anywhere near my house I'll be—"

"Far, far away," Joe said.

"You can help Lt. Crandall by doing what he says," Rick added. "I know it sucks, son, and I'll do my best to help keep your mind off your mom. We'll swim, shoot baskets, whatever it takes."

"Can I come, too?" Matt asked.

Luke gawked at his friend. "You'd do that?"

"Heck, yeah."

Luke's hair was so blond it nearly looked white. He lowered his head, then raised it to focus on Joe. "You swear to call me no matter what?"

Joe felt a helpless rage. He wanted to promise the boy he'd find his mother and bring her back safe. However, that was unrealistic and a long shot. Yet, he could honor this request. "No matter what, Luke. The moment I learn anything, you'll know in the next minute."

Ten minutes later, Joe entered his garage to return to the division. His cell phone rang and he answered, "Crandall."

"Joe, it's Harry. Got a match on those prints. You pegged this one. They match an ex-convict by the name of Drake Maxwell."

Chapter Forty-eight

With the boys in Rick's care and two unmarked units parked near Mel's property, Joe headed downtown. He needed to assemble a task force, access Maxwell's prison photos for patrol and go over phone records he'd acquired via emergency subpoena.

On the way, he also placed another call to the Cañon City Chief of Police and left voice mail. Undoubtedly, Chief Clayborn Morrison from Riverside had called his counterpart by now to list Drake Maxwell as the most viable suspect for the off-duty correction officer's murder. But the Chief hadn't known when he'd talked to Joe that Maxwell's prints had been confirmed on Melanie's cell phone. Joe had been a fool not to trust his instincts.

At four-fifteen the next morning, existing on a diet of stale bagels and caffeine, he rubbed his eyes. An equally exhausted-looking Bruce Bennett knocked on his door.

Joe tightened his stubble-covered jaw. "What are you doing here at this hour?"

"Believe it or not, I do work for a living. Campaign by day, prosecute by night. I heard, Joe. I can't tell you how sorry I am."

Joe's throat clogged. He couldn't have told the D.A. to go to hell if he wanted to.

"This may strain our already tenuous friendship, but I have to ask. Are you sure she didn't go willingly?"

At the ludicrous statement Joe opened his right-hand drawer and removed a plastic evidence bag. Inside lay Mel's mutilated cell phone.

He also removed the phone logs from both her cellular carrier and landline. Melanie had a very small social circle. Joe had successfully identified each call, marking them with a yellow highlighter. The log included one long distance call to Peter Walford in Kansas City, several calls to Warden Simon Rivers, while the rest were local, placed or received from either Mel's place of employment, Luke, Matt or Joe.

Bruce said, "Okay, you've done your homework. She appears legit. What are the chances she's still alive?"

Joe buried his face in his hands. "Get out, Bruce."

The D.A. dropped into a chair. "No can do, pal. I should go to Gallegos and demand you recuse yourself from this investigation."

Ready to tear Bruce from limb to limb, Joe lifted his head.

"Can't promise he won't learn it from someone else, but the chief won't hear it from me. Find Maxwell, Joe. Nail the son of a bitch, and let me know how I can help."

Any chance for Joe to express his gratitude was waylaid by his ringing cell phone. "Crandall," he said. He listened and the boulder crushing his chest slightly lifted. He ended the call. "Two men were caught trying to break into Melanie's house. Cops are bringing them in for questioning."

Mel opened the bathroom door to the sound of screaming. She ran through the convenience store aisles, desperate to find the source and end someone's agony. But when she rounded the corner, she'd lost her way. Snow covered the ground and she started to shiver. Ten feet in front of her stood a leering Drake Maxwell. In his arms, he held a child. Kicking and crying, tears streamed down the little guy's blond freckled face, and when he saw her, he held out his arms and sobbed, "Mommy, Mommy!"

Mel startled awake. Heart on fire, she'd been gripped in the culmination of nightmares and memories of yesterday. She also realized something else. She was freezing. Probably because she no longer had the benefit of the only warmth she'd had all night, Drake's body heat. He'd left her alone. She lay still, listening for signs of activity overhead. Nothing.

During the night her subconscious had clued her into something else. Drake had named his partner. *Ramirez.* That name matched the prescription bottle in the bathroom. So did Maria own this house? Was Ramirez her husband, her brother?

She was still bound tight, but her kidnapper had made a mistake. He'd forgotten to put the duct tape over her mouth, and she knew the location of the phone. Now if only she could get to it she could summon help and get the hell out of here.

Mel finagled her body to an upright position. Unlike yesterday, the basement was pitch black, but earlier she'd counted twelve narrow steps. Now the question remained, tied up, and in the dark, could she make it up those stairs? Screw that insane thought. This was her life on the line. A more apt question remained, what happened if she didn't?

As Joe and Bruce neared interrogation, the D.A. conveniently excused himself. "These jokers have more civil rights than all the honest folks in the building, Joe. I know you're hot, but don't blow this case."

Hot was the cleaned up version of how he felt, and Melanie Norris would never be just a case to him.

A uniformed officer handed Joe the rap sheets of the men seated in Interrogation Rooms A and B. He'd busted these two before. Roscoe Mercer and Melvin "Skinny" Thomas were smalltime thugs with no history of violence. Each had served time in the East Cañon Correctional Facility, which is probably where they'd hooked up with Maxwell in the first place.

Studying their sheets, Joe wouldn't have found it odd they'd graduated from stolen vehicles to houses. But to choose Mel's house just hours after she'd gone missing?

Massaging the rioting muscles in his neck, he had to stop thinking of her in the past tense. He'd promised Luke he wouldn't give up hope, but with each passing hour, the chances of finding her alive grew less likely.

Detective Dale Abernathy, the lead man Joe had worked with on the McPherson arson case, exited the room housing Roscoe Mercer. "We always get the fun jobs, huh, L.T.?" Dale nodded over his shoulder. "This one's strung tighter than a turkey at Thanksgiving. Wants a public defender now."

"Get him one," Joe said. "But hold him off for a while. Let's see if we can't enlist Mr. Mercer's cooperation."

Joe entered the tiny room, introduced himself to a black man, who doubled as a freight train, and sat down in a chair.

Seated at the tiny table, Roscoe Mercer looked like a fourth grader held back for preschool. "I remember you," he said.

Joe narrowed his eyes. What Mercer remembered was a by-the-book-cop who'd treated him fairly. Things were about to change.

"We've called your attorney. He'll be here any minute, at which time he'll tell you to shut up, he'll wheel and deal, and you'll go back to prison." Joe linked his fingers and circled his thumbs back and forth. "Is that how you see things happening, Mr. Mercer?"

Mercer leaned back in his chair and nodded.

"You think attempted breaking and entering holds a minimal sentence, is that it?"

"I know it does." The ex-con shrugged. "I won't do a year. I'll get three squares and free cable. Hell, on the outside I have to pay for it." Mercer flexed his bouncer-sized arms, then folded them. "No one's ever been crazy enough to mess with me. Frankly, the joint's my idea of a vacation."

Stupid fuck. Joe wanted to kick the legs out from under his chair. "Too bad it's not breaking and entering we're charging you with."

"Huh?"

"The charge is first degree kidnapping, potentially murder." Joe paused to let the charge sink in.

Confidence fled the big man's face. "But it wasn't kidnapping. Me and Skinny never made it inside the house."

It was Joe's turn to feel confused. His lie was about to become fact—the suspect's attorney would show up at any time. "Where's the woman, Mercer?"

"Who?"

"Melanie Norris. She's missing, and you were found breaking into her home."

"We weren't sent to get no woman. Me and Skinny, we saw a house that looked easy, we took it."

"Really." Joe felt rage seizing him. He'd personally left lights on in the house and secured the windows and doors. Of all the houses on the block that looked easy, Mel's house was hardly the one. "Drake Maxwell tell you to hit that house?"

Mercer's eyes darted away from Joe, then back again. "Don't know anybody by that name."

"Is that so?" Joe stood. In one fell swoop he did what he'd resisted doing moments before.

Mercer and his chair toppled backward.

Applying his weight, Joe pinned his forearm against the asshole's windpipe. "I ain't got time to play with you, Mercer, so here's what's going down. I don't give a damn about my badge on this one. The lady you took, she's mine. If anything happens to her, that cell you call a country club will be your casket. I'll spend every dime I have to make sure someone on the inside sticks you. You'll never know who or when, and you'll never be safe."

Mercer struggled for breath, the healthy color leaving his face, forming a grayish hue.

The door opened and Det. Abernathy barged in. "Lieutenant! Sir. Lt. Crandall, let him go."

Somewhere in the back of his mind, Joe heard the detective's voice, but his ability to reason had deserted him. Abernathy's powerful arms pulled Joe away from the scum on the floor. With both men breathing hard, and Mercer clutching his throat, Abernathy said, "Get hold of yourself, L.T. The PDA's on her way up."

Joe didn't give a damn. He was running on fury, worry and adrenaline. If he couldn't strangle Mercer, he'd just as soon throw the son of a bitch through the one-way mirror.

Abernathy righted the suspect's chair, then extended his hand. Helping the man to his feet, he said, "Mr. Mercer? Do you wish to press charges against the lieutenant?"

Rubbing his neck and glaring, Mercer cleared his throat.

A woman wearing a public defender's badge stood in the doorway. "What's going on here?"

Mercer cast a wary glance from Abernathy to Joe, then balled his hands into fists. "You call these things you give us to sit in chairs? Damned thing collapsed out from under me." To the woman he said, "You my lawyer, lady?"

"I am."

"It's about time you got here. You might want to tell Skinny I'm talking. These SOBs think I kidnapped some dame. That wasn't part of the deal, and I ain't going down for something I didn't do."

Chapter Forty-nine

Mel lay in the basement counting. Where did criminals disappear to in the early morning hours? Certainly not church or to visit their mothers. Maybe they'd gone for coffee. When she'd reached thirty and heard nothing but quiet above her, she didn't care where they'd slithered off to. She had only a fraction of time to make her move.

Damn, it was dark. The basement stairs were somewhere to her left and about twelve feet away. With her hands tied behind her back, her ankles bound, she'd be forced to hop. The hard cement floor beneath her discouraged that thought, so she rolled.

It turned out to be a brilliant idea, because she made quick progress. When she neared what she thought was the base of the stairs, she slowed. Her head hurt enough without adding a self-inflicted blow to it.

Forced to use her nose, cheek and mouth to feel her way, she lifted her head. She strained her neck, and although Mel was panting like an Olympian, she managed to place it on the bottom step. Success. Now it was a matter of climbing to a sitting position and using her butt and her legs. Doing just that, she breathlessly traveled from step to step.

Drake had taken her watch, but she suspected she'd accomplished this feat in under ten minutes. And as beams of early morning light poured through the basement windows, at last she could see. The winter solstice had passed, the days were getting longer, which she estimated made it around seven. Yet, the house remained eerily quiet.

She pressed her ear to the door.

Nothing.

Okay. Good. Time to get through it. Holding her breath and commanding her heart to slow, she reminded herself she was close. Although there was still the huge challenge of standing and positioning her body just right so she could get her hands around the knob.

She could do this. She had to do this.

Using the door at her back as leverage, she pushed herself up. Her cautious stance accomplished, she was no longer grateful for the light. Facing a harrowing flight of stairs below, with no free limbs to break her fall, she'd be lucky to end up with only one broken bone if she fell.

Quit being a coward, think of your son, and get through that door.

Fumbling with bound hands, she finally found the knob and turned, but the door wouldn't budge.

No!

She'd been sure there wasn't a lock. Did she dare push? Damn it, what choice did she have? Careful not to shove too hard, lest the momentum backfire and propel her to the cement floor, she applied her weight. The door gave, but didn't open.

Tears of frustration welled and she knew. Drake must've blocked the basement's exit.

With her heart jack-hammering, she pressed her back against the door, and furtively lowered herself once again to sit on the top step.

That's when she heard the outside kitchen door open, followed by footfalls, Drake's hated voice and the man she suspected to be Ramirez.

Slink down the stairs, Mel. Get back to the mattress. In moments they'll come for you.

Someone spoke; she leaned close to the door.

"Mercer doesn't answer his phone. Something's wrong."

"Relax. He probably turned it off during the break-in and forgot to turn it back on."

"I don't know, Max. It's been too long. I told him to call the moment he had the kid. If the cops latched on to him, he could tell them about the hits, how to find us."

"It's not Mercer I'm worried about. Mercer wouldn't rat us out, it's Skinny I'm not too sure of."

"I'm not willing to chance either of them. We're out of here. Go get—"

Mel started to scramble. A phone rang, however, and she stayed perilously glued to the door.

Ramirez answered. "Where are you?" He paused. "Took you long enough. You get the kid?" Another brief silence later, he said, "Good. Bring him here." . . . "Why not? . . . "The entire car?". . . "Shit. Where'd you take him?" . . . "Yeah?" . . ."Skinny's old lady must've loved that one." . . ."Well, bring me evidence you got him. We can't get the broad to cooperate without proof."

Every ounce of stamina drained from her body, leaving Mel empty. It wasn't possible. They couldn't have Luke. What did they mean the entire car? Had he become sick? Were they talking about blood? And why couldn't they bring him here? Had they hurt him?

Oh, god, Joe, I counted on you. Why didn't you protect him?

"Get the woman, Max."

The sound of a chair scraping back was followed by the basement door swinging open.

And even as Maxwell bellowed, Mel made no attempt to get away. He grabbed her and hauled her into the kitchen. She didn't cry out. She couldn't. Her son was in the hands of madmen. Mel no longer had the strength to scream.

Chapter Fifty

"Very good, Mercer," Joe said as the ex-convict ended the call. "If you ever decide to go straight, you should try acting."

Along with several detectives, SWAT team members, the man nicknamed Skinny sat in a chair looking on. By his unrelenting glare, he didn't appear happy that Mercer had agreed to wear a wire and cooperate with police. That was okay with Joe. Not only had Roscoe Mercer identified every member of the Chaos Bandits, the police had these men as accessories to felony kidnapping. Melvin "Skinny" Thomas wasn't going to see the outside world anytime soon.

"Who's got Skinny's cell phone?" Joe asked.

A vice cop stepped forward. "I win that prize."

"If it rings, keep your answers short. Don't tip our hand."

"Not a chance."

Bruce Bennett entered as Joe and the other officer's strapped on their Kevlar vests. "You understand what we want you to do, Mr. Mercer?" the D.A. asked.

Mercer reached for Luke's practice jersey. Upon Joe's request a patrolman had swung by Mel's house and picked it up. "Walk in to Ramirez's house and show 'em this jersey."

Joe lowered his head, hoping to God Mel could forgive him for using this tactic. They needed to establish her whereabouts before they swarmed the house. "Great," Joe said. "Then what?"

"If the woman's around I say, 'What's your name, pretty lady?' If she's not, I say, 'Where's the dame?'"

Pretty straightforward, Joe thought. Conceptually it should work, letting law enforcement know if it was safe to raid, using force. Too often, though, a kink found its way into the system.

Marksman Sam Ortega crossed the room. "We're ready when you are, Lieutenant."

Joe was pleased to see the man, who not too many weeks ago had been suspended for taking down a crazed meth dealer. Evidently, he'd been reinstated to active duty.

Joe nodded. He directed an officer to take Skinny back to a holding cell. Joe hadn't even had to assign a group for this op. As soon as the callout went down, men stepped forward, the majority off duty, Ortega among them.

Clearing his throat, Joe said, "Thanks. Give me a second, then let's do it." He reached for the phone on his belt, walked to the window overlooking the lofts next door, then dialed Mel's son.

Out of breath the boy answered after several rings. "Lt. Crandall?"

"Yeah, Luke, it's me. Where are you?"

"I'm with Matt and Coach. We're at school shooting baskets. What's going on?"

"We believe we found your mom, and at this point, we think she's okay. She's being held against her will, and part of Maxwell's scheme is to make her believe they have you."

"What? That's crazy. Why would—"

"Luke, listen to me. I hate to do this to you. Tell Coach to take you to his house and stay put and out of sight. I'm sure these people don't travel in the same circles as any of you, but the media may be onto this kidnapping. If they see you out and about, or try to interview you when we've convinced them you're being held someplace else, it could go bad for your mom."

A moment's silence occurred on the line before Luke said, "Got it."

"Do I need to relay this information to your Coach?"

"No, sir. I'll do it. Find my mom."

"That's the plan. Tell Matt I love him. Your father would be proud, Luke. I'm damn impressed as well. You boys be strong."

Surrounded by patrol cars, Joe and the team walked to an unmarked van while Mercer slid into a blue Ford Focus. "Can you hear me?" the black man asked as he switched on the ignition.

"Copy," the technician inside the van said.

"Just want you to know," Mercer added. "If Ramirez and Maxwell smell a trap, you'll never identify all my body parts. Take that up with the judge when you're talking reduced sentence."

"Will do, Mr. Mercer," the D.A. replied. "Help us get Mrs. Norris out alive and it will buy you a great deal of leniency."

Mrs. Norris alive. Taking slow, steady breaths, Joe entered the back of the vehicle and sat beside Bruce and the rest of the team.

The van started to move. The countdown was on.

Chapter Fifty-one

Free of her bonds, Mel sat at the kitchen table, pressing a palm to her injured cheek.

Ramirez took a dishtowel and filled it with ice. Handing it to her, he said, "Damn, Max. Stop using her for a freaking punching bag. She walks in the bank all banged up, she'll attract attention before she makes it to the teller."

Mel took the ice pack and gingerly placed it against her jaw. "It doesn't matter if you beat me to a pulp, I'm not robbing a bank."

Drake, who was sitting next to her, leaned forward. "You'll do whatever we tell you if you want your brat to live."

"How do I know you have him? I want to talk to him."

"We can arrange that," Ramirez cut in. "But not yet. Your boy didn't like our surprise visit. Puked his guts out. My men doused him with Dramamine so he's sleeping. He's safe, so far. I give you my word."

She squeezed her eyes shut. "Your word means nothing to me. I'll do as you say, but only if you release my son."

"Release? I don't think so. But I will see that you talk to him." Ramirez's cell phone rang. "This may be Skinny right now." He checked the number and frowned. "*Hola,* Tess. What can I do for you?". . . "Skinny?" . . . "No, *chica.* He's not with you?" The gang leader's voice went from reasonable to undiluted panic. "He didn't bring you a visitor?". . ."No, Tess, call no one. You talk to no one, understand?". . . "No. Sit tight. You'll hear from me."

A mask of fury came over Ramirez's face as he disconnected the call. He picked up a glass, threw it against the sink where it shattered. "It's a set up. They're on to us. Grab your shit, Max. *Ándale.*"

As Drake vaulted down the stairs, Ramirez raked a hand through his hair. He pivoted and advanced on her. Mel's heart slammed in her chest. "So it appears we don't have your fucking kid after all." He removed his switchblade and pressed it to her throat. "Change of plans, *chica.* We no longer have a reason to keep you alive."

Chapter Fifty-two

Acting as lead officer, Joe directed the cop driving the white utility van to park fifty meters away from the home of Maria Ramirez, sister of longtime gangbanger and thug, Denny Ramirez. Two days before New Year's Eve, for once Joe was grateful for the cold. It was likely the curious onlookers were staying inside due to the weather as police quarantined the area around 1301 Presidential Drive.

"C.W.'s moving, L.T."

Mercer, the C.W. or Cooperating Witness as the mobile tech referred to him, drove his blue Ford Focus and parked in a cul-de-sac of the middle-class, well-maintained eastside neighborhood. For a moment the man just sat there. Then murmuring, "Here goes everything," he got out of the car, Luke's practice jersey in hand.

"All units prepare to move on my say so," Joe said. Wearing jeans and a T-shirt under a bomber jacket, he felt for the Glock, tucked in his shoulder holster and slipped out of the van. He started walking, his destination the eastside of Ramirez's house.

Mercer rang the bell, then pressed the buzzer again, finally pounding until he said into the mic strapped to his chest, "What gives?"

"Try the back door," Joe said. "Unit five, C.W.'s moving to the rear of the property."

"Copy that unit one. Visual on C.W."

A full thirty seconds of knocking yielded no response. Warrant in hand, with the D.A. looking on, Joe and Sam Ortega kicked in the front door, while cops from all directions swarmed the premises.

"Police," Joe yelled, and entered what appeared to be a vacant residence.

Weapons raised, law enforcement converged on every room, quickly discovering the place was empty.

Joe's gut roiled as he said into his shoulder mic, "All clear."

"Check this out," Sam said, pointing to a chip in the wall, broken glass in the sink, counters and floor. "Somebody's either a careless housekeeper, or a tad upset."

Joe moved to the table to view a wadded towel containing ice cubes. Touching it, he said, "Ice hasn't begun to melt. We just missed them, damn it."

"Lieutenant! Sgt. Ortega! Down here," a man shouted.

Joe rushed down the stairs into an unfinished basement. The only furnishing was a single mattress and chair. In the patrolman's hands, he held several strands of rope. Someone had been held here, and it didn't take a genius I.Q. to figure out who.

"No blood," Bruce said. "I'll take that as a positive."

Joe saw nothing remotely encouraging about the situation. He picked up the mattress, threw it against the wall and roared, "Shit."

Speechless, the men in the room stared. But Joe's outburst had not only lessened his tension, it led to revealing a stack of literature and brochures. Bruce lowered himself to the floor and picked up several flyers. "Good thing we have a warrant to search. Maybe someday you'll share that fact-finding technique with me. Looks like somebody's planning a trip near the equator."

Joe squatted beside him. "And scouting out banks."

"You thinking what I'm thinking?" Bruce asked.

"Oh, yeah," Joe said. "I've seen this one coming. Our boys have moved onto the big time."

Chapter Fifty-three

Mel wasn't ready to die. But with her hands bound and trapped in the backseat of Drake Maxwell's two-door Jeep, she saw no way to avoid the outcome or outwit her captors. She caught a glimpse of her face in the glass. Bruised, beaten . . . a victim. As she'd been fifteen years earlier. Except that fifteen years later, she'd made a difference in a young boy's life.

Or so she hoped. How her death would affect him remained to be seen. God, she wasn't ready. She thought of Joe, and a smile came to her face. He'd kept Luke safe after all. If Skinny's woman, or whoever she was, hadn't called, Joe's ruse might have worked.

Thanks, Joe. Mel thought of the special night he'd given her and she blinked back tears. If she had nothing else to hold on to as she left this world, she would treasure that memory.

From the passenger seat, Ramirez broke into her muse and flashed his blade. "I'll make this quick, *chica*, I promise you. Max wanted to do the honors, but we agreed no noise."

Shaking her head, she glared at the bastard. "Where are you taking me?"

Drake laughed. "Old Stage Road. Don't worry. You'll have company. We'll dump you next to Sanchez's body so you won't be lonely."

"Sanchez?" Mel asked.

"Like you, bitch, someone who crossed us. It might not be a lifetime in prison," Drake said. "But somehow dumping you next to him is fitting."

They were driving toward the mountains. Throat dry, heart pounding, her mind began to shut down and she accepted her fate. Until self-preservation came calling one last time. "If you spare me, I'll do the robbery. I'll get your money, Drake." To say what came next made her shudder with revulsion. "But I don't ever want to go back to prison. Take me with you?"

He met her gaze in the rearview mirror. Laughing, taunting, victorious. He lifted his foot off the gas pedal.

"Max, no. *Hombre*, she's bluffing. Let's off her, do the job and catch a plane. The cops, they're on to us."

"You and I are the only ones who know about the job," Drake argued. "We shared it with no one."

"You are one crazy son of a bitch. *Before* we had her kid. Now we have nothing."

"We have something," Max retorted. "Melanie's downfall is her conscience. She's fucking *weak*."

Mel held her breath. She might have bought herself time, but what were they talking about? She leaned back in the seat, lowered her head and squeezed her eyes closed. Drake whipped a U-turn. Opening her eyes at the abrupt change in direction, that's when she saw the pen. Located under the driver's seat, it wasn't quite close enough to grasp with two free hands. It would be nearly impossible with her wrists tied. Luckily, this time her feet weren't bound. Keeping her face impassive, she stretched. Little by little, she worked it in her direction.

Upfront, Drake and Ramirez lowered their voices, which given the engine noise and tires rotating beneath her, they needn't have bothered. Clearly, though, they were plotting their next moves and Mel's involvement in it. She'd maneuvered the pen now directly under her foot. Would they notice? Did she dare? She held her breath and waited. And when Drake took the next curve at a high rate of speed, she complained loudly for him to slow down, then let herself tumble to the floorboard. Once she had the pen firmly in her grasp, she struggled to sit up again.

She met Drake's laughing gaze in the rearview mirror. With pen in hand, she tucked it under her thigh and silently laughed back. Without paper, it might not do her any good. But prison had taught her one thing: the simplest items made the most effective weapons.

Chapter Fifty-four

Outside in Ramirez's driveway, Joe set up a makeshift command post. Bruce paced and men waited for orders, while Joe and Det. Abernathy studied the clues left under Maxwell's mattress.

"It's definitely one of these, L.T.," Dale said, handing over two bank flyers. "There's stars and scribbling all over them."

"I agree," Joe said. "From the looks of things, they were planning to hit one of these banks tomorrow."

"Were?" Bruce asked.

"We upset their little scheme," Joe replied. "Since we're on to them, they'll change their plans."

Dale shook his head. "I don't think so. They've gone through too much trouble to abort now. They're desperate, plus in order to get to Brazil, they'll need *dinero*. They'll be anxious to get out of town."

"You think they'll hit it today?" Joe asked.

"Yes, sir. Sooner rather than later."

Joe glanced around. From across the street, neighbors were taking an avid interest in what his team was doing. Uniformed officers kept them from interfering. "Where's Mercer?"

Wearing the handcuffs again, an officer led Mercer from a patrol car and brought him forward.

"Whose low-rider in the garage?" Joe asked.

"Ramirez's," Mercer said.

"And Maxwell, what does he drive?"

Mercer squinted. "Brown Jeep Wrangler, I think."

Joe said, "Sam, split up. Your team takes Liberty National Bank. Dale, you and your men come with me. We rendezvous at Assurance Bank."

"Got it."

"Joe," Bruce said. "May I remind you you're expending police resources on a long shot? APBs are out, Highway Patrol's on alert."

"Melanie's shop is two minutes away from Assurance. I was wrong to not make more waves about the prison guard. I'm not making the same mistake twice." Then recalling Luke's words, Joe said, "Besides, I can't just sit around doing nothing. And right now, a long shot's all we got."

Sam Ortega ended the argument by saying, "Let's roll, people. A woman's life is on the line."

Chapter Fifty-five

Mel tried to get Ramirez's comb through her tangled, riot of hair. It did little good. She looked as if she'd been through a war.

She had.

From over his shoulder, Ramirez studied her. "She looks bad, Max. She'll walk into the bank and it's over."

"Shut up." Drake was sweating now. He wore dark glasses, but beneath them Mel suspected his eyes bore the glazed look of a crazy. Fifteen years ago, she'd witnessed that look as he attacked the clerk. Careful to keep her hands out of sight, she tucked the pen into her sleeve.

The bank came into view and every nerve in Mel's body activated.

Drake parked the Jeep. He took a baseball cap from the floorboard, then paused.

Don't change your mind now. He had his plan; she had hers.

He put on the cap, retrieved a gun from the glove box and removed the clip. Tossing the clip back into the box, he said, "This one's for show. Walk up to that teller you know so well, show her the piece, tell her if she pushes the alarm, your partner starts shooting, and demand money.

"I'll be right behind you, Melanie. One trick and I waste everybody. Remember the clerk? You wouldn't let one man die. This time? You'll be a corpse, and you'll die with a ton of blood on your hands."

"Don't hurt anybody, Drake. That's the deal. I'll get you your money, then we'll go."

He grinned. "See there, Ramirez. Didn't I tell you? Perfect. Keep the motor running. We'll be right back."

Drake helped her climb out of the Jeep, shoved the gun in his belt, closing his jacket over it. He wore tan pans and his look was casual.

Mel glanced toward the mountains, toward Pikes Peak, and swallowed her fear. This was it. Someone was going down. All she could hope was it wouldn't be her.

Chapter Fifty-six

"ETA, five minutes," Dale shouted into the handheld radio as he and Joe sped down Garden of Gods Boulevard. Joe gripped the armrest. Bruce was right. What were the chances Maxwell would hit the bank at this particular time? All Joe had to go on was that he'd interrupted their scheme. And experience, of course. Criminals got stupid and greedy. They wouldn't walk away with nothing.

Melanie. Screw this insane world. Joe thought of her laugh, her passionate kiss, her beautiful body. The old adage, *the good die young* stuck in his head and his eyes filled.

The late December day might be cold, but the Colorado sun was intense. He wiped at his eyes, pretending to adjust his sunglasses.

Dale said, "For what it's worth, L.T. I hope your lady's okay."

Joe shot Dale a glance. *His lady*. The entire force knew. Joe didn't give a damn.

Chapter Fifty-seven

Mel walked with Drake across the sparsely populated parking lot like she was trudging through swampland. The majority of cars utilized the drive-thru, thank God, but there were always the few who preferred to go inside, and, of course, the bank employees.

Her mind raced for options. If she did as Drake wanted and approached the teller, she faced prison. There was no way, with her record and her history with Drake, that an ambitious prosecutor wouldn't convince a judge and jury she'd been in on the robbery all along. She pictured a smug Bruce Bennett grandstanding before the jury, and her heart seized.

Luke.

He'd end up with his grandparents after all. She gripped the pen in her sleeve and willed her kidnapper to make a careless mistake. But he'd moved a good two feet away from her as they approached the bank. Not only did Drake have a loaded gun tucked inside his belt, he possessed superior strength. To carry out her plan, she needed the element of surprise, she needed the luck that had deserted her for the last twenty-four hours, and, unfortunately, she needed the scum of the earth close by.

Her gaze traveled the lot. Perhaps if she made a break for it. Could she get behind one of the distant vehicles, hide until help came? No. She'd be dead with a bullet in her back before she got ten feet.

Joe. Where was he? Was he frantic? Looking for her? Mel squeezed her eyes shut, dismissing the useless questions. Joe couldn't help her now.

Drake and Ramirez had planned their strategy well. They'd parked away from other vehicles, so once Drake and Mel left the bank with the money, Ramirez would hit the gas and they'd make a quick escape. She wasn't under any illusion they would let her live if she went along with their plans. Though she'd said she'd go with Drake, he hated her too much to let that happen. After she robbed the bank, he would either leave her for the cops or murder her on the spot.

Sweat beaded her forehead. She forced her breathing to even. She wasn't against praying, and was doing it nonstop anyway, but right now, she had to help herself.

A maroon minivan drove into the parking lot, and though Mel silently intoned the driver to keep going, he pulled into a slot a few spaces down from where Ramirez sat ready to make his getaway.

"Keep walking," Drake said. "Just what we need for you to do this job.

Another customer."

But the driver wasn't a he. She was a woman. A young blonde, who hopped out of the van and slid open the passenger door. A toddler's wails filled the parking lot, and the woman's frustration became evident. "All right, Vanessa, Mommy's coming." Her shoulders sagged. "Jeremy, honey, where's your shoe?" Clearly, the young mom had her hands full.

Noting Drake's sardonic interest in the scene, Mel increased her pace. The woman had no idea that the longer she took to care for her fretting children, the longer she might stay alive. A shoe flew out of the van and landed a few feet from Drake. Catching Mel's stunned reaction, he stopped, lowered his sunglasses and flashed her a wink. Then ambling to where it lay, he picked up the toddler's sneaker.

"Drake, no." Her heart began a staccato drumming. She'd seen this look before. The early dawn morning he'd walked into a convenience store and made small talk with the clerk he'd later tried to kill. She hadn't recognized it then, but she did now. Drake enjoyed killing. If Mel didn't do exactly what he said, these people would die.

"Excuse me," he said, as he walked toward the hapless young woman. "Looks like your little man dropped this."

With her back to Drake, the woman stiffened. Most assuredly, the nearness of a stranger while she wrestled a child out of a car seat brought out her need to protect. But as she turned, took one look at Drake's handsome façade and her child's belonging in his hand, she, like so many others, failed to recognize the danger.

"Oh, jeeze, Jeremy. I'm sorry, sir." She took the shoe from Drake and started to go about her business.

"Need some help?"

Mel wanted to scream. What the hell was he doing? She glanced over her shoulder to where Ramirez sat waiting in the idling Jeep. He seemed equally confused and outraged over his partner's actions and pounded the steering wheel.

"If you don't mind, I could really use the stroller in the back." The woman unlocked the rear door with her access key. "I wouldn't be here if I wasn't overdrawn."

Drake presented her with his most charming smile. Raising his eyebrows at Mel, he said, "Not us. We're here to make a withdrawal."

The bastard. He was already at work setting up Mel as his accomplice. By including her in his conversation, though, it provided her with a chance to intervene. "Yes, dear, but if we don't hurry, we'll face *charges*."

Drake pulled the stroller out of the rear compartment and set it up. The mom, who was settling both toddlers into their seats, shot Mel a less than approving look.

"My wife," he explained as they crossed the parking lot. "She only thinks of herself."

Watching Mel carefully, he held the bank door open for the blonde as she negotiated the children in their double stroller inside. But before Mel could move past him, he grabbed her arm. She stifled a gasp. This was the first time he'd come close enough, but his manacle-like grip held her immobile.

His restless gaze darted around the lobby. "Those brats, Melanie? They'll go first. I swear it. Just like we discussed. Walk up to the teller, show her the gun. Any funny business, I blow these people away."

As the young mother pushed her treasured cargo toward the patrons in line, Mel knew how a convict felt when his time was up on Death Row. Her steps hesitant, she scanned the customers at the teller windows. From the familiar, friendly faces behind them, to the loan officers behind glass-walled partitions, to the chatty customer-service representative at a nearby desk, whom did she select to place even at greater risk?

Fresh bouquets sat on various counters and desks, emitting their floral scents, a direct contradiction to Mel's unwashed body since being Drake's prisoner.

To keep these people alive, he left her no choice. She would have to rob the bank. Her shoulders slumped from the weight of her concern.

Luke. Would he ever forgive her?

Joe. Would he think he'd been right in the first place?

A silver-haired woman in bifocals left her office concentrating on paperwork. Just for a second she focused on Mel, and in that instant, she mouthed the word, "Help."

The employee's gaze seemed to narrow beneath the glasses, but in the next moment she resumed perusing the forms. Had she gotten the message?

"Go," Drake said. He let go of her arm and gave Mel a small push.

"I can't do this," she murmured when they'd walked farther into the lobby.

"Have it your way, babe." His hand traveled toward the gun stashed in his belt and hidden by his sports coat.

Mel had no doubt he would fulfill the threat. He might even be hoping she'd refuse so he could let loose his need to kill. But for the first time she was free, and at the same time close enough to Drake to take her one and only shot at escaping this nightmare. She yanked the pen from her sleeve.

Reverting back fifteen years, she relived her fear of the trucker, the female convicts holding her down, and fast forwarded to the last terrifying twenty-four hours.

Aided by the strength of these memories, she attacked. Jabbing the bastard's neck with the pointed end of the pen, Mel screamed, "Get down, get down, get down!"

Children cried, customers scrambled, bank employees hit the ground.

And as sirens blared from the outside, Drake went for his gun. But before he could fire, Mel tugged the unloaded weapon from inside her windbreaker, and slammed the butt against his cheekbone.

Then from out of nowhere the silver-haired lady appeared. Carrying one of the bank's massive ledgers, she formed a batter-like stance and struck Drake in the back of the head.

The bastard went down, losing control of the gun.

His dive to retrieve it had Mel sliding across the marble floor to beat him to it.

Feat accomplished, she jumped to her feet, raised the gun and aimed it at him.

At that moment, Joe and another police officer burst through the doors, weapons drawn.

Mel glared at the man on the floor. The pain in her jaw was nothing compared to her time in prison, the years she'd spent living a lie, or the fear for her son. She tightened her grip, loving the feel of her finger on the trigger and finally having the upper hand on her enemy.

Vaguely aware of Joe coming near, but trapped in a fugue of then and now, she kept the gun pointed directly at Drake's face. He lay writhing; calling her every vile name that came to his lips.

The gun shook in her hand, but she never altered her target.

"Don't do it, Mel."

Anger replaced the fear she'd underwent just moments before. She itched to pull the trigger. It would be so easy, *so warranted.* She ground her teeth. The urge to kill Drake Maxwell was as prevalent as her need for air. She could do it. Rid the world of the menace, and for her trouble, a jury of her peers would send her back to prison.

"Mel."

She raised her gaze to find that Joe and the cop beside him had their weapons trained on her.

She'd given Joe her heart, and although his panicked expression belied his actions, she couldn't believe what she was seeing. "He hurt me, Joe. He would've hurt Luke."

Joe lowered the firearm to his side and took a small step forward. Holding his free hand out to her, he kept his voice soft. "Baby, I know. I *know*. But it's over. Put down the gun."

Her stomach rolled. "Kind of like old times, isn't it, Officer Crandall? If I run . . ."

"I'll chase you. Melanie, I'll have to. Baby, I love you. Please. We've got lots of innocent people in here. What do you say? Put down the gun."

The oxygen seeped from her lungs. Mel searched Joe's face to find him in agony. As much as she detested Drake Maxwell, she loved Joe Crandall more. Tears filled her eyes. Seduced by his words, and utterly exhausted, she allowed the gun to slip from her fingers.

It fell to the floor at the same time Drake pulled a Derringer from an ankle holster and got off a shot. A new contingent of screaming and panic erupted. The rest swirled around her in slow motion. Mel collapsed as Joe fired. The last thing she saw before everything went black was Joe's bullet's objective. It hit her nemesis squarely between the eyes.

Chapter Fifty-eight

The morning after the shooting, Mel sat up in her hospital bed, her injured arm bandaged and in a sling. She tried not to frown as yet another nurse came in to take her blood pressure. "Excuse me," Mel said. "Can you tell me when the doctor will be by? It's been three days since I've seen my son, and I want to go home."

The nurse patted her arm. "You're not the doctor's only patient, dear. Try to relax and I'll give him a call."

Mel looked to the ceiling and blew out a frustrated breath.

"She's right, Mom," the young man said in the doorway. "You need to *chillax.*"

Mel squealed and held out her good arm. "Luke! Oh my God. Luke!" Her son crossed the room and she crushed him in her one-armed embrace. For days she'd been crying tears of sorrow, today she shed happy ones. Brushing the blond hair out of his eyes, she studied the endearing face she thought she might never see again. "I was so worried about you."

"*You* were? What do you think you did to me? You made the papers, Mom. The kids at school are calling you an Amazon warrior. They think it's pretty sweet you brought down an ex-con as bad as Maxwell."

She blushed at her son's praise, but wasn't about to take all the credit. "Actually Lt. Crandall had something to do with it, and so did the bank manager." Dorothy Hayward, the woman who'd used the bank ledger to bring Maxwell's rampage to a halt, had paid Mel a visit earlier that morning. Mel's silent plea for help had gotten Dorothy's attention, and it was then that she said she'd recognized the vulgar man who'd pretended to be a potential bank customer the day before.

"I would've done much, much more to keep you safe," Mel said.

It was Luke's turn to turn red. "Hope you don't mind, but I brought company."

Supporting herself with her good arm, she shifted awkwardly. Joe and Matt stood in the outside hall. She smiled and waved them inside.

Matt entered the room, bobbing his head like the proverbial cool cat. "Somebody must have connections. Check out all these flowers."

"You think?" Mel laughed. Her boss had spared no expense to fill the hospital room with exquisite arrangements. Lenora Sims had sent her a bouquet, too.

Across the room, Luke rifled through all the well wishes and zoned in on a box of chocolate. "Crandall, get over here."

Joe used the boys' distraction to join her in a chair by the bed. "How's the arm?"

"It looks pretty awful, but they tell me it's just a flesh wound, and I'll be fine." She winked. "Want to see?"

"No. I faint at the sight of blood. Especially yours." He took her hand and brought it to his lips. Then turning it, he kissed her palm. "I thought I'd go out of my mind, Mel."

She squeezed his hand. "Did I thank you, Joe? When I think of everything I stood to lose, I don't think I'll ever be able to repay you."

He rose from the chair, scooted next to her and pulled her into his arms. "No problem. I've already come up with the terms. You're not leaving my bed for weeks."

She looked toward the boys and sent Joe a censuring look.

As much as she'd tried to banish the memories of the last two days, they surfaced. "That man named Ramirez?" she asked. The moment he'd heard sirens, the gang leader had fled the scene.

"He's in custody. The Sheriff's office provided backup and cornered him a few miles from the bank. He made a critical mistake in bragging to you about killing one of his gang members. We've located Ernesto Sanchez's body. Ramirez will be going away for a very long time."

Sagging with relief, she breathed deeply and closed her eyes. Drake Maxwell was dead; Ramirez was going back to prison. That's all she needed to know. "Good. Can we talk about something else then, please?"

"Love to. Let's talk about us."

Us. The word conjured up all the longing and dread she'd been avoiding in recent weeks. She emitted a bitter, humorless laugh. "As much as I'm grateful you kept me and my son alive, Lieutenant, I'm afraid there's still no *us.*"

"I don't agree," Joe said.

A knock on the door interrupted their conversation. Bruce Bennett stood in the doorway. At the D.A.'s presence, Mel yanked her hand out of Joe's. She stiffened, expecting him to move away as well. When he remained steadfast by her side, the logical part of her brain cried *your career*, while the part that was in love, rejoiced.

"May I come in?" the prosecutor asked. In his left hand he carried a briefcase.

She looked to the boys. There was no way she would rehash the events of her kidnapping in front of them, or let Bennett insinuate she was a criminal in front of her son. Luke had been through enough. "This isn't a good time, Mr. Bennett." She lowered her voice and lifted an eyebrow. "Do I need a lawyer? I'm not seventeen anymore, and I promise you, he *won't* be a public defender."

Luke and Matt paused in their chocolate raid across the room.

"No. You don't need a criminal lawyer, but perhaps a civil one to see to certain aspects taking place. Also, when you're ready, Mrs. Norris, the police department and the district attorney's office have a little gift we'd like to bestow on you."

"Really?" Luke tossed a piece of chocolate back into the box, and wandered close to her bedside. "Mom, talk to the man."

She eyed Joe warily, then refocused on Bennett. "What kind of civil aspect? Is someone suing me? And what could you possibly mean about a gift?"

"It's a plaque actually," the D.A. said. He opened the briefcase to remove a framed award. "It reads, 'In grateful appreciation, the City of Colorado Springs acknowledges Melanie Norris for her part in the apprehension of the Chaos Bandits.' Signed The Honorable Sanderson Carter, Mayor, Arthur Gallegos, Chief of Police and Bruce Bennett, El Paso County District Attorney."

She couldn't be hearing right. Stunned, she reached for the plaque, blinking away the

tears that blurred her vision. But it was true, signatures and all. Wondering if one could die of happiness, she ran a finger over the lettering. "Wow. Oh, wow."

Joe kissed her forehead and tightened his hold.

"One more thing," the D.A. went on. "The CSPD thought of one more way it might show its gratitude." He removed a manila envelope and handed it to her.

"I can't look." Overwhelmed, she passed it to Joe.

He opened it and inspected the pages. In a husky voice, he said, "It's a petition, Mel, containing a boatload of signatures by quite a few men and women on the force."

"A petition? To whom?"

"The governor." His Adam's apple convulsed as he struggled to speak. "It's a request to expunge your criminal conviction."

The culmination of the past few days and that remarkable act of kindness renewed the water works. She stifled a sob. Expunge? It was more than she'd ever dreamt of. "You're serious?"

"Absolutely," Bruce said, pointing. "As a matter of fact, if you'll look here, the signatures include not only the police department, but the employees of the Department of Corrections. Notice the first signature.

She leaned over to view the papers in Joe's hands. At Warden Simon River's influential scrawl, she knew their friendship was intact and her heart overflowed.

"Members of my staff insisted on signing as well," the D.A. said.

Mel pressed a trembling hand to her mouth. "I—I don't know what to say Mr. Bennett, thank you."

The D.A. made an awkward attempt to move toward her, then stopped.

She'd never seen him exhibit the least bit of timidity, but he did so now. He cleared his throat. "I'm running for office, Mrs. Norris. Joe's a good friend, and in the future, we're bound to cross paths.

"Since you're soon to be a voting member of society, I'd consider it a personal favor if you'd call me Bruce." He did step closer then. "And maybe someday you might even find it in your heart to think of me as someone you can trust."

Mel supposed this was the closest thing to an apology she would ever receive from this man. Reconciling his cold, unfeeling treatment of her in the past would take a very forgiving person. But Bennett had obviously gone to a great deal of trouble on her behalf. She swallowed hard, grateful the doctor chose that moment to enter.

Release forms in hand, he said, "I understand someone's anxious to go home. But since you're throwing a party, I can back later."

"Oh, no, you don't." The knowledge that he was joking didn't quell her anxiety or the fact she'd been stuck in this bed for an entire day. Mel extended her good hand for the clipboard. "No offense, Doctor, but I'm sick of your hospital."

Epilogue

Melanie shoveled compost into a large rectangular ceramic pot and smiled as Joe's daughter added her share. Mel was showing Trish how to transplant individual herbs from their tiny plastic containers into a transportable herb garden, which the girl could take home with her at the end of the summer. By the intense look on the soon to be twelve-year-old's face, she was enjoying the process.

Cradling the root ball, Mel held it close to the girl's nose "Smell, Trish."

She sniffed and scrunched up her face. "What is it?"

"Sage," Mel said. "Later, we'll make potpourri if you like."

"Cool," she replied.

Footsteps sounded above in the kitchen and Trish raised her pretty brunette head.

"That'll be your dad," Mel said.

"Where is everybody?" Joe called from the kitchen door.

Mel winked at the girl. "On three." In unison, they hollered, "Down here, *Commander.*"

His footfalls on her wooden steps sounded like an army of elephants. Smiling, Joe met Mel's gaze, then that of his daughter's as he entered the basement. "I'd tell you to stop with the commander jazz, but when my two favorite ladies say it . . ."

Trish, who'd flown in to spend the next three months with her dad, grinned up at him. He brushed the dirt off her face with the pad of his thumb.

"I happen to think it's great when a daughter's proud of her father," Mel countered.

"Me, too. But I've been a commander for three months now. Hey, you," Joe said to Trish. "Mrs. Harmon's out front waiting to take you and Lindsey swimming."

The girl's eyes went wide. "Sweet. See you later, Melanie."

Her footsteps were considerably lighter than Joe's as she tore up the stairs.

"Don't think I didn't notice she didn't say goodbye to me. You've created a monster there, woman." He took in the plant-filled basement, which he'd warned was on the verge of becoming a rain forest.

"As long as she likes me, I'd say it's worth it, wouldn't you?"

He glanced down. "Wearing your ring?"

"Right here, Com—Joe," she said, teasing him and tugging off her left work glove.

He held her hand, turning it to admire the pear-shaped diamond. Then bringing her hand to his lips, he brushed them over her knuckles, which left her anticipating later.

"Feel like taking a drive with me?" he asked.

With the boys practicing in Denver for an invitational tournament and Trish off with friends, Mel's Saturday was suddenly free. She pulled off her other glove and set it upon the shelf over her grow boxes and next to the humidity gauge. "Sure. What do you have in mind?"

He lowered his head to kiss her. "You'll see."

Twenty minutes later when they turned on to Thirtieth Street, Mel wondered if he'd planned a walk in The Garden of the Gods. But before he got to the national landmark, famous for its three-hundred-foot red sandstone formations, he traveled farther west toward the mountains.

It was early June and snow still capped Pikes Peak. Wherever Joe was taking her, it didn't matter. Some things never changed. Alone-time with Joe was a precious commodity.

As he drove the Mustang through a neighborhood zoned for horse property, Mel let him have his fun.

Some of the surrounding homes were well-maintained, while others had major landscaping issues. Still, others needed paint and major exterior renovations.

Finally, when Joe turned into the loosely graveled drive, which technically had more dirt than rock, her curiosity couldn't be silenced. "Okay. What gives?"

He drove down the path and parked in front of an enormous colonial-type house set back from the driveway. With ample parking, it had two-stories and a three-car garage, but clearly the structure, which wept for several coats of paint, had to be more than fifty years old.

"What do you think?" he asked.

She stared up at the potential cash drain, in truth, a little horrified. "Is it haunted?"

"I hope not," Joe replied. "It's for sale."

"No! Somebody's willing to give up all *this*?"

"Funny. I thought you were a woman with an open mind. You staying in here, or coming with me?"

"I haven't decided." But even as she said it, she stepped out of the car.

They toured the house, which thankfully didn't need as much upkeep on the inside as it did on the outside. Warped, scuffed-up wood floors, an outdated kitchen, five bedrooms and four full bathrooms, the unloved home had family written all over it. And if someone had taken better care of it, it might have been a showplace.

They climbed the circular staircase to the bedrooms. And when Joe opened the door to the master, she gasped. This room, too, required updating, but it was more of a suite than a bedroom. Her mind was already at work taking down the hideous orange and gold wallpaper.

Joe walked to the window and looked out to what she suspected was the backyard. "What do you think of the view?"

She came to stand beside him, ready to ask what they could possibly do with an old barn, when she saw it. "Oh my gosh, is that a greenhouse back there?"

Returning one of his typical half-smiles, he said, "You'd be more qualified to answer that question than me."

"What are we doing here?" She searched his face.

"Just looking, sweetheart. Just looking."

"Be right back." Grinning, she rushed toward the door.

"Melanie?"

In the doorway, she pivoted.

Joe held out a key. "You'll need this."

Outside and several seconds later, she slid the key into the flimsy lock of an A-frame-styled greenhouse close to the size of the one Carl had built for her in Cañon City. Once she opened the door, however, she discovered this one stripped bare. Still, there was no mistaking the familiar smell of fertilizer, loam and the plants that at one time must have thrived here.

She traced a hand over dirty, grimy ancient windows, took in the old-fashioned attic fan and the transparent panels overhead, and her half-empty glass filled with hope.

"What do you think?" he asked from the door.

Smiling, she turned to give him her thoughts when she saw what looked like a set of drawings in his hand.

"I guess I'm afraid to think anything until I know what you have in mind." Her voice carried throughout the vast empty space. "How did you find it?"

Tapping the rolled-up drawings against his thigh, he came toward her. "I told Lenora Sims if she ever came across something in our price range that had a greenhouse on the property to give me a call."

Mel laughed. "Well, this certainly seems like it's in our budget."

"Was I wrong not to talk to you first?" He turned suddenly serious, his ordinarily confident baritone voice uncertain. "To ask if you even wanted to move? I know how much work and pride you've put into the one you have now. But when people get married, they generally live together."

She walked toward him. "They generally do. What's in your hand, Joe?"

"Architectural plans. Not for the main house," he added quickly. "For the greenhouse. If we buy this place, the remodel in this area alone will take significant cash."

Mel's throat tightened with every spoken word. Simon had once called Joe a walk-away. The warden couldn't have been more wrong. A walk-away was an unscrupulous fiend, a womanizer, a love 'em and leave 'em type. The term hardly fit the man who'd arrested her, antagonized her, saved her life and then taught her the meaning of love.

Wrapping her arms around him, she whispered, "I'm not marrying you for your money. Joe. Nor am I afraid of hard work."

"Is that a yes, Mel? You're willing to move? You like the place?"

"I *love* the place, and I love you."

"What a relief," he said, bowing his head to kiss her. "Because in case I haven't mentioned it, the feeling's mutual."

Acknowledgements

So many helped with this book, I couldn't possibly name them all. However, I would be remiss in not naming specifically Robin Searle, Misty Evans, Jean Willett, Julie Rowe, Annette Dashofy, Renee Ryan and Anne Marie Becker and, of course, my wonderful mom, Irma Barnes who is my biggest fan and first reader. Special thanks to Pam McCutcheon who was the first published author to read it from start to finish. To the El Paso County Sheriff's Office and their outstanding Citizens Academy, to Crimescenewriters, a Yahoo loop I co-own with retired veteran police officer Wally Lind, I thank you and all the members of the loop for their assistance. To Bell Bridge Books, and my editor Pat Van Wie, a heartfelt thank you for your vision, logic and expertise, and to my husband, Les, I couldn't have written this book without your love and support. To my best friend in the world, Moreen Drake, one of my mentors Dianne Drake and to my sister Maria Gravina, thank you for the use of your names. While my characters are evil, the three of you are wonderful, and I love you. Finally, any mistakes are my own, and not any of those who tried their best to convey police work and what goes on inside the head of a cop.

About the Author

Donnell Ann Bell is as at home in nonfiction as she is in fiction. She has worked for a weekly business publication and a monthly parenting magazine, has a background in court reporting, has worked with kids and engineers, and has volunteered for law enforcement and other organizations. She is co-owner of Crimescenewriters, a Yahoo group for mystery/suspense writers, 2000 members strong, and formed by a retired police officer. She is also a graduate of the El Paso County Sheriff's Citizens Academy. The recipient of numerous awards for her fiction writing, including a two-time finalist for Romance Writers of America's prestigious Golden Heart®, Donnell was raised in New Mexico's Land of Enchantment and today calls Colorado home. http://donnellannbell.com/